DIANA PALMER

Christmas with the Rancher

MILLS & BOON

All the characters in this book have no existence outside the imagination of the author, and have no relation whatsoever to anyone bearing the same name or names. They are not even distantly inspired by any individual known or unknown to the author, and all the incidents are pure invention.

Mills & Boon, an imprint of Harlequin (UK) Limited, Eton House, 18-24 Paradise Road, Richmond, Surrey TW9 1SR

ISBN: 978 0 263 91021 6

009-1013

Harlequin (UK) policy is to use papers that are natural, renewable and recyclable products and made from wood grown in sustainable forests. The logging and manufacturing processes conform to the legal environmental regulations of the country of origin.

Printed and bound in Spain
by Blackprint CPI, Barcelona

The Rancher

The prolific author of over one hundred books, **Diana Palmer** got her start as a newspaper reporter. A multi-*New York Times* bestselling author and one of the top ten romance writers in America, she has a gift for telling the most sensual tales with charm and humour. Diana lives with her family in Georgia.

Dear Reader,

You probably think this story is about Cort Brannt, the brother of my heroine, Morie Brannt, in *Wyoming Tough.* Well, it's not. It's actually about the rooster who belongs to Cort's neighbour. A red rooster came into my yard several weeks ago. I tried to run him off, but he kept coming back. I discovered that roosters can fly, because he jumped a seven-foot-high solid wooden fence to keep coming into my yard. I have lots of grass and a garden, which means bugs and worms and nice edibles. He wouldn't leave.

Over the weeks, people who work for me in the yard tried to catch him. Some of the neighbours got into the act. I especially wanted him gone because every time I went out to feed the birds or look at my garden, he would attack me. I was spurred three times, and I have the scars to prove it. So the rooster had to go. That presented a problem. I didn't want him killed or eaten, which left his fate up to me, since his owner apparently moved away and left him behind. (I don't blame him. If you knew this rooster, you wouldn't blame him, either!)

Our nice Mr Martin, who looks after the koi and goldfish ponds for us, had a friend who knew how to catch chickens. He also kept chickens. So he just walked into the backyard, picked the rooster up and carried him off. My jaw is still dropping. Anyway, the rooster is very happy, has many hens to court, and I am happy because I can walk to my pumpkin patch without being mauled on the way.

Cort Brannt is going to have the same problem. His nice little frumpy neighbour has a pet rooster named Pumpkin and she loves him. She loves Cort, too, but Cort loves Odalie Everett, who wants to train as a soprano and sing in the great opera houses of the world. Ah, the eternal triangle. It will all end well, I promise. And Pumpkin will have a happy future. Just like my unwanted red rooster visitor.

Hope you like the book. It has roots in Branntville, Texas, and King Brannt is Cort's dad.

Your greatest fan,

Diana Palmer

Chapter One

Maddie Lane was worried. She was standing in her big yard, looking at her chickens, and all she saw was a mixture of hens. There were red ones and white ones and gray speckled ones. But they were all hens. Someone was missing: her big Rhode Island Red rooster, Pumpkin.

She knew where he likely was. It made her grind her teeth together. There was going to be trouble, again, and she was going to be on the receiving end of it.

She pushed back her short, wavy blond hair and grimaced. Her wide gray eyes searched the yard, hoping against hope that she was mistaken, that Pumpkin had only gone in search of bugs, not cowboys.

"Pumpkin?" she called loudly.

Great-Aunt Sadie came to the door. She was slight

and a little dumpy, with short, thin gray hair, wearing glasses and a worried look.

"I saw him go over toward the Brannt place, Maddie," she said as she moved out onto the porch. "I'm sorry."

Maddie groaned aloud. "I'll have to go after him. Cort will kill me!"

"Well, he hasn't so far," Sadie replied gently. "And he could have shot Pumpkin, but he didn't..."

"Only because he missed!" Maddie huffed. She sighed and put her hands on her slim hips. She had a boyish figure. She wasn't tall or short, just sort of in the middle. But she was graceful, for all that. And she could work on a ranch, which she did. Her father had taught her how to raise cattle, how to market them, how to plan and how to budget. Her little ranch wasn't anything big or special, but she made a little money. Things had been going fine until she decided she wanted to branch out her organic egg-laying business and bought Pumpkin after her other rooster was killed by a coyote, along with several hens. But now things weren't so great financially.

Maddie had worried about getting a new rooster. Her other one wasn't really vicious, but she did have to carry a tree branch around with her to keep from getting spurred. She didn't want another aggressive one.

"Oh, he's gentle as a lamb," the former owner assured her. "Great bloodlines, good breeder, you'll get along just fine with him!"

Sure, she thought when she put him in the chicken yard and his first act was to jump on her foreman, old Ben Harrison, when he started to gather eggs.

"Better get rid of him now," Ben had warned as she doctored the cuts on his arms the rooster had made even through the fabric.

"He'll settle down, he's just excited about being in a new place," Maddie assured him.

Looking back at that conversation now, she laughed. Ben had been right. She should have sent the rooster back to the vendor in a shoebox. But she'd gotten attached to the feathered assassin. Sadly, Cort Brannt hadn't.

Cort Matthew Brannt was every woman's dream of the perfect man. He was tall, muscular without making it obvious, cultured, and he could play a guitar like a professional. He had jet-black hair with a slight wave, large dark brown eyes and a sensuous mouth that Maddie often dreamed of kissing.

The problem was that Cort was in love with their other neighbor, Odalie Everett. Odalie was the daughter of big-time rancher Cole Everett and his wife, Heather, who was a former singer and songwriter. She had two brothers, John and Tanner. John still lived at home, but Tanner lived in Europe. Nobody talked about him.

Odalie loved grand opera. She had her mother's clear, beautiful voice and she wanted to be a professional soprano. That meant specialized training.

Cort wanted to marry Odalie, who couldn't see him for dust. She'd gone off to Italy to study with some famous voice trainer. Cort was distraught and it didn't help that Maddie's rooster kept showing up in his yard and attacking him without warning.

"I can't understand why he wants to go all the way over there to attack Cort," Maddie said aloud. "I mean, we've got cowboys here!"

"Cort threw a rake at him the last time he came over here to look at one of your yearling bulls," Sadie reminded her.

"I throw things at him all the time," Maddie pointed out.

"Yes, but Cort chased him around the yard, picked him up by his feet, and carried him out to the hen yard to show him to the hens. Hurt his pride," Sadie continued. "He's getting even."

"You think so?"

"Roosters are unpredictable. That particular one," she added with a bite in her voice that was very out of character, "should have been chicken soup!"

"Great-Aunt Sadie!"

"Just telling you the way it is," Sadie huffed. "My brother—your granddaddy—would have killed him the first time he spurred you."

Maddie smiled. "I guess he would. I don't like killing things. Not even mean roosters."

"Cort would kill him for you if he could shoot straight," Sadie said with veiled contempt. "You load that .28 gauge shotgun in the closet for me, and I'll do it."

"Great-Aunt Sadie!"

She made a face. "Stupid thing. I wanted to pet the hens and he ran me all the way into the house. Pitiful, when a chicken can terrorize a whole ranch. You go ask

Ben how he feels about that red rooster. I dare you. If you'd let him, he'd run a truck over it!"

Maddie sighed. "I guess Pumpkin is a terror. Well, maybe Cort will deal with him once and for all and I can go get us a nice rooster."

"In my experience, no such thing," the older woman said. "And about Cort dealing with him…" She nodded toward the highway.

Maddie grimaced. A big black ranch truck turned off the highway and came careening down the road toward the house. It was obviously being driven by a maniac.

The truck screeched to a stop at the front porch, sending chickens running for cover in the hen yard because of the noise.

"Great," Maddie muttered. "Now they'll stop laying for two days because he's terrified them!"

"Better worry about yourself," Great-Aunt Sadie said. "Hello, Cort! Nice to see you," she added with a wave and ran back into the house, almost at a run.

Maddie bit off what she was going to say about traitors. She braced herself as a tall, lean, furious cowboy in jeans, boots, a chambray shirt and a black Stetson cocked over one eye came straight toward her. She knew what the set of that hat meant. He was out for blood.

"I'm sorry!" she said at once, raising her hands, palms out. "I'll do something about him, I promise!"

"Andy landed in a cow patty," he raged in his deep voice. "That's nothing compared to what happened to the others while we were chasing him. I went headfirst into the dipping tray!"

She wouldn't laugh, she wouldn't laugh, she wouldn't…

"Oh, hell, stop that!" he raged while she bent over double at the mental image of big, handsome Cort lying facedown in the stinky stuff they dipped cattle in to prevent disease.

"I'm sorry. Really!" She forced herself to stop laughing. She wiped her wet eyes and tried to look serious. "Go ahead, keep yelling at me. Really. It's okay."

"Your stupid rooster is going to feed my ranch hands if you don't keep him at home!" he said angrily.

"Oh, my, chance would be a fine thing, wouldn't it?" she asked wistfully. "I mean, I guess I could hire an off-duty army unit to come out here and spend the next week trying to run him down." She gave him a droll look. "If you and your men can't catch him, how do you expect me to catch him?"

"I caught him the first day he was here," he reminded her.

"Yes, but that was three months ago," she pointed out. "And he'd just arrived. Now he's learned evasion techniques." She frowned. "I wonder if they've ever thought of using roosters as attack animals for the military? I should suggest it to someone."

"I'd suggest you find some way to keep him at home before I resort to the courts."

"You'd sue me over a chicken?" she exclaimed. "Wow, what a headline that would be. Rich, Successful Rancher Sues Starving, Female Small-Rancher for Rooster Attack. Wouldn't your dad love reading that headline in the local paper?" she asked with a bland smile.

His expression was growing so hard that his high cheekbones stood out. "One more flying red feather attack and I'll risk it. I'm not kidding."

"Oh, me, neither." She crossed her heart. "I'll have the vet prescribe some tranquilizers for Pumpkin to calm him down," she said facetiously. She frowned. "Ever thought about asking your family doctor for some? You look very stressed."

"I'm stressed because your damned rooster keeps attacking me! On my own damned ranch!" he raged.

"Well, I can see that it's a stressful situation to be in," she sympathized. "With him attacking you, and all." She knew it would make him furious, but she had to know. "I hear Odalie Everett went to Italy."

The anger grew. Now it was cold and threatening. "Since when is Odalie of interest to you?"

"Just passing on the latest gossip." She peered at him through her lashes. "Maybe you should study opera..."

"You venomous little snake," he said furiously. "As if you could sing a note that wasn't flat!"

She colored. "I could sing if I wanted to!"

He looked her up and down. "Sure. And get suddenly beautiful with it?"

The color left her face.

"You're too thin, too flat-chested, too plain and too untalented to ever appeal to me, just in case you wondered," he added with unconcealed distaste.

She drew herself up to her full height, which only brought the top of her head to his chin, and stared at him with ragged dignity. "Thank you. I was wondering why men don't come around. It's nice to know the reason."

Her damaged pride hit him soundly, and he felt small. He shifted from one big booted foot to the other. "I didn't mean it like that," he said after a minute.

She turned away. She wasn't going to cry in front of him.

Her sudden vulnerability hurt him. He started after her. "Listen, Madeline," he began.

She whirled on her booted heel. Her pale eyes shot fire at him. Her exquisite complexion went ruddy. Beside her thighs, her hands were clenched. "You think you're God's gift to women, don't you? Well, let me tell you a thing or two! You've traded on your good looks for years to get you what you want, but it didn't get you Odalie, did it?"

His face went stony. "Odalie is none of your damned business," he said in a soft, dangerous tone.

"Looks like she's none of yours, either," she said spitefully. "Or she'd never have left you."

He turned around and stomped back to his truck.

"And don't you dare roar out of my driveway and scare my hens again!"

He slammed the door, started the truck and deliberately gunned the engine as he roared out toward the main highway.

"Three days they won't lay, now," Maddie said to herself. She turned, miserable, and went up the porch steps. Her pride was never going to heal from that attack. She'd had secret feelings for Cort since she was sixteen. He'd never noticed her, of course, not even to tease her as men sometimes did. He simply ignored her existence most of the time, when her rooster wasn't attacking him. Now she knew why. Now she knew what he really thought of her.

Great-Aunt Sadie was waiting by the porch screen door. She was frowning. "No call for him to say that about you," she muttered. "Conceited man!"

Maddie fought tears and lost.

Great-Aunt Sadie wrapped her up tight and hugged her. "Don't you believe what he said. He was just mad and looking for a way to hurt you because you mentioned his precious Odalie. She's too good for any cowboy. At least, she thinks she is."

"She's beautiful and rich and talented. But so is Cort," Maddie choked out. "It really would have been a good match, to pair the Everett's Big Spur ranch with Skylance, the Brannt ranch. What a merger that would be."

"Except that Odalie doesn't love Cort and she probably never will."

"She may come home with changed feelings," Maddie replied, drawing away. "She might have a change of heart. He's always been around, sending her flowers, calling her. All that romantic stuff. The sudden stop might open her eyes to what a catch he is."

"You either love somebody or you don't," the older woman said quietly.

"You think?"

"I'll make you a nice pound cake. That will cheer you up."

"Thanks. That's sweet of you." She wiped her eyes. "Well, at least I've lost all my illusions. Now I can just deal with my ranch and stop mooning over a man who thinks he's too good for me."

"No man is too good for you, sweetheart," Great-Aunt Sadie said gently. "You're pure gold. Don't you ever let anyone tell you different."

She smiled.

When she went out late in the afternoon to put her hens in their henhouse to protect them from overnight predators, Pumpkin was right where he should be—back in the yard.

"You're going to get me sued, you red-feathered problem child," she muttered. She was carrying a small tree branch and a metal garbage can lid as she herded her hens into the large chicken house. Pumpkin lowered his head and charged her, but he bounced off the lid.

"Get in there, you fowl assassin," she said, evading and turning on him.

He ran into the henhouse. She closed the door behind him and latched it, leaned back against it with a sigh.

"Need to get rid of that rooster, Miss Maddie," Ben murmured as he walked by. "Be delicious with some dumplings."

"I'm not eating Pumpkin!"

He shrugged. "That's okay. I'll eat him for you."

"I'm not feeding him to you, either, Ben."

He made a face and kept walking.

She went inside to wash her hands and put antibiotic

cream on the places where her knuckles were scraped from using the garbage can lid. She looked at her hands under the running water. They weren't elegant hands. They had short nails and they were functional, not pretty. She remembered Odalie Everett's long, beautiful white fingers on the keyboard at church, because Odalie could play as well as she sang. The woman was gorgeous, except for her snobbish attitude. No wonder Cort was in love with her.

Maddie looked in the mirror on the medicine cabinet above the sink and winced. She really was plain, she thought. Of course, she never used makeup or perfume, because she worked from dawn to dusk on the ranch. Not that makeup would make her beautiful, or give her bigger breasts or anything like that. She was basically just pleasant to look at, and Cort wanted beauty, brains and talent.

"I guess you'll end up an old spinster with a rooster who terrorizes the countryside."

The thought made her laugh. She thought of photographing Pumpkin and making a giant Wanted poster, with the legend, Wanted: Dead or Alive. She could hardly contain herself at the image that presented itself if she offered some outlandish reward. Men would wander the land with shotguns, looking for a small red rooster.

"Now you're getting silly," she told her image, and went back to work.

Cort Brannt slammed out of his pickup truck and into the ranch house, flushed with anger and self-contempt.

His mother, beautiful Shelby Brannt, glanced up as he passed the living room.

"Wow," she murmured. "Cloudy and looking like rain."

He paused and glanced at her. He grimaced, retraced his steps, tossed his hat onto the sofa and sat down beside her. "Yeah."

"That rooster again, huh?" she teased.

His dark eyes widened. "How did you guess?"

She tried to suppress laughter and lost. "Your father came in here bent over double, laughing his head off. He said half the cowboys were ready to load rifles and go rooster-hunting about the time you drove off. He wondered if we might need to find legal representation for you…?"

"I didn't shoot her," he said. He shrugged his powerful shoulders and let out a long sigh, his hands dangling between his splayed legs as he stared at the carpet. "But I said some really terrible things to her."

Shelby put down the European fashion magazine she'd been reading. In her younger days, she had been a world-class model before she married King Brannt. "Want to talk about it, Matt?" she asked gently.

"Cort," he corrected with a grin.

She sighed. "Cort. Listen, your dad and I were calling you Matt until you were teenager, so it's hard…"

"Yes, well, you were calling Morie 'Dana,' too, weren't you?"

Shelby laughed. "It was an inside-joke. I'll tell it to you one day." She smiled. "Come on. Talk to me."

His mother could always take the weight off his shoulders. He'd never been able to speak so comfortably about personal things to his father, although he loved the older man dearly. He and his mother were on the same wavelength. She could almost read his mind.

"I was pretty mad," he confessed. "And she was cracking jokes about that stupid rooster. Then she made a crack about Odalie and I just, well, I just lost it."

Odalie, she knew, was a sore spot with her son. "I'm sorry about the way things worked out, Cort," she said gently. "But there's always hope. Never lose sight of that."

"I sent her roses. Serenaded her. Called her just to talk. Listened to her problems." He looked up. "None of that mattered. That Italian voice trainer gave her an invitation and she got on the next plane to Rome."

"She wants to sing. You know that. You've always known it. Her mother has the voice of an angel, too."

"Yes, but Heather never wanted fame. She wanted Cole Everett," he pointed out with a faint smile.

"That was one hard case of a man," Shelby pointed out. "Like your father." She shook her head. "We had a very, very rocky road to the altar. And so did Heather and Cole."

She continued pensively. "You and Odalie's brother, John Everett, were good friends for a while. What happened there?"

"His sister happened," Cort replied. "She got tired of having me at their place all the time playing video games with John and was very vocal about it, so he stopped inviting me over. I invited him here, but he got into rodeo and then I never saw him much. We're still friends, in spite of everything."

"He's a good fellow."

"Yeah."

Shelby got up, ruffled his hair and grinned. "You're a good fellow, too."

He laughed softly. "Thanks."

"Try not to dwell so much on things," she advised. "Sit back and just let life happen for a while. You're so intense, Cort. Like your dad," she said affectionately, her dark eyes soft on his face. "One day Odalie may discover that you're the sun in her sky and come home. But you have to let her try her wings. She's traveled, but only with her parents. This is her first real taste of freedom. Let her enjoy it."

"Even if she messes up her life with that Italian guy?"

"Even then. It's her life," she reminded him gently. "You don't like people telling you what to do, even if it's for your own good, right?"

He glowered at her. "If you're going to mention that time you told me not to climb up the barn roof and I didn't listen…"

"Your first broken arm," she recalled, and pursed her lips. "And I didn't even say I told you so," she reminded him.

"No. You didn't." He stared at his linked fingers. "Maddie Lane sets me off. But I should never have said she was ugly and no man would want her."

"You said that?" she exclaimed, wincing. "Cort…!"

"I know." He sighed. "Not my finest moment. She's not a bad person. It's just she gets these goofy notions about animals. That rooster is going to hurt somebody bad one day, maybe put an eye out, and she thinks it's funny."

"She doesn't realize he's dangerous," she replied.

"She doesn't want to realize it. She's in over her head with these expansion projects. Cage-free eggs. She hasn't got the capital to go into that sort of operation, and she's probably already breaking half a dozen laws by selling them to restaurants."

"She's hurting for money," Shelby reminded somberly. "Most ranchers are, even us. The drought is killing us. But Maddie only has a few head of cattle and she can't buy feed for them if her corn crop dies. She'll have to sell at a loss. Her breeding program is already losing money." She shook her head. "Her father was a fine rancher. He taught your father things about breeding bulls. But Maddie just doesn't have the experience. She jumped in at the deep end when her father died, but it was by necessity, not choice. I'm sure she'd much rather be drawing pictures than trying to produce calves."

"Drawing." He said it with contempt.

She stared at him. "Cort, haven't you ever noticed that?" She indicated a beautiful rendering in pastels of a fairy in a patch of daisies in an exquisite frame on the wall.

He glanced at it. "Not bad. Didn't you get that at an art show last year?"

"I got it from Maddie last year. She drew it."

He frowned. He actually got up and went to look at the piece. “She drew that?” he asked.

“Yes. She was selling two pastel drawings at the art show. This was one of them. She sculpts, too—beautiful little fairies—but she doesn’t like to show those to people. I told her she should draw professionally, perhaps in graphic design or even illustration. She laughed. She doesn’t think she’s good enough.” She sighed. “Maddie is insecure. She has one of the poorest self-images of anyone I know.”

Cort knew that. His lips made a thin line. He felt even worse after what he’d said to her. “I should probably call and apologize,” he murmured.

“That’s not a bad idea, son,” she agreed.

“And then I should drive over there, hide in the grass and shoot that damned red-feathered son of a…!”

“Cort!”

He let out a harsh breath. “Okay. I’ll call her.”

“Roosters don’t live that long,” she called after him. “He’ll die of old age before too much longer.”

“With my luck, he’ll hit fifteen and keep going. Animals that nasty never die!” he called back.

He wanted to apologize to Maddie. But when he turned on his cell phone, he realized that he didn’t even know her phone number. He tried to look it up on the internet, but couldn’t find a listing.

He went back downstairs. His mother was in the kitchen.

“Do you know the Lanes’ phone number?” he asked.

She blinked. "Well, no. I don't think I've ever tried to call them, not since Pierce Lane died last year, anyway."

"No number listed, anywhere," he said.

"You might drive by there later in the week," she suggested gently. "It's not that far."

He hesitated. "She'd lock the doors and hide inside when I drove up," he predicted.

His mother didn't know what to say. He was probably right.

"I need to get away," he said after a minute. "I'm wired like a piano. I need to get away from the rooster and Odalie and…everything."

"Why don't you go to Wyoming and visit your sister?" she suggested.

He sighed. "She's not expecting me until Thursday."

She laughed. "She won't care. Go early. It would do both of you good."

"It might at that."

"It won't take you long to fly up there," she added. "You can use the corporate jet. I'm sure your father wouldn't mind. He misses Morie. So do I."

"Yeah, I miss her, too," he said. He hugged his mother. "I'll go pack a bag. If that rooster shows up looking for me, put him on a plane to France, would you? I hear they love chicken over there. Get him a business-class ticket. If someone can ship a lobster from Maine," he added with a laugh, referring to a joke that had gone the rounds years before, "I can ship a chicken to France."

"I'll take it under advisement," she promised.

* * *

His mother was right, Cort thought that evening. He loved being with his sister. He and Morie were a lot alike, from their hot tempers to their very Puritan attitudes. They'd always been friends. When she was just five, she'd followed her big brother around everywhere, to the amusement of his friends. Cort was tolerant and he adored her. He never minded the kidding.

"I'm sorry about your rooster problems," Morie told him with a gentle laugh. "Believe me, we can understand. My poor sister-in-law has fits with ours."

"I like Bodie," he said, smiling. "Cane sure seems different these days."

"He is. He's back in therapy, he's stopped smashing bars and he seems to have settled down for good. Bodie's wonderful for him. She and Cane have had some problems, but they're mostly solved now," she said. She smiled secretly. "Actually, Bodie and I are going to have a lot more in common for the next few months."

Cort was quick. He glanced at her in the semidarkness of the front porch, with fireflies darting around. "A baby?"

She laughed with pure delight. "A baby," she said, and her voice was like velvet. "I only found out a little while ago. Bodie found out the day you showed up." She sighed. "So much happiness. It's almost too much to bear. Mal's over the moon."

"Is it a boy or a girl? Do you know yet?"

She shook her head. "Too early to tell. But we're not

going to ask. We want it to be a surprise, however old-fashioned that might be."

He chuckled. "I'm going to be an uncle. Wow. That's super. Have you told Mom and Dad?"

"Not yet. I'll call Mom tonight, though."

"She'll be so excited. Her first grandchild."

Morie glanced at him. "You ever going to get married?" she asked.

"Sure, if Odalie ever says yes." He sighed. "She was warming up to me there just for a while. Then that Italian fellow came along and offered her voice training. He's something of a legend among opera stars. And that's what she wants, to sing at the Met." He grimaced. "Just my luck, to fall in love with a woman who only wants a career."

"I believe her mother was the same way, wasn't she?" Morie asked gently. "And then she and Cole Everett got really close. She gave up being a professional singer to come home and have kids. Although she still composes. That Wyoming group, Desperado, had a major hit from a song she wrote for them some years ago."

"I think she still composes. But she likes living on a ranch. Odalie hates it. She says she's never going to marry a man who smells like cow droppings." He looked at one of his big boots, where his ankle was resting on his other knee in the rocking chair. "I'm a rancher, damn it," he muttered. "I can't learn another trade. Dad's counting on me to take over when he can't do the work anymore."

"Yes, I know," she said sadly. "What else could you do?"

“Teach, I guess,” he replied. “I have a degree in animal husbandry.” He made a face. “I’d rather be shot. I’d rather let that red-feathered assassin loose on my nose. I hate the whole idea of routine.”

“Me, too,” Morie confessed. “I love ranching. I guess the drought is giving Dad problems, too, huh?”

“It’s been pretty bad,” Cort agreed. “People in Oklahoma and the other plains states are having it worse, though. No rain. It’s like the Dust Bowl in the thirties, people are saying. So many disaster declarations.”

“How are you getting around it?”

“Wells, mostly,” he said. “We’ve drilled new ones and filled the tanks to the top. Irrigating our grain crops. Of course, we’ll still have to buy some feed through the winter. But we’re in better shape than a lot of other cattle producers. Damn, I hate how it’s going to impact small ranchers and farmers. Those huge combines will be standing in the shadows, just waiting to pounce when the foreclosures come.”

“Family ranches are going to be obsolete one day, like family farms,” Morie said sadly. “Except, maybe, for the big ones, like ours.”

“True words. People don’t realize how critical this really is.”

She reached over and squeezed his hand. “That’s why we have the National Cattleman’s Association and the state organizations,” she reminded him. “Now stop worrying. We’re going fishing tomorrow!”

“Really?” he asked, delighted. “Trout?”

“Yes. The water’s just cold enough, still. When it

heats up too much, you can't eat them." She sighed. "This may be the last chance we'll get for a while, if this heat doesn't relent."

"Tell me about it. We hardly had winter at all in Texas. Spring was like summer, and it's gone downhill since. I'd love to stand in a trout stream, even if I don't catch a thing."

"Me, too."

"Does Bodie fish?"

"You know, I've never asked. We'll do that tomorrow. For now," she said, rising, "I'm for bed." She paused and hugged him. "It's nice to have you here for a while."

"For me, too, little sis." He hugged her back, and kissed her forehead. "See you in the morning."

Chapter Two

Maddie hadn't thought about Cort for one whole hour. She laughed at herself while she fed her hens. Pumpkin was in the henhouse, locked in for the time being, so that she could feed the chickens without having to defend herself.

The laughter died away as she recalled the things Cort had said to her. She was ugly and flat-chested and he could never be attracted to her. She looked down at her slender body and frowned. She couldn't suddenly become beautiful. She didn't have the money to buy fancy clothes that flattered her, like Odalie did. In fact, her wardrobe was two years old.

When her father had been dying of cancer, every penny they had was tied up trying to keep up with doctor bills that the insurance didn't cover. Her father did carry life insurance, which was a lucky break because at his death, it was enough to pay back everybody.

But things were still hard. This year, they'd struggled to pay just the utility bills. It was going to come down to a hard choice, sell off cattle or sell off land. There was a developer who'd already been to see Maddie about selling the ranch. He wanted to build a huge hotel and amusement park complex. He was offering her over a million dollars, and he was persistent.

"You just run a few head of cattle here, don't you?" the tall man in the expensive suit said, but his smile didn't really reach his eyes. He was an opportunist, looking for a great deal. He thought Maddie would be a pushover once he pulled out a figure that would tempt a saint.

But Maddie's whole heritage was in that land. Her great-grandfather had started the ranch and suffered all sorts of deprivations to get it going. Her grandfather had taken over where he left off, improving both the cattle herd and the land. Her father had toiled for years to find just the right mix of grasses to pursue a purebred cattle breeding herd that was now the envy of several neighbors. All that would be gone. The cattle sold off, the productive grasslands torn up and paved for the complex, which would attract people passing by on the long, monotonous interstate highway that ran close to the border of the ranch.

"I'll have to think about it," she told him, nodding. Her smile didn't reach her eyes, either.

He pursed his lips. "You know, we're looking at other land in the area, too. You might get left out in the cold if we find someone who's more enthusiastic about the price we're offering."

Maddie didn't like threats. Even nice ones, that came with soft words and smiles.

"Whatever," she said. She smiled again. "I did say I'd have to think about it."

His smile faded, and his eyes narrowed. "You have a prime location here, only one close neighbor and a nearby interstate. I really want this place. I want it a lot."

"Listen, I hate being pressured…!"

He held up both hands. "Okay! But you think about it. You think hard." His expression became dangerous-looking. "We know how to deal with reluctant buyers. That's not a threat, it's just a statement. Here's my card."

She took it gingerly, as if she thought it had germs.

He made a huffing sound and climbed back into his fantastically expensive foreign car. He roared out of the driveway, scattering chickens.

She glared after it. No more eggs for two more days, she thought irritably. She'd rather starve than sell the ranch. But money was getting very tight. The drought was going to be a major hit to their poor finances, she thought dismally.

"Miss Maddie, you got that rooster locked up?" Ben called at the fence, interrupting her depressing reverie.

She turned. "Yes, Ben, he's restrained." She laughed.

"Thanks." He grimaced. "Going to feed the livestock and I'd just as soon not be mauled in the process."

"I know." She glanced at the wire door behind which Pumpkin was calling to the hens in that odd tone that roosters used when there was some special treat on the ground for them. It was actually a handful of mealworms that Maddie had tossed in the henhouse to keep him occupied while she locked him in.

Two of the hens went running to the door.

"He's lying," Maddie told them solemnly. "He's already eaten the mealworms, he just wants out."

"Cort left town, you hear?" Ben asked.

Her heart jumped. "Where did he go?" she asked miserably, waiting to hear that he'd flown to Italy to see Odalie.

"Wyoming, one of his cowboys said, to see his sister."

"Oh."

"Mooning over that Odalie girl, I guess," he muttered. "She said she hated men who smelled like cattle. I guess she hates her dad, then, because he made his fortune on the Big Spur raising cattle, and he still does!"

"She's just been spoiled," Maddie said quietly.

Ben glanced at her irritably. "She was mean to you when you were in school. Your dad actually went to the school to get it stopped. He went to see Cole Everett about it, too, didn't he?"

"Yes." She flushed. She didn't like remembering that situation, although Odalie had quickly stopped victimizing her after her father got involved.

"Had a nasty attitude, that one," Ben muttered. "Looked down her nose at every other girl and most of the boys. Thought she was too good to live in a hick town in Texas." His eyes narrowed. "She's going to come a cropper one day, you mark my words. What's that quote, 'pride goeth after a fall'? And she's got a lot farther to fall than some women."

"There's another quote, something about love your enemies?" she teased.

"Yes, well, she's given a lot of people reason to put that one into practice."

Maddie grimaced. "It must be nice, to have beauty and talent. I'd settle for one or the other myself." She laughed.

"You ought to be selling them little fairy statues you make," he advised. "Prettiest little things I ever saw. That one you sent my granddaughter for her birthday sits in the living room, because her mother loves to look at it. One of her friends has an art gallery in San Antonio. She said," he emphasized, "that you could make a fortune with those things."

Maddie flushed. "Wow."

"Not that those pretty drawings are bad, either. Sold one to Shelby Brannt, didn't you?"

"Yes." She'd loved the idea of Cort having to see her artwork every day, because she knew that Shelby had mounted it on a wall in the dining room of her home. But he probably never even looked at it. Though cultured, Cort had little use for art or sculpture. Unless it was a sculpture of one of the ranch's prize bulls. They had one done in bronze. It sat on the mantel in the living room of the Brannt home.

"Ought to paint that rooster while he's still alive," Ben said darkly.

"Ben!"

He held up both hands. "Didn't say I was going to hurt him."

"Okay."

"But somebody else might." He pursed his lips. "You know, he could be the victim of a terrible traffic accident one day. He loves to run down that dirt road in front of the house."

"You bite your tongue," she admonished.

"Spoilsport."

"That visitor who came the other day, that developer, you see him again?" Ben asked curiously.

"No, but he left his name." She pulled his business card out of her pocket and held it up. "He's from Las Vegas. He wants to build a hotel and amusement park complex right here." She looked around wistfully. "Offered me a million dollars. Gosh, what I could do with that!"

"You could sell and throw away everything your family worked for here?" Ben asked sadly. "My great-grandfather started working here with your great-grandfather. Our families have been together all that time." He sighed. "Guess I could learn to use a computer and make a killing with a dot-com business," he mused facetiously.

"Aw, Ben," she said gently. "I don't want to sell up. I was just thinking out loud." She smiled, and this time it was genuine. "I'd put a lot of people out of work, and God knows what I'd do with all the animals who live here."

"Especially them fancy breeding bulls and cows,"

he replied. "Cort Brannt would love to get his hands on them. He's always over here buying our calves."

"So he is."

Ben hesitated. "Heard something about that developer, that Archie Lawson fellow."

"You did? What?"

"Just gossip, mind."

"So? Tell me!" she prodded.

He made a face. "Well, he wanted a piece of land over around Cheyenne, on the interstate. The owner wouldn't sell. So cattle started dying of mysterious causes. So did the owner's dog, a big border collie he'd had for years. He hired a private investigator, and had the dog autopsied. It was poison. They could never prove it was Lawson, but they were pretty sure of it. See, he has a background in chemistry. Used to work at a big government lab, they say, before he started buying and selling land."

Her heart stopped. "Oh, dear." She bit her lip. "He said something about knowing how to force deals…"

"I'll get a couple of my pals to keep an eye on the cattle in the outer pastures," Ben said. "I'll tell them to shoot first and ask questions later if they see anybody prowling around here."

"Thanks, Ben," she said heavily. "Good heavens, as if we don't already have enough trouble here with no rain, for God knows how long."

"Everybody's praying for it." He cocked his head. "I know a Cheyenne medicine man. Been friends for a couple of years. They say he can make rain."

"Well!" She hesitated. "What does he charge?"

"He doesn't. He says he has these abilities that God gave him, and if he ever takes money for it, he'll lose it. Seems to believe it, and I hear he's made rain at least twice in the area. If things go from bad to worse, maybe we should talk to him."

She grinned. "Let's talk to him."

He chuckled. "I'll give him a call later."

Her eyebrows arched. "He has a telephone?"

"Miss Maddie," he scoffed, "do you think Native American people still live in teepees and wear head-dresses?"

She flushed. "Of course not," she lied.

"He lives in a house just like ours, he wears jeans and T-shirts mostly and he's got a degree in anthropology. When he's not fossicking, they say he goes overseas with a group of mercs from Texas for top secret operations."

She was fascinated. "Really!"

"He's something of a local celebrity on the rez. He lives there."

"Could you call him and ask him to come over when he has time?"

He laughed. "I'll do that tonight."

"Even if he can't make rain, I'd love to meet him," she said. "He sounds very interesting."

"Take my word for it, he is. Doesn't talk much, but when he does, it's worth hearing. Well, I'll get back to work."

"Thanks, Ben."

He smiled. "My pleasure. And don't let that developer bully you," he said firmly. "Maybe you need to talk to

Cort's dad and tell him what's going on. He's not going to like that, about the development. It's too close to his barns. In these hard times, even the Brannts couldn't afford to build new ones with all that high tech they use."

"Got a point. I'll talk to him."

Maddie went back to the house. She put the feed basket absently on the kitchen counter, mentally reviewing all the things she had planned for the week. She missed Cort already. But at least it meant the rooster was likely to stay at home. He only went over to the Brannt ranch when Cort was in residence, to attack him.

"Better wash those eggs and put them in the refrigerator," Great-Aunt Sadie advised. "They're the ones for the restaurant, aren't they?"

"Yes. Old Mr. Bailey said his customers have been raving about the taste of his egg omelets lately." She laughed. "I'll have to give my girls a treat for that."

Great-Aunt Sadie was frowning. "Maddie, did you ever look up the law about selling raw products?"

Maddie shook her head. "I meant to. But I'm sure it's not illegal to sell eggs. My mother did it for years before she died…."

"That was a long time ago, honey. Don't you remember that raid a few years ago on those poor farmers who were selling raw milk?" She made a face. "What sort of country do we live in? Sending an armed raid team after helpless farmers for selling milk!"

Maddie felt uneasy. "I'd forgotten that."

"I hadn't. In my day we had homemade butter and we could drink all the raw milk we wanted—didn't have all this fancy stuff a hundred years ago and it seems to me people were a whole lot healthier."

"You weren't here a hundred years ago," Maddie pointed out with a grin. "Anyway, the government's not going to come out here and attack me for selling a few eggs!"

She did look on the internet for the law pertaining to egg production and found that she was in compliance. In fact, there were even places in the country licensed to sell raw milk. She'd have to tell Great-Aunt Sadie about that, she mused. Apparently armed teams weren't raiding farms out west.

Meanwhile, a day later, she did call King Brannt. She was hesitant about it. Not only was he Cort's father, he had a reputation in the county for being one tough customer, and difficult to get along with. He had a fiery temper that he wasn't shy about using. But the developer's determination to get the Lane ranch could have repercussions. A lot of them.

She picked up the phone and dialed the ranch.

The housekeeper answered.

"Could I speak to King Brannt, please?" she asked. "It's Maddie Lane."

There was a skirl of laughter. "Yes, you've got a rooster named Pumpkin."

Maddie laughed. "Is he famous?"

"He is around here," the woman said. "Cort isn't laughing, but the rest of us are. Imagine having a personal devil in the form of a little red rooster! We've been teasing Cort that he must have done something terrible that we don't know about."

Maddie sighed. "I'm afraid Pumpkin has it in for Cort. See, he picked him up by the feet and showed him to my girls, my hens, I mean, and hurt his pride. That was when he started looking for Cort."

"Oh, I see. It's vengeance." She laughed again. "Nice talking to you, I'll go get Mr. Brannt. Take just a minute..."

Maddie held on. Her gaze fell on one of her little fairy statues. It was delicate and beautiful; the tiny face perfect, lovely, with sculpted long blond hair, sitting on a stone with a butterfly in its hand. It was a new piece, one she'd just finished with the plastic sculpture mix that was the best on the market. Her egg money paid for the materials. She loved the little things and could never bear to sell one. But she did wonder if there was a market for such a specialized piece.

"Brannt," a deep voice said curtly.

She almost jumped. "Mr. Brannt? It's... I mean I'm Maddie Lane. I live on the little ranch next door to yours," she faltered.

"Hi, Maddie," he said, and his voice lost its curt edge and was pleasant. "What can I do for you?"

"I've got sort of a situation over here. I wanted to tell you about it."

"What's wrong? Can we help?"

"That's so nice of you." She didn't add that she'd been told some very scary things about his temper. "It's this developer. He's from Las Vegas..."

"Yes. Archie Lawson. I had him investigated."

"He's trying to get me to sell my ranch to him. I don't want to. This ranch has been in my family for generations. But he's very pushy and he made some threats."

"He's carried them out in the past," King said, very curtly. "But you can be sure I'm not going to let him hurt you or your cattle herd. I'll put on extra patrols on the land boundary we share, and station men at the cabin out there. We use it for roundup, but it's been vacant for a week or so. I'll make sure someone's there at all times, and we'll hook up cameras around your cattle herd and monitor them constantly."

"You'd do that for me?" she faltered. "Cameras. It's so expensive." She knew, because in desperation she'd looked at them and been shocked at the prices for even a cheap system.

"I'd do that for you," he replied. "You have one of the finest breeding herds I know of, which is why we buy so many of your young bulls."

"Why, thank you."

"You're welcome. You see, it's looking out for our interests as well as yours. I can't have a complex so close to my barns, or my purebred herd. The noise of construction would be bad enough, but the constant traffic would injure production."

"Yes, I know what you mean."

"Besides that, Lawson is unscrupulous. He's got his fingers in lots of dirty pies. He's had several brushes with the law, too."

"I'm not surprised. He was a little scary."

"Don't you worry. If he comes back and makes any threat at all, you call over here. If you can't find me, talk to Cort. He'll take care of it."

She hesitated. "Actually Cort isn't speaking to me right now."

There was a pause. "Because of the rooster?" His voice was almost smiling.

"Actually because I made a nasty crack about Odalie Everett," she confessed heavily. "I didn't mean to. He made me mad. I guess he was justified to complain. Pumpkin is really mean to him."

"So I heard. That rooster has had brushes with several of our cowboys." She could tell that he was trying not to laugh.

"The man who sold him to me said he was real gentle and wouldn't hurt a fly. That's sort of true. I've never seen Pumpkin hurt a fly." She laughed. "Just people."

"You need a gentle rooster, especially if you're going to be selling eggs and baby chicks."

"The baby chick operation is down the road, but I'm doing well with my egg business."

"Glad to hear it. Our housekeeper wants to get on your customer list, by the way."

"I'll talk to her, and thanks!"

He chuckled. "My pleasure."

"If Mr. Lawson comes back, I'll let you know."

"Please do. The man is trouble."

"I know. Thanks again, Mr. Brannt. I feel better now."

"Your dad was a friend of mine," he said quietly. "I miss him. I know you do, too."

"I miss him a lot," she said. "But Great-Aunt Sadie and I are coping. It's just this ranching thing," she added miserably. "Dad was good at it, he had charts in the barn, he knew which traits to breed for, all that technical stuff. He taught me well, but I'm not as good as he was at it. Not at all. I like to paint and sculpt." She hesitated. "Creative people shouldn't have to breed cattle!" she burst out.

He laughed. "I hear you. Listen, suppose I send Cort over there to help you with the genetics? He's even better at it than I am. And I'm good. No conceit, just fact."

She laughed, too. "You really are. We read about your bulls in the cattle journals." She paused. "I don't think Cort would come."

"He'll come." He sounded certain of it. "He needs something to take his mind off that woman. She's a sweet girl, in her way, but she's got some serious growing up to do. She thinks the world revolves around her. It doesn't."

"She's just been a little spoiled, I think." She tried to be gracious.

"Rotten," he replied. "My kids never were."

"You and Mrs. Brannt did a great job with yours. And John Everett is a really nice man. So the Everetts did a great job there, too." She didn't mention the second Everett son, Tanner. The Everetts never spoke about him. Neither did anyone else. He was something of a mystery man. But gossip was that he and his dad didn't get along.

"They did a great job on John, for sure." He let out a breath. "I just wish Cort would wake up. Odalie is never going to settle in a small community. She's meant for high society and big cities. Cort would die in a high-rise apartment. He's got too much country in him, although he'd jump at the chance if Odalie would offer him one. Just between us," he added quietly, "I hope she doesn't. If she makes it in opera, and I think she can, what would Cort do with himself while she trained and performed? He'd be bored out of his mind. He doesn't even like opera. He likes country-western."

"He plays it very well," Maddie said softly. "I loved coming to the barbecue at your place during the spring sale and hearing him sing. It was nice of you to invite all of us. Even old Ben. He was over the moon."

He laughed. "You're all neighbors. I know you think of Ben as more family than employee. His family has worked for your family for four generations."

"That's a long time," she agreed. "I'm not selling my place," she added firmly. "No matter what that fancy Las Vegas man does."

"Good for you. I'll help you make sure of that. I'll send Cort on over."

"He's back from visiting his sister?" she stammered.

"Yes. Got back yesterday. They went trout fishing."

She sighed. "I'd love to go trout fishing."

"Cort loves it. He said they did close the trout streams for fishing a couple of days after he and Dana—Morie, I mean, went. The heat makes it impossible. "

"That's true." She hesitated. "Why do you call Morie Dana?" she blurted out.

He laughed. "When Shelby was carrying them, we called them Matt and Dana. Those were the names we picked out. Except that two of our friends used those names for theirs and we had to change ours. It got to be a habit, though, until the kids were adolescents.

"Hey, Cort," she heard King call, his hand covering the receiver so his voice was a little muffled.

"Yes, Dad?" came the reply.

"I want you to go over to the Lane place and give Maddie some help with her breeding program."

"The hell I will!" Cort burst out.

The hand over the phone seemed to close, because the rest of it was muffled. Angry voices, followed by more discussion, followed like what seemed a string of horrible curses from Cort.

King came back on the line. "He said he'd be pleased to come over and help," he lied. "But he did ask if you'd shut your rooster up first." He chuckled.

"I'll put him in the chicken house right now." She tried not to sound as miserable as she felt. She knew Cort didn't want to help her. He hated her. "And thank you again."

"You're very welcome. Call us if you need help with Lawson. Okay?"

"Okay."

True to his father's words, Cort drove up in front of the house less than an hour later. He wasn't slamming doors or scattering chickens this time, either. He looked almost pleasant. Apparently his father had talked to him very firmly.

Maddie had combed her hair and washed her face.

She still wasn't going to win any beauty contests. She had on her nicest jeans and a pink T-shirt that said La Vie en Rose.

It called attention, unfortunately, to breasts that were small and pert instead of big and tempting. But Cort was looking at her shirt with his lips pursed.

"The world through rose-colored glasses?" he mused. "You speak French."

"Of course. French, Spanish and enough German to get me arrested in Munich. We do cattle deals all over the world," he added.

"Yes, I remember." She swallowed, hard, recalling the things he'd said at their last unfortunate meeting. "Your father said you could help me figure out Dad's breeding program."

"I think so. I helped him work up the new one before he passed away," he added quietly. "We were all shocked by how fast it happened."

"So were we," Maddie confessed. "Two months from the time he was diagnosed until he passed on." She drew in a long breath. "He hated tests, you know. He wouldn't go to the doctor about anything unless he was already at death's door. I think the doctor suspected something, but Dad just passed right over the lecture about tests being necessary and walked out. By the time they diagnosed the cancer, it was too late for anything except radiation. And somebody said that they only did that to help contain the pain." Her pale eyes grew sad. "It was terrible, the pain. At the last, he was so sedated that he hardly knew me. It was the only way he could cope."

"I'm sorry," he said. "I haven't lost parents, but I lost both my grandparents. They were wonderful people. It was hard to let them go."

"Life goes on," she said quietly. "Everybody dies. It's just a matter of how and when."

"True."

She swallowed. "Dad kept his chalkboard in the barn, and his books in the library, along with his journals. I've read them all, but I can't make sense of what he was doing. I'm not college educated, and I don't really know much about animal husbandry. I know what I do from watching Dad."

"I can explain it to you."

She nodded. "Thanks."

She turned and led the way to the house.

"Where's that...rooster?" he asked.

"Shut up in the henhouse with a fan."

"A fan?" he exclaimed and burst out laughing.

"It really isn't funny," she said softly. "I lost two of my girls to the heat. Found them dead in the henhouse, trying to lay. I had Ben go and get us a fan and install it there. It does help with the heat, a little at least."

"My grandmother used to keep hens," he recalled. "But we only have one or two now. Foxes got the rest." He glanced at her. "Andie, our housekeeper, wants to get on your egg customer list for two dozen a week."

She nodded. "Your dad mentioned that. I can do that. I've got pullets that should start laying soon. My flock is growing by leaps and bounds." She indicated the large fenced chicken yard, dotted with all sorts of chickens.

The henhouse was huge, enough to accommodate them all, complete with perches and ladders and egg boxes and, now, a fan.

"Nice operation."

"I'm going to expand it next year, if I do enough business."

"Did you check the law on egg production?"

She laughed. "Yes, I did. I'm in compliance. I don't have a middleman, or I could be in trouble. I sell directly to the customer, so it's all okay."

"Good." He shrugged, his hands in his jean pockets. "I'd hate to have to bail you out of jail."

"You wouldn't," she sighed.

He stopped and looked down at her. She seemed so dejected. "Yes, I would," he said, his deep voice quiet and almost tender as he studied her small frame, her short wavy blond hair, her wide, soft gray eyes. Her complexion was exquisite, not a blemish on it except for one small mole on her cheek. She had a pretty mouth, too. It looked tempting. Bow-shaped, soft, naturally pink…

"Cort?" she asked suddenly, her whole body tingling, her heart racing at the way he was staring at her mouth.

"What? Oh. Yes. The breeding books." He nodded. "We should get to it."

"Yes." She swallowed, tried to hide her blush and opened the front door.

Chapter Three

Maddie couldn't help but stare at Cort as he leaned over the desk to read the last page of her father's breeding journal. He was the handsomest man she'd ever seen. And that physique! He was long and lean, but also muscular. Broad-shouldered, narrow-hipped, and in the opening of his chambray shirt, thick curling black hair peeked out.

She'd never been overly interested in intimacy. Never having indulged, she had no idea how it felt, although she'd been reading romance novels since her early teens. She did know how things worked between men and women from health class. What she didn't know was why women gave in to men. She supposed it came naturally.

Cort felt her eyes on him and turned, so that he was

looking directly into her wide, shocked gray eyes. His own dark ones narrowed. He knew that look, that expression. She was trying to hide it, but he wasn't fooled.

"Take a picture," he drawled, because her interest irritated him. She wasn't his type. Not at all.

Her reaction shamed him. She looked away, cleared her throat and went beet-red. "Sorry," she choked. "I was just thinking. You were sort of in the way. I was thinking about my fairies..."

He felt guilty. That made him even more irritable. "What fairies?"

She stumbled and had to catch herself as she went past him. She was so embarrassed she could hardly even walk.

She went to the shelf where she'd put the newest one. Taking it down very carefully, she carried it to the desk and put it in front of him.

He caught his breath. He picked it up, delicately for a man with such large, strong hands, and held it up to his eyes. He turned it. He was smiling. "This is really beautiful," he said, as if it surprised him. He glanced at her. "You did this by yourself?"

She moved uneasily. "Yes," she muttered. What did he think—that she had somebody come in and do the work so she could claim credit for it?

"I didn't mean it like that, Maddie," he said gently. The sound of her name on his lips made her tingle. She didn't dare look up, because her attraction to him would surely show. He knew a lot more about women than she knew about men. He could probably tell already that she liked him. It had made him mad. So she'd have to hide it.

"Okay," she said. But she still wouldn't look up.

He gave the beautiful little statuette another look before he put it down very gently on the desk. "You should be marketing those," he said firmly. "I've seen things half as lovely sell for thousands of dollars."

"Thousands?" she exclaimed.

"Yes. Sometimes five figures. I was staying at a hotel in Arizona during a cattlemen's conference and a doll show was exhibiting at the same hotel. I talked to some of the artists." He shook his head. "It's amazing how much collectors will pay for stuff like that." He indicated the fairy with his head. "You should look into it."

She was stunned. "I never dreamed people would pay so much for a little sculpture."

"Your paintings are nice, too," he admitted. "My mother loves the drawing you did. She bought it at that art show last year. She said you should be selling the sculptures, too."

"I would. It's just that they're like my children," she confessed, and flushed because that sounded nutty. "I mean…well, it's hard to explain."

"Each one is unique and you put a lot of yourself into it," he guessed. "So it would be hard to sell one."

"Yes." She did look up then, surprised that he was so perceptive.

"You have the talent. All you need is the drive."

"Drive." She sighed. She smiled faintly. "How about imminent starvation? Does that work for drive?"

He laughed. "We wouldn't let you starve. Your bull calves are too valuable to us," he added, just when she thought he might actually care.

"Thanks," she said shyly. "In that journal of Dad's—" she changed the subject "—he talks about heritability traits for lean meat with marbling to produce cuts that health-conscious consumers will buy. Can you explain to me how I go about producing herd sires that carry the traits we breed for?"

He smiled. "It's complicated. Want to take notes?"

She sighed. "Just like going back to school." Then she remembered school, and the agonies she went through in her junior and senior years because of Odalie Everett, and her face clenched.

"What's wrong?" he asked, frowning.

She swallowed. She almost said what was wrong. But she'd been down that road with him already, making comments she shouldn't have made about Odalie. She wasn't going to make him mad. Not now, when he was being pleasant and helpful.

"Nothing. Just a stray thought." She smiled. "I'll get some paper and a pencil."

After a half hour she put down the pencil. "It's got to be like learning to speak Martian," she muttered.

He laughed out loud. "Listen, I didn't come into the world knowing how this stuff worked, either. I had to learn it, and if my dad hadn't been a patient man, I'd have jumped off a cliff."

"Your dad is patient?" she asked, and couldn't help sounding surprised.

"I know he's got a reputation for being just the opposite. But he really is patient. I had a hard time with algebra in high school. He'd take me into the office every night and go over problems with me until I understood how to do them. He never fussed, or yelled, or raised his voice. And I was a problem child." He shook his head. "I'm amazed I got through my childhood in one piece. I've broken half the bones in my body at some point, and I know my mother's gray hairs are all because of me. Morie was a little lady. She never caused anybody any trouble."

"I remember," Maddie said with a smile. "She was always kind to me. She was a couple of years ahead of me, but she was never snobby."

His dark eyes narrowed. "There's a hidden comment in there."

She flushed. "I didn't mention anybody else."

"You meant Odalie," he said. "She can't help being beautiful and rich and talented," he pointed out. "And it wasn't her fault that her parents put her in public school instead of private school, where she might have been better treated."

"Better treated." She glared at him. "Not one teacher or administrator ever had a bad word to say about her, even though she bullied younger girls mercilessly and spent most of her time bad-mouthing people she didn't like. One year she had a party for our whole class, at the ranch. She invited every single girl in the class—except me."

Cort's eyes narrowed. "I'm sure it wasn't intentional."

"My father went to see her father, that's how unintentional it was," she replied quietly. "When Cole Everett knew what she'd done to me, he grounded her for a month and took away her end-of-school trip as punishment."

"That seems extreme for not inviting someone to a party," he scoffed.

"I guess that's because you don't know about the other things she did to me," she replied.

"Let me guess—she didn't send you a Valentine's Day card, either," he drawled in a tone that dripped sarcasm.

She looked at him with open sadness. "Sure. That's it. I held a grudge because she didn't send me a holiday card and my father went to see the school principal and Odalie's father because he liked starting trouble."

Cort remembered her father. He was the mildest, most forgiving man anywhere around Branntville. He'd walk away from a fight if he could. The very fact that he got involved meant that he felt there was more than a slight problem.

But Cort loved Odalie, and here was this bad-tempered little frump making cracks about her, probably because she was jealous.

"I guess if you don't have a real talent and you aren't as pretty, it's hard to get along with someone who has it all," he commented.

Her face went beet-red. She stood up, took her father's

journal, closed it and put it back in the desk drawer. She faced him across the width of the desk.

"Thank you for explaining the journal to me," she said in a formal tone. "I'll study the notes I took very carefully."

"Fine." He started to leave, hesitated. He turned and looked back at her. He could see an unusual brightness in her eyes. "Look, I didn't mean to hurt your feelings. It's just, well, you don't know Odalie. She's sweet and kind, she'd never hurt anybody on purpose."

"I don't have any talent, I'm ugly and I lie." She nodded. "Thanks."

"Hell, I never said you lied!"

She swallowed. Loud voices and curses made her nervous. She gripped the edge of the desk.

"Now what's wrong?" he asked angrily.

She shook her head. "Nothing," she said quickly.

He took a sudden, quick step toward her. She backed up, knocked over the desk chair and almost fell again getting it between him and herself. She was white in the face.

He stopped in his tracks. His lips fell open. In all his life, he'd never seen a woman react that way.

"What the hell is wrong with you?" he asked, but not in a loud or menacing tone.

She swallowed. "Nothing. Thanks for coming over."

He scowled. She looked scared to death.

Great-Aunt Sadie had heard a crash in the room. She opened the door gingerly and looked in. She glanced from Maddie's white face to Cort's drawn one. "Maddie, you okay?" she asked hesitantly, her eyes flicking back and forth to Cort's as if she, too, was uneasy.

"I'm fine. I just…knocked the chair over." She laughed, but it was a nervous, quick laugh. "Cort was just leaving. He gave me lots of information."

"Nice of him," Sadie agreed. She moved closer to Maddie, as if prepared to act as a human shield if Cort took another step toward the younger woman. "Good night, Cort."

He wanted to know what was wrong. It was true he'd said some mean things, but the fear in Maddie's eyes, and the looks he was getting, really disturbed him. He moved to the door, hesitated. "If you need any more help…" he began.

"I'll call. Sure. Thanks for offering." Maddie's voice sounded tight. She was standing very still. He was reminded forcibly of deer's eyes in headlights.

"Well, I'll get on home. Good night."

"Night," Maddie choked out.

He glanced from one woman to the other, turned and pulled the door closed behind him.

Maddie almost collapsed into the chair. Tears were running down her cheeks. Great-Aunt Sadie knelt beside the chair and pulled her close, rocking her. "There, there, it's all right. He's gone. What happened?"

"I mentioned about Odalie not inviting me to the party and he said I was just jealous of her. I said something, I don't…remember what, and he started toward me, all mad and impatient…" She closed her eyes, shivering. “I can’t forget. All those years ago, and I still can’t forget!”

“Nobody ever told Cort just what Odalie did to you, did they?”

“Apparently not,” Maddie said heavily. She wiped her eyes. “Her dad made her apologize, but I know she never regretted it.” She drew in a breath. “I told her that one day somebody was going to pay her back for all the mean things she did.” She looked up. “Cort thinks she’s a saint. If he only knew what she’s really like…”

“It wouldn’t matter,” the older woman said sadly. “Men get hooked on a pretty face and they’d believe white was black if the woman told them it was. He’s infatuated, baby. No cure for that but time.”

“I thought he was so sexy.” Maddie laughed. She brushed at her eyes again. “Then he lost his temper like that. He scared me,” she said on a nervous smile.

“It’s all right. Nobody’s going to hurt you here. I promise.”

She hugged the older woman tight. “Thanks.”

“At the time, that boy did apologize, and he meant it,” Sadie reminded her. “He was as much a victim as you were.”

“Yes, but he got in trouble and he should have. No man, even an angry young one with justification, should ever do what he did to a girl. He didn’t have nightmares for a month, either, did he, or carry emotional scars that never go away? Sad thing about him,” she added quietly, “he died overseas when a roadside bomb blew up when he was serving in the Middle East. With a temper like that, I often wondered what he might do to a woman if he got even more upset than he was at me that time."

"No telling. And just as well we don't have to find out." Her face hardened. "But you're right about that Odalie girl. Got a bad attitude and no compassion for anybody. One of these days, life is going to pay her out in her own coin. She'll be sorry for the things she's done, but it will be too late. God forgives," she added. "But there's a price."

"What's that old saying, 'God's mill grinds slowly, but relentlessly'?"

"Something like that. Come on. I'll make you a nice cup of hot coffee."

"Make that a nice cup of hot chocolate instead," Maddie said. "I've had a rough day and I want to go to bed."

"I don't blame you. Not one bit."

Cort was thoughtful at breakfast the next morning. He was usually animated with his parents while he ate. But now he was quiet and retrospective.

"Something wrong?" his dad asked.

Cort glanced at him. He managed a smile. "Yeah. Something." He sipped coffee. "I went over her dad's journal with Maddie. We had sort of an argument and I started toward her while I was mad." He hesitated. "She knocked over a chair getting away from me. White in the face, shaking all over. It was an extreme reaction. We've argued before, but that's the first time she's been afraid of me."

"And you don't understand why." His father's expression was troubled.

"I don't." Cort's eyes narrowed. "But you do, don't you?"

He nodded.

"King, should you tell him?" Shelby asked worriedly.

"I think I should, honey," he said gently, and his dark eyes smiled with affection. "Somebody needs to."

"Okay then." She got up with her coffee. "You men talk. I'm going to phone Morie and see how she's doing."

"Give her my love," King called after her.

"Mine, too," Cort added.

She waved a hand and closed the door behind her.

"Tell me," Cort asked his dad.

King put down his coffee cup. "In her senior year, Maddie was Odalie's worst enemy. There was a boy, seemingly a nice boy, who liked Maddie. But Odalie liked him, and she was angry that Maddie, a younger girl who wasn't pretty or rich or talented, seemed to be winning in the affection sweepstakes."

"I told Maddie, Odalie's not like that," Cort began angrily.

King held up a hand. "Just hear me out. Don't interrupt."

Cort made a face, but he shut up.

"So Odalie and a girlfriend got on one of the social websites and started posting things that she said Maddie told her about the boy. She said Maddie thought he was a hick, that his mother was stupid, that both his parents couldn't even pass a basic IQ test."

"What? That's a lie…!"

"Sit down!" King's voice was soft, but the look in his eyes wasn't. Cort sat.

"The boy's mother was dying of cancer. He was outraged and furious at what Maddie had allegedly said about his family. His mother had just been taken to the hospital, not expected to live. She died that same day. He went to school just to find Maddie. She was in the library." He picked up his cup and sipped coffee. "He jerked her out of her chair, slapped her over a table and pulled her by her hair to the window. He was in the act of throwing her out—and it was on the second floor—when the librarian screamed for help and two big, stronger boys restrained him, in the nick of time."

Cort's face froze. "Maddie told you that?"

"Her father's lawyer told Cole Everett that," came the terse reply. "There were at least five witnesses. The boy was arrested for assault. It was hushed up, because that's what's done in small communities to protect the families. Odalie was implicated, because the attorney hired a private investigator to find the source of the allegations. They traced the posts to her computer."

Cort felt uneasy. He was certain Odalie couldn't have done such a thing. "Maybe somebody used her computer," he began.

"She confessed," King said curtly.

Cort was even more uneasy now.

"Cole Everett had his own attorney speak to the one Maddie's father had hired. They worked out a compromise that wouldn't involve a trial. But Odalie had to toe the line from that time forward. They put her on probation, you see. She had first-offender status, so her record was wiped when she stayed out of trouble for the next two years. She had a girlfriend who'd egged her on. The girlfriend left town shortly thereafter."

"Yes," Cort replied, relaxing. "I see now. The girlfriend forced her to do it."

King made a curt sound deep in his throat. "Son, nobody forced her to do a damned thing. She was jealous of Maddie. She was lucky the boy didn't kill Maddie, or she'd have been an accessory to murder." He watched Cort's face pale. "That's right. And I don't think even Cole Everett could have kept her out of jail if that had happened."

Cort leaned back in his chair. "Poor Odalie."

"Funny," King said. "I would have said, 'Poor Maddie.'"

Cort flushed. "It must have been terrible for both of them, I suppose."

King just shook his head. He got up. "Blind as a bat," he mused. "Just like me, when I was giving your mother hell twice a day for being engaged to my little brother. God, I hated him. Hated them both. Never would admit why."

"Uncle Danny?" Cort exclaimed. "He was engaged to Mom?"

"He was. It was a fake engagement, however." He chuckled. "He was just trying to show me what my feelings for Shelby really were. I forgave him every minute's agony. She's the best thing that ever happened to me. I didn't realize how deeply a man could love a woman.

All these years," he added in a soft tone, "and those feelings haven't lessened a bit. I hope you find that sort of happiness in your life. I wish it for you."

"Thanks," Cort said. He smiled. "If I can get Odalie to marry me, I promise you, I'll have it."

King started to speak, but thought better of it. "I've got some book work to do."

"I've got a new video game I'm dying to try." Cort chuckled. "It's been a long day."

"I appreciate you going over to talk to Maddie."

"No problem. She just needed a few pointers."

"She's no cattlewoman," King said worriedly. "She's swimming upstream. She doesn't even like cattle. She likes chickens."

"Don't say chickens," Cort pleaded with a groan.

"Your problem isn't with chickens, it's with a rooster."

"I'd dearly love to help him have a fatal heart attack," Cort said irritably.

"He'll die of old age one day." His dad laughed.

"Maddie said that developer had been putting pressure on her to sell," King added solemnly. "I've put on some extra help to keep an eye over that way, just to make sure her breeding stock doesn't start dying mysteriously."

"What?" Cort asked, shocked. "She didn't say anything about that."

"Probably wouldn't, to you. It smacks of weakness to mention such things to the enemy."

"I'm not the enemy."

King smiled. "Aren't you?"

He left his son sitting at the table, deep in thought.

* * *

Maddie was working in the yard when the developer drove up a week later. She leaned on the pitchfork she was using to put hay into a trough, and waited, miserable, for him to get out of his car and talk to her.

"I won't sell," she said when he came up to her. "And in case you feel like high pressure tactics, my neighbor has mounted cameras all over the ranch." She flushed at his fury.

"Well, how about that?" he drawled, and his eyes were blazing with anger. He forced a smile. "You did know that cameras can be disabled?" he asked.

"The cameras also have listening devices that can pick up a whisper."

He actually seemed to go pale. He looked at the poles that contained the outside lighting and mumbled a curse under his breath. There was some sort of electronic device up there.

"I'll come back again one day and ask you the same question," he promised, but he smiled and his voice was pleasant. "Maybe you'll change your mind."

"We also have cowboys in the line cabins on the borders of this ranch. Mr. Brannt is very protective of me since my father died. He buys many of our young breeding bulls," she added for good measure.

He was very still. "King Brannt?"

"Yes. You've heard of him, I gather."

He didn't reply. He turned on his heel and marched back to his car. But this time he didn't spin his wheels.

Maddie almost fell over with relief.

Just as the developer left, another car drove up, a sleek Jaguar, black with silver trim. Maddie didn't recognize it. Oh, dear, didn't some hit men drive fancy cars…?

The door opened and big John Everett climbed out of the low-slung luxury car, holding on to his white Stetson so that it wouldn't be dislodged from his thick head of blond hair. Maddie almost laughed with relief.

John grinned as he approached her. He had pale blue eyes, almost silver-colored, like his dad's, and he was a real dish. He and Odalie both had their mother's blond fairness, instead of Cole Everett's dark hair and olive complexion.

"What the hell's wrong with you?" he drawled. "Black cars make you twitchy or something?"

"I think hit men drive them, is all."

He burst out laughing. "I've never shot one single person. A deer or two, maybe, in season." He moved toward her and stopped, towering over her. His pale eyes were dancing on her flushed face. "I ran into King Brannt at a cattlemen's association meeting last night. He said you were having some problems trying to work out your father's breeding program. He said Cort explained it to you."

"Uh, well, yes, sort of." It was hard to admit that even taking notes, she hadn't understood much of what Cort had told her.

"Cort tried to tutor me in biology in high school. I got a D on the test. He's good at genetics, lousy at trying to explain them." He shoved his hat back on his head and grinned. "So I thought, maybe I'll come over and have a try at helping you understand it."

"You're a nice guy, John," she said gently. And he was. At the height of his sister's intimidation, John had been on Maddie's side.

He shrugged. "I'm the flower of my family." His face hardened. "Even if she is my sister, Odalie makes me ashamed sometimes. I haven't forgotten the things she did to you."

"We all make mistakes when we're young," she faltered, trying to be fair.

"You have a gentle nature," he observed. "Like Cort's mother. And mine," he added with a smile. "Mom can't bear to see anything hurt. She cried for days when your father's lawyer came over and told her and Dad what Odalie had done to you."

"I know. She called me. Your dad did, too. They're good people."

"Odalie might be a better person if she had a few disadvantages," John said coldly. "As things stand, she'll give in to Cort's persuasion one day and marry him. He'll be in hell for the rest of his life. The only person she's ever really loved is herself."

"That's harsh, John," she chided gently.

"It's the truth, Maddie." He swung his pointing finger at her nose. "You're like my mother…she'd find one nice thing to say about the devil." He smiled. "I'm in the mood to do some tutoring today. But I require payment. Your great-aunt makes a mean cup of coffee, and I'm partial to French vanilla."

"That's my favorite."

He chuckled. "Mine, too." He went back to the car, opened the passenger seat, took out a big box and a bag. "So since I drink a lot of it, I brought my own."

She caught her breath. It was one of those European coffee machines that used pods. Maddie had always wanted one, but the price was prohibitive.

"Sad thing is it only brews one cup at a time, but we'll compensate." He grinned. "So lead the way to the kitchen and I'll show you how to use it."

Two cups of mouthwatering coffee later, they were sitting in Maddie's father's office, going over breeding charts. John found the blackboard her father had used to map out the genetics. He was able to explain it so simply that Maddie understood almost at once which herd sires to breed to which cows.

"You make it sound so simple!" she exclaimed. "You're a wonder, John!"

He laughed. "It's all a matter of simplification," he drawled. He leaned back in the chair and sketched Maddie's radiant face with narrowed pale blue eyes. "You sell yourself short. It's not that you can't understand. You just have to have things explained. Cort's too impatient."

She averted her eyes. Mention of Cort made her uneasy.

"Yes, he loses his temper," John said thoughtfully. "But he's not dangerous. Not like that boy."

She paled. "I can't talk about it."

"You can, and you should," he replied solemnly.

"Your father was advised to get some counseling for you, but he didn't believe in such things. That boy had a record for domestic assault, did you ever know? He beat his grandmother almost to death one day. She refused to press charges, or he would have gone to jail. His parents jumped in and got a fancy lawyer and convinced the authorities that he wasn't dangerous. I believe they contributed to the reelection campaign of the man who was police chief at the time as well."

"That's a harsh accusation," she said, shocked.

"It's a harsh world, and politics is the dirtiest business in town. Corruption doesn't stop at criminals, you know. Rich people have a way of subverting justice from time to time."

"You're rich, and you don't do those types of things."

"Yes, I am rich," he replied honestly. "And I'm honest. I have my own business, but I didn't get where I am by depending on my dad to support me."

She searched his eyes curiously. "Is that a dig at Cort?"

"It is," he replied quietly. "He stays at home, works on the ranch and does what King tells him to do. I told him some time ago that he's hurting himself by doing no more than wait to inherit Skylance, but he just nods and walks off."

"Somebody will have to take over the ranch when King is too old to manage it," she pointed out reasonably. "There isn't anybody else."

John grimaced. "I suppose that's true. But it's the same with me. Can you really see Odalie running a ranch?" He burst out laughing. "God, she might chip a fingernail!"

She grinned from ear to ear.

"Anyway, I was a maverick. I wanted my own business. I have a farm-equipment business and I also specialize in marketing native grasses for pasture improvement."

"You're an entrepreneur," she said with a chuckle.

"Something like that, I guess." He cocked his head and studied her. "You know I don't date much."

"Yes. Sort of like me. I'm not modern enough for most men."

"I'm not modern enough for most women," he replied, and smiled. "Uh, there's going to be a dressy party over at the Hancock place to introduce a new rancher in the area. I wondered if you might like to go with me?"

"A party?" she asked. She did have one good dress. She'd bought it for a special occasion a while ago, and she couldn't really afford another one with the ranch having financial issues. But it was a nice dress. Her eyes brightened. "I haven't been to a party in a long time. I went with Dad to a conference in Denver before he got sick."

"I remember. You looked very nice."

"Well, I'd be wearing the same dress I had on then," she pointed out.

He laughed. "I don't follow the current fashions for women," he mused. "I'm inviting you, not the dress."

"In that case," she said with a pert smile, "I'd be delighted!"

Chapter Four

Some men dragged their feet around the room and called it dancing. John Everett could actually dance! He knew all the Latin dances and how to waltz, although he was uncomfortable with some of the newer ways to display on a dance floor. Fortunately the organizers of the party were older people and they liked older music.

Only a minute into an enthusiastic samba, John and Maddie found themselves in the middle of the dance floor with the other guests clapping as they marked the fast rhythm.

"We should take this show on the road." John chuckled as they danced.

"I'm game. I'll give up ranching and become a professional samba performer, if you'll come, too," she suggested.

"Maybe only part of the year," he mused. "We can't let our businesses go to pot."

"Spoilsport."

He grinned.

While the two were dancing, oblivious to the other guests, a tall, dark man in a suit walked in and found himself a flute of champagne. He tasted it, nodding to other guests. Everyone was gathered around the dance floor of the ballroom in the Victorian mansion. He wandered to the fringes and caught his breath. There, on the dance floor, was Maddie Lane.

She was wearing a dress, a sheath of black slinky material that dipped in front to display just a hint of the lovely curve of her breasts and display her long elegant neck and rounded arms. Her pale blond hair shone like gold in the light from the chandeliers. She was wearing makeup, just enough to enhance what seemed to be a rather pretty face, and the pretty calves of her legs were displayed to their best advantage from the arch of her spiked high-heel shoes. He'd rarely seen her dressed up. Not that he'd been interested in her or anything.

But there she was, decked out like a Christmas tree, dancing with his best friend. John didn't date anybody. Until now.

Cort Brannt felt irritation rise in him like bile. He scowled at the display they were making of themselves. Had they no modesty at all? And people were clapping like idiots.

He glared at Maddie. He remembered the last time he'd seen her. She backed away from Cort, but she was dancing with John as if she really liked him. Her face was radiant. She was smiling. Cort had rarely seen her smile at all. Of course, usually he was yelling at her or making hurtful remarks. Not much incentive for smiles.

He sipped champagne. Someone spoke to him. He just nodded. He was intent on the dancing couple, focused and furious.

Suddenly he noticed that the flute was empty. He turned and went back to the hors d'oeuvres table and had them refill it. But he didn't go back to the dance floor. Instead he found a fellow cattleman to talk to about the drought and selling off cattle.

A few minutes later he was aware of two people helping themselves to punch and cake.

"Oh, hi, Cort," John greeted him with a smile. "I didn't think you were coming."

"Hadn't planned to," Cort said in a cool tone. "My dad had an emergency on the ranch, so I'm filling in. One of the officers of the cattlemen's association is here." He indicated the man with a nod of his head. "Dad wanted me to ask him about any pending legislation that might help us through the drought. We've heard rumors, but nothing substantial."

"My dad was wondering the same." John frowned. "You okay?"

"I'm fine," Cort said, making sure that he enunciated as plainly as possible. He stood taller, although he still wasn't as tall, or as big, as his friend. "Why do you ask?"

"Because that's your second glass of champagne and you don't drink," John said flatly.

Cort held the flute up and looked at it. It was empty. "Where did that go?" he murmured.

"Just a guess, but maybe you drank it?" John replied.

Cort set the flute on the spotless white tablecloth and looked down at Maddie. "You're keeping expensive company these days."

She was shocked at the implication.

"Hold it right there," John said, and his deep tone was menacing. "I invited her."

"Got plans, have you?" Cort replied coldly.

"Why shouldn't I?" came the droll reply. "Oh, by the way, Odalie says her Italian voice teacher is an idiot. He doesn't know beans about how to sing, and he isn't teaching her anything. So she thinks she may come home soon."

Maddie felt her heart sink. Cort's expression lightened. "You think she might?"

"It's possible. You should lay off that stuff."

Cort glanced at the flute. "I suppose so."

"Hey, John, can I talk to you for a minute?" a man called to him. "I need a new combine!"

"I need a new sale," John teased. He glanced at Maddie. "I won't be a minute, okay?"

"Okay," she said. But she was clutching her small evening bag as if she was afraid that it might escape. She started looking around for someone, anyone, to talk to besides Cort Brannt.

While she was thinking about running, he slid his big hand into her small one and pulled her onto the dance floor. He didn't even ask. He folded her into his arms and led her to the lazy, slow rhythm.

He smelled of spicy, rich cologne. He was much taller than she was, so her she couldn't see his face. She felt his cheek against the big wave of blond hair at her temple and her body began to do odd things. She felt uneasy, nervous. She felt…safe, excited.

"Your hand is like ice," he murmured as he danced with her around the room.

"They get cold all the time," she lied.

He laughed deep in his throat. "Really."

She wondered why he was doing this. Surely he should be pleased about Odalie's imminent reappearance in his life. He hated Maddie. Why was he dancing with her?

"I've never raised my hand to a woman," he said at her ear. "I never would, no matter how angry I was."

She swallowed and stopped dancing. She didn't want to talk about that.

He coaxed her eyes up. His were dark, narrow, intent. He was remembering what his father had told him, about the boy who tried to throw Maddie out a second-story window because of Odalie's lies. He didn't want to believe that Odalie had meant that to happen. Surely her female visitor had talked her into putting those nasty things about the boy and his family on the internet. But however it had happened, the thought of someone manhandling Maddie made him angry. It upset him.

He didn't really understand why. He'd never thought of her in any romantic way. She was just Pierce Lane's daughter. He'd known her since she was a child, watched her follow her dad around the ranch. She was always petting a calf or a dog, or carrying chickens around because she liked the sounds they made.

"Why are you watching me like that?" she faltered.

"You love animals, don't you?" he asked, and there was an odd, soft glow about his dark eyes. "I remember you carrying Mom's chickens around like cuddly toys when you'd come over to the ranch with your dad. You were very small then. I had to rescue you from one of the herding dogs. You tried to pet him, and he wasn't a pet."

"His name was Rowdy," she recalled. "He was so pretty."

"We never let anybody touch those dogs except the man who trains and uses them. They have to be focused. You didn't know." He smiled. "You were a cute little kid. Always asking questions, always curious about everything."

She shifted uncomfortably. He wasn't dancing and they were drawing attention.

He looked around, cocked an eyebrow and moved her back around the room in his arms. "Sorry."

She didn't know what to think. She was tingling all over. She wanted him to hold her so close that she could feel every inch of his powerful frame against her. She wanted him to bend his head and kiss her so hard that her lips would sting. She wanted…something. Something more. She didn't understand these new and unexpected longings. It was getting hard to breathe and her heartbeat was almost shaking her. She couldn't bear it if he noticed.

He did notice. She was like melting ice in his arms. He felt her shiver when he drew her even closer, so that her soft, pert little breasts were hard against his chest through the thin suit jacket he was wearing. He liked the way she smelled, of wildflowers in the sun.

He drank in that scent. It made his head swim. His arm contracted. He was feeling sensations that he'd almost forgotten. Odalie didn't like him close to her, so his longing for her had been stifled. But Maddie was soft and warm and receptive. Too receptive.

His mouth touched her ear. "You make me hungry," he whispered roughly.

"Ex-excuse me?" she stammered.

"I want to lay you down on the carpet and kiss your breasts until my body stops hurting."

She caught her breath and stopped dancing. She pushed back from him, her eyes blazing, her face red with embarrassment. She wanted to kick him in the shin, but that would cause more problems.

She turned away from him, almost shivering with the emotions he'd kindled in her, shocked at the things he'd said to her. She almost ran toward John, who was walking toward her, frowning.

"What is it?" he asked suddenly, putting his arm around her.

She hid her face against him.

He glared at Cort, who was approaching them with more conflicting emotions than he'd ever felt in his life.

"You need to go home," John told Cort in a patient tone that was belied by his expression. "You've had too much to drink and you're going to make a spectacle of yourself and us if you keep this up."

"I want to dance with her," Cort muttered stubbornly.

"Well, it's pretty obvious that she doesn't want to dance with you." John leaned closer. "I can pick you up over my shoulder and carry you out of here, and I will."

"I'd like to see you try it," Cort replied, and his eyes blazed with anger.

Another cattleman, seeing a confrontation building, came strolling over and deliberately got between the two men.

"Hey, Cort," he said pleasantly, "I need to ask you about those new calves your dad's going to put up at the fall production sale. Can I ride home with you and see them?"

Cort blinked. "It's the middle of the night."

"The barn doesn't have lights?" the older man asked, raising an eyebrow.

Cort was torn. He knew the man. He was from up around the Frio river. He had a huge ranch, and Cort's dad was hungry for new customers.

"The barn has lights. I guess we could…go look at the calves." He was feeling very light-headed. He wasn't used to alcohol. Not at all.

"I'll drive you home," the rancher said gently. "You can have one of your cowboys fetch your car, can't you?"

"Yeah. I guess so."

"Thanks," John told the man.

He shrugged and smiled. "No problem."

He indicated the door. Cort hesitated for just a minute. He looked back at Maddie with dark, stormy eyes, long enough that she dropped her own like hot bricks. He gave John a smug glance and followed the visiting cattleman out the door.

"Oh, boy," John said to himself. "Now we get to the complications."

"Complications?" Maddie was only half listening. Her eyes were on Cort's long, elegant back. She couldn't remember ever being so confused.

After the party was over, John drove her to her front door and cut off the engine.

"What happened?" he asked her gently, because she was still visibly upset.

"Cort was out of line," she murmured without lifting her eyes.

"Not surprising. He doesn't drink. I can't imagine what got him started."

"I guess he's missing your sister," she replied with a sigh. She looked up at him. "She's really coming home?"

"She says she is," he told her. He made a face. "That's Odalie. She always knows more than anybody else about any subject. My parents let her get away with being sassy because she was pretty and talented." He laughed shortly. "My dad let me have it if I was ever rude or impolite or spoke out of turn. My brother had it even rougher."

She cocked her head. "You never talk about Tanner."

He grimaced. "I can't. It's a family thing. Maybe I'll

tell you one day. Anyway, Dad pulled me up short if I didn't toe the line at home." He shook his head. "You wouldn't believe how many times I had to clean the horse stalls when I made him mad."

"Odalie is beautiful," Maddie conceded, but in a subdued tone.

"Only a very few people know what she did to you," John said quietly. "It shamed the family. Odalie was only sorry she got caught. I think she finally realized how tragic the results could have been, though."

"How so?"

"For one thing, she never spoke again to the girlfriend who put her up to it," he said. "After she got out of school, she stopped posting on her social page and threw herself into studying music."

"The girlfriend moved away, didn't she, though?"

"She moved because threats were made. Legal ones," John confided. "My dad sent his attorneys after her. He was pretty sure that Odalie didn't know how to link internet sites and post simultaneously, which is what was done about you." He touched her short hair gently. "Odalie is spoiled and snobbish and she thinks she's the center of the universe. But she isn't cruel."

"Isn't she?"

"Well, not anymore," he added. "Not since the lawyers got involved. You weren't the only girl she victimized. Several others came forward and talked to my dad when they heard about what happened to you in the library. He was absolutely dumbfounded. So was my mother." He shook his head. "Odalie never got over what they said to her. She started making a real effort to consider the feelings of other people. Years too late, of course, and she's still got that bad attitude."

"It's a shame she isn't more like your mother," Maddie said gently, and she smiled. "Mrs. Everett is a sweet woman."

"Yes. Mom has an amazing voice and is not conceited. She was offered a career in opera but she turned it down. She liked singing the blues, she said. Now, she just plays and sings for us, and composes. There's still the occasional journalist who shows up at the door when one of her songs is a big hit, like Desperado's."

"Do they still perform…I mean Desperado?" she qualified.

"Yes, but not so much. They've all got kids now. It makes it tough to go on the road, except during summer holidays."

She laughed. "I love their music."

"Me, too." He studied her. "Odd."

"What is?"

"You're so easy to talk to. I don't get along with most women. I'm strung up and nervous and the aggressive ones make me uncomfortable. I sort of gave up dating after my last bad experience." He laughed. "I don't like women making crude remarks to me."

"Isn't it funny how things have changed?" she wondered aloud. "Not that I'm making fun of you. It's just that women used to get hassled. They still do, but it's turned around somewhat—now men get it, too."

"Yes, life is much more complicated now."

"I really enjoyed the party. Especially the dancing."

"Me, too. We might do that again one day."

She raised both eyebrows. "We might?"

He chuckled. "I'll call you."

"That would be nice."

He smiled, got out, went around and opened the door for her. He seemed to be debating whether or not to kiss her. She liked that lack of aggression in him. She smiled, went on tiptoe and kissed him right beside his chiseled mouth.

"Thanks again," she said. "See you!"

She went up the steps and into the house. John Everett stood looking after her wistfully. She thought he was nice. She liked him. But when she'd come off the dance floor trailing Cort Brannt, she'd been radiating like a furnace. Whether she knew it or not, she was in love with Cort. Shame, he thought as he drove off. She was just the sort of woman he'd like to settle down with. Not much chance of that, now.

Maddie didn't sleep at all. She stared at the ceiling. Her body tingled from the long contact with Cort's. She could feel his breath on her forehead, his lips in her hair. She could hear what he'd whispered.

She flushed at the memory. It had evoked incredible hunger. She didn't understand why she had these feelings now, when she hadn't had them for that boy who'd tried to hurt her so badly. She'd really thought she was crazy about him. But it was nothing like this.

Since her bad experience, she hadn't dated much. She'd seen her father get mad, but it was always quick and never physical. She hadn't been exposed to men who hit women. Now she knew they existed. It had been a worrying discovery.

Cort had frightened her when he'd lost his temper so violently in her father's office. She didn't think he'd attack her. But she'd been wary of him, until they danced together. Even if he was drunk, it had been the experience of a lifetime. She thought she could live on it forever, even if Odalie came home and Cort married her. He was never going to be happy with her, though. Odalie loved herself so much that there was no room in her life for a man.

If only the other woman had fallen in love with the Italian voice trainer and married him. Then Cort would have to let go of his unrequited feelings for Odalie, and maybe look in another direction. Maybe look in Maddie's direction.

On the other hand, he'd only been teasing at the dance. He wasn't himself.

Cold sober, he'd never have anything to do with Maddie. Probably, he'd just been missing Odalie and wanted a warm body to hold. Yes. That was probably it.

Just before dawn she fell asleep, but all too soon it was time to get up and start doing the chores around the ranch.

She went to feed her flock of hens, clutching the metal garbage can lid and the leafy limb to fend off Pumpkin. Somewhere in the back of her mind, she realized that it was going to come down to a hard decision one day.

Pumpkin protected her hens, yes; he would be the bane of predators everywhere. But he was equally dangerous to people. What if he flew up and got one of her cowboys in the eye? She'd been reading up on rooster behavior, and she'd read some horror stories.

There had been all sorts of helpful advice, like giving him special treats and being nice to him. That had resulted in more gouges on her legs, even through her slacks, where his spurs had landed. Then there was the advice about having his spurs trimmed. Good advice, but who was going to catch and hold him while someone did that? None of her cowboys were lining up to volunteer.

"You problem child," she told Pumpkin as he chased her toward the gate. "One day, I'll have to do something about you!"

She got through the gate in the nick of time and shut it, hard. At least he wasn't going to get out of there, she told herself. She'd had Ben go around the perimeter of the large fenced area that surrounded the henhouse and plug any openings where that sneaky feathered fiend could possibly get out. If she kept him shut up, he couldn't hurt anybody, and the fence was seven feet high. No way he was jumping that!

She said so to Ben as she made her way to the barn to check on a calf they were nursing; it had dropped late and its mother had been killed by predators. They found it far on the outskirts of the ranch. They couldn't figure how it had wandered so far, but then, cattle did that. It was why you brought pregnant cows up close to the barn, so that you'd know when they were calving. It was especially important to do that in winter, just before the spring calves were due.

She looked over the gate at the little calf in the stall and smiled. “Pretty boy,” she teased.

He was a purebred Santa Gertrudis bull. Some were culled and castrated and became steers, if they had poor conformation or were less than robust. But the best ones were treated like cattle royalty, spoiled rotten and watched over. This little guy would one day bring a handsome price as a breeding bull.

She heard a car door slam and turned just as Cort came into the barn.

She felt her heartbeat shoot off like a rocket.

He tilted his hat back and moved to the stall, peering over it. “That’s a nice young one,” he remarked.

“His mother was killed, so we’re nursing him,” she faltered.

He frowned. “Killed?”

“Predators, we think,” she replied. “She was pretty torn up. We found her almost at the highway, out near your line cabin. Odd, that she wandered so far.”

“Very odd,” he agreed.

Ben came walking in with a bottle. “’Day, Cort,” he said pleasantly.

“How’s it going, Ben?” the younger man replied.

“So far so good.”

Maddie smiled as Ben settled down in the hay and fed the bottle to the hungry calf.

“Poor little guy,” Maddie said.

“He’ll make it,” Ben promised, smiling up at her.

"Well, I'll leave you to it," Maddie said. She was reluctant to be alone with Cort after the night before, but she couldn't see any way around it.

"You're up early," she said, fishing for a safe topic.

"I didn't sleep." He stuck his hands into his pockets as he strolled along with her toward the house.

"Oh?"

He stopped, so that she had to. His eyes were bloodshot and they had dark circles under them. "I drank too much," he said. "I wanted to apologize for the way I behaved with you."

"Oh." She looked around for anything more than one syllable that she could reply with. "That's…that's okay."

He stared down at her with curiously intent eyes. "You're incredibly naive."

She averted her eyes and her jaw clenched. "Yes, well, with my background, you'd probably be the same way. I haven't been anxious to repeat the mistakes of the past with some other man who wasn't what he seemed to be."

"I'm sorry. About what happened to you."

"Everybody was sorry," she replied heavily. "But nobody else has to live with the emotional baggage I'm carrying around."

"How did you end up at the party with John?"

She blinked. "Well, he came over to show me some things about animal husbandry, and he asked me to go with him. It was sort of surprising, really. He doesn't date anybody."

"He's had a few bad experiences with women. So have I."

She'd heard about Cort's, but she wasn't opening that topic with him. "Would you like coffee?" she asked. "Great-Aunt Sadie went shopping, but she left a nice coffee cake baking in the oven. It should be about ready."

"Thanks. I could use a second cup," he added with a smile.

But the smile faded when he saw the fancy European coffee machine on the counter. "Where the hell did you buy that?" he asked.

She flushed. "I didn't. John likes European coffee, so he brought the machine and the pods over with him."

He lifted his chin. "Did he, now? I gather he thinks he'll be having coffee here often, then?"

She frowned. "He didn't say anything about that."

He made a huffing sound in his throat, just as the stove timer rang. Maddie went to take the coffee cake out of the oven. She was feeling so rattled, it was a good thing she'd remembered that it was baking. She placed it on a trivet. It smelled of cinnamon and butter.

"My great-aunt can really cook," she remarked as she took off the oven mitts she'd used to lift it out.

"She can, can't she?"

She turned and walked right into Cort. She hadn't realized he was so close. He caught her small waist in his big hands and lifted her right onto the counter next to the coffee cake, so that she was even with his dark, probing eyes.

"You looked lovely last night," he said in a strange, deep tone. "I've never really seen you dressed up before."

"I…I don't dress up," she stammered. He was tracing

her collarbone and the sensations it aroused were delicious and unsettling. "Just occasionally."

"I didn't know you could do those complicated Latin dances, either," he continued.

"I learned them from watching television," she said.

His head was lower now. She could feel his breath on her lips; feel the heat from his body as he moved closer, in between her legs so that he was right up against her.

"I'm not in John Everett's class as a dancer," he drawled, tilting her chin up. "But, then, he's not in my class…at this…"

His mouth slowly covered hers, teasing gently, so that he didn't startle her. He tilted her head just a little more, so that her mouth was at just the right angle. His firm lips pushed hers apart, easing them back, so that he had access to the soft, warm depths of her mouth.

He kissed her with muted hunger, so slowly that she didn't realize until too late how much a trap it was. He grew insistent then, one lean hand at the back of her head, holding it still, as his mouth devoured her soft lips.

"Sweet," he whispered huskily. "You taste like honey…."

His arms went under hers and around her, lifting her, so that her breasts were flattened against his broad, strong chest.

Involuntarily her cold hands snaked around his neck. She'd never felt hunger like this. She hadn't known it was possible. She let him open her mouth with his, let him grind her breasts against him. She moaned softly as sensations she'd never experienced left her helpless, vulnerable.

She felt his hand in her hair, tangling in it, while he kissed her in the soft silence of the kitchen. It was a moment out of time when she wished it could never end, that she could go on kissing him forever.

But just when he lifted his head, and looked into her eyes, and started to speak...

A car pulled up at the front porch and a door slammed.

Maddie looked into Cort's eyes with shock. He seemed almost as unsettled as she did. He moved back, helping her off the counter and onto her feet. He backed up just as Great-Aunt Sadie walked in with two bags of groceries.

"Didn't even have fresh mushrooms, can you believe it?" she was moaning, her mind on the door that was trying to close in her face rather than the two dazed people in the kitchen.

"Here, let me have those," Cort said politely, and he took the bags and put them on the counter. "Are there more in the car?" he asked.

"No, but thank you, Cort," Sadie said with a warm smile.

He grinned. "No problem." He glanced at Maddie, who still looked rattled. "I have to go. Thanks for the offer of coffee. Rain check?" he added, and his eyes were almost black with feeling.

"Oh, yes," Maddie managed breathlessly. "Rain check."

He smiled at her and left her standing there, vibrating with new hope.

Chapter Five

Maddie still couldn't believe what had happened right there in her kitchen. Cort had kissed her, and as if he really did feel something for her. Besides that, he was very obviously jealous of John Everett. She felt as if she could actually walk on air.

"You look happier than I've seen you in years, sweetie," Great-Aunt Sadie said with a smile.

"I am."

Sadie grinned. "It's that John Everett, isn't it?" she teased. She indicated the coffeemaker. "Thought he was pretty interested. I mean, those things cost the earth. Not every man would start out courting a girl with a present like that!"

"Oh. Well, of course, I like John," Maddie stammered. And then she realized that she couldn't very well tell her great-aunt what was going on. Sadie might start gossiping. Maddie's ranch hands had friends who worked for the Brannts. She didn't want Cort to think she was telling tales about him, even in an innocent way. After all, it might have been a fluke. He could be missing Odalie and just reacted to Maddie in unexpected ways.

"He's a dish," Sadie continued as she peeled potatoes in the kitchen. "Handsome young man, just like his dad." She grimaced. "I'm not too fond of his sister, but, then, no family is perfect."

"No." She hesitated. "Sadie, do you know why nobody talks about the oldest brother, Tanner?"

Sadie smiled. "Just gossip. They said he and his dad had a major falling out over his choice of careers and he packed up and went to Europe. That was when he was in his late teens. As far as I know, he's never contacted the family since. It's a sore spot with the Everetts, so they don't talk about him anymore. Too painful, I expect."

"That's sad."

"Yes, it is. There was a rumor that he was hanging out with some dangerous people as well. But you know what rumors are."

"Yes," Maddie said.

"What was Cort doing over here earlier in the week?" Sadie asked suddenly.

"Oh, he was just…giving me some more pointers on dad's breeding program," Maddie lied.

"Scared you to death, too," Sadie said irritably. "I don't think he'd hurt you, but he's got a bad temper, sweetie."

Maddie had forgotten that, in the new relationship she seemed to be building with Cort. "People say his father was like that, when he was young. But Shelby married him and tamed him," she added with a secret smile.

Sadie glanced at her curiously. "I guess that can happen. A good woman can be the salvation of a man. But just…be careful."

"I will," she promised. "Cort isn't a mean person."

Sadie gave her a careful look. "So that's how it is."

Maddie flushed. "I don't know what you mean."

"John likes you, a lot," she replied.

Maddie sighed. "John's got a barracuda for a sister, too," she reminded the older woman. "No way in the world am I having her for a sister-in-law, no matter how nice John is."

Sadie grimaced. "Should have thought of that, shouldn't I?"

"I did."

She laughed. "I guess so. But just a suggestion, if you stick your neck out with Cort," she added very seriously. "Make him mad. Make him really mad, someplace where you can get help if you need to. Don't wait and find out when it's too late if he can't control his temper."

"I remember that boy in high school," Maddie reminded her. "He didn't stop. Cort frightened me, yes, but when he saw I was afraid, he started apologizing. If he couldn't control his temper, he'd never have been able to stop."

Sadie looked calmer. "No. I don't think he would."

"He's still apologizing for it, in fact," Maddie added.

Sadie smiled and her eyes were kind. "All right, then. I won't harp on it. He's a lot like his father, and his dad is a good man."

"They're all nice people. Morie was wonderful to me in school. She stuck up for me when Odalie and her girlfriend were making my life a daily purgatory."

"Pity Odalie never really gets paid back for the things she does," Sadie muttered."

Maddie hugged her. "That mill grinds slowly but relentlessly," she reminded her. She grinned. "One day..."

Sadie laughed. "One day."

Maddie let her go with a sigh. "I hope I can learn enough of this stuff not to sink dad's cattle operation," she moaned. "I wasn't really faced with having to deal with the breeding aspect until now, with roundup ahead and fall breeding standing on the line in front of me. Which bull do I put on which cows? Gosh! It's enough to drive you nuts!"

"Getting a lot of help in that, though, aren't you?" Sadie teased. "Did you tell Cort that John had been coaching you, too?"

"Yes." She sighed. "Cort wasn't overjoyed about it, either. But John makes it understandable." She threw up her hands. "I'm just slow. I don't understand cattle. I love to paint and sculpt. But Dad never expected to go so soon and have to leave me in charge of things. We're going in the hole because I don't know what I'm doing." She glanced at the older woman. "In about two years, we're going to start losing customers. It terrifies me. I don't want to lose the ranch, but it's going to go downhill without dad to run it." She toyed with a bag on the counter. "I've been thinking about that developer..."

"Don't you dare," Sadie said firmly. "Darlin', do you realize what he'd do to this place if he got his hands on it?" she exclaimed. "He'd sell off all the livestock to anybody who wanted it, even for slaughter, and he'd rip the land to pieces. All that prime farmland, gone, all the native grasses your dad planted and nurtured, gone. This house—" she indicated it "—where your father and your grandfather and I were born! Gone!"

Maddie felt sick. "Oh, dear."

"You're not going to run the ranch into the ground. Not when you have people, like King Brannt, who want to help you get it going again," she said firmly. "If you ever want to sell up, you talk to him. I'll bet he'd offer for it and put in a manager. We could probably even stay on and pay rent."

"With what?" Maddie asked reasonably. "Your social security check and my egg money?" She sighed. "I can't sell enough paintings or enough eggs to pay for lunch in town," she added miserably. "I should have gone to school and learned a trade or something." She grimaced. "I don't know what to do."

"Give it a little time," the older woman said gently. "I know it's overwhelming, but you can learn. Ask John to make you a chart and have Ben in on the conversation. Your dad trusted Ben with everything, even the finances. I daresay he knows as much as you do about things."

"That's an idea." She smiled sadly. "I don't really

want to sell that developer anything. He's got a shady look about him."

"You're telling me."

"I guess I'll wait a bit."

"Meanwhile, you might look in that bag I brought home yesterday."

"Isn't it groceries…dry goods?"

"Look."

She peered in the big brown bag and caught her breath. "Sculpting material. Paint! Great-Aunt Sadie!" she exclaimed, and ran and hugged the other woman. "That's so sweet of you!"

"Looking out for you, darling," she teased. "I want you to be famous so those big TV people will want to interview me on account of we're related!" She stood up and struck a pose. "Don't you think I'd be a hit?"

Maddie hugged her even tighter. "I think you're already a hit. Okay. I can take a hint. I'll get to work right now!"

Sadie chortled as she rushed from the room.

Cort came in several days later while she was retouching one of the four new fairies she'd created, working where the light was best, in a corner of her father's old office. She looked up, startled, when Great-Aunt Sadie let him in.

She froze. "Pumpkin came after you again?" she asked, worried.

"What?" He looked around, as if expecting the big red rooster to appear. "Oh, Pumpkin." He chuckled. "No.

He was in the hen yard giving me mean looks, but he seems to be well contained."

"Thank goodness!"

He moved to the table and looked at her handiwork. "What a group," he mused, smiling. "They're all beautiful."

"Thanks." She wished she didn't sound so breathless, and that she didn't have paint dabbed all over her face from her days' efforts. She probably looked like a painting herself.

"Going to sell them?"

"Oh, I couldn't," she said hesitantly. "I mean, I…well, I just couldn't."

"Can't you imagine what joy they'd bring to other people?" he asked, thinking out loud. "Why do you think doll collectors pay so much for one-of-a-kind creations like those? They build special cabinets for them, take them out and talk to them…"

"You're kidding!" she exclaimed, laughing. "Really?"

"This one guy I met at the conference said he had about ten really rare dolls. He sat them around the dining room table every night and talked to them while he ate. He was very rich and very eccentric, but you get the idea. He loved his dolls. He goes to all the doll collector conventions. In fact, there's one coming up in Denver, where they're holding a cattlemen's workshop." He smiled. "Anyway, your fairies wouldn't be sitting on a shelf collecting dust on the shelf of a collector like that. They'd be loved."

"Wow." She looked back at the little statuettes. "I never thought of it like that."

"Maybe you should."

She managed a shy smile. He looked delicious in a pair of beige slacks and a yellow, very expensive pull-over shirt with an emblem on the pocket. Thick black hair peeked out where the top buttons were undone. She wondered how his bare chest would feel against her hands. She blushed. "What can I do for you?" she asked quickly, trying to hide her interest.

Her reaction to him was amusing. He found it really touching. Flattering. He hadn't been able to get her out of his mind since he'd kissed her so hungrily in her kitchen. He'd wanted to come back sooner than this, but business had overwhelmed him.

"I have to drive down to Jacobsville, Texas, to see a rancher about some livestock," he said. "I thought you might like to ride with me."

She stared at him as if she'd won the lottery. "Me?"

"You." He smiled. "I'll buy you lunch on the way. I know this little tearoom off the beaten path. We can have high tea and buttermilk pie."

She caught her breath. "I used to hear my mother talk about that one. I've never had high tea. I'm not even sure what it is, exactly."

"Come with me and find out."

She grinned. "Okay! Just let me wash up first."

"Take your time. I'm not in any hurry."

"I'll just be a few minutes."

She almost ran up the staircase to her room.

Cort picked up one of the delicate little fairies and stared at it with utter fascination. It was ethereal, beautiful, stunning. He'd seen such things before, but never anything so small with such personality. The little fairy had short blond hair, like Maddie's, and pale eyes. It amused him that she could paint something so tiny. He noted the magnifying glass standing on the table, and realized that she must use it for the more detailed work. Still, it was like magic, making something so small look so realistic.

He put it down, very carefully, and went into the kitchen to talk to Sadie while he waited for Maddie to get ready.

"Those little fairies she makes are amazing," he commented, lounging against the counter.

Sadie smiled at him. "They really are. I don't know how she does all that tiny detailed work without going blind. The little faces are so realistic. She has a gift."

"She does. I wish she'd do something with it."

"Me, too," Sadie replied. "But she doesn't want to sell her babies, as she calls them."

"She's sitting on a gold mine here." Cort sighed. "You know, breeding herd sires is hard work, even for people who've done it for generations and love it."

She glanced at him and she looked worried. "I know. She doesn't really want to do it. My nephew had to toss her in at the deep end when he knew his cancer was fatal." She shook her head. "I hate it for her. You shouldn't be locked into a job you don't want to do. But she's had no training. She really can't do anything else."

"She can paint. And she can sculpt."

"Yes, but there's still the ranch," Sadie emphasized.

"Any problem has a solution. It's just a question of finding it." He sighed. "Ben said you'd had another cow go missing."

"Yes." She frowned. "Odd thing, too, she was in a pasture with several other cows, all of them healthier than her. I can't think somebody would steal her."

"I know what you mean. They do wander off. It's just that it looks suspicious, having two go missing in the same month."

"Could it be that developer man?"

Cort shook his head. "I wouldn't think so. We've got armed patrols and cameras mounted everywhere. If anything like that was going on, we'd see it."

"I suppose so."

There was the clatter of footsteps almost leaping down the staircase.

"Okay, I'm ready," Maddie said, breathless. She was wearing jeans and boots and a pretty pink button-up blouse. She looked radiant.

"Where are you off to?" Sadie asked, laughing.

"I'm going to Jacobsville with Cort to look at livestock."

"Oh." Sadie forced a smile. "Well, have fun, then."

Cort started the sleek two-seater Jaguar. He glanced at Maddie, who was looking at everything with utter fascination.

"Not quite like your little Volkswagen, huh?" he teased.

"No! It's like a spaceship or something."

"Watch this."

As he started the car, the air vents suddenly opened up and the Jaguar symbol lit up on a touch screen between the steering wheel and the glove compartment. At the same time, the gearshift rose up from the console, where it had been lying flat.

"Oh, gosh!" she exclaimed. "That's amazing!"

He chuckled. "I like high-tech gadgets."

"John has one of these," she recalled.

His eyes narrowed. "So he does. I rode him around in mine and he found a dealership the next day. His is more sedate."

"I just think they're incredible."

He smiled. "Fasten your seat belt."

"Oops, sorry, wasn't thinking." She reached up and drew it between her breasts, to fasten it beside her hip.

"I always wear my seat belt," he said. "Dad refused to drive the car until we were all strapped in. He was in a wreck once. He said he never forgot that he'd be dead except for the seat belt."

"My dad wasn't in a wreck, but he was always careful about them, too." She put her strappy purse on the floorboard. "Did Odalie come home?" she asked, trying not to sound too interested.

"Not yet," he said. He had to hide a smile, because the question lacked any subtlety.

"Oh."

He was beginning to realize that Odalie had been a major infatuation for him. Someone unreachable that he'd dreamed about, much as young boys dreamed about movie stars. He knew somewhere in the back of his mind that he and Odalie were as different as night and day. She wanted an operatic career and wasn't interested in fitting him into that picture. Would he be forever hanging around opera houses where she performed, carrying bags and organizing fans? Or would he be in Texas, waiting for her rare visits? She couldn't have a family and be a performer, not in the early stages of her career, maybe never. Cort wanted a family. He wanted children.

Funny, he'd never thought of himself as a parent before. But when he'd listened to Maddie talk about her little fairy sculptures and spoke of them as her children, he'd pictured her with a baby in her arms. It had shocked him how much he wanted to see that for real.

"You like kids, don't you?" he asked suddenly.

"What brought that on?" She laughed.

"What you said, about your little fairy sculptures. They're beautiful kids."

"Thanks." She looked out the window at the dry, parched grasslands they were passing through. "Yes, I love kids. Oh, Cort, look at the poor corn crops! That's old Mr. Raines's land, isn't it?" she added. "He's already holding on to his place by his fingernails I guess he'll have to sell if it doesn't rain."

"My sister said they're having the same issues up in Wyoming." He glanced at her. "Her husband knows a medicine man from one of the plains tribes. She said that he actually did make it rain a few times. Nobody understands how, and most people think it's fake, but I wonder."

"Ben was talking about a Cheyenne medicine man who can make rain. He's friends with him. I've known people who could douse for water," she said.

"Now, there's a rare talent indeed," he commented. He pursed his lips. "Can't Ben do that?"

"Shh," she said, laughing. "He doesn't want people to think he's odd, so he doesn't want us to tell anybody."

"Still, you might ask him to go see if he could find water. If he does, we could send a well-borer over to do the job for him."

She looked at him with new eyes. "That's really nice of you."

He shrugged. "I'm nice enough. From time to time." He glanced at her pointedly. "When women aren't driving me to drink."

"What? I didn't drive you to drink!"

"The hell you didn't," he mused, his eyes on the road so that he missed her blush. "Dancing with John Everett. Fancy dancing. Latin dancing." He sighed. "I can't even do a waltz."

"Oh, but that doesn't matter," she faltered, trying to deal with the fact that he was jealous. Was he? That was how it sounded! "I mean, I think you dance very nicely."

"I said some crude things to you," he said heavily. "I'm really sorry. I don't drink, you see. When I do…" He let the sentence trail off. "Anyway, I apologize."

"You already apologized."

"Yes, but it weighs on my conscience." He stopped

at a traffic light. He glanced at her with dark, soft eyes. “John’s my friend. I think a lot of him. But I don’t like him taking you out on dates and hanging around you.”

She went beet-red. She didn’t even know what to say.

“I thought it might come as a shock,” he said softly. He reached a big hand across the console and caught hers in it. He linked her fingers with his and looked into her eyes while he waited for the lights to change. “I thought we might take in a movie Friday night. There’s that new Batman one.”

“There’s that new Ice Age one,” she said at the same time.

He gave her a long, amused look. “You like cartoon movies?”

She flushed. “Well…”

He burst out laughing. “So do I. Dad thinks I’m nuts.”

“Oh, I don’t!”

His fingers contracted around hers. “Well, in that case, we’ll see the Ice Age one.”

“Great!”

The light changed and he drove on. But he didn’t let go of her hand.

High tea was amazing! There were several kinds of tea, china cups and saucers to contain it, and little cucumber sandwiches, chicken salad sandwiches, little cakes and other nibbles. Maddie had never seen anything like it. The tearoom was full, too, with tourists almost overflowing out of the building, which also housed an antique shop.

"This is awesome!" she exclaimed as she sampled one thing after another.

"Why, thank you." The owner laughed, pausing by their table. "We hoped it would be a success." She shook her head. "Everybody thought we were crazy. We're from Charleston, South Carolina. We came out here when my husband was stationed in the air force base at San Antonio, and stayed. We'd seen another tearoom, way north, almost in Dallas, and we were so impressed with it that we thought we might try one of our own. Neither of us knew a thing about restaurants, but we learned, with help from our staff." She shook her head. "Never dreamed we'd have this kind of success," she added, looking around. "It's quite a dream come true."

"That cameo," Maddie said hesitantly, nodding toward a display case close by. "Does it have a story?"

"A sad one. The lady who owned it said it was handed down in her family for five generations. Finally there was nobody to leave it to. She fell on hard times and asked me to sell it for her." She sighed. "She died a month ago." She opened the case with a key and pulled out the cameo, handing it to Maddie. It was black lacquer with a beautiful black-haired Spanish lady painted on it. She had laughing black eyes and a sweet smile. "She was so beautiful."

"It was the great-great-grandmother of the owner. They said a visiting artist made it and gave it to her. She and her husband owned a huge ranch, from one of those Spanish land grants. Pity there's nobody to keep the legend going."

"Oh, but there is." Cort took it from the woman and handed it to Maddie. "Put it on the tab, if you will," he told the owner. "I can't think of anyone who'll take better care of her."

"No, you can't," Maddie protested, because she saw the price tag.

"I can," Cort said firmly. "It was a family legacy. It still is." His dark eyes stared meaningfully into hers. "It can be handed down, to your own children. You might have a daughter who'd love it one day."

Maddie's heart ran wild. She looked into Cort's dark eyes and couldn't turn away.

"I'll put the ticket with lunch," the owner said with a soft laugh. "I'm glad she'll have a home," she added gently.

"Can you write down the woman's name who sold it to you?" Maddie asked. "I want to remember her, too."

"That I can. How about some buttermilk pie? It's the house specialty," she added with a grin.

"I'd love some."

"Me, too," Cort said.

Maddie touched the beautiful cheek of the cameo's subject. "I should sculpt a fairy who looks like her."

"Yes, you should," Cort agreed at once. "And show it with the cameo."

She nodded. "How sad," she said, "to be the last of your family."

"I can almost guarantee that you won't be the last of yours," he said in a breathlessly tender tone.

She looked up into his face and her whole heart was in her eyes.

He had to fight his first impulse, which was to drag her across the table into his arms and kiss the breath out of her.

She saw that hunger in him and was fascinated that she seemed to have inspired it. He'd said that she was plain and uninteresting. But he was looking at her as if he thought her the most beautiful woman on earth.

"Dangerous," he teased softly, "looking at me like that in a public place."

"Huh?" She caught her breath as she realized what he was saying. She laughed nervously, put the beautiful cameo beside her plate and smiled at him. "Thank you, for the cameo."

"My pleasure. Eat up. We've still got a long drive ahead of us!"

Jacobsville, Texas, was a place Maddie had heard of all her life, but she'd never seen it before. In the town square, there was a towering statue of Big John Jacobs, the founder of Jacobsville, for whom Jacobs County was named. Legend had it that he came to Texas from Georgia after the Civil War, with a wagonload of black sharecroppers. He also had a couple of Comanche men who helped him on the ranch. It was a fascinating story, how he'd married the spunky but not so pretty daughter of a multimillionaire and started a dynasty in Texas.

Maddie shared the history with Cort as they drove down a long dirt road to the ranch, which was owned by Cy Parks. He was an odd sort of person, very reticent, with jet-black hair sprinkled with silver and piercing green eyes. He favored one of his arms, and Maddie could tell that it had been badly burned at some point. His wife was a plain little blonde woman who wore glasses and obviously adored her husband. The feeling seemed to be mutual. They had two sons who were in school, Lisa explained shyly. She was sorry she couldn't introduce them to the visitors.

Cy Parks showed them around his ranch in a huge SUV. He stopped at one pasture and then another, grimacing at the dry grass.

"We're having to use up our winter hay to feed them," he said with a sigh. "It's going to make it a very hard winter if we have to buy extra feed to carry us through." He glanced at Cort and laughed. "You'll make my situation a bit easier if you want to carry a couple of my young bulls home with you."

Cort grinned, too. "I think I might manage that. Although we're in the same situation you are. Even my sister's husband, who runs purebred cattle in Wyoming, is having it rough. This drought is out of anybody's experience. People are likening it to the famous Dust Bowl of the thirties."

"There was another bad drought in the fifties," Parks added. "When we live on the land, we always have issues with weather, even in good years. This one has been a disaster, though. It will put a lot of the family farms and ranches out of business." He made a face. "They'll be bought up by those damned great combines, corporate ranching, I call it. Animals pumped up with drugs, genetically altered—damned shame. Pardon the language," he added, smiling apologetically at Maddie.

"She's lived around cattlemen all her life," Cort said affectionately, smiling over the back of the seat at her.

"Yes, I have." Maddie laughed. She looked into Cort's dark eyes and blushed. He grinned.

They stopped at the big barn on the way back and Cy led them through it to a stall in the rear. It connected to a huge paddock with plenty of feed and fresh water.

"Now this is my pride and joy," he said, indicating a sleek, exquisite young Santa Gertrudis bull.

"That is some conformation," Cort said, whistling. "He's out of Red Irony, isn't he?" he added.

Cy chuckled. "So you read the cattle journals, do you?"

"All of them. Your ranch has some of the best breeding stock in Texas. In the country, in fact."

"So does Skylance," Parks replied. "I've bought your own bulls over the years. And your father's," he added to Maddie. "Good stock."

"Thanks," she said.

"Same here," Cort replied. He drew in a breath. "Well, if this little fellow's up for bids, I'll put ours in."

"No bids. He's yours if you want him." He named a price that made Maddie feel faint, but Cort just smiled.

"Done," he said, and they shook hands.

On the way back home, Maddie was still astonished at the price. "That's a fortune," she exclaimed.

"Worth every penny, though," Cort assured her. "Healthy genetics make healthy progeny. We have to put new bulls on our cows every couple of years to avoid any defects. Too much inbreeding can be dangerous to the cattle and disastrous for us."

"I guess so. Mr. Parks seems like a very nice man," she mused.

He chuckled. "You don't know his history, do you? He led one of the most respected groups of mercenaries in the world into small wars overseas. His friend Eb Scott still runs a world-class counterterrorism school on his ranch. He was part of the merc group, along with a couple of other citizens of Jacobsville."

"I didn't know!"

"He's a good guy. Dad's known him for years."

"What a dangerous way to make a living, though."

"No more dangerous than dealing with livestock," Cort returned.

That was true. There were many pitfalls of working with cattle, the least of which was broken bones. Concussions could be, and sometimes were, fatal. You could drown in a river or be trampled…the list went on and on.

"You're very thoughtful," Cort remarked.

She smiled. "I was just thinking."

"Me, too." He turned off onto a side road that led to a park. "I want to stretch my legs for a bit. You game?"

"Of course."

He pulled into the car park and led the way down a small bank to the nearby river. The water level was down, but flowing beautifully over mossy rocks, with mesquite trees drooping a little in the heat, but still pretty enough to catch the eye.

"It's lovely here."

"Yes." He turned and pulled her into his arms, looking down into her wide eyes. "It's very lovely here." He bent his head and kissed her.

Chapter Six

Maddie's head was swimming. She felt the blood rush to her heart as Cort riveted her to his long, hard body and kissed her as if he might never see her again. She pressed closer, wrapping her arms around him, holding on for dear life.

His mouth tasted of coffee. It was warm and hard, insistent as it ground into hers. She thought if she died now, it would be all right. She'd never been so happy.

She heard a soft groan from his mouth. One lean hand swept down her back and pressed her hips firmly into his. She stiffened a little. She didn't know much about men, but she was a great reader. The contours of his body had changed quite suddenly.

"Nothing to worry about," he whispered into her mouth. "Just relax..."

She did. It was intoxicating. His free hand went under her blouse and expertly unclasped her bra to give free rein to his searching fingers. They found her breast and teased the nipple until it went hard. He groaned and bent his head, putting his mouth right over it, over the cloth. She arched up to him, so entranced that she couldn't even find means to protest.

"Yes," he groaned. "Yes, yes…!"

Her hands tangled in his thick black hair, tugging it closer. She arched backward, held by his strong arms as he fed on the softness of her breast under his demanding mouth. His hand at her back was more insistent now, grinding her against the growing hardness of his body.

She was melting, dying, starving to death. She wanted him to take off her clothes; she wanted to lie down with him and she wanted something, anything that would ease the terrible ache in her young body.

And just when she was certain that it would happen, that he wasn't going to stop, a noisy car pulled into the car park above and a car door slammed.

She jerked back from him, tugging down her blouse, shivering at the interruption. His eyes were almost black with hunger. He cursed under his breath, biting his lip as he fought down the need that almost bent him over double.

From above there were children's voices, laughing and calling to each other. Maddie stood with her back to him, her arms wrapped around her body, while she struggled with wild excitement, embarrassment and confusion. He didn't like her. He thought she was ugly. But he'd kissed her as if he were dying for her mouth. It was one big puzzle…

She felt his big, warm hands on her shoulders. "Don't sweat it," he said in a deep, soft tone. "Things happen."

She swallowed and forced a smile. "Right."

He turned her around, tipping her red face up to his eyes. He searched them in a silence punctuated with the screams and laughter of children. She was very pretty like that, her mouth swollen from his kisses, her face shy, timid. He was used to women who demanded. Aggressive women. Even Odalie, when he'd kissed her once, had been very outspoken about what she liked and didn't like. Maddie simply…accepted.

"Don't be embarrassed," he said softly. "Everything's all right. But we should probably go now. It's getting late."

She nodded. He took her small hand in his, curled his fingers into hers and drew her with him along the dirt path that led back up to the parking lot.

Two bedraggled parents were trying to put out food in plastic containers on a picnic table, fighting the wind, which was blowing like crazy in the sweltering heat. They glanced at the couple and grinned.

Cort grinned back. There were three children, all under school age, one in his father's arms. They looked happy, even though they were driving a car that looked as if it wouldn't make it out of the parking lot.

"Nice day for a picnic," Cort remarked.

The father made a face. "Not so much, but we've got a long drive ahead of us and it's hard to sit in a fast-food joint with this company." He indicated the leaping, running toddlers. He laughed. "Tomorrow, they'll be hijacking my car," he added with an ear-to-ear smile, "so we're enjoying it while we can."

"Nothing like kids to make a home a home," the mother commented.

"Nice looking kids, too," Cort said.

"Very nice," Maddie said, finally finding her voice.

"Thanks," the mother said. "They're a handful, but we don't mind."

She went back to her food containers, and the father went running after the toddlers, who were about to climb down the bank.

"Nice family," Cort remarked as they reached his car.

"Yes. They seemed so happy."

He glanced down at her as he stopped to open the passenger door. He was thoughtful. He didn't say anything, but his eyes were soft and full of secrets. "In you go."

She got in, fastened her seat belt without any prompting and smiled all the way back home.

Things were going great, until they got out of the car in front of Maddie's house. Pumpkin had found a way out of the hen enclosure. He spotted Cort and broke into a halting run, with his head down and his feathers ruffled.

"No!" Maddie yelled. "Pumpkin, no!"

She tried to head him off, but he jumped at her and she turned away just in time to avoid spurs in her face. "Cort, run! It's okay, just run!" she called when he hesitated.

He threw his hands up and darted toward his car. "You have to do something about that damned rooster, Maddie!" he called back.

"I know," she wailed. "I will, honest! I had fun. Thanks so much!"

He threw up his hands and dived into the car. He started it and drove off just before Pumpkin reached him.

"You stupid chicken! I'm going to let Ben eat you, I swear I am!" she raged.

But when he started toward her, she ran up the steps, into the house and slammed the door.

She opened her cell phone and called her foreman.

"Ben, can you please get Pumpkin back into the hen lot and try to see where he got out? Be sure to wear your chaps and carry a shield," she added.

"Need to eat that rooster, Maddie," he drawled.

"I know." She groaned. "Please?"

There was a long sigh. "All right. One more time…" He hung up.

Great-Aunt Sadie gave her a long look. "Pumpkin got out again?"

"Yes. There must be a hole in the fence or something," she moaned. "I don't know how in the world he does it!"

"Ben will find a way to shut him in, don't worry. But you are going to have to do something, you know. He's dangerous."

"I love him," Maddie said miserably.

"Well, sometimes things we love don't love us back and should be made into chicken and dumplings," Sadie mused with pursed lips.

Maddie made a face at her. She opened her shoulder bag and pulled out a box. “I want to show you something. Cort bought it for me.”

“Cort’s buying you presents?” Sadie exclaimed.

“It’s some present, too,” Maddie said with a flushed smile.

She opened the box. There, inside, was the hand-painted cameo of the little Spanish lady, with a card that gave all the information about the woman, now deceased, who left it with the antiques dealer.

“She’s lovely,” Sadie said, tracing the face with a forefinger very gently.

“Read the card.” Maddie showed it to her.

When Sadie finished reading it, she was almost in tears. “How sad, to be the last one in your family.”

“Yes. But this will be handed down someday.” She was remembering the family at the picnic tables and Cort’s strange smile, holding hands with him, kissing him. “Someday,” she said again, and she sounded as breathless as she felt.

Sadie didn’t ask any questions. But she didn’t have to. Maddie’s bemused expression told her everything she needed to know. Apparently Maddie and Cort were getting along very well, all of a sudden.

Cort walked into the house muttering about the rooster.

“Trouble again?” Shelby asked. She was curled up on the sofa watching the news, but she turned off the television when she saw her son. She smiled, dark-eyed and still beautiful.

“The rooster,” he sighed. He tossed his hat into a chair and dropped down into his father’s big recliner. “I bought us a bull. He’s very nice.”

“From Cy Parks?”

He nodded. “He’s quite a character.”

“So I’ve heard.”

“I bought Maddie a cameo,” he added. “In that tea-room halfway between here and Jacobsville. It’s got an antiques store in with it.” He shook his head. “Beautiful thing. It’s hand-painted…a pretty Spanish lady with a fan, enameled. She had a fit over it. The seller died recently and had no family.”

“Sad. But it was nice of you to buy it for Maddie.”

He pursed his lips. “When you met Dad, you said you didn’t get along.”

She shivered dramatically. “That’s putting it mildly. He hated me. Or he seemed to. But when my mother, your grandmother, died, I was alone in a media circus. They think she committed suicide and she was a big-name movie star, you see. So there was a lot of publicity. I was almost in hysterics when your father showed up out of nowhere and managed everything.”

“Well!”

“I was shocked. He’d sent me home, told me he had a girlfriend and broke me up with Danny. Not that I needed breaking-up, Danny was only pretending to be engaged to me to make King face how he really felt.

But it was fireworks from the start." She peered at him through her thick black eyelashes. "Sort of the way it was with you and Maddie, I think."

"It's fireworks, now, too. But of a different sort," he added very slowly.

"Oh?" She didn't want to pry, but she was curious.

"I'm confused. Maddie isn't pretty. She can't sing or play anything. But she can paint and sculpt and she's sharp about people." He grimaced. "Odalie is beautiful, like the rising sun, and she can play any instrument and sing like an angel."

"Accomplishments and education don't matter as much as personality and character," his mother replied quietly. "I'm not an educated person, although I've taken online courses. I made my living modeling. Do you think I'm less valuable to your father than a woman with a college degree and greater beauty?"

"Goodness, no!" he exclaimed at once.

She smiled gently. "See what I mean?"

"I think I'm beginning to." He leaned back. "It was a good day."

"I'm glad."

"Except for that damned rooster," he muttered. "One of these days…!"

She laughed.

He was about to call Maddie, just to talk, when his cell phone rang.

He didn't recognize the number. He put it up to his ear. "Hello?"

"Hello, Cort," Odalie's voice purred in his ear. "Guess what, I'm home! Want to come over for supper tonight?"

He hesitated. Things had just gotten complicated.

Maddie half expected Cort to phone her, after their lovely day together, but he didn't. The next morning, she heard a car pull up in the driveway and went running out. But it wasn't Cort. It was John Everett.

She tried not to let her disappointment show. "Hi!" she said. "Would you like a cup of very nice European coffee from a fancy European coffeemaker?" she added, grinning.

He burst out laughing. "I would. Thanks. It's been a hectic day and night."

"Has it? Why?" she asked as they walked up the steps.

"I had to drive up to Dallas-Fort Worth airport to pick up Odalie yesterday."

Her heart did a nosedive. She'd hoped against hope that the other woman would stay in Italy, marry her voice teacher, get a job at the opera house, anything but come home, and especially right now! She and Cort were only just beginning to get to know each other. It wasn't fair!

"How is she?" she asked, her heart shattering.

"Good," he said heavily. "She and the voice teacher disagreed, so she's going to find someone in this country to take over from him." He grimaced. "I don't know who. Since she knows more than the voice trainers do, I don't really see the point in it. She can't take criticism."

She swallowed, hard, as she went to work at the coffee machine. “Has Cort seen her?”

“Oh, yes,” he said, sitting down at the little kitchen table. “He came over for supper last night. They went driving.”

She froze at the counter. She didn’t let him see her face, but her stiff back was a good indication of how she’d received the news.

“I’m really sorry,” he said gently. “But I thought you should know before you heard gossip.”

She nodded. Tears were stinging her eyes, but she hid them. “Thanks, John.”

He drew in a long breath. “She doesn’t love him,” he said. “He’s just a habit she can’t give up. I don’t think he loves her, either, really. It’s like those crushes we get on movie stars. Odalie is an image, not someone real who wants to settle down and have kids and live on a ranch. She can't stand cattle!”

She started the coffee machine, collected herself, smiled and turned around. “Good thing your parents don’t mind them,” she said.

“And I’ve told her so. Repeatedly.” He studied her through narrowed eyes. His thick blond hair shone like pale yellow diamonds in the overhead light. He was so good-looking, she thought. She wished she could feel for him what she felt for Cort.

“People can’t help being who they are,” she replied quietly.

“You’re wise for your years,” he teased.

She laughed. “Not so wise, or I’d get out of the cattle business.” She chuckled. “After we have coffee, want to have another go at explaining genetics to me? I'm a lost cause, but we can try."

"You're not a lost cause, and I'd love to try."

Odalie was irritable and not trying to hide it. "What's the matter with you?" she snapped at Cort. "You haven't heard a word I've said."

He glanced at her and grimaced. "Sorry. We've got a new bull coming. I'm distracted."

Her pale blue eyes narrowed. "More than distracted, I think. What's this I hear about you taking that Lane girl with you to buy the new bull?"

He gave her a long look and didn't reply.

She cleared her throat. Cort was usually running after her, doing everything he could to make her happy, make her smile. She'd come home to find a stranger, a man she didn't know. Her beauty hadn't interested the voice trainer; her voice hadn't really impressed him. She'd come home with a damaged ego and wanted Cort to fix it by catering to her. That hadn't happened. She'd invited him over today for lunch and he'd eaten it in a fog. He actually seemed to not want to be with her, and that was new and scary.

"Well, she's plain as toast," Odalie said haughtily. "She has no talent and she's not educated."

He cocked his head. "And you think those are the most important character traits?"

She didn't like the way he was looking at her. "None of my friends had anything to do with her in school," she muttered.

"You had plenty to do with that, didn't you?" Cort asked with a cold smile. "I believe attorneys were involved…?"

"Cort!" She went flaming red. She turned her head. "That was a terrible misunderstanding. And it was Millie who put me up to it. That's the truth. I didn't like Maddie, but I'd never have done it if I'd realized what that boy might do." She bit her lip. She'd thought about that a lot in recent weeks, she didn't know why. "He could have killed her. I'd have had it on my conscience forever," she added in a strange, absent tone.

Cort was not impressed. This was the first time he'd heard Odalie say anything about the other woman that didn't have a barb in it, and even this comment was self-centered. Though it was small, he still took her words as a sign that maybe she was changing and becoming more tolerant…

"Deep thoughts," he told her.

She glanced at him and smiled. "Yes. I've become introspective. Enjoy it while it lasts." She laughed, and she was so beautiful that he was really confused.

"I love your car," she said, glancing out the window. "Would you let me drive it?"

He hesitated. She was the worst driver he'd ever known. "As long as I'm in it," he said firmly.

She laughed. "I didn't mean I wanted to go alone," she teased.

She knew where she wanted to drive it, too. Right past Maddie Lane's house, so that she'd see Odalie with Cort. So she'd know that he was no longer available. Odalie seemed to have lost her chance at a career in opera, but here was Cort, who'd always loved her. Maybe she'd settle down, maybe she wouldn't, but Cort was hers. She wanted Maddie to know it.

She'd never driven a Jaguar before. This was a very fast, very powerful, very expensive two-seater. Cort handed her the key.

She clicked it to open the door. She frowned. "Where's the key?" she asked.

"You don't need a key. It's a smart key. You just keep it in your pocket or lay it in the cup holder."

"Oh."

She climbed into the car and put the smart key in the cup holder.

"Seat belt," he emphasized.

She glared at him. "It will wrinkle my dress," she said fussily, because it was delicate silk, pink and very pretty.

"Seat belt or the car doesn't move," he repeated.

She sighed. He was very forceful. She liked that. She smiled at him prettily. "Okay."

She put it on, grimacing as it wrinkled the delicate fabric. Oh, well, the dry cleaners could fix it. She didn't want to make Cort mad. She pushed the button Cort showed her, the button that would start the car, but nothing happened.

"Brake," he said.

She glared at him. "I'm not going fast enough to brake!"

"You have to put your foot on the brake or it won't start," he explained patiently.

"Oh."

She put her foot on the brake and it started. The air vents opened and the touch screen came on. "It's like something out of a science-fiction movie," she said, impressed.

"Isn't it, though?" He chuckled.

She glanced at him, her face radiant. "I have got to have Daddy get me one of these!" she exclaimed.

Cort hoped her father wouldn't murder him when he saw what they cost.

Odalie pulled the car out of the driveway in short jerks. She grimaced. "I haven't driven in a while, but it will come back to me, honest."

"Okay. I'm not worried." He was petrified, but he wasn't showing it. He hoped he could grab the wheel if he had to.

She smoothed out the motions when she got onto the highway. "There, better?" she teased, looking at him.

"Eyes on the road," he cautioned.

She sighed. "Cort, you're no fun."

"It's a powerful machine. You have to respect it. That means keeping your eyes on the road and paying attention to your surroundings."

"I'm doing that," she argued, looking at him again.

He prayed silently that they'd get home again.

She pulled off on a side road and he began to worry.

"Why are we going this way?" he asked suspiciously.

"Isn't this the way to Catelow?" she asked in all innocence.

"No, it's not," he said. "It's the road that leads to the Lane ranch."

"Oh, dear, I don't want to go there. But there's no place to turn off," she worried. "Anyway, the ranch is just ahead, I'll turn around there."

Cort had to bite his lip to keep from saying something.

Maddie was out in the yard with her garbage can lid. This time Pumpkin had gotten out of the pen when she was looking. He'd jumped a seven-foot-high fence. If she hadn't seen it with her own eyes, she'd never have believed it.

"Pumpkin, you fool!" she yelled at him. "Why can't you stay where I put you? Get back in there!"

But he ran around her. This time he wasn't even trying to spur her. He ran toward the road. It was his favorite place, for some reason, despite the heat that made the ribbon of black asphalt hotter than a frying pan.

"You come back here!" she yelled.

Just as she started after him, Odalie's foot hit the accelerator pedal too hard, Cort called out, Odalie looked at him instead of the road…

Maddie heard screaming. She was numb. She opened her eyes and there was Cort, his face contorted with horror. Beside him, Odalie was screaming and crying.

"Just lie still," Cort said hoarsely. "The ambulance is on the way. Just lie still, baby."

"I hit her, I hit her!" Odalie screamed. "I didn't see her until it was too late! I hit her!"

"Odalie, you have to calm down. You're not helping!" Cort snapped at her. "Find something to cover her. Hurry!"

"Yes…there's a blanket…in the backseat, isn't there…?"

Odalie fetched it with cold, shaking hands. She drew it over Maddie's prone body. There was blood. So much blood. She felt as if she were going to faint, or throw up. Then she saw Maddie's face and tears ran down her cheeks. "Oh, Maddie," she sobbed, "I'm so sorry!"

"Find something to prop her head, in case her spine is injured," Cort gritted. He was terrified. He brushed back Maddie's blond hair, listened to her ragged breathing, saw her face go even paler. "Please hurry!" he groaned.

There wasn't anything. Odalie put her beautiful white leather purse on one side of Maddie's head without a single word, knowing it would ruin the leather and not caring at all. She put her knit overblouse on the other, crumpled up. She knelt in the dirt road beside Maddie and sat down, tears in her eyes. She touched Maddie's arm. "Help is coming," she whispered brokenly. "You hold on, Maddie. Hold on!"

Maddie couldn't believe it. Her worst enemy was sitting beside her in a vision of a horrifically expensive pink silk dress that was going to be absolutely ruined, and apparently didn't mind at all.

She tried to speak. "Pum…Pumpkin?" she rasped.

Cort looked past her and grimaced. He didn't say anything. He didn't have to.

Maddie started to cry, great heaving sobs.

"We'll get you another rooster," Cort said at once. "I'll train him to attack me. Anything. You just have to…hold on, baby," he pleaded. "Hold on!"

She couldn't breathe. "Hurts," she whispered as sensation rushed back in and she began to shudder.

Cort was in hell. There was no other word that would express what he felt as he saw her lying there in bloody clothing, maybe dying, and he couldn't do one damned thing to help her. He was sick to his soul.

He brushed back her hair, trying to remember anything else, anything that would help her until the ambulance arrived.

"Call them again!" Odalie said firmly.

He did. The operator assured them that the ambulance was almost there. She began asking questions, which Cort did his best to answer.

"Where's your great-aunt?" he asked Maddie softly.

"Store," she choked out.

"It's okay, I'll call her," he said when she looked upset.

Odalie had come out of her stupor and she was checking for injuries while Cort talked to the 911 operator. "I don't see anything that looks dangerous, but I'm afraid to move her," she said, ignoring the blood in her efforts to give aid. "There are some abrasions, pretty raw ones. Maddie, can you move your arms and legs?" she asked in a voice so tender that Maddie thought maybe she really was just dreaming all this.

She moved. "Yes," she said. "But…it hurts…"

"Move your ankles."

"Okay."

Odalie looked at Cort with horror.

"I moved...them," Maddie said, wincing. "Hurts!"

"Please, ask them to hurry," Cort groaned into the phone.

"No need," Odalie said, noting the red-and-white vehicle that was speeding toward them.

"No sirens?" Cort asked blankly.

"They don't run the sirens or lights unless they have to," the operator explained kindly. "It scares people to death and can cause wrecks. They'll use them to get the victim to the hospital, though, you bet," she reassured him.

"Thanks so much," Cort said.

"I hope she does well."

"Me, too," he replied huskily and hung up.

Odalie took one of the EMTs aside. "She can't move her feet," she whispered.

He nodded. "We won't let her know."

They went to the patient.

Maddie wasn't aware of anything after they loaded her into the ambulance on a backboard. They talked to someone on the radio and stuck a needle into her arm. She slept.

When she woke again, she was in a hospital bed with two people hovering. Cort and Odalie. Odalie's dress was dirty and bloodstained.

"Your...beautiful dress," Maddie whispered, wincing.

Odalie went to the bed. She felt very strange. Her whole life she'd lived as if there was nobody else around. She'd never been in the position of nursing anybody—her parents and brother had never even sprained a hand. She'd been petted, spoiled, praised, but never depended upon.

Now here was this woman, this enemy, whom her actions had placed almost at death's door. And suddenly she was needed. Really needed.

Maddie's great-aunt had been called. She was in the waiting room, but in no condition to be let near the patient. The hospital staff had to calm her down, she was so terrified.

They hadn't told Maddie yet. When Sadie was calmer, they'd let her in to see the injured woman.

"Your great-aunt is here, too," Odalie said gently. "You're going to be fine."

"Fine." Maddie felt tears run down her cheeks. "So much…to be done at the ranch, and I'm stove up…!"

"I'll handle it," Cort said firmly. "No worries there."

"Pumpkin," she sobbed. "He was horrible. Just horrible. But I loved him." She cried harder.

Odalie leaned down and kissed her unkempt hair. "We'll find you another horrible rooster. Honest."

Maddie sobbed. "You hate me."

"No," Odalie said softly. "No, I don't. And I'm so sorry that I put you in here. I was driving." She bit her lip. "I wasn't watching the road," she said stiffly. "God, I'm sorry!"

Maddie reached out a lacerated hand and touched Odalie's. "I ran into the road after Pumpkin…I wasn't looking. Not your fault. My fault."

Odalie was crying, too. "Okay. Both our faults. Now we have to get you well."

"Both of us," Cort agreed, touching Maddie's bruised cheek.

Maddie swallowed, hard. She wanted to say something else, but they'd given her drugs to make her comfortable, apparently. She opened her mouth to speak and went right to sleep.

Chapter Seven

"Is she going to be all right?" Great-Aunt Sadie asked when Odalie and Cort dropped into chairs in the waiting room while Maddie was sleeping.

"Yes, but it's going to be a long recovery," Cort said heavily.

"You can't tell her," Odalie said gently, "but there seems to be some paralysis in her legs. No, it's all right," she interrupted when Sadie looked as if she might start crying. "We've called one of the foremost orthopedic surgeons in the country at the Mayo Clinic. We're flying him down here to see her. We'll go from there, once he's examined her."

"But the expense," Sadie exclaimed.

"No expense. None. This is my fault and I'm paying for it," Odalie said firmly.

"It's my car, I'm helping," Cort added.

She started crying again. "It's so nice of you, both of you."

Odalie hugged her. "I'm so sorry," she said sadly. "I didn't mean to hit her. I wasn't looking, and I should have been."

Sadie hugged her back. "Accidents happen," she sobbed. "It was that stupid rooster, wasn't it?"

"It was." Cort sighed. "He ran right into the road and Maddie ran after him. The road was clear and then, seconds later, she was in the middle of it."

Odalie couldn't confess that she'd gone that way deliberately to show Maddie she was with Cort. She was too ashamed. "She'll be all right," she promised.

"Oh, my poor little girl," Sadie said miserably. "She'll give up, if she knows she might not be able to walk again. She won't fight!"

"She will. Because we'll make her," Odalie said quietly.

Sadie looked at her with new eyes. Her gaze fell to Odalie's dress. "Oh, your dress," she exclaimed.

Odalie just smiled. "I can get another dress. It's Maddie I'm worried about." It sounded like a glib reply, but it wasn't. In the past few hours, Odalie's outlook had totally shifted from herself to someone who needed her. She knew that her life would never be the same again.

A sheriff's deputy came into the waiting room, spotted Odalie and Cort and approached them, shaking his head.

"I know," Odalie said. "It's my fault. I was driving his

car—" she indicated Cort "—and not looking where I was going. Maddie ran out into the road after her stupid rooster, trying to save him. She's like that."

The deputy smiled. "We know all that from the re-creation of the scene that we did," he said. "It's very scientific," he added. "How is she?"

"Bad," Odalie said heavily. "They think she may lose the use of her legs. But we've called in a world-famous surgeon. If anything can be done, it will be. We're going to take care of her."

The deputy looked at the beautiful woman, at her bloodstained, dirty, expensive dress, with kind eyes. "I know some women who would be much more concerned with the state of their clothing than the state of the victim. Your parents must be very proud of you, young lady. If you were my daughter, I would be."

Odalie flushed and smiled. "I feel pretty guilty right now. So thanks for making me feel better."

"You going to charge her?" Cort asked.

The deputy shook his head. "Probably not, as long as she survives. In the law, everything is intent. You didn't mean to do it, and the young lady ran into the road by her own admission." He didn't add that having to watch the results of the accident day after day would probably be a worse punishment than anything the law could prescribe. But he was thinking it.

"That doesn't preclude the young lady pressing charges, however," the deputy added.

Odalie smiled wanly. "I wouldn't blame her if she did."

He smiled back. "I hope she does well."

"So do we," Odalie agreed. "Thanks."

He nodded and went back out again.

"Tell me what the doctor said about her legs," Sadie said sadly, leaning toward them.

Odalie took a long breath. She was very tired and she had no plans to go home that night. She'd have to call her family and tell them what was happening here. She hadn't had time to do that yet, nor had Cort.

"He said that there's a great deal of bruising, with inflammation and swelling. That can cause partial paralysis, apparently. He's started her on anti-inflammatories and when she's able, he'll have her in rehab to help get her moving," she added gently.

"But she was in so much pain…surely they won't make her get up!" Sadie was astonished.

"The longer she stays there, the stronger the possibility that she won't ever get up, Sadie," Odalie said gently. She patted the other woman's hands, which were resting clenched in her lap. "He's a very good doctor."

"Yes," Sadie said absently. "He treated my nephew when he had cancer. Sent him to some of the best oncologists in Texas." She looked up. "So maybe it isn't going to be permanent?"

"A good chance. So you stop worrying. We all have to be strong so that we can make her look ahead instead of behind, so that we can keep her from brooding." She bit her lower lip. "It's going to be very depressing for her, and it's going to be a long haul, even if it has a good result."

"I don't care. I'm just so happy she's still alive," the older woman cried.

"Oh, so am I," Odalie said heavily. "I can't remember ever feeling quite so bad in all my life. I took my eyes off the road, just for a minute." Her eyes closed and she shuddered. "I'll be able to hear that horrible sound when I'm an old lady..."

Cort put his arm around her. "Stop that. I shouldn't have let you drive the car until you were familiar with it. My fault, too. I feel as bad as you do. But we're going to get Maddie back on her feet."

"Yes," Odalie agreed, forcing a smile. "Yes, we are."

Sadie wiped her eyes and looked from one young determined face to the other. Funny how things worked out, she was thinking. Here was Odalie, Maddie's worst enemy, being protective of her, and Cort just as determined to make her walk again when he'd been yelling at her only a week or so earlier. What odd companions they were going to be for her young great-niece. But what a blessing.

She considered how it could have worked out, if Maddie had chased that stupid red rooster out into the road and been hit by someone else, maybe someone who ran and left her there to die. It did happen. The newspapers were full of such cases.

"What are you thinking so hard about?" Cort asked with a faint smile.

Sadie laughed self-consciously. "That if she had to get run over, it was by such nice people who stopped and rendered aid."

"I know what you mean," Cort replied. "A man was killed just a couple of weeks ago by a hit-and-run driver who was drunk and took off. The pedestrian died. I wondered at the time if his life might have been spared, if the man had just stopped to call an ambulance before he ran." He shook his head. "So many cases like that."

"Well, you didn't run, either of you." Sadie smiled. "Thanks, for saving my baby."

Odalie hugged her again, impulsively. "For the foreseeable future, she's my baby, too," she said with a laugh. "Now, how about some coffee? I don't know about you, but I'm about to go to sleep out here and I have no intention of leaving the hospital."

"Nor do I," Cort agreed. He stood up. "Let's go down to the cafeteria and see what we can find to eat, too. I just realized I'm starving."

The women smiled, as they were meant to.

Maddie came around a long time later, or so it seemed. A dignified man with black wavy hair was standing over her with a nurse. He was wearing a white lab coat with a stethoscope draped around his neck.

"Miss Lane?" the nurse asked gently. She smiled. "This is Dr. Parker from the Mayo Clinic. He's an orthopedic specialist, and we'd like him to have a look at your back. If you don't mind."

Maddie cleared her throat. She didn't seem to be in pain, which was odd. She felt very drowsy. "Of course," she said, puzzled as to why they would have such a famous man at such a small rural hospital.

"Just a few questions first," he said in a deep, pleasant tone, "and then I'll examine you." He smiled down at her.

"Okay."

The pain came back as the examination progressed, but he said it was a good sign. Especially the pain she felt in one leg. He pressed and poked and asked questions while he did it. After a few minutes she was allowed to lie down in the bed, which she did with a grimace of pure relief.

"There's a great deal of edema—swelling," he translated quietly. "Bruising of the spinal column, inflammation, all to be expected from the trauma you experienced."

"I can't feel my legs. I can't move them," Maddie said with anguish in her wan face.

He dropped down elegantly into the chair by her bed, crossed his legs and picked up her chart. "Yes, I know. But you mustn't give up hope. I have every confidence that you'll start to regain feeling in a couple of weeks, three at the outside. You have to believe that as well." He made notations and read what her attending physician had written in the forms on the clipboard, very intent on every word. "He's started you on anti-inflammatories," he murmured. "Good, good, just what I would have advised. Getting fluids into you intravenously, antibiotics…" He stopped and made another notation. "And then, physical therapy."

"Physical therapy." She laughed and almost cried. "I can't stand up!"

"It's much more than just exercise," he said and

smiled gently. “Heat, massage, gentle movements, you’ll see. You’ve never had physical therapy I see.”

She shook her head. “I’ve never really had an injury that required it.”

“You’re very lucky, then,” he said.

“You think I’ll walk again?” she prompted, her eyes wide and full of fear.

“I think so,” he said. “I won’t lie to you, there’s a possibility that the injury may result in permanent disability.” He held up a hand when she seemed distraught. “If that happens, you have a wonderful support group here. Your family. They’ll make sure you have everything you need. You’ll cope. You’ll learn how to adapt. I’ve seen some miraculous things in my career, Miss Lane,” he added. “One of my newest patients lost a leg overseas in a bombing. We repaired the damage, got him a prosthesis and now he’s playing basketball.”

She caught her breath. “Basketball?”

He grinned, looking much younger. “You’d be amazed at the advances science has made in such things. Right now, they’re working on an interface that will allow quadriplegics to use a computer with just thought. Sounds like science fiction, doesn’t it? But it’s real. I watched a video of a researcher who linked a man’s mind electronically to a computer screen, and he was able to move a curser just with the power of his thoughts.” He shook his head. “Give those guys ten years and they’ll build something that can read minds.”

“Truly fascinating,” she agreed.

“But right now, what I want from you is a promise

that you'll do what your doctor tells you and work hard at getting back on your feet," he said. "No brooding. No pessimism. You have to believe you'll walk again."

She swallowed. She was bruised and broken and miserable. She drew in a breath. "I'll try," she said.

He stood up and handed the chart to the nurse with a smile. "I'll settle for that, as long as it's your very best try," he promised. He shook hands with her. "I'm going to stay in touch with your doctor and be available for consultation. If I'm needed, I can fly back down here. Your friends out there sent a private jet for me." He chuckled. "I felt like a rock star."

She laughed, then, for the first time since her ordeal had begun.

"That's more like it," he said. "Ninety-nine percent of recovery is in the mind. You remember that."

"I'll remember," she promised. "Thanks for coming all this way."

He threw up a hand. "Don't apologize for that. It got me out of a board meeting," he said. "I hate board meetings."

She grinned.

Later, after she'd been given her medicines and fed, Odalie and Cort came into the private room she'd been moved to.

"Dr. Parker is very nice," she told them. "He came all the way from the Mayo Clinic, though…!"

"Whatever it takes is what you'll get," Odalie said with a smile.

Maddie grimaced as she looked at Odalie's beautiful pink dress, creased and stained with blood and dirt. "Your dress," she moaned.

"I've got a dozen pretty much just like it," Odalie told her. "I won't even miss it." She sighed. "But I really should go home and change."

"Go home and go to bed," Maddie said softly. "You've done more than I ever expected already…"

"No," Odalie replied. "I'm staying with you. I got permission."

"But there's no bed," Maddie exclaimed. "You can't sleep in a chair…!"

"There's a rollaway bed. They're bringing it in." She glanced at Cort with a wicked smile. "Cort gets to sleep in the chair."

He made a face. "Don't rub it in."

"But you don't have to stay," Maddie tried to reason with them. "I have nurses. I'll be fine, honest I will."

Odalie moved to the bed and brushed Maddie's unkempt hair away from her wan face. "You'll brood if we leave you alone," she said reasonably. "It's not as if I've got a full social calendar these days, and I'm not much for cocktail parties. I'd just as soon be here with you. We can talk about art. I majored in it at college."

"I remember," Maddie said slowly. "I don't go to college," she began.

"I'll wager you know more about it than I do," Odalie returned. "You had to learn something of anatomy to make those sculptures so accurate."

"Well, yes, I did," Maddie faltered. "I went on the internet and read everything I could find."

"I have all sorts of books on medieval legends and romances, I'll bring them over for you to read when they let you go home. Right now you have to rest," Odalie said.

Maddie flushed. "That would be so nice of you."

Odalie's eyes were sad. "I've been not so nice to you for most of the time we've known one another," she replied. "You can't imagine how I felt, after what happened because I let an idiot girl talk me into telling lies about you online. I've had to live with that, just as you have. I never even said I was sorry for it. But I am," she added.

Maddie drew in a breath. She was feeling drowsy. "Thanks," she said. "It means a lot."

"Don't you worry about a thing," Odalie added. "I'll take care of you."

Maddie flushed. She'd never even really had a girlfriend, and here was Odalie turning out to be one.

Odalie smiled. "Now go to sleep. Things will look brighter tomorrow. Sometimes a day can make all the difference in how we look at life."

"I'll try."

"Good girl." She glanced at Cort. "Can you drive me home and bring me back?"

"Sure," he said. "I need a change of clothes, too. I'll drop you off at Big Spur, go home and clean up and we'll both come back. We need to tell our parents what's going on, too."

"John will be beside himself," Odalie said without

thinking. “All I’ve heard since I got home is how sweet Maddie is,” she added with a smile.

She didn’t see Cort’s expression, and she couldn’t understand why Maddie suddenly looked so miserable at the mention of her brother’s name.

“Well, don’t worry about that right now,” Odalie said quickly. “But I’m sure he’ll be in to see you as soon as he knows what happened.”

Maddie nodded.

“I’ll be right out,” Cort said, smiling at Odalie.

“Sure. Sleep tight,” she told Maddie. She hesitated. “I’m sorry about your rooster, too. Really sorry,” she stammered, and left quickly.

Maddie felt tears running down her cheeks.

Cort picked a tissue out of the box by the bed, bent down and dabbed at both her eyes. “Stop that,” he said softly. “They’ll think I’m pinching you and throw me out.”

She smiled sadly. “Nobody would ever think you were mean.”

“Don’t you believe it.”

“You and Odalie…you’ve both been so kind,” she said hesitantly. “Thank you.”

“We feel terrible,” he replied, resting his hand beside her tousled hair on the pillow. “It could have been a worse tragedy than it is. And Pumpkin…” He grimaced and dabbed at more tears on her face. “As much as I hated him, I really am sorry. I know you loved him.”

She sniffed, and he dabbed at her nose, too. “He was so mean,” she choked out. “But I really did love him.”

"We'll get you a new rooster. I'll train him to attack me," he promised.

She laughed through her tears.

"That's better. The way you looked just now was breaking my heart."

She searched his eyes. He wasn't joking. He meant it.

He brushed back her hair. "God, I don't know what I would have done if you'd died," he whispered hoarsely. He bent and crushed his mouth down over hers, ground into it with helpless need. After a few seconds, he forced himself to pull back. "Sorry," he said huskily. "Couldn't help myself. I was terrified when I saw you lying there so still."

"You were?" She looked fascinated.

He shook his head and forced a smile. "Clueless," he murmured. "I guess that's not such a bad thing. Not for the moment anyway." He bent and brushed his mouth tenderly over hers. "I'll be back. Don't go anywhere."

"If I tried to, three nurses would tackle me, and a doctor would sit on me while they sent for a gurney," she assured him, her eyes twinkling.

He wrinkled his nose and kissed her again. "Okay. He stood up. "Anything you want me to bring you?"

"A steak dinner, two strawberry milkshakes, a large order of fries…"

"For that, they'd drag me out the front door and pin me to a wall with scalpels," he assured her.

She sighed. "Oh, well. It was worth a try. They fed me green gelatin." She made a face.

"When we get you out of here, I'll buy you the tastiest steak in Texas, and that's a promise. With fries."

"Ooooh," she murmured.

He grinned. "Incentive to get better. Yes?"

She nodded. "Yes." The smile faded. "You don't have to come back. Odalie, either. I'll be okay."

"We're coming back, just the same. We'll drop Great-Aunt Sadie off at the house, but she can stay at Skylance if she's nervous about being there alone. She's been a real trooper, but she's very upset."

"Can I see her?"

"For just a minute. I'll bring her in. You be good."

She nodded.

Great-Aunt Sadie was still crying when she went to the bed and very carefully bent down to hug Maddie. "I'm so glad you're going to be all right," she sobbed.

Maddie touched her gray hair gently. "Can't kill a weed." She laughed.

"You're no weed, my baby." She smoothed back her hair. "You keep getting better. I'll bring your gown and robe and slippers and some cash when I come back. Here. This is for the machines if you want them to get you anything…"

"Put that back," Cort said, "Maddie won't need cash."

"Oh, but—" Sadie started to argue.

"It won't do any good," Cort interrupted with a grin. "Ask my dad."

"He's right," Maddie said drowsily. "I heard one of

his cowboys say that it's easier to argue with a signpost, and you'll get further."

"Stop bad-mouthing me. Bad girl," he teased.

She grinned sleepily.

"You go to sleep," he told her. "Odalie and I will be back later, and we'll bring Sadie in the morning."

"You're a nice boy, Cort," Sadie said tearfully.

He hugged her. "You're a nice girl," he teased. "Good night, honey," he told Maddie, and didn't miss the faint blush in her cheeks as she registered the endearment.

"Good night," she replied.

She drifted off to sleep before they got out of the hospital. In her mind, she could still hear that soft, deep voice drawling "honey."

The next morning, Maddie opened her eyes when she heard a commotion.

"I can't bathe her with you sitting there," the nurse was saying reasonably.

Cort frowned as he stood up. "I know, I know. Sorry. I only fell asleep about four," he added with a sheepish smile.

The nurse smiled back. "It's all right. A lot of patients don't have anybody who even cares if they live or die. Your friend's very fortunate that the two of you care so much."

"She's a sweet girl," Odalie said gently.

"So are you," Cort said, and smiled warmly at her.

She flushed a little.

Maddie, watching, felt her heart sink. They'd both been so caring and attentive that she'd actually forgotten how Cort felt about Odalie. And now it seemed that Odalie was seeing him with new eyes.

Cort turned, but Maddie closed her eyes. She couldn't deal with this. Not now.

"Tell her we went to have breakfast and we'll be back," Cort said, studying Maddie's relaxed face.

"I will," the nurse promised.

Cort let Odalie go out before him and closed the door as he left.

"Time to wake up, sweetie," the nurse told Maddie. "I'm going to give you your bath and then you can have breakfast."

"Oh, is it morning?" Maddie asked, and pretended to yawn. "I slept very well."

"Good. Your friends went to have breakfast. That handsome man said they'd be back," she added with a laugh. "And that woman. What I wouldn't give to be that beautiful!"

"She sings like an angel, too," Maddie said.

"My, my, as handsome as he is, can you imagine what beautiful children they'd have?" the nurse murmured as she got her things together to bathe Maddie.

"Yes, wouldn't they?" Maddie echoed.

Something in her tone made the other woman look at her curiously.

But Maddie just smiled wanly. "They've both been very kind," she said. "They're my neighbors."

"I see."

No, she didn't, but Maddie changed the subject to a

popular television series that she watched. The nurse watched it, too, which gave them a talking point.

Later, Sadie came in with a small overnight bag.

"I brought all your stuff," she told Maddie. "You look better," she lied, because Maddie was pale and lethargic and obviously fighting pain.

"It's a little worse today," she replied heavily. "You know what they say about injuries, they're worse until the third day and then they start getting better."

"Who said that?" Sadie wondered.

"Beats me, but I've heard it all my life. Did you bring me anything to read?" she added curiously.

"I didn't. But somebody else did." She glanced at the door. Odalie came in with three beautifully illustrated fairy-tale books. After breakfast, both Odalie and Cort had gone home to change, and then picked up Great-Aunt Sadie when returning to the hospital.

"I bought these while I was in college," Odalie said, handing one to Maddie. "I thought they had some of the most exquisite plates I'd ever seen."

And by plates, she meant paintings. Maddie caught her breath as she opened the book and saw fairies, like the ones she made, depicted in a fantasy forest with a shimmering lake.

"Oh, this is…it's beyond words," she exclaimed, breathlessly turning pages.

"Yes. I thought you'd like them." She beamed. "These are updated versions of the ones I have. I bought these for you."

"For me?" Maddie looked as if she'd won the lottery. "You mean it?"

"I mean it. I'm so glad you like them."

"They're beautiful," she whispered reverently. She traced one of the fairies. "I have my own ideas about faces and expressions, but these are absolutely inspiring!"

"Fantasy art is my favorite."

"Mine, too." She looked up, flushing a little. "How can I ever thank you enough?"

"You can get better so that my conscience will stop killing me," Odalie said gently.

Maddie smiled. "Okay. I promise to try."

"I'll settle for that."

"I put your best gowns and slippers in the bag," Sadie told her. "And Cort brought you something, too."

"Cort?"

She looked toward the door. He was smiling and nodding at the nurses, backing into the room. Behind his back was a strange, bottom-heavy bear with a big grin and bushy eyebrows.

He turned into the room and handed it to Maddie. "I don't know if they'll let you keep it, but if they won't, I'll let Sadie take him home and put him in your room. His name's Bubba."

"Bubba?" She burst out laughing as she took the bear from him. It was the cutest stuffed bear she'd ever seen. "Oh, he's so cute!"

"I'm glad you like him. I wanted to smuggle in a steak, but they'd have smelled it at the door."

"Thanks for the thought," she said shyly.

"You're welcome."

"Bears and books." She sighed. "I feel spoiled."

"I should hope so," Odalie said with a grin. "We're doing our best."

"When we get you out of here, we're taking you up to Dallas and we'll hit all the major museums and art galleries," Cort said, dropping into a chair. "Culture. Might give you some new ideas for your paintings and sculptures."

"Plus we bought out an art supply store for you," Odalie said with twinkling eyes. "You'll have enough to make all sorts of creations when you get home."

"Home." Maddie looked from one of them to the other. "When? When can I go home?"

"In a few days." Cort spoke for the others. "First they have to get you stabilized. Then you'll be on a regimen of medicine and physical therapy. We'll go from there."

Maddie drew in a long breath. It sounded like an ordeal. She wasn't looking forward to it. And afterward, what if she could never walk again? What if…?

"No pessimistic thoughts." Odalie spoke for the visitors. "You're going to get well. You're going to walk. Period."

"Absolutely," Sadie said.

"Amen," Cort added.

Maddie managed a sheepish smile. With a cheering section like that, she thought, perhaps she could, after all.

Chapter Eight

The third day was definitely the worst. Maddie was in incredible pain from all the bruising. It was agony to move at all, and her legs were still numb. They kept her sedated most of the day. And at night, as usual, Cort and Odalie stayed with her.

"How are you getting away with this?" Maddie asked Odalie when Cort left to get them both a cup of coffee.

"With this?" Odalie asked gently.

"Staying in the room with me," she replied drowsily. "I thought hospitals made people leave at eight-thirty."

"Well, they mostly do," Odalie said sheepishly. "But, you see, Cort's Dad endowed the new pediatric unit, and mine paid for the equipment in the physical therapy unit. So, they sort of made an exception for us."

Maddie laughed in spite of the pain. "Oh, my."

"As my dad explained it, you can do a lot of good for other people and help defray your own taxes, all at once. But, just between us, my dad would give away money even if it didn't help his tax bill. So would Cort's. It's just the sort of people they are."

"It's very nice of them." She shifted and grimaced. "How are things at my ranch, do you know?" she asked worriedly.

"Great. Not that the boys don't miss you. But Cort's been over there every day getting roundup organized and deciding on your breeding program. I hope you don't mind."

"Are you kidding? I make fairies…I don't know anything about creating bloodlines." She sighed. "My dad knew all that stuff. He was great at it. But he should have had a boy who'd have loved running a ranch. I just got stuck with it because there was nobody else he could leave it to."

"Your father must have known that you'd do the best you could to keep it going," Odalie said gently.

"I am. It's just I have no aptitude for it, that's all."

"I think…"

"Finally!" John Everett said as he walked in, frowning at his sister. "There was such a conspiracy of silence. I couldn't get Cort to tell me where you were. I called every hospital in Dallas…"

"I left you seven emails and ten text messages!" Odalie gasped. "Don't tell me you never read them?"

He glowered at her. "I don't read my personal email because it's always advertisements, and I hate text messages. I disabled them from coming to my phone. You couldn't have called me in Denver and told me what happened?"

Odalie would have told him that Cort talked her out of it, but he was mad, and John in a temper would discourage most people from confessing that.

"Sorry," she said instead.

He turned his attention to Maddie and grimaced. The bruises were visible around the short-sleeved gown she was wearing. "Poor little thing," he said gently. "I brought you flowers."

He opened the door and nodded to a lady standing outside with a huge square vase full of every flower known to man—or so it seemed. "Right over there looks like a good place," he said, indicating a side table.

The lady, probably from the gift shop, smiled at Maddie and placed the flowers on the table. "I hope you feel better soon," she told her.

"The flowers are just lovely," Maddie exclaimed.

"Thanks," the lady replied, smiled at John and left them to it.

"Oh, how beautiful. Thanks, John!" she exclaimed.

Odalie looked very uncomfortable. John didn't even look at her. He went to the bedside, removed his Stetson and sat down in the chair by the bed, grasping one of Maddie's hands in his. "I've been beside myself since I knew what happened. I wanted to fly right home, but I was in the middle of negotiations for Dad and I couldn't. I did try to call your house, but nobody answered, and I didn't have your cell phone number." He glared at his sister again. "Nobody would even tell me which hospital you were in!"

"I sent you emails," Odalie said again.

"The telephone has a voice mode," he drawled sarcastically.

Odalie swallowed hard and got to her feet. "Maybe I should help Cort carry the coffee," she said. "Do you want some?"

"Don't be mean to her," Maddie said firmly. "She's been wonderful to me."

John blinked. He glanced at Odalie with wide-eyed surprise. "Her?"

"Yes, her," Maddie replied. "She hasn't left me since I've been in here. She brought me books…"

"Her?" John exclaimed again.

Odalie glared at him. "I am not totally beyond redemption," she said haughtily.

"Maybe I have a fever," John mused, touching his forehead as he looked back down into Maddie's eyes. "I thought you said she stayed with you in the hospital. She hates hospitals."

"She's been here all night every night," Maddie said softly. She smiled at Odalie. "She's been amazing."

Odalie went beet-red. She didn't know how to handle the compliment. She'd had so many, all her life, about her beauty and her talent. But nobody had ever said she was amazing for exhibiting compassion. It felt really good.

"It was my fault, what happened," Odalie said quietly. "I was driving."

"Who the hell let you drive a car?" John exclaimed.

"I did," Cort said heavily as he joined them. He looked at John's hand holding Maddie's and his dark eyes began to burn with irritation. "Don't hold her hand, it's bruised," he blurted out before he thought.

John's blue eyes twinkled suddenly. "It is?" He turned it over and looked at it. "Doesn't look bruised. That hurt?" he asked Maddie.

"Well, no," she answered. The way Cort was looking at John was very odd.

"Yes, he let me drive because I badgered him into it," Odalie broke in. "Poor Maddie tried to save her rooster and ran out into the road. I didn't see her until it was too late."

"Oh, no," John said, concerned. "Will you be all right?" he asked Maddie.

"I'm going to be fine," she assured him with more confidence than she really felt.

"Yes, she is," Odalie said, smiling. "We're all going to make sure of it."

"What about Pumpkin?" John asked.

Odalie tried to stop him from asking, but she was too late.

"It's all right," Maddie said gently. "I'm getting used to it. Pumpkin…didn't make it."

Sadie had told her that Ben had buried the awful rooster under a mesquite tree and even made a little headstone to go on the grave. Considering how many scars Ben had, it was quite a feat of compassion.

"I'll get you a new rooster," John said firmly.

"Already taken care of," Cort replied. "You're in my seat, bro."

John gave him a strange look. "Excuse me?"

"That's my seat. I've got it just the way I like it, from sleeping in it for two nights."

John was getting the picture. He laughed inside. Amazing how determined Cort was to get him away from Maddie. He glanced at his sister, who should be fuming. But she wasn't. Her eyes were smiling. She didn't even seem to be jealous.

Maddie was so out of it that she barely noticed the by-play. The sedative was working on her. She could barely keep her eyes open.

As she drifted off, Cort was saying something about a rooster with feathers on his feet....

A week after the accident, Maddie began to feel her back again. It was agonizing pain. Dr. Brooks came in to examine her, his face impassive as he had her grip his fingers. He used a pin on the bottom of her feet, and actually grinned when she flinched.

"I'm not going to be paralyzed?" she asked, excited and hopeful.

"We can't say that for sure," Dr. Brooks said gently. "Once the swelling and edema are reduced, there may be additional injuries that become apparent. But I will say it's a good sign."

She let out a breath. "I'd have coped," she assured him. "But I'm hoping I won't have to."

He smiled and patted her on the shoulder. "One step

at a time, young lady. Recovery first, then rehabilitation with physiotherapy. Meanwhile I'm going to consult with your orthopedic surgeon and put in a call to a friend of mine, a neurologist. We want to cover all our bases."

"You're being very cautious," she murmured.

"I have to be. The fact that you got excellent immediate care at the scene is greatly in your favor, however. Cort knew exactly what to do, and the paramedics followed up in textbook perfection. However," he added with a smile, "my personal opinion is your condition comes from bad bruising and it is not a permanent injury. We saw nothing on the tests that indicated a tearing of the spinal cord or critical damage to any of your lumbar vertebrae."

"You didn't say," she replied.

"Until the swelling goes down, we can't be absolutely sure of anything, which is why I'm reluctant to go all bright-eyed over a cheery prognosis," he explained. "But on the evidence of what I see, I think you're going to make a complete recovery."

She beamed. "Thank you!"

He held up a hand. "We'll still wait and see."

"When can I go home?" she asked.

"Ask me next week."

She made a face. "I'm tired of colored gelatin," she complained. "They're force feeding me water and stuff with fiber in it."

"To keep your kidney and bowel function within acceptable levels," he said. "Don't fuss. Do what they tell you."

She sighed. "Okay. Thanks for letting Cort and Odalie stay with me at night. One of the nurses said you spoke to the administrator himself."

He shrugged. "He and I were at med school together. I beat him at chess regularly."

She laughed. "Can you thank him for me? You don't know what it meant, that they wanted to stay."

"Yes, I do," he replied solemnly. "I've never seen anybody do a greater turnaround than your friend Odalie." He was the doctor who'd treated Maddie after the boy tried to throw her out of the window at school. He'd given a statement to the attorneys who went to see Cole Everett, as well. He shook his head. "I've known your families since you were children. I know more about Odalie than most people do. I must say, she's impressed me. And I'm hard to impress."

Maddie smiled. "She's impressed me, too. I never expected her to be so compassionate. Of course, it could be guilt," she said hesitantly. She didn't add that Odalie could be trying to win back Cort. She made a face. "I'm ashamed that I said that."

"Don't be. It's natural to be suspicious of someone who's been nothing short of an enemy. But this time, I believe her motives are quite sincere."

"Thanks. That helps."

He smiled. "You keep improving. I'll be back to see you from time to time. But I'm pleased with the progress I see."

"Thanks more for that."

He chuckled. "I love my job," he said at the door.

* * *

Late at night, Maddie was prey to her secret fears of losing the use of her legs. Despite Dr. Brooks's assurances, she knew that the prognosis could change. The traumatic nature of her injury made it unpredictable.

"Hey," Cort said softly, holding her hand when she moved restlessly in bed. "Don't think about tomorrow. Just get through one day at a time."

She rolled her head on the pillow and looked at him with tormented eyes. Odalie was sound asleep on the rollaway bed nearby, oblivious. But last night, it had been the other woman who'd been awake while Cort slept, to make sure Maddie had anything she needed.

"It's hard not to think about it," she said worriedly. "I'm letting everybody at the ranch down...."

"Baloney," he mused, smiling. "I've got Ben and the others organized. We're making progress on your breeding program." He made a face. "John went over there today to oversee things while I was here with you."

"John's your best friend," she reminded him.

He didn't want to tell her that he was jealous of his friend. He'd wanted to thump John when he walked in and found him holding Maddie's hand. But he was trying to be reasonable. He couldn't be here and at the ranch. And John was talented with breeding livestock. He'd learned from Cole Everett, whose skills were at least equal with King Brannt's and, some people said, just a tad more scientific.

"That's nice of John," she remarked.

He forced a smile. "Yeah. He's a good guy."

She searched his eyes.

"Oh, hell," he muttered, "he's got an honors degree in animal husbandry. I've got an associate's."

She brightened. "Doesn't experience count for something?" she teased lightly.

He chuckled deep in his throat. "Nice of you, to make me feel better, when I've landed you in that hospital bed," he added with guilt in his eyes.

She squeezed his hand. "My dad used to say," she said softly, "that God sends people into our lives at various times, sometimes to help, sometimes as instruments to test us. He said that you should never blame people who cause things to happen to you, because that might be a test to teach you something you needed to know." She glanced at Odalie. "I can't be the only person who's noticed how much she's changed," she added in a low tone. "She's been my rock through all this. You have, too, but…"

"I understand." He squeezed her hand back, turning it over to look at the neat, clean fingernails tipping her small, capable fingers. "I've been very proud of her."

"Me, too," Maddie confessed. "Honestly this whole experience has changed the way I look at the world, at people."

"Your dad," he replied, "was a very smart man. And not just with cattle."

She smiled. "I always thought so. I do miss him."

He nodded. "I know you do."

He put her hand back on the bed. "You try to go back

to sleep. Want me to call the nurse and see if she can give you something else for pain?"

She laughed softly and indicated the patch on her arm. "It's automatic. Isn't science incredible?"

"Gets more incredible every day," he agreed. He got up. "I'm going for more coffee. I won't be long."

"Thanks. For all you're doing," she said seriously.

He stared down at her with quiet, guilty eyes. "It will never be enough to make up for what happened."

"That's not true," she began.

"I'll be back in a bit." He left her brooding.

"You have to try to make Cort stop blaming himself," Maddie told Odalie the next day after she'd had breakfast and Cort had gone to the ranch for a shower and change of clothes. Odalie would go when he returned, they'd decided.

"That's going to be a tall order," the other woman said with a gentle smile.

"If there was a fault, it was Pumpkin's and mine," Maddie said doggedly. "He ran out into the road and I chased after him without paying any attention to traffic."

Odalie sat down in the seat beside the bed, her face covered in guilt. "I have a confession," she said heavily. "You're going to hate me when you hear it."

"I couldn't hate you after all you've done," came the soft reply. "It isn't possible."

Odalie flushed. "Thanks," she said in a subdued tone. She drew in a deep breath. "I drove by your place deliberately. Cort had been talking about you when I got home. I was jealous. I wanted you to see me with him." She averted her eyes. "I swear to God, if I'd had any idea what misery and grief I was going to cause, I'd never have gotten in the car at all!"

"Oh, goodness," Maddie said unsteadily. But she was much more unsettled by Odalie's jealousy than she was of her actions. It meant that Odalie cared for Cort. And everybody knew how he felt about her; he'd never made any secret of it.

But Maddie had been hurt, and Cort felt responsible. So he was paying attention to Maddie instead of Odalie out of guilt.

Everything became clear. Maddie felt her heart break. But it wasn't Odalie's fault. She couldn't force Cort not to care about her.

Odalie's clear blue eyes lifted and looked into Maddie's gray ones. "You care for him, don't you?" she asked heavily. "I'm so sorry!"

Maddie reached out a hand and touched hers. "One thing I've learned in my life is that you can't make people love you," she said softly. She drew in a long breath and stared at the ceiling. "Life just doesn't work that way."

"So it seems..." Odalie said, and her voice trailed away. "But you see the accident really was my fault."

Maddie shook her head. She wasn't vindictive. She smiled. "It was Pumpkin's."

Odalie felt tears streaming down her cheeks. "All this time, all I could think about is the things I did to you when we were in school. I'm so ashamed, Maddie."

Maddie was stunned.

"I put on a great act for the adults. I was shy and sweet and everybody's idea of the perfect child. But when they weren't looking, I was horrible. My parents didn't know how horrible until your father came to the house with an attorney, and laid it out for them." She grimaced. "I didn't know what happened to you. There was gossip, but it was hushed up. And gossip is usually exaggerated, you know." She picked at her fingernail, her head lowered. "I pretended that I didn't care. But I did." She looked up. "It wasn't until the accident that I really faced up to the person I'd become." She shook her own head. "I didn't like what I saw."

Maddie didn't speak. She just listened.

Odalie smiled sadly. "You know, I've spent my life listening to people rave about how pretty I was, how talented I was. But until now, nobody ever liked me because I was kind to someone." She flushed red. "You needed me. That's new, having somebody need me." She grinned. "I really like it."

Maddie burst out laughing.

Odalie laughed, too, wiping at tears. "Anyway, I apologize wholeheartedly for all the misery I've caused you, and I'm going to work really hard at being the person I hope I can be."

"I don't know what I would have done without you," Maddie said with genuine feeling. "Nobody could have been kinder."

"Some of that was guilt. But I really like you," she said, and laughed again sheepishly. "I never knew what beautiful little creatures you could create from clay and paint."

"My hobby." She laughed.

"It's going to be a life-changing hobby. You wait."

Maddie only smiled. She didn't really believe that. But she wanted to.

Cort came back later and Odalie went home to freshen up.

Cort dropped into the chair beside Maddie's bed with a sigh. "I saw your doctor outside, doing rounds. He thinks you're progressing nicely."

She smiled. "Yes, he told me so. He said I might be able to go home in a few days. I'll still have to have physical therapy, though."

"Odalie and I will take turns bringing you here for it," he said, answering one of her fears that her car wouldn't stand up to the demands of daily trips, much less her gas budget.

"But, Cort," she protested automatically.

He held up a hand. "It won't do any good," he assured her.

She sighed. "Okay. Thanks, then." She studied his worn face. "Odalie's been amazing, hasn't she?"

He laughed. "Oh, I could think of better words. She really shocked me. I wouldn't have believed her capable of it."

"I know."

"I'm very proud of her," he said, smiling wistfully. He was thinking what a blessing it was that Odalie hadn't shown that side of herself to him when he thought he was in love with her. Because with hindsight, he realized that it was only an infatuation. He'd had a crush on Odalie that he'd mistaken for true love.

Maddie couldn't hear his thoughts. She saw that wistful smile and thought he was seeing Odalie as he'd always hoped she could be, and that he was more in love with her than ever before.

"So am I," she replied.

He noted the odd look in her eyes and started to question it when his mother came in with Heather Everett. Both women had been visiting every day. This time they had something with them. It was a beautiful arrangement of orchids.

"We worked on it together," Heather said, smiling. She was Odalie, aged, still beautiful with blue eyes and platinum blond hair. A knockout, like dark-eyed, dark-haired Shelby Brannt, even with a sprinkle of gray hairs.

"Yes, and we're not florists, but we wanted to do something personal," Shelby added.

Heather put it on the far table, by the window, where it caught the light and looked exotic and lush.

"It's so beautiful! Thank you both," Maddie enthused.

"How are you feeling, sweetheart?" Shelby asked, hovering.

"The pain is easing, and I have feeling in my legs," she said, the excitement in her gray eyes. "The doctor thinks I'll walk again."

"That's wonderful news," Shelby said heavily. "We've been so worried."

"All of us," Heather agreed. She smiled. "It's worse for us, because Odalie was driving."

"Odalie has been my rock in a storm," Maddie said gently. "She hasn't left me, except to freshen up, since they brought me in here. I honestly don't know how I would have made it without her. Or without Cort," she added, smiling at him. "They've stopped me from brooding, cheered me up, cheered me on…they've been wonderful."

Shelby hugged her tall son. "Well, of course, I think so." She laughed. "Still, it's been hard on all three families," she added quietly. "It could have been even more of a tragedy if—"

"I'm going to be fine," Maddie interrupted her.

"Yes, she is," Cort agreed. He smiled at Maddie. His dark eyes were like velvet. There was an expression in them that she'd never noticed before. Affection. Real affection.

She smiled back, shyly, and averted her eyes.

"Odalie wants you to talk to one of our friends, who has an art gallery in Dallas," Heather said. "She thinks your talent is quite incredible."

"It's not, but she's nice to say so…" Maddie began.

"They're her kids," Cort explained to the women, and Maddie's eyes widened. "Don't deny it, you told me so," he added, making a face at her. "She puts so much of herself into them that she can't bear to think of selling one."

"Well, I know it sounds odd, but it's like that with me and the songs I compose," Heather confessed, and flushed a little when they stared at her. "I really do put my whole heart into them. And I hesitate to share that with other people."

"Desperado owes you a lot for those wonderful songs." Shelby chuckled. "And not just money. They've made an international reputation with them."

"Thanks," Heather said. "I don't know where they come from. It's a gift. Truly a gift."

"Like Odalie's voice," Maddie replied. "She really does sing like an angel."

Heather smiled. "Thank you. I've always thought so. I wanted her to realize her dream, to sing at the Met, at the Italian opera houses." She looked introspective. "But it doesn't look like she's going to do that at all."

"Why not?" Shelby asked, curious.

Heather smiled. "I think she's hungry for a home of her own and a family. She's been talking about children lately."

"Has she?" Cort asked, amused.

He didn't seem to realize that Maddie immediately connected Heather's statement with Odalie's changed nature and Cort's pride in her. She added those facts together and came up with Cort and Odalie getting married.

It was so depressing that she had to force herself to smile and pretend that she didn't care.

"Can you imagine what beautiful children she'll have?" Maddie asked with a wistful smile.

"Well, yours aren't going to be ugly," Cort retorted. Then he remembered that he'd called Maddie that, during one of their arguments, and his face paled with shame.

Maddie averted her eyes and tried not to show what she was feeling. "Not like Odalie's," she said. "Is she thinking about getting married?" she asked Heather.

"She says she is," she replied. "I don't know if she's really given it enough thought, though," she added with sadness in her tone. "Very often, we mistake infatuation for the real thing."

"You didn't," Shelby teased before anyone could react to Heather's statement. "You knew you wanted to marry Cole before you were even an adult."

Heather saw Maddie's curious glance. "Cole's mother married my father," she explained. "There was some terrible gossip spread, to the effect that we were related by blood. It broke my heart. I gave up on life. And then the truth came out, and I realized that Cole didn't hate me at all. He'd only been shoving me out of his life because he thought I was totally off-limits, and his pride wouldn't let him admit how thoroughly he'd accepted the gossip for truth."

"You made a good match." Shelby smiled.

"So did you, my friend." Heather laughed. "Your road to the altar was even more precarious than mine."

Shelby beamed. "Yes, but it was worth every tear." She hugged her son. "Look at my consolation prize!"

But when the women left, and Cort walked them out to the parking lot, Maddie was left with her fears and insecurities.

Odalie wanted to marry and raise a family. She'd seen how mature and caring Cort was, and she wanted to drive him by Maddie's house because she was jealous of her. She'd wanted Maddie to see her with Cort.

She could have cried. Once, Odalie's feelings wouldn't have mattered. But since she'd been in the hospital, Maddie had learned things about the other woman. She genuinely liked her. She was like the sister Maddie had never had.

What was she going to do? Cort seemed to like Maddie now, but she'd been hurt and it was his car that had hit her. Certainly he felt guilty. And nobody could deny how much he'd loved Odalie. He'd grieved for weeks after she left for Italy.

Surely his love for her hadn't died just because Maddie had been in an accident. He'd told Maddie that she was ugly and that she didn't appeal to him as a man, long before the wreck. That had been honest; she'd seen it in his dark eyes.

Now he was trying to make up for what had happened. He was trying to sacrifice himself to Maddie in a vain attempt to atone for her injuries. He was denying himself Odalie out of guilt.

Maddie closed her eyes. She couldn't have that. She wanted him to be happy. In fact, she wanted Odalie to be happy. Cort would be miserable if he forced himself into a relationship with Maddie that he didn't feel.

So that wasn't going to be allowed to happen. Maddie was going to make sure of it.

Chapter Nine

By the end of the second week after the accident, Maddie was back home, with a high-tech wheelchair to get around the house in.

Odalie and Cort had insisted on buying her one to use while she was recuperating, because she still couldn't walk, even though the feeling had come back into her legs. She was exhilarated with the doctor's cautious prognosis that she would probably heal completely after several months.

But she'd made her friends promise to get her an inexpensive manual wheelchair. Of course, they'd said, smiling.

Then they walked in with a salesman who asked questions, measured her and asked about her choice of colors. Oh, bright yellow, she'd teased, because she was sure they didn't make a bright yellow wheelchair. The only ones she'd seen were black and ugly and plain, and they all looked alike. She'd dreaded the thought of having to sit in one.

A few days later, the wheelchair was delivered. It came from Europe. It was the most advanced wheelchair of its type, fully motorized, able to turn in its own circumference, able to lift the user up to eye level with other people, and all-terrain. Oh, and also, bright yellow in color.

"This must have cost a fortune!" Maddie almost screamed when she saw it. "I said something inexpensive!"

Cort gave her a patient smile. "You said inexpensive. This is inexpensive," he added, glancing at Odalie.

"Cheap," the blonde girl nodded. She grinned unrepentantly. "When you get out of it, you can donate it to someone in need."

"Oh. Well." The thought that she would get out of it eventually sustained her. "I can donate it?"

Odalie nodded. She smiled.

Cort smiled, too.

"Barracudas," she concluded, looking from one to the other. "I can't get around either one of you!"

They both grinned.

She laughed. "Okay. Thanks. Really. Thanks."

"You might try it out," Odalie coaxed.

"Yes, in the direction of the hen yard," Cort added.

She looked from one of them to the other. They had very suspicious expressions. "Okay."

She was still learning to drive it, but the controls were straightforward, and it didn't take long to learn them. The salesman had come out with it, to further explain its operation.

It had big tires, and it went down steps. That was a revelation. It didn't even bump very much. She followed Cort and Odalie over the sandy yard to the huge enclosure where her hens lived. It was grassy, despite the tendency of chickens to scratch and eat the grass, with trees on one side. The other contained multiple feeders and hanging waterers. The enormous henhouse had individual nests and cowboys cleaned it out daily. There was almost no odor, and the hens were clean and beautiful.

"My girls look very happy," Maddie said, laughing.

"They have a good reason to be happy." Cort went into the enclosure, and a minute later, he came back out, carrying a large red rooster with a big comb and immaculate feathers.

He brought him to Maddie. The rooster looked sort of like Pumpkin, but he was much bigger. He didn't seem at all bothered to be carried under someone's arm. He handed the rooster to Maddie.

She perched him on her jean-clad lap and stared at him. He cocked his head and looked at her and made a sort of purring sound.

She was aghast. She looked up at Cort wide-eyed.

"His name's Percival," Cort told her with a chuckle. "He has impeccable bloodlines."

She looked at the feathery pet again. "I've never seen a rooster this tame," she remarked.

"That's from those impeccable bloodlines." Odalie giggled. "All their roosters are like this. They're even guaranteed to be tame, or your money back. So he's sort of returnable. But you won't need to return him. He's been here for a week and he hasn't attacked anybody yet. Considering his age, he's not likely to do it."

"His age?" Maddie prompted.

"He's two," Cort said. "Never attacked anybody on the farm for all that time. The owners' kids carry the roosters around with them all the time. They're gentled. But they're also bred for temperament. They have exceptions from time to time. But Percy's no exception. He's just sweet."

"Yes, he is." She hugged the big rooster, careful not to hug him too closely, because chickens have no diaphragm and they can be smothered if their chests are compressed for too long. "Percy, you're gorgeous!"

He made that purring sound again. Almost as if he were laughing. She handed him back to Cort. "You've got him separate from the girls?"

He nodded. "If you want biddies, we can put him with them in time for spring chicks. But they know he's nearby, and so will predators. He likes people. He hates predators. The owner says there's a fox who'll never trouble a henhouse again after the drubbing Percy gave him."

Maddie laughed with pure joy. "It will be such a relief not to have to carry a limb with me to gather eggs," she said. The smile faded. "I'll always miss Pumpkin," she said softly, "but even I knew that something had to give eventually. He was dangerous. I just didn't have the heart to do anything about him."

"Providence did that for you," Cort replied. He smiled warmly. Maddie smiled back but she avoided his eyes.

That bothered him. He put Percy back in the enclosure in his own fenced area, very thoughtful. Maddie was polite, but she'd been backing away from him for days now. He felt insecure. He wanted to ask her what was wrong. Probably, he was going to have to do that pretty soon.

Maddie went to work on her sculptures with a vengeance, now that she had enough materials to produce anything she liked.

Her first work, though, was a tribute to her new friend. She made a fairy who looked just like Odalie, perched on a lily pad, holding a firefly. She kept it hidden when Cort and Odalie came to see her, which was pretty much every single day. It was her secret project.

She was so thrilled with it that at first she didn't even want to share it with them. Of all the pieces she'd done, this was her best effort. It had been costly, too. Sitting in one position for a long time, even in her cushy imported wheelchair, was uncomfortable and took a toll on her back.

"You mustn't stress your back muscles like this," the therapist fussed when she went in for therapy, which she did every other day. "It's too much strain so early in your recovery."

She smiled while the woman used a heat lamp and

massage on her taut back. “I know. I like to sculpt things. I got overenthusiastic.”

“Take frequent breaks,” the therapist advised.

“I’ll do that. I promise.”

She was walking now, just a little at a time, but steadily. Cort had bought a unit for her bathtub that created a Jacuzzi-like effect in the water. It felt wonderful on her sore and bruised back. He’d had a bar installed, too, so that she could ease herself up out of the water and not have to worry about slipping.

Odalie brought her exotic cheeses and crackers to eat them with, having found out that cheese was pretty much Maddie’s favorite food. She brought more art books, and classical music that Maddie loved.

Cort brought his guitar and sang to her. That was the hardest thing to bear. Because Maddie knew he was only doing it because he thought Maddie had feelings for him. It was humiliating that she couldn’t hide them, especially since she knew that he loved Odalie and always would.

But she couldn’t help but be entranced by it. She loved his deep, rich voice, loved the sound of the guitar, with its mix of nylon and steel strings. It was a classical guitar. He’d ordered it from Spain. He played as wonderfully as he sang.

When he’d played *“Recuerdos de la Alhambra”* for her, one of the most beautiful classical guitar compositions ever conceived, she wept like a baby.

“It is beautiful, isn’t it?” he asked, drying her tears with a handkerchief. “It was composed by a Spaniard,

Francisco Tárrega, in 1896." He smiled. "It's my favorite piece."

"Mine, too," she said. "I had a recording of guitar solos on my iPod with it. But you play it just as beautifully as that performer did. Even better than he did."

"Thanks." He put the guitar back into its case, very carefully. "From the time I was ten, there was never any other instrument I wanted to play. I worried my folks to death until they bought me one. And Morie used to go sit outside while I practiced, with earplugs in." He chuckled, referring to his sister.

"Poor Morie," she teased.

"She loves to hear me play, now. She said it was worth the pain while I learned."

She grinned. "You know, you could sing professionally."

He waved that thought away. "I'm a cattleman," he replied. "Never wanted to be anything else. The guitar is a nice hobby. But I don't think I'd enjoy playing and singing as much if I had to do it all the time."

"Good point."

"How's that sculpture coming along?"

Her eyes twinkled. "Come see."

She turned on the wheelchair and motored herself into the makeshift studio they'd furnished for her in her father's old bedroom. It had just the right airy, lighted accommodation that made it a great place to work. Besides that, she could almost feel her father's presence when she was in it.

"Don't tell her," she cautioned as she uncovered a mound on her worktable. "It's going to be a surprise."

"I promise."

She pulled off the handkerchief she'd used to conceal the little fairy sculpture. The paint was dry and the glossy finish she'd used over it gave the beautiful creature an ethereal glow.

"It looks just like her!" Cort exclaimed as he gently picked it up.

She grinned. "Do you think so? I did, but I'm too close to my work to be objective about it."

"It's the most beautiful thing you've done yet, and that's saying something." He looked down at her with an odd expression. "You really have the talent."

She flushed. "Thanks, Cort."

He put the sculpture down and bent, brushing his mouth tenderly over hers. "I have to be so careful with you," he whispered at her lips. "It's frustrating, in more ways than one."

She caught her breath. She couldn't resist him. But it was tearing her apart, to think that he might be caught in a web of deception laced by guilt. She looked up into his eyes with real pain.

He traced her lips with his forefinger. "When you're back on your feet," he whispered, "we have to talk."

She managed a smile. "Okay." Because she knew that, by then, she'd find a way to ease his guilt, and Odalie's, and step out of the picture. She wasn't going to let them sacrifice their happiness for her. That was far too much.

He kissed her again and stood up, smiling. "So when are you going to give it to her?"

"Tomorrow," she decided.

"I'll make sure she comes over."

"Thanks."

He shrugged and then smiled. "She's going to be over the moon when she sees it."

That was an understatement. Odalie cried. She turned the little fairy around and around in her elegant hands, gasping at the level of detail in the features that were so exactly like her own.

"It's the most beautiful gift I've ever been given."

She put it down, very gently, and hugged Maddie as carefully as she could. "You sweetie!" she exclaimed. "I'll never be able to thank you. It looks just like me!"

Maddie chuckled. "I'm glad you like it."

"You have to let me talk to my friend at the art gallery," Odalie said.

Maddie hesitated. "Maybe someday," she faltered. "Maybe."

"But you have so much talent, Maddie. It's such a gift."

Maddie flushed. "Thanks."

Odalie kept trying, but she couldn't move the other girl. Not at all.

"Okay," she relented. "You know your own mind. Oh, goodness, what is that?" she exclaimed, indicating a cameo lying beside another fairy, a black-haired one sitting on a riverbank holding a book.

Maddie told her the story of the antique dealer and the cameo that had no family to inherit.

"What an incredible story," Odalie said, impressed. "She's quite beautiful. You can do that, from a picture?"

Maddie laughed. "I did yours from the one in our school yearbook," she said, and this time she didn't flinch remembering the past.

Odalie looked uncomfortable, but she didn't refer to it. Perhaps in time she and Maddie could both let go of that terrible memory. "Maddie, could you do one of my great-grandmother if I brought you a picture of her? It's a commission, now..."

Maddie held up a hand. "No. I'd love to do it. It's just a hobby, you know, not a job. Just bring me a picture."

Odalie's eyes were unusually bright. "Okay. I'll bring it tomorrow!"

Maddie laughed at her enthusiasm. "I'll get started as soon as I have it."

The picture was surprising. "This is your grandmother?" Maddie asked, because it didn't look anything like Odalie. The subject of the painting had red hair and pale green eyes.

"My great-grandmother," Odalie assured her, but she averted her eyes to another sculpture while she said it.

"Oh. That explains it. Yes, I can do it."

"That's so sweet of you, Maddie."

"It's nothing at all."

It took two weeks. Maddie still had periods of discomfort that kept her in bed, but she made sure she walked and moved around, as the therapist and her doctor had told her to do. It was amazing that, considering the impact of the car, she hadn't suffered a permanent disability. The swelling and inflammation had been pretty bad, as was the bruising, but she wasn't going to lose the use of her legs. The doctor was still being cautious about that prognosis. But Maddie could tell from the way she was healing that she was going to be all right. She'd never been more certain of anything.

She finished the little fairy sculpture on a Friday. She was very pleased with the result. It looked just like the photograph, but with exquisite detail. This fairy was sitting on a tree stump, with a small green frog perched on her palm. She was laughing. Maddie loved the way it had turned out. But now it was going to be hard to part with it. She did put part of herself into her sculptures. It was like giving herself away with the art.

She'd promised Odalie, though, so she had to come to terms with it.

Odalie was overwhelmed with the result. She stared at it and just shook her head. "I can't believe how skilled you are," she said, smiling at Maddie. "This is so beautiful. She'll, I mean my mother, will love it!"

"Oh, it's her grandmother," Maddie recalled.

"Yes." Odalie still wouldn't meet her eyes, but she laughed. "What a treat this is going to be! Can I take it with me?" she asked.

Maddie only hesitated for a second. She smiled. "Of course you can."

"Wonderful!"

She bent and hugged Maddie gently. "Still doing okay?" she asked worriedly.

Maddie nodded. "Getting better all the time, thanks

to a small pharmacy of meds on my bedside table," she quipped.

"I'm so glad. I mean that," she said solemnly. "The day you can walk to your car and drive it, I'll dance in the yard."

Maddie laughed. "Okay. I'll hold you to that!"

Odalie just grinned.

Cort came over every day. Saturday morning he went to the barn to study the charts he and John Everett had made. John had just come over to bring Maddie flowers. She was sitting on the porch with Great-Aunt Sadie. As soon as John arrived, Cort came back from the barn and joined the group on the porch. The way Cort glared at him was surprising.

"They'll give her allergies," Cort muttered.

John gave him a stunned look, and waved around the yard at the blooming crepe myrtle and jasmine and sunflowers and sultanas and zinnias. "Are you nuts?" he asked, wide-eyed. "Look around you! Who do you think planted all these?"

Cort's dark eyes narrowed. He jammed his hands into his jean pockets. "Well, they're not in the house, are they?" he persisted.

John just laughed. He handed the pot of flowers to Great-Aunt Sadie, who was trying not to laugh. "Can you put those inside?" he asked her with a smile. "I want to check the board in the barn and see how the breeding program needs to go."

"I sure can," Sadie replied, and she went into the house.

Maddie was still staring at John with mixed feelings. "Uh, thanks for the flowers," she said haltingly. Cort was looking irritated.

"You're very welcome," John said. He studied her for a long moment. "You look better."

"I feel a lot better," she said. "In fact, I think I might try to walk to the barn."

"In your dreams, honey," Cort said softly. He picked her up, tenderly, and cradled her against his chest. "But I'll walk you there."

John stared at him intently. "Should you be picking her up like that?" he asked.

Cort wasn't listening. His dark eyes were probing Maddie's gray ones with deep tenderness. Neither of them was looking at John, who suddenly seemed to understand what was going on around him.

"Darn, I left my notes in the car," he said, hiding a smile. "I'll be right back."

He strode off. Cort bent his head. "I thought he'd never leave," he whispered, and brought his mouth down, hard, on Maddie's.

"Cort…"

"Shh," he whispered against her lips. "Don't fuss. Open your mouth…!"

The kiss grew hotter by the second. Maddie was clinging to his neck for dear life while he crushed her breasts into the softness of his blue-checked shirt and devoured her soft lips.

He groaned harshly, but suddenly he remembered where they were. He lifted his head, grateful that his back was to the house, and John's car. He drew in a long breath.

"I wish you weren't so fragile," he whispered. He kissed her shocked eyes shut. "I'm starving."

Her fingers teased the hair at the back of his head. "I could feed you a biscuit," she whispered.

He smiled. "I don't want biscuits." He looked at her mouth. "I want you."

Her face flamed with a combination of embarrassment and sheer delight.

"But we can talk about that later, after I've disposed of John's body," he added, turning to watch the other man approach, his eyes buried in a black notebook.

"Wh-h-hat?" she stammered, and burst out laughing at his expression.

He sighed. "I suppose no war is ever won without a few uncomfortable battles," he said under his breath.

"I found them," John said with a grin, waving the notebook. "Let's have a look at the breeding strategy you've mapped out, then."

"I put it all on the board," Cort replied. He carried Maddie into the barn and set her on her feet very carefully, so as not to jar her spine. "It's right there," he told John, nodding toward the large board where he'd indicated which bulls were to be bred to which heifers and cows.

John studied it for a long moment. He turned and

looked at Cort curiously. "This is remarkable," he said. "I would have gone a different way, but yours is better."

Cort seemed surprised. "You've got a four-year degree in animal husbandry," he said. "Mine is only an associate's degree."

"Yes, but you've got a lifetime of watching your father do this." He indicated the board. "I've been busy studying and traveling. I haven't really spent that much time observing. It's rather like an internship, and I don't have the experience, even if I have the education."

"Thanks," Cort said. He was touchy about his two-year degree. He smiled. "Took courses in diplomacy, too, did you?" he teased.

John bumped shoulders with him. "You're my best friend," he murmured. "I'd never be the one to try to put you down."

Cort punched his shoulder gently. "Same here."

Maddie had both hands on her slender hips as she stared at the breeding chart. "Would either of you like to try to translate this for me?" She waved one hand at the blackboard. "Because it looks like Martian to me!"

Both men burst out laughing.

Cort had to go out of town. He was worried when he called Maddie to tell her, apologizing for his absence.

"Mom and Dad will look out for you while I'm gone," he promised. "If you need anything, you call them. I'll phone you when I get to Denver."

Her heart raced. "Okay."

"Will you miss me?" he teased.

She drew in a breath. "Of course," she said.

There was a pause. "I'll miss you more," he said quietly. His deep voice was like velvet. "What do you want me to bring you from Denver?"

"Yourself."

There was a soft chuckle. "That's a deal. Talk to you later."

"Have a safe trip."

He sighed. "At least Dad isn't flying me. He flies like he drives. But we'll get there."

The plural went right over her head. She laughed. She'd heard stories about King Brannt's driving. "It's safer than driving, everybody says so."

"In my dad's case, it's actually true. He flies a lot better than he drives."

"I heard that!" came a deep voice from beside him.

"Sorry, Dad," Cort replied. "See you, Maddie."

He hung up. She held the cell phone to her ear for an extra minute, just drinking in the sound of his voice promising to miss her.

While Cort was away, Odalie didn't come, either. But even though she called, Maddie missed her daily visits. She apologized over the phone. She was actually out of town, but her mother had volunteered to do any running-around that Maddie needed if Sadie couldn't go.

Maddie thanked her warmly. But when she hung up she couldn't help but wonder at the fact that Cort and Odalie were out of town at the same time. Had Odalie gone to Denver with Cort and they didn't want to tell her? It was worrying.

She rode her wheelchair out to the hen enclosure. Ben was just coming out of it with the first of many egg baskets. There were a lot of hens, and her customer list for her fresh eggs was growing by the week.

"That's a lot of eggs," she ventured.

He chuckled. "Ya, and I still have to wash 'em and check 'em for cracks."

"I like Percy," she remarked.

"I love Percy," Ben replied. "Never saw such a gentle rooster."

"Thanks. For what you did for Pumpkin's grave," she said, averting her eyes. She still cried easily when she talked about him.

"It was no problem at all, Miss Maddie," he said gently.

She looked over her hens with proud eyes. "My girls look good."

"They do, don't they?" he agreed, then added, "Well, I should get to work."

"Ben, do you know where Odalie went?" she asked suddenly.

He bit his lip.

"Come on," she prodded. "Tell me."

He looked sad. "She went to Denver, Miss Maddie. Heard it from her dad when I went to pick up feed in town."

Maddie's heart fell to her feet. But she smiled. "She and Cort make a beautiful couple," she remarked, and tried to hide the fact that she was dying inside.

"Guess they do," he said. He tried to say something

else, but he couldn't get the words to come out right. "I'll just go get these eggs cleaned."

She nodded. The eyes he couldn't see were wet with tears.

It seemed that disaster followed disaster. While Cort and Odalie were away, bills flooded the mailbox. Maddie almost passed out when she saw the hospital bill. Even the minimum payment was more than she had in the bank.

"What are we going to do?" she wailed.

Sadie winced at her expression. "Well, we'll just manage," she said firmly. "There's got to be something we can sell that will help pay those bills." She didn't add that Cort and Odalie had promised they were taking care of all that. But they were out of town, and Sadie knew that Maddie's pride would stand in the way of asking them for money. She'd never do it.

"There is something," Maddie said heavily. She looked up at Sadie.

"No," Sadie said shortly. "No, you can't!"

"Look at these bills, Sadie," she replied, and spread them out on the table. "There's nothing I can hock, nothing I can do that will make enough money fast enough to cover all this. There just isn't anything else to do."

"You aren't going to talk to that developer fellow?"

"Heavens, no!" Maddie assured her. "I'll call a real estate agent in town."

"I think that's..."

Just as she spoke, a car pulled up in the yard.

"Well, speak of the devil," Maddie muttered.

The developer climbed out of his car, looked around and started for the front porch.

"Do you suppose we could lock the door and pretend to be gone?" Sadie wondered aloud.

"No. We're not hiding. Let him in," Maddie said firmly.

"Don't you give in to his fancy talk," Sadie advised.

"Never in a million years. Let him in."

The developer, Arthur Lawson, came in the door with a smug look on his face. "Miss Lane," he greeted. He smiled like a crocodile. "Bad news does travel fast. I heard you were in an accident and that your bills are piling up. I believe I can help you."

Maddie looked at Sadie. Her expression was eloquent.

Archie Lawson grinned like the barracuda he was.

"I heard that your neighbors have gone away together," he said with mock sympathy. "Just left you with all those medical bills to pay, did they?"

Maddie felt terrible. She didn't want to say anything unkind about Odalie and Cort. They'd done more than most people could have expected of them. But Maddie was left with the bills, and she had no money to pay them with. She'd read about people who didn't pay their hospital bill on time and had to deal with collectors' agencies. She was terrified.

"They don't say I have to pay them at once," Maddie began.

"Yes, but the longer you wait, the higher the interest they charge," he pointed out.

"Interest?"

"It's such and such a percent," he continued. He sat

down without being asked in her father's old easy chair. "Let me spell it out for you. I can write you a check that will cover all those medical bills, the hospital bill, everything. All you have to do is sign over the property to me. I'll even take care of the livestock. I'll make sure they're sold to people who will take good care of them."

"I don't know," Maddie faltered. She was torn. It was so quick...

"Maddie, can I talk to you for a minute?" Sadie asked tersely. "It's about supper," she lied.

"Okay."

She excused herself and followed Sadie into the kitchen.

Sadie closed the door. "Listen to me, don't you do that until you talk to Mr. Brannt," Sadie said firmly. "Don't you dare!"

"But, Sadie," she said in anguish, "we can't pay the bills, and we can't expect the Brannts and the Everetts to keep paying them forever!"

"Cort said he'd take care of the hospital bill, at least," Sadie reminded her.

"Miss Lane?" Lawson called. "I have to leave soon!"

"Don't let him push you into this," Sadie cautioned. "Make him wait. Tell him you have to make sure the estate's not entailed before you can sell, you'll have to talk to your lawyer!"

Maddie bit her lower lip.

"Tell him!" Sadie said, gesturing her toward the porch.

Maddie took a deep breath and Sadie opened the door for her to motor through.

"Sadie was reminding me that we had a couple of outstanding liens on the property after Dad died," Maddie lied. "I'll have to talk to our attorney and make sure they've been lifted before I can legally sell it to you."

"Oh." He stood up. "Well." He glared. "You didn't mention that earlier."

"I didn't think you thought I was going to sell the ranch today," Maddie said, and with a bland smile. "That's all. You wouldn't want to find out later that you didn't actually own it…?"

"No. Of course not." He made a face. "All right, I'll be back in, say, two days? Will that give you enough time?"

"Yes," Maddie said.

He picked up his briefcase and looked around the living room. "This house will have to be torn down. But if you want some pictures and stuff, I can let you have it after we wrap up the sale. The furniture's no loss." He laughed coldly. "I'll be in touch. And if your answer is no—well, don't be surprised if your cattle suddenly come down with unusual diseases. Anthrax always comes to mind… And if federal agencies have to be called in, your operation will be closed down immediately."

He left and Maddie had to bite back curses. "The furniture's no loss," she muttered. "These are antiques! And anthrax! What kind of horrible person would infect defenseless animals! Maddie went inside, a chill settling in her heart.

"Nasty man. You can't let him have our house!" Sadie glared out the window as the developer drove off.

Maddie leaned back in her chair. "I wish I didn't," she said heavily. "But I don't know what else to do." She felt sick to her soul at the man's threats. "Cort is going to marry Odalie, you know."

Sadie wanted to argue, but she didn't know how to. It seemed pretty obvious that if he hadn't told Maddie he was leaving with Odalie, he had a guilty conscience and was trying to shield her from the truth.

"Should have just told you, instead of sneaking off together," Sadie muttered.

"They didn't want to hurt me," Maddie said heavily. "It's pretty obvious how I feel about Cort, you know."

"Still…"

Maddie looked at the bills lying open on the table. She leaned forward with her face in her hands. Her heart was breaking. At least she might be able to walk eventually. But that still left the problem of how she was going to walk herself out of this financial mess. The ranch was all she had left for collateral.

Collateral! She turned to Sadie. "We can take out a mortgage, can't we?" she asked Sadie.

Sadie frowned. "I don't know. Best you should call the lawyer and find out."

"I'll do that right now!"

She did at least have hope that there were options. A few options, at least.

But the lie she'd told Lawson turned out to be the truth.

"I'm really sorry, Maddie," Burt Davies told her. "But

your dad did take out a lien on the property when he bought that last seed bull. I've been keeping up the payments out of the ranch revenues when I did the bills for you the past few months."

"You mean, I can't sell or even borrow on the ranch."

"You could sell," he admitted. "If you got enough for it that would pay off the lien... But, Maddie, that land's been in your family for generations. You can't mean to sell it."

She swallowed. "Burt, I've got medical bills I can't begin to pay."

"Odalie and Cort are taking care of those," he reminded her. "Legally, even if not morally, they're obligated to."

"Yes, but, they're getting married, don't you see?" she burst out. "I can't tie them up with my bills."

"You can and you will, if I have to go to court for you," Burt said firmly. "The accident wasn't your fault."

"Yes, it was," she said in a wan tone. "I ran out in the road to save my stupid rooster, who died anyway. As for guilt, Odalie and Cort have done everything humanly possible for me since the wreck. Nobody could fault them for that."

"I know, but…"

"If I sell the ranch," she argued gently, "I can pay off all my debts and I won't owe anyone anything."

"That's bad legal advice. You should never try to act as your own attorney."

She laughed. "Yes, I know. Okay, I'll think about it for a couple of days," she said.

"You think about it hard," he replied. "No sense in letting yourself be forced into a decision you don't want to make."

"All right. Thanks, Burt."

She hung up. "Life," she told the room at large, "is just not fair."

The next day, Ben came walking in with a sad expression. "Got bad news," he said.

"What now?" Maddie asked with a faint smile.

"Lost two more purebred cows. They wandered off."

"All right, that's more than coincidence," she muttered. She moved to the phone, picked it up and called King Brannt.

"How many cows does that make?" King asked, aghast.

"Four, in the past few weeks," she said. "Something's not right."

"I agree. I'll get our computer expert to check those recordings and see if he can find anything."

"Thanks, Mr. Brannt."

He hesitated. "How are things over there?"

She hesitated, too. "Just fine," she lied. "Fine."

"Cort's coming home day after tomorrow," he added.

"I hope he and Odalie have had a good time," she said, and tried not to sound as hurt as she felt. "They've both been very kind to me. I owe them a lot."

"Maddie," he began slowly, "about that trip they took—"

"They're my friends," she interrupted. "I want them

to be happy. Look I have to go, okay? But if you find out anything about my cows, can you call me?"

"Sure."

"Thanks, Mr. Brannt."

She hung up. She didn't think she'd ever felt so miserable in her whole young life. She loved Cort. But he was never going to be hers. She realized now that he'd been pretending, to keep her spirits up so that she wouldn't despair. But he'd always loved Odalie, and she'd always known it. She couldn't expect him to give up everything he loved just to placate an injured woman, out of guilt. She wasn't going to let him do it.

And Odalie might have been her enemy once, but that was certainly no longer the case. Odalie had become a friend. She couldn't have hard feelings toward her....

Oh, what a bunch of bull, she told herself angrily. Of course she had hard feelings. She loved Cort. She wanted him! But he loved Odalie and that was never going to change. How would it feel, to let a man hang around just because he felt guilty that you'd been hurt? Knowing every day that he was smiling and pretending to care, when he really wanted that beautiful golden girl, Odalie Everett, and always would?

No. That would cheat all three of them. She had to let him go. He belonged to Odalie, and Maddie had always known it. She was going to sell the ranch to that terrible developer and make herself homeless out of pride, because she didn't want her friends to sacrifice any more than they already had for her.

That developer, could he have been responsible for

her lost cows? But why would he hurt the livestock when he was hoping to buy the ranch? No. It made no sense. None at all.

Later, with her door closed, she cried herself to sleep. She couldn't stop thinking about Cort, about how tender he'd been to her, how kind. Surely he hadn't been able to pretend the passion she felt in his long, hard, insistent kisses? Could men pretend to want a woman?

She wished she knew. She wanted to believe that his hints at a shared future had been honest and real. But she didn't dare trust her instincts. Not when Cort had taken Odalie with him to Denver and hidden it from Maddie.

He hadn't wanted her to know. That meant he knew it would hurt her feelings and he couldn't bear to do it, not after all she'd been through.

She wiped her eyes. Crying wasn't going to solve anything. After all, what did she have to be sad about? There was a good chance that she would be able to walk normally again, when she was through recuperating. She'd still have Great Aunt Sadie, and the developer said that he'd let her have her odds and ends out of the house.

The developer. She hated him. He was willing to set her up, to let her whole herd of cattle be destroyed, her breeding stock, just to get his hands on the ranch. She could tell someone, Mr. Brannt, maybe. But it would be her word against Lawson's. She had so much to lose. What if he could actually infect her cattle? Better to let her cattle be sold at auction to someone than risk having them destroyed. She couldn't bear to step on a spider, much less watch her prize cattle, her father's prize cattle, be exterminated.

No, she really didn't have a choice. She was going to lose the ranch one way or another, to the developer or to bill collectors.

She got up and went to the kitchen to make coffee. It was two in the morning, but it didn't matter. She was never going to sleep anyway.

She heard a sound out in the yard. She wished she kept a dog. She'd had one, but it had died not long after her father did. There was nothing to alert her to an intruder's presence anymore. She turned out the lights and motored to the window, hoping the sound of the wheelchair wouldn't be heard outside.

She saw something shadowy near the barn. That was where the surveillance equipment was set up.

She turned on all the outside lights, opened the door and yelled, "Who's out there?!" The best defense was offense, she told herself.

There was startled movement, a dark blur going out behind the barn. Without a second thought, she got her cell phone and called the sheriff.

The sheriff's department came, and so did King Brannt. He climbed out of his ranch pickup with another man about two steps behind the tall deputy.

Maddie rolled onto the porch. She'd been afraid to go outside until help arrived. She was no match, even with two good legs, for someone bent upon mischief.

"Miss Lane?" the deputy asked.

"Yes, sir," she said. "Someone was out here. I turned on the outside lights and yelled. Whoever it was ran."

The deputy's lips made a thin line.

"Yes, I know," she said heavily. "Stupid thing to do, opening the door. But I didn't go outside, and the screen was latched."

He didn't mention that any intruder could have gone through that latched screen like it was tissue paper.

"Miss Lane's had some threats," King commented. "This is Blair, my computer expert. We set up surveillance cameras on the ranch at cross fences to see if we could head off trouble." He smiled. "Looks like we might have succeeded."

"Have you noticed anything suspicious?" the deputy asked.

She grimaced. "Well, I've had a couple of cows found dead. Predators," she said, averting her eyes.

"Anyone prowling around the house, any break-ins?" he persisted.

"No, sir."

The deputy turned to King. "Mr. Brannt, I'd like to see what those cameras of yours picked up, if anything."

"Sure. Come on, Blair." He turned to Maddie. "You should go back inside, honey," he said gently. "Just in case."

"Okay." She went very quickly. She didn't want any of the men to ask her more questions. She was afraid of what Lawson might do if he was backed into a corner. She didn't want the government to come over and shut her cattle operation down, even if it meant giving away the ranch.

* * *

Later, the deputy came inside, asked more questions and had her write out a report for him in her own words. He took that, and statements from King and Blair and told Maddie to call if she heard anything else.

"Did you find anything?" she asked worriedly.

"No," the deputy said. "But my guess is that someone meant to disable that surveillance equipment."

"Mine, too," King replied. "Which is why I've just sent several of my cowboys out to ride fence lines and watch for anything suspicious."

"That's very nice of you," she commented.

He shrugged. "We're neighbors and I like your breeding bulls," he told her.

"Well, thanks, just the same."

"If you think of anything else that would help us, please get in touch with me," the deputy said, handing her a card.

"I'll do that," she promised. "And thanks again."

King didn't leave when the deputy did. Sadie was making coffee in the kitchen, her face lined with worry.

"It will be all right," she assured the older woman.

"No, it won't," Sadie muttered. She glanced at Maddie. "You should tell him the truth. He's the one person who could help you!"

"Sadie!" Maddie groaned.

King pulled Blair aside, spoke to him in whispers, and sent him off. He moved into the kitchen, straddled a chair at the table and perched his Stetson on a free chair.

"Okay," he said. "No witnesses. Let's have it."

Maddie went pale.

King laughed softly. "I'm not an ogre. If you want my word that I won't tell anyone what you say, you have it."

Maddie bit her lower lip. "That developer," she said after a minute. "He said that he could bring in a federal agency and prove that my cattle had anthrax."

"Only if he put it there to begin with," King said, his dark eyes flashing with anger.

"That's what I think he means to do," she said. "I don't know what to do. The bills are just burying me..."

He held up a hand. "Cort and Odalie are taking care of those," he said.

"Yes, but they've done too much already, I'm not a charity case!" she burst out.

"It was an accident that they caused, Maddie," he said gently.

"I caused it, by running into the road," she said miserably.

"Accidents are things that don't happen on purpose," he said with a faint grin. "Now, listen, whatever trouble you're in, that developer has no right to make threats to do harm to your cattle."

"It would be my word against his," she sighed.

"I'd take your word against anyone else's, in a heartbeat," he replied. "You let me handle this. I know how to deal with people like Lawson. "

"He's really vindictive."

"He won't get a chance to be vindictive. I promise." He got up. "I won't stay for coffee, Sadie, I've got a lot of phone calls to make."

"Thanks, Mr. Brannt," Maddie said gently. "Thanks a lot."

He put a hand on her shoulder. "We take care of our own," he said. "Cort will be back day after tomorrow."

"So will that developer," she said worriedly. So many complications, she was thinking. Poor Cort, he'd feel even more guilty.

"He won't stay long," King drawled, and he grinned. "Cort will make sure of that, believe me."

Chapter Ten

Maddie was on pins and needles Saturday morning. It was worrying enough to know that Cort and Odalie were coming back. She'd have to smile and pretend to be happy for them, even though her heart was breaking.

But also she was going to have to face the developer. She didn't know what King Brannt had in mind to save her from him. She might have to go through with signing the contracts to ensure that her poor cattle weren't infected. She hadn't slept a wink.

She and Sadie had coffee and then Maddie wandered around the house in her wheelchair, making ruts.

"Will you relax?" Sadie said. "I know it's going to be all right. You have to trust that Mr. Brannt knows what to do."

"I hope so. My poor cattle!"

"Is that a car?"

Even as she spoke a car drove up in front of the house and stopped. "Mr. Lawson, no doubt. I hope he's wearing body armor," she muttered, and she wheeled her chair to the front porch.

But it wasn't the developer. It was Odalie and Cort. They were grinning from ear to ear as they climbed out of his Jaguar and came to the porch.

Just what I need right now, Maddie thought miserably. But she put on a happy face. "You're both home again. And I guess you have news?" she added. "I'm so happy for you."

"For us?" Cort looked at Odalie and back at Maddie blankly. "Why?"

They followed her into the house. She turned the chair around and swallowed. "Well," she began uneasily.

Odalie knew at once what she thought. She came forward. "No, it's not like that," she said quickly. "There was a doll collectors' convention at the hotel where the cattlemen were meeting. I want you to see this." She pulled a check out of her purse and handed it to Maddie.

It was a good thing she was sitting down. The check was for five figures. Five high figures. She looked at Odalie blankly.

"The fairy," she said, smiling. "I'm sorry I wasn't honest with you. It wasn't my great-grandmother's picture. It was a collector's. He wanted a fairy who looked like her to add to his collection, and I said I knew someone who would do the perfect one. So I flew to Denver to take him the one you made from the photograph."

Odalie's blue eyes were soft. "He cried. He said the old lady was the light of his life… She was the only person in his family who didn't laugh and disown him when he said he wanted to go into the business of doll collecting. She encouraged him to follow his dream. He's worth millions now and all because he followed his dream." She nodded at the check. "He owns a doll boutique in Los Angeles. He ships all over the world. He said he'd pay that—" she indicated the check again "—for every fairy you made for him. And he wants to discuss licensing and branding. He thinks you can make a fortune with these. He said so."

Maddie couldn't even find words. The check would pay her medical bills, buy feed and pay taxes. It would save the ranch. She was sobbing and she didn't even realize it until Odalie took the check back and motioned to Cort.

Cort lifted her out of the wheelchair and cradled her against him. "You'll blot the ink off the check with those tears, sweetheart." He chuckled, and kissed them away. "And just for the record, Odalie and I aren't getting married."

"You aren't?" she asked with wet eyes.

"We aren't." Odalie giggled. "He's my friend. I love him. But not like that," she added softly.

"And she's my friend," Cort added. He smiled down at Maddie. "I went a little goofy over her, but, then, I got over it."

"Gee, thanks," Odalie said with amused sarcasm.

"You know what I mean." He laughed. "You're beautiful and talented."

"Not as talented as *our* friend over there." She indicated Maddie, with a warm smile. "She has magic in her hands."

"And other places," Cort mused, looking pointedly at her mouth.

She hid her face against him. He cuddled her close.

"Oh, dear," Sadie said from the doorway. "Maddie, he's back! What are you going to tell him?"

"Tell who?" Cort asked. He turned. His face grew hard. "Oh. Him. My dad gave me an earful about him when I got home."

He put Maddie gently back down into the wheelchair.

"You didn't encourage him?" he asked her.

She grimaced. "The medical bills and doctor bills and feed bills all came in at once," she began miserably. "I couldn't even pay taxes. He offered me a fortune…"

"We're paying the medical bills," Odalie told her firmly. "We even said so."

"It's not right to ask you," Maddie said stubbornly.

"That's okay. You're not asking. We're telling." Odalie said.

"Exactly." Cort was looking more dangerous by the second as the developer got out of his car with a briefcase. "My dad said you've had more cows killed over here, too."

"Yes." She was so miserable she could hardly talk.

"Dad found out a lot more than that about him. He was arrested up in Billings, Montana, on charges of intimidation and poisoning in another land deal," Cort added. "He's out on bond, but apparently it didn't teach him a thing."

"Well, he threatened to plant anthrax in my herd and have the feds come out and destroy them," she said sadly. "He says if I don't sell to him, he'll do it. I think he will."

"He might have," Cort said mysteriously. "Good thing my dad has a real suspicious nature and watches a lot of spy films."

"Excuse me?" Maddie inquired.

He grinned. "Wait and see, honey." He bent and kissed the tip of her nose.

Odalie laughed softly. "One fried developer, coming right up," she teased, and it was obvious that she wasn't jealous of Maddie at all.

There was a tap at the door and the developer walked right in. He was so intent on his contracts that he must not have noticed the other car in the driveway. "Miss Lane, I've brought the paper...work—" He stopped dead when he saw her companions.

"You can take your paperwork and shove it," Cort said pleasantly. He tilted his Stetson over one eye and put both hands on his narrow hips. "Or you can argue. Personally, I'd love it if you argued."

"She said she wanted to sell," the developer shot back. But he didn't move a step closer.

"She changed her mind," Cort replied.

"You changed it for her," the developer snarled. "Well,

she can just change it right back. Things happen sometimes when people don't make the right decisions."

"You mean diseases can be planted in cattle?" Odalie asked sweetly.

The older man gave her a wary look. "What do you mean?"

"Maddie told us how you threatened her," Cort said evenly.

Lawson hesitated. "You can't prove that."

Cort smiled. "I don't have to." He pulled out a DVD in a plastic sleeve and held it up. "You're very trusting, Lawson. I mean, you knew there was surveillance equipment all over the ranch, but you didn't guess the house and porch were wired as well?"

Lawson looked a lot less confident. "You're bluffing."

Cort didn't look like he was bluffing. "My dad has a call in to the district attorney up in Billings, Montana. I believe you're facing indictment there for the destruction of a purebred herd of Herefords because of suspected anthrax?"

"They can't prove that!"

"I'm afraid they can," Cort replied. "There are two witnesses, one of whom used to work with you," he added easily. "He's willing to testify to save his butt." He held up the DVD. "This may not be admissible in court, but it will certainly help to encourage charges against you here for the loss of Miss Lane's purebred stock."

"You wouldn't dare!" the developer said harshly.

"I would dare," Cort replied.

The developer gripped his briefcase tighter. "On second thought," he said, looking around with disdain, "I've decided I don't want this property. It's not good enough for the sort of development I have in mind, and the location is terrible for business. Sorry," he spat at Maddie. "I guess you'll have to manage some other way to pay your medical bills."

"Speaking of medical bills," Cort said angrily, and stepped forward.

"Now, Cort," Maddie exclaimed.

The developer turned and almost ran out of the house to his car. He fumbled to start it and managed to get it in gear just before Cort got to him. He sped out the driveway, fishtailing all the way.

Cort was almost bent over double laughing when he went back into the house. He stopped when three wide-eyed females gaped at him worriedly.

"Oh, I wasn't going to kill him," he said, still laughing. "But I didn't mind letting him think I might. What do you want to bet that he's out of town by tonight and can't be reached by telephone?"

"I wouldn't bet against that," Odalie agreed.

"Me, neither," Sadie said.

"Dad said that Lawson's in more trouble than he can manage up in Billings already. I don't expect he'll wait around for more charges to be filed here."

"Are you going to turn that DVD over to the district attorney?" she asked, nodding toward the jacketed disc.

He glanced at her. "And give up my best performance of 'Recuerdos de la Alhambra?' he exclaimed. "I'll never get this good a recording again!"

Maddie's eyes brightened. "You were bluffing!"

"For all I was worth." He chuckled.

"Cort, you're wonderful!"

He pursed his lips. "Am I, now?"

"We could take a vote," Odalie suggested. "You've got mine."

"And mine!" Sadie agreed. "Oh, Maddie, you'll have a way to make a living now," she exclaimed, indicating the little fairy. "You won't have to sell our ranch!"

"No, but we still have the problem of running it," Maddie said heavily. "If I'm going to be spending my life sculpting, and thanks to you two, I probably will—" she grinned "—who's going to manage the ranch?"

"I think we can work something out about that," Cort told her, and his dark eyes were flashing with amusement. "We'll talk about it later."

"Okay," she said. "Maybe Ben could manage it?"

Cort nodded. "He's a good man, with a good business head. We'll see."

We'll see? She stared at him as if she'd never seen him before. It was an odd statement. But before she could question it, Sadie went into the kitchen.

"Who wants chocolate pound cake?" she asked.

Three hands went up, and all discussion about the ranch went away.

Maddie wanted to know all about the doll collector. He was a man in his fifties, very distinguished and he had a collection that was famous all over the world.

"There are magazines devoted to collectors," Odalie

said excitedly. "They showcased his collection last year. I met him when we were at the Met last year during opera season. We spoke and he said that he loved small, very intricate work. When I saw your sculptures, I remembered him. I looked him up on his website and phoned him. He said he was always looking for new talent, but he wanted to see what you could do. So I asked him for a photo of someone he'd like made into a sculpture and he faxed me the one I gave you."

"I will never be able to repay you for this," Maddie said fervently.

"Maddie, you already have, over and over," Odalie said softly. "Most especially with that little fairy statue that looks just like me." She shook her head. "I've never owned anything so beautiful."

"Thanks."

"Besides, you're my best friend," Odalie said with a gamine grin. "I have to take care of you."

Maddie felt all warm inside. "I'll take care of you, if you ever need me to," she promised.

Odalie flushed. "Thanks."

"This is great cake," Cort murmured. "Can you cook?" he asked Maddie.

"Yes, but not so much right now." She indicated the wheelchair with a grimace.

"Give it time," he said gently. He smiled, and his whole face grew radiant as he looked at her. "You'll be out of that thing before you know it."

"You think so?" she asked.

He nodded. "Yes, I do."

She smiled. He smiled back. Odalie smiled into her cake and pretended not to notice that they couldn't take their eyes off each other.

Odalie said her goodbyes and gave Maddie the collector's telephone number so that she could thank him personally for giving her fairy a good home. But Cort lingered.

He bent over the wheelchair, his hands on the arms, and looked into Maddie's eyes. "Later we'll talk about going behind my back to do business with a crook."

"I was scared. And not just that he might poison my cattle. There were so many bills!"

He brushed his mouth over her lips. "I told you I'd take care of all those bills."

"But they all came due, and you've done so much… I couldn't ask…"

He was kissing her. It made talking hard.

She reached up with cold, nervous hands and framed his face in them. She looked into his eyes and saw secrets revealed there. Her breath caught. "It isn't Odalie," she stammered. "It's me."

He nodded. And he didn't smile. "It was always you. I just didn't know it until there was a good chance that I was going to lose you." He smiled tightly then. "Couldn't do that. Couldn't live, if you didn't."

She bit her lip, fighting tears.

He kissed them away. "I don't have a life without you," he whispered at her nose. "So we have to make plans."

"When?" she asked, bursting with happiness.

"When you're out of that wheelchair," he said. He gave her a wicked smile. "Because when we start talking, things are apt to get, well, physical." He wiggled his eyebrows.

She laughed.

He laughed.

He kissed her affectionately and stood back up. "I'll drive Odalie home. I'll call you later. And I'll see you tomorrow. And the day after. And the day after. And the day after that..."

"And the day after that?" she prompted.

"Don't get pushy," he teased.

He threw up a hand and went out to the car. This time, when he drove off with Odalie, Maddie didn't go through pangs of jealousy. The look in his eyes had been as sweet as a promise.

Epilogue

Physical therapy seemed to go on forever. The days turned to weeks, the leaves began to fall. The cows grew big with calves. Rain had come in time for some of the grain crops to come to harvest, and there would be enough hay, hopefully, to get them through the winter. Maddie's legs were growing stronger. Little by little, she made progress.

Odalie and Cort were still around, prodding her, keeping her spirits up during the long mending process. She didn't let herself get discouraged. She created new fairies and Odalie shipped them off, carefully packed, to a man named Angus Moore, who acted as Maddie's agent and sold her dainty little creations for what amounted to a small fortune for the artist.

The developer, sure enough, left town and left no forwarding address. Gossip was that the authorities wanted to talk to him about several cases of dead cattle on properties he'd tried to buy in several states. Maddie hoped they caught up with him one day.

Meanwhile, Cort came over every night for supper. He brought his guitar most nights, and serenaded Maddie on the porch until the nights got too cold for that. Then he serenaded her in the living room, by the fireplace with its leaping flames while she curled up under a blanket on the sofa.

From time to time, when Sadie was occupied in the kitchen, he curled up under the blanket with her.

She loved his big hands smoothing her bare skin under her shirt, the warmth and strength of them arousing sensations that grew sweeter by the day. He was familiar to her now. She had no fear of his temper. He didn't lose it with her, although he'd been volatile about a man who left a gate open and cattle poured through it onto the highway. At least none of the cattle was injured, and no cars were wrecked.

"He was just a kid," Cort murmured against her collarbone. "He works for us after school. Usually does a pretty good job, too, cleaning out the stables."

She arched her back and winced.

"Damn." He lifted his head and his hands stilled on her body. "Too soon."

She looked miserable.

He laughed. He peered toward the doorway before he slid the hem of her T-shirt up under her chin and looked at the pert little breasts he'd uncovered. "Buried treasure," he whispered, "and I'm a pirate..."

She moaned.

"Stop that. She'll hear you."

She bit her lip and gave him an anguished look. He grinned before he bent his head again, producing even more eloquent sounds that were, thankfully, soon muffled by his mouth.

But things between them were heating up more every day. She had his shirt unbuttoned just before he eased over her. Her hard-tipped breasts nestled into the thick hair on his muscular chest and one long, powerful leg eased between both of hers. He levered himself down very gently while he was kissing her, but she felt the quick, hard swell of him as he began to move helplessly on her, grinding his hips into hers.

"Oh, God," he bit off. He jerked himself back and up, to sit beside her on the sofa with his head bent, shuddering.

"I'm sorry," she whispered shakily.

He drew in short, harsh breaths while his hands worked at buttoning up the shirt. "Well, I'm not," he murmured, glancing down at her. He groaned. "Honey, you have to cover those up or we're going to be back at first base all over again!"

She looked down and flushed a little as she pulled her shirt down and fumbled behind her to do up the bra again. "First base."

He laughed softly. "First base."

She beamed at him. "I'm getting better every day. It won't be long."

"It had better not be," he sighed. "I think I'll die of it pretty soon."

"No!"

"Just kidding." He turned on the sofa and looked down at her with warm, dark, possessive eyes. "I talked to a minister."

"You did? What did he have to say?"

He traced her nose. "We have to have a marriage license first."

Her heart jumped. They'd been kissing and petting for quite a long time, and he'd insinuated, but he'd never actually asked.

"I thought we might get one with flowers and stuff. You know. So it would look nice framed on the wall."

"Framed."

He nodded. His eyes were steady on her face. "Madeline Edith Lane, will you do me the honor of becoming my wife?" he asked softly.

She fought tears. "Yes," she whispered. "Yes!"

He brushed the tears away, his eyes so dark they seemed black. "I'll love you all my life," he whispered. "I'll love you until the sun burns out."

"I'll love you longer," she whispered back, and it was all there, in her eyes and his.

He smiled slowly. "And we'll have beautiful kids," he said softly. He pushed back her hair. "Absolutely beautiful. Like you."

Now she was really bawling.

He pulled her gently into his arms and across his lap, and rocked her and kissed away the tears.

Sadie came walking in with coffee and stopped dead. "Oh, goodness, what's wrong?"

"I told her we were going to have beautiful kids," he said with a chuckle. "She's very emotional."

"Beautiful kids? You're going to get married?" Sadie exclaimed.

"Yes." Maddie smiled.

"Whoopee!"

"Oh, dear!" Maddie exclaimed.

Sadie looked down at the remains of the glass coffeepot and two ceramic mugs. "Oh, dear," she echoed.

Cort just laughed. But then, like the gentleman he was, he went to help Sadie clean up the mess.

They were married at Christmas. Maddie was able to wear an exquisite designer gown that Odalie had insisted on buying for her, as her "something new." It was an A-line gown of white satin with cap sleeves and a lacy bodice that went up to encase her throat like a high-necked Victorian dress.

There was a train, also of delicate white lace, and a fingertip veil with lace and appliquéd roses. She wore lace gloves and carried a bouquet of white roses. There was a single red rose in the center of the bouquet. One red rose for true love, Cort had insisted, and white ones for purity because in a modern age of easy virtue, Maddie was a throwback to Victorian times. She went to her marriage a virgin, and never apologized once for not following the crowd.

She walked down the aisle on the arm of Cole Everett, who had volunteered to give her away. Odalie was her maid of honor. Heather Everett and Shelby Brannt were her matrons of honor. Four local girls she'd known all her life were bridesmaids, and John Everett was Cort's best man.

At an altar with pots of white and red roses they were married in the local Methodist church, where all three families were members. The minister had preached the funeral of most of their deceased kin. He was elderly and kind, and beloved of the community.

When he pronounced Cort and Maddie man and wife, Cort lifted the veil, ignoring the flash from the professional photographer's camera, and closed in to kiss his new bride.

Nobody heard him when he bent, very low, and whispered, "First base."

Nobody heard the soft, mischievous laughter the comment provoked from the bride. There was a huge reception. John Everett stopped by the table where Cort and Maddie were cutting the wedding cake.

"So, tell me, Cort," John said when the photographer finished shooting the cake-eating segment, "if I'm really the best man, why are you married to my girl?"

"Now, a remark like that could get you punched," Cort teased, catching the other man around the neck, "even at a wedding."

John chuckled, embracing him in a bear hug. "I was

just kidding. No doubt in my mind from the beginning where her heart was." He indicated a beaming Maddie.

Cort glanced at her and smiled. "What an idiot I was," he said, shaking his head. "I almost lost her."

"Crazy, the way things turn out," John mused, his eyes on Odalie as she paused to speak to Maddie. "My sister, Attila the Hun, is ending up as Maddie's best friend. Go figure."

"I wouldn't have believed it myself. Odalie's quite a girl."

John smiled. "I thought it would be you and Odalie, eventually."

Cort shook his head. "We're too different. Neither of us would fit in the other's world. It took me a long time to realize that. But I saw my future in Maddie's eyes. I always will. I hope Odalie finds someone who can make her half as happy as I am today. She deserves it."

John nodded. "I'm very proud of her. She's matured a lot in the past few months." He turned back to Cort. "Christmas is next week. You guys coming home for it or not?"

"Oh, we have to…my folks would kill us, to say nothing of Sadie." He indicated the older woman in her pretty blue dress talking to some other people. "Maddie's like the daughter she never had. They can't have Christmas without us," he stated. "We're just going down to Panama City for a couple of days. Maybe later I can take Maddie to Europe and show her the sights. Right now, even a short plane trip is going to make her uncomfortable, much less a long one to somewhere exotic."

"I don't think Maddie will mind where you go, as long as she's with you," John said. "I wish you all the best. You know that."

"Thanks, bro."

"And when you come home, maybe we can crack open some new video games, now that my sister won't complain about my having you over," he added with a sigh.

Cort just grinned.

The hotel was right on the beach. It was cold in Panama City, but not so cold that they couldn't sit on the patio beyond the glass sliding doors and look at the cold moonlight on the ocean.

Predictably, they'd barely made it into the hotel room when all the months of pent-up anguished desire were taken off the bridle for the first time.

He tried to be gentle, he really did, but his body was shivering with need long before he could do what he wanted to do: to show his love for Maddie.

Not that she noticed. She was with him every step of the way, even when the first encounter stung and made her cry out.

"This is part of it," he gritted, trying to slow down. "I'm so sorry!"

"Don't…sweat it," she panted, moving up to meet the furious downward motion of his hips. "You can hang out…the bedsheet in the morning…to prove I was a virgin…!"

"Wha-a-at?" he yelped, and burst out laughing even as his body shuddered with the beginning of ecstasy.

"First…base," she choked out, and bit him.

It was the most glorious high he'd ever experienced. He groaned and groaned as his body shuddered over hers. The pleasure was exquisite. He felt it in every cell of his body, with every beat of his heart. He could hear his own heartbeat, the passion was so violent.

Under him, her soft body was rising and falling like a pistol as she kept pace with his need, encouraged it, fanned the flames and, finally, glued itself to his in an absolute epiphany of satisfaction that convulsed both of them as they almost passed out from the climax.

She clung to him, shivering with pleasure in the aftermath. Neither of them could stop moving, savoring the dregs of passion until they drained the cup dry.

"Wow," she whispered as she looked into his eyes.

"Wow," he whispered back. He looked down their bodies to where they were joined. They hadn't even thought of turning out the lights. He was glad. Looking at her, like this, was a joy he hadn't expected.

"Beautiful," he breathed.

She smiled slowly. "And to think I was nervous about the first time," she said.

"Obviously unnecessary, since I have skills far beyond those of most mortal men…*oof!*"

She'd hit him. She grinned, though. And then she wiggled her eyebrows and moved her hips ever so slowly. Despite the sting, and the discomfort, pleasure welled up like water above a dam in a flood.

"Oh, yes," she whispered as he began to move, looking straight into her eyes. "Yes. Do that."

He smiled. "This," he murmured, "is going to be indescribable."

And it was.

When they got back, in time for the Christmas celebrations at Skylance, nobody could understand why, when Cort whispered, "first base," Maddie almost fell down laughing. But that was one secret neither one of them ever shared with another living soul.

* * * * *

Christmas Cowboy

Chapter One

It was the holiday season in Jacobsville, Texas. Gaily colored strands of lights crisscrossed the main street, and green garlands and wreaths graced each telephone pole along the way. In the center of town, all the small maple trees that grew out of square beds at intervals along the sidewalk were decorated with lights as well.

People were bundled in coats, because even in south Texas it was cold in late November. They rushed along with shopping bags full of festively wrapped presents to go under the tree. And over on East Main Street, the Optimist Club had its yearly Christmas tree lot open already. A family of four was browsing its sawdust-covered grounds, early enough to have the pick of the beautifully shaped fir trees, just after Thanksgiving.

Dorie Wayne gazed at her surroundings the way a child would look through a store window at toys she couldn't afford. Her hand went to the thin scar down an otherwise perfect cheek and she shivered. How long ago it seemed that she stood right here on this street corner in front of the Jacobsville Drugstore, and backed away from Corrigan Hart. It had been an instinctive move; at eighteen, he'd frightened her. He was so very masculine, a mature man with a cold temper and an iron will. He'd set his sights on Dorie, who found him fearful instead of attractive, despite the fact that any single woman hereabouts would have gone to him on her knees.

She recalled his jet black hair and pale, metallic eyes. She'd wondered at first if it wasn't her fairness that attracted him, because he was so dark. Dorie had hair so blond it was almost platinum, and it was cut short, falling into natural thick waves. Her complexion was delicate and fair, and she had big gray eyes, just a shade darker than Corrigan's. He was very handsome—unlike his brothers. At least, that was what people said. Dorie hadn't gotten to meet the others when she left Jacobsville. And only Corrigan and three of his brothers lived in Jacobsville. The fifth Hart male wasn't talked about, ever. His name wasn't even known locally.

Corrigan and three of his four brothers had come down to Jacobsville from San Antonio eight years ago to take over the rich cattle operation their grandfather had left to them in his will.

It had been something of a local joke that the Harts had no hearts, because they seemed immune to women. They kept to themselves and there was no gossip about them with women. But that changed when Dorie attended a local square dance and found herself whirling around the floor in Corrigan Hart's arms.

Never one to pull his punches, he made his intentions obvious right at the start. He found her attractive. He was drawn to her. He wanted her. Just like that.

There was never any mention of marriage, engagement or even some furtive live-in arrangement. Corrigan said often that he wasn't the marrying kind. He didn't want ties. He made that very clear, because there was never any discussions of taking her to meet his brothers. He kept her away from their ranch.

But despite his aversion to relationships, he couldn't seem to see enough of Dorie. He wanted her and with every new kiss Dorie grew weaker and hungrier for him.

Then one spring day, he kissed her into oblivion,

picked her up in his arms and carried her right into her own bedroom the minute her father left for his weekly poker game.

Despite the drugging effect of masterful kisses and the poignant trembling his expert hands aroused, Dorie had come to her senses just barely in time and pushed him away. Dazed, he'd looked down at her with stunned, puzzled eyes, only belatedly realizing that she was trying to get away, not closer.

She remembered, red-faced even now, how he'd pulled away and stood up, breathing raggedly, eyes blazing with frustrated desire. He'd treated her to a scalding lecture about girls who teased. She'd treated him to one about confirmed bachelors who wouldn't take no for an answer, especially since she'd told him she wasn't the sleep-around sort.

He didn't buy that, he'd told her coldly. She was just holding out for marriage, and there was no hope in that direction. He wanted to sleep with her, and she sure seemed to want him, too. But he didn't want her for keeps.

Dorie had been in love with him, and his emotional rejection had broken something fragile inside her. But she hadn't been about to let him see her pain.

He'd gone on, in the same vein. One insult had led to another, and once he'd gotten really worked up, he'd stormed out the door. His parting shot had been that she must be nuts if she thought he was going to buy her being a virgin. There was no such thing anymore, even at the young age of eighteen.

His rejection had closed doors between them. Dorie couldn't bear the thought of staying in Jacobsville and having everybody know that Corrigan Hart had thrown her aside because she wouldn't sleep with him. And everybody *would* know, somehow. They always knew the secret things in small towns.

That very night Dorie had made up her mind to take up her cousin Belinda's offer to come to New York and get into modeling. Certainly Dorie had the looks and figure for it. She might be young, but she had poise and grace and an exquisite face framed by short, wavy blond hair. Out of that face, huge gray eyes shone like beacons, mirroring happiness or sorrow.

After that sordid evening, Dorie cut her losses and bought a bus ticket.

She'd been standing right here, on this very corner, waiting for the bus to pick her up in front of this drugstore, when Corrigan had found her.

Her abrupt withdrawal from him had halted him in his tracks. Whatever he'd been going to say, her shamed refusal to look at him, combined with her backward steps, stopped him. She was still smarting from his angry words, as well as from her own uninhibited behavior. She was ashamed that she'd given him such license with her body now that she knew there had only been desire on his part.

He hadn't said a single word before the bus stopped for her. He hadn't said a word as she hurriedly gave her ticket to the driver, got on the bus and waited for it to leave without looking his way again. He'd stood there in the trickling rain, without even a raincoat, with his hands deep in his jean pockets, and watched the bus pull away from the curb. That was how Dorie had remembered him all the long years, a lonely fading figure in the distance.

She'd loved him desperately. But her own self-respect wouldn't let her settle for a furtive affair in the goldfish-bowl atmosphere of Jacobsville. She'd wanted a home, a husband, children, everything.

Corrigan had only wanted to sleep with her.

She'd gone, breathless and sick at heart, all the way to New York City, swearing her father to absolute secrecy about her movements.

There had been a letter, a few weeks after her arrival, from her father. In it, he told her that he'd seen Corrigan only once since her departure, and that he was now hot in pursuit of a rich divorcée with sophistication dripping from her fingers. If Dorie had any parting regrets about her decision to leave town, that was the end of them. Corrigan had made his feelings plain, if he was seeing some woman already.

Dorie wondered if her father hadn't said something unpleasant to Corrigan Hart about his daughter's sudden departure from home. It would have been like him. He was fiercely protective of his only child, especially since the death of her mother from heart disease some years past. And his opinion about philandering men was obvious to everyone.

He believed in the old-fashioned sort of courtship, the kind that ended in marriage. Only a handful of conventional people were left, he told Dorie over and over. Such people were the cornerstones of social order. If they all fell, chaos reigned. A man who loved a woman would want to give her, and his children, his name. And Corrigan, he added, had made it clear to the whole town that he wanted no part of marriage or a family. Dorie would have been asking for heartbreak if she'd given in to Corrigan's selfish demands.

Her father was dead now. Dorie had come home for the funeral as well as to dispose of the house and property and decide her own future. She'd started out with such hopes of becoming a successful model. Her eyes closed and she shivered unconsciously at the memories.

"Dorie?"

She turned at the hesitant sound of her name. The face took a little longer to recognize. "Abby?" she said. "Abby Clark!"

"Abby Ballenger," the other woman corrected with a grin. "I married Calhoun."

"Calhoun!" Dorie was momentarily floored. The younger Ballenger brother had been a rounder and a half, and he was married? And to Abby, of all people, the shy and sweet girl for whom Calhoun and Justin had shared guardianship following the death of their parents.

"Surprising, isn't it?" Abby asked, hugging the other woman. "And there's more. We have three sons."

"I haven't been away that long, have I?" Dorie asked hesitantly.

"Eight years," came the reply. Abby was a little older, but she still had the same pretty gray-blue eyes and dark hair, even if it had silver threads now. "Justin married Shelby Jacobs just after I married Calhoun. They have three sons, too," she added on a sigh. "Not a girl in the bunch."

Dorie shook her head. "For heaven's sake!"

"We heard that you were in modeling..." Her voice trailed away as she saw the obvious long scar on the once-perfect cheek. "What happened?"

Dorie's eyes were all but dead. "Not much. I decided that modeling wasn't for me." She laughed at some private joke. "I went back to school and completed a course in business. Now I work for a group of attorneys. I'm a stenographer." Her gaze fell. "Jacobsville hasn't changed a bit."

"Jacobsville never changes," Abby chuckled. "I find it comforting." The laughter went out of her eyes. "We all heard about your father. I'm sorry. It must have been a blow."

"He'd been in the nursing home near me for some time, but he always said he wanted to be buried here. That's why I brought him home. I appreciated so many people coming to the funeral. It was kind."

"I suppose you noticed one missing face in the crowd?" Abby asked carefully, because she knew how persistent Corrigan Hart had been in his pursuit of Dorie.

"Yes." She twisted her purse in her hands. "Are they still making jokes about the Hart boys?"

"More than ever. There's never been the slightest hint of gossip about any of them and a woman. I guess they're all determined to die single. Especially Corrigan. He's turned into a recluse. He stays out at the ranch all the time now. He's never seen."

"Why?"

Abby seemed evasive. "He doesn't mix and nobody knows much about his life. Odd, isn't it, in a town this small, where we mostly know each other's business, that he isn't talked about? But he stays out of sight and none of the other boys ever speak about him. He's become the original local mystery."

"Well, don't look at me as if I'm the answer. He couldn't get rid of me fast enough," she said with a twinge of remaining bitterness.

"That's what you think. He became a holy terror in the weeks after you left town. Nobody would go near him."

"He only wanted me," Dorie said doggedly.

Abby's eyes narrowed. "And you were terrified of him," she recalled. "Calhoun used to joke about it. You were such an innocent and Corrigan was a rounder. He said it was poetic justice that rakes got caught by innocents."

"I remember Calhoun being a rake."

"He was," Abby recalled. "But not now. He's reformed. He's the greatest family man I could have imagined, a doting father and a wonderful husband." She sobered. "I'm sorry things didn't work out for you and Corrigan. If you hadn't taken off like that, I think he might have decided that he couldn't live without you."

"God forbid," she laughed, her eyes quick and nervous. "He wasn't a marrying man. He said so, frequently. And I was raised…well, you know how Dad was. Ministers have a decidedly conventional outlook on life."

"I know."

"I haven't had such a bad time of it," she lied,

grateful that her old friend couldn't read minds. She smiled. "I like New York."

"Do you have anyone there?"

"You mean a boyfriend, or what do they call it, a significant other?" she murmured. "No. I…don't have much to do with men."

There was a strangely haunted look about her that Abby quickly dispelled with an offer of coffee and a sandwich in the local café.

"Yes, thanks, I'm not hungry but I'd love some hot chocolate."

"Great!" Abby said. "I've got an hour to kill before I have to pick my two oldest boys up at school and the youngest from kindergarten. I'll enjoy your company."

The café was all but empty. It was a slow day, and except for a disgruntled looking cowboy sitting alone at a corner table, it was deserted.

Barbara, the owner, took their orders with a grin. "Nice to have pleasant company," she said, glaring toward the cowboy in the corner. "He brought a little black cloud in with him, and it's growing." She leaned closer. "He's one of the Hart employees," she whispered. "Or, he was until this morning. It seems that Corrigan fired him."

The sound of the man's name was enough to make Dorie's heart race, even after so many years. But she steeled herself not to let it show. She had nothing left to offer Corrigan, even if he was still interested in her. And that was a laugh. If he'd cared even a little, he'd have come to New York looking for her all those years ago.

"Fired him?" Abby glanced at the man and scowled. "But that's Buck Wyley," she protested. "He's the Harts' foreman. He's been with them since they came here."

"He made a remark Corrigan didn't like. He got knocked on his pants for his trouble and summarily fired." Barbara shrugged. "The Harts are all high-tempered, but until now I always thought Corrigan was fair. What sort of boss fires a man with Christmas only three weeks away?"

"Ebenezer Scrooge?" Abby ventured dryly.

"Buck said he cut another cowboy's wages to the bone for leaving a gate open." She shook her head. "Funny, we've heard almost nothing about Corrigan for years, and all of a sudden he comes back into the light like a smoldering madman."

"So I noticed," Abby said.

Barbara wiped her hands on a dishcloth. "I don't know what happened to set him off after so many years. The other brothers have been more visible lately, but not Corrigan. I'd wondered if he'd moved away for a while. Nobody even spoke of him." She glanced at Dorie with curious eyes. "You're Dorothy

Wayne, aren't you?" she asked then, smiling. "I thought I recognized you. Sorry about your pa."

"Thanks," Dorie said automatically. She noticed how Barbara's eyes went to the thin scar on her cheek and flitted quickly away.

"I'll get your order."

Barbara went back behind the counter and Abby's puzzled gaze went to the corner.

"Having a bad day, Buck?" she called.

He sipped black coffee. "It couldn't get much worse, Mrs. Ballenger," he replied in a deep, pleasant tone. "I don't suppose Calhoun and Justin are hiring out at the feedlot?"

"They'd hire you in a minute, and you know it," Abby told him. She smiled. "Why don't you go out there and..."

"Oh, the devil!" Buck muttered, his black eyes flashing. He got to his feet and stood there, vibrating, as a tall, lean figure came through the open door.

Dorie actually caught her breath. The tall man was familiar to her, even after all those years. Dressed in tight jeans, with hand-tooled boots and a chambray shirt and a neat, spotless white Stetson atop his black hair, he looked formidable, even with the cane he was using for support.

He didn't look at the table where Dorie was sitting, which was on the other side of the café from Buck.

"You fired me," Buck snapped at him. "What do

you want, another punch at me? This time, you'll get it back in spades, gimpy leg or not!"

Corrigan Hart just stared at the man, his pale eyes like chrome sparkling in sunlight.

"Those purebred Angus we got from Montana are coming in by truck this morning," he said. "You're the only one who knows how to use the master program for the computerized herd records."

"And you need me," Buck agreed with a cold smile. "For how long?"

"Two weeks," came the curt reply. "You'll work that long for your severance pay. If you're still of a mind to quit."

"Quit, hell!" Buck shot back, astonished. "You fired me!"

"I did not!" the older man replied curtly. "I said you could mind your own damned business or get out."

Buck's head turned and he stared at the other man for a minute. "If I come back, you'd better keep your fists to yourself from now on," he said shortly.

The other man didn't blink. "You know why you got hit."

Buck glanced warily toward Dorie and a ruddy color ran along his high cheekbones. "I never meant it the way you took it," he retorted.

"You'll think twice before you presume to make such remarks to me again, then, won't you?"

Buck made a movement that his employer took for assent.

"And your Christmas bonus is now history!" he added.

Buck let out an angry breath, almost spoke, but crushed his lips together finally in furious submission.

"Go home!" the older man said abruptly.

Buck pulled his hat over his eyes, tossed a dollar bill on the table with his coffee cup and strode out with barely a tip of the hat to the women present, muttering under his breath as he went.

The door closed with a snap. Corrigan Hart didn't move. He stood very still for a moment, as if steeling himself.

Then he turned, and his pale eyes stared right into Dorie's. But the anger in them eclipsed into a look of such shock that Dorie blinked.

"What happened to you?" he asked shortly.

She knew what he meant without asking. She put a hand self-consciously to her cheek. "An accident," she said stiffly.

His chin lifted. The tension in the café was so thick that Abby shifted uncomfortably at the table.

"You don't model now," he continued.

The certainty in the statement made her miserable. "No. Of course I don't."

He leaned heavily on the cane. "Sorry about your father," he said curtly.

She nodded.

His face seemed pinched as he stared at her. Even across the room, the heat in the look was tangible to Dorie. Her hands holding the mug of hot chocolate went white at the knuckles from the pressure of them around it.

He glanced at Abby. "How are things at the feedlot?"

"Much as usual," she replied pleasantly. "Calhoun and Justin are still turning away business. Nice, in the flat cattle market this fall."

"I agree. We've culled as many head as possible and we're venturing into new areas of crossbreeding. Nothing but purebreds now. We're hoping to pioneer a new breed."

"Good for you," Abby replied.

His eyes went back to Dorie. They lingered on her wan face, her lack of spirit. "How long are you going to stay?" he asked.

The question was voiced in such a way it seemed like a challenge. Her shoulders rose and fell. "Until I tie up all the loose ends, I suppose. They've given me two weeks off at the law firm where I work."

"As an attorney?"

She shook her head. "A stenographer."

He scowled. "With your head for figures?" he asked shortly.

Her gaze was puzzled. She hadn't realized that he was aware of her aptitude for math.

"It's a waste," he persisted. "You'd have been a natural at bookkeeping and marketing."

She'd often thought so, too, but she hadn't pursued her interest in that field. Especially after her first attempt at modeling.

He gave her a calculating stare. "Clarisse Marston has opened a boutique in town. She designs women's clothes and has them made up at a local textile plant. She sells all over the state."

"Yes," Abby added. "In fact, she's now doing a lot of designing for Todd Burke's wife, Jane—you know, her signature rodeo line of sportswear."

"I've heard of it, even in New York," Dorie admitted.

"The thing Clarisse doesn't have is someone to help her with marketing and bookkeeping." He shook his head. "It amazes me that she hasn't gone belly-up already."

Abby started to speak, but the look on Corrigan's face silenced her. She only smiled at Dorie.

"This is your home," Corrigan persisted quietly. "You were born and raised in Jacobsville. Surely having a good job here would be preferable to being a stenographer in New York. Unless," he added slowly, "there's some reason you want to stay there."

His eyes were flashing. Dorie looked into the film on her cooling hot chocolate. "I don't have anyone in New York." She shifted her legs. "I don't have anyone here, either, now."

"But you do," Abby protested. "All your friends."

"Of course, she may miss the bright lights and excitement," Corrigan drawled.

She looked at him curiously. He was trying to goad her. Why?

"Is Jacobsville too small for you now, city girl?" he persisted with a mocking smile.

"No, it isn't that at all," she said. She cleared her throat.

"Come home," Abby coaxed.

She didn't answer.

"Still afraid of me?" Corrigan asked with a harsh laugh when her head jerked up. "That's why you left. Is it why you won't come back?"

She colored furiously, the first trace of color that had shown in her face since the strange conversation began.

"I'm not...afraid of you!" she faltered.

But she was, and he knew it. His silver eyes narrowed and that familiar, mocking smile turned up his thin upper lip. "Prove it."

"Maybe Miss Marston doesn't want a bookkeeper."

"She does," he returned.

She hesitated. "She might not like me."

"She will."

She let out an exasperated sigh. "I can't make a decision that important in a few seconds," she told him. "I have to think about it."

"Take your time," he replied. "Nobody's rushing you."

"It would be lovely if you came back, though," Abby said with a smile. "No matter how many friends we have, we can always use one more."

"Exactly," Corrigan told her. His eyes narrowed. "Of course, you needn't consider me in your decision. I'm not trying to get you to come back for my sake. But I'm sure there are plenty of other bachelors left around here who'd be delighted to give you a whirl, if you needed an incentive."

His lean face was so hard and closed that not one flicker of emotion got away from it.

Abby was eyeing him curiously, but she didn't say a word, not even when her gaze fell to his hand on the silver knob of the cane and saw it go white from the pressure.

He eased up on the handle, just the same. "Well?"

"I'd like to," Dorie said quietly. She didn't look at

him. Odd, how his statement had hurt, after all those years. She looked back on the past with desperation these days, wondering how her life would have been if she hadn't resisted him that night he'd tried to carry her to bed.

She hadn't wanted an affair, but he was an honorable man, in his fashion. Perhaps he would have followed up with a proposal, despite his obvious distaste for the married state. Or perhaps he wouldn't have. There might have been a child…

She grimaced and lifted the cup of chocolate to her lips. It was tepid and vaguely distasteful.

"Go see Clarisse, why don't you?" he added. "You've nothing to lose, and a lot to gain. She's a sweet woman. You'll like her."

Did he? She didn't dare wonder about that, or voice her curiosity. "I might do that," she replied.

The tap of the cane seemed unusually loud as he turned back to the door. "Give the brothers my best," Corrigan told Abby. He nodded and was gone.

Only then did Dorie look up, her eyes on his tall, muscular body as he walked carefully back to the big double-cabbed black ranch pickup truck he drove.

"What happened to him?" Dorie asked.

Abby sipped her own hot chocolate before she answered. "It happened the week after you left town. He went on a hunting trip in Montana with some other men. During a heavy, late spring snow, Corrigan and another man went off on their own in a four-wheel-drive utility vehicle to scout another section of the hunting range."

"And?" Dorie prompted.

"The truck went over a steep incline and overturned. The other man was killed outright. Corrigan was pinned and couldn't get free. He lay there most of the night and into the next day before the party came looking for them and found him. By that time, he was unconscious. The impact broke his leg in two places, and he had frostbite as well. He almost died."

Dorie caught her breath. "How horrible!"

"They wanted to amputate the leg, but..." she shrugged. "He refused them permission to operate, so they did the best they could. The leg is usable, just, but it will always be stiff. They said later that it was a miracle he didn't lose any toes. He had just enough sense left to wrap himself in one of those thin thermal sheets the men had carried on the trip. It saved him from a dangerous frostbite."

"Poor man."

"Oh, don't make that mistake," Abby mused. "Nobody is allowed to pity Corrigan Hart. Just ask his brothers."

"All the same, he never seemed the sort of man to lose control of anything, not even a truck."

"He wasn't himself but he didn't lose control, either."

"I beg your pardon?"

Abby grimaced. "He and the other man, the one who was driving, had been drinking. He blamed himself not only for the wreck, but for the other man's death. He knew the man wasn't fit to drive but he didn't try to stop him. They say he's been punishing himself ever since. That's why he never comes into town, or has any social life. He's withdrawn into himself and nobody can drag him back out. He's become a hermit."

"But, why?"

"Why was he drinking, you mean?" Abby said, and Dorie nodded. Still, Abby hesitated to put it into words.

"Tell me," came the persistent nudge from Dorie.

Abby's eyes were apologetic. "Nobody knows, really. But the gossip was that he was trying to get over losing you."

Chapter Two

"But he wanted to lose me," Dorie exclaimed, shocked. "He couldn't get out of my house fast enough when I refused...refused him," she blurted. She clasped her hands together. "He accused me of being frigid and a tease..."

"Corrigan was a rounder, Dorie," Abby said gently. "In this modern age, even in Jacobsville, a lot of girls are pretty sophisticated at eighteen. He wouldn't have known about your father being a minister, because he'd retired from the church before the Harts came to take over their grandfather's ranch. He was probably surprised to find you less accommodating than other girls."

"Surprised wasn't the word," Dorie said miserably. "He was furious."

"He did go to the bus depot when you left."

"How did you know that?"

"Everybody talked about it," Abby admitted. "It was generally thought that he went there to stop you."

"He didn't say a word," came the quiet reply. "Not one word."

"Maybe he didn't know what to say. He was probably embarrassed and upset about the way he'd treated you. A man like that might not know what to do with an innocent girl."

Dorie laughed bitterly. "Sure he did. You see her off and hope she won't come back. He told me that he had no intention of marrying."

"He could have changed his mind."

Dorie shook her head. "Not a chance. He never talked about us being a couple. He kept reminding me that I was young and that he liked variety. He said that we shouldn't think of each other in any serious way, but just enjoy each other while it lasted."

"That sounds like a Hart, all right," Abby had to admit. "They're all like Corrigan. Apparently they have a collective bad attitude toward women and think of them as minor amusements."

"He picked on the wrong girl," Dorie said. She finished her hot chocolate. "I'd never even had a real boyfriend when he came along. He was so forceful and demanding and inflexible, so devoid of tenderness when he was with me." She huddled closer into her sweater. "He came at me like a rocket. I couldn't run, I couldn't hide, he just kept coming." Her eyes closed on a long sigh. "Oh, Abby, he scared me to death. I'd been raised in a such a way that I couldn't have an affair, and I knew that was all he wanted. I ran, and kept running. Now I can't stop."

"You could, if you wanted to."

"The only way I'd come back is with a written guarantee that he wanted nothing more to do with me," she said with a cold laugh. "Otherwise, I'd never feel safe here."

"He just told you himself that he had no designs on you," Abby reminded her. "He has other interests."

"Does he? Other…women interests?"

Abby clasped her fingers together on the table. "He goes out with a rich divorcée when he's in need of company," she said. "That's been going on for a long time now. He probably was telling the truth when he said that he wouldn't bother you. After all, it's been eight years." She studied the other woman. "You want to come home, don't you?"

Caught off guard, Dorie nodded. "I'm so alone," she confessed. "I have bolts and chains on my door and I live like a prisoner when I'm not at work. I rarely ever go outside. I miss trees and green grass."

"There's always Central Park."

"You can't plant flowers there," she said, "or have a dog or cat in a tiny apartment like mine. I want to sit out in the rain and watch the stars at night. I've dreamed of coming home."

"Why haven't you?"

"Because of the way I left," she confessed. "I didn't want any more trouble than I'd already had. It was bad enough that Dad had to come and see me, that I couldn't come home."

"Because of Corrigan?"

"What?" For an instant, Dorie's eyes were frightened. Then they seemed to calm. "No, it was for another reason altogether, those first few years. I couldn't risk coming here, where it's so easy to find people…" She closed up when she realized what she was saying. "It was a problem I had, in New York. That's all I can tell you. And it's over now. There's no more danger from that direction. I'm safe."

"I don't understand."

"You don't need to know," Dorie said gently. "It wouldn't help matters to talk about it now. But I would like to come back home. I seem to have spent most of my life on the run."

What an odd turn of phrase, Abby thought, but she didn't question it. She just smiled. "Well, if you decide to come back, I'll introduce you to Clarisse. Just let me know."

Dorie brightened. “All right. Let me think about it for a day or two, and I’ll be in touch with you.”

“Good. I’ll hold you to that.”

For the next two days, Dorie thought about nothing else except coming back to her hometown. While she thought, she wandered around the small yard, looking at the empty bird feeders and the squirrel feeder nearby. She saw the discarded watering pot, the weed-bound flower beds. Her father’s long absence had made its mark on the little property. It needed a loving hand to restore it.

She stood very still as an idea formed in her mind. She didn’t have to sell the property. She could keep it. She could live here. With her math skills, and the bookkeeping training she’d had in business school, she could open a small bookkeeping service of her own. Clarisse could be a client. She could have others. She could support herself. She could leave New York.

The idea took wing. She was so excited about it that she called Abby the next morning when she was sure that the boys would be in school.

She outlined the idea to her friend. “Well, what do you think?” she asked enthusiastically.

“I think it’s a great idea!” Abby exclaimed. “And the perfect solution. When are you going to start?”

“Next week,” she said with absolute certainty. “I’ll

use the Christmas vacation I would have had as my notice. It will only take a couple of days to pack up the few things I have. I'll have to pay the rent, because I signed a lease, but if things work out as I hope they will, that won't be a problem. Oh, Abby, it's like a dream!"

"Now you sound more like the Dorothy I used to know," Abby told her. "I'm so glad you're coming home."

"So am I," Dorie replied, and even as she said it, she tried not to think of the complications that could arise. Corrigan was still around. But he'd made her a promise of sorts, and perhaps he'd keep it. Anyway, she'd worry about that situation later.

A week later, Dorie was settled into her father's house, with all her bittersweet memories of him to keep her company. She'd shipped her few big things, like her piano, home by a moving service. Boxes still cluttered the den, but she was beginning to get her house into some sort of order.

It needed a new roof, and some paint, as well as some plumbing work on the leaky bathtub faucet. But those were minor inconveniences. She had a good little nest egg in her savings account and it would tide her over, if she was careful, until she could be self-supporting in her business again.

She had some cards and stationery printed and put an ad in the Jacobsville weekly newspaper. Then she settled in and began to work in the yard, despite the cold weather. She was finding that grief had to be worked through. It didn't end at the funeral. And the house was a constant reminder of the old days when she and her father had been happy.

So it was a shock to find Corrigan Hart on her doorstep the first Saturday she was in residence.

She just stared at him at first, as if she'd been stunned. In fact, she was. He was the last person she'd have expected to find on her doorstep.

He had a bouquet of flowers in the hand that wasn't holding the cane and his hat. He proferred them brusquely.

"Housewarming present," he said.

She took the pretty bouquet and belatedly stood aside. "Would you like to come in? I could make coffee."

He accepted the invitation, placing his hat on the rack by the door. He kept the cane and she noticed that he leaned on it heavily as he made his way to the nearest easy chair and sat down in it.

"They say damp weather is hard on injured joints," she remarked.

His pale eyes speared into her face, with an equal mixture of curiosity and irritation. "They're right," he drawled. "Walking hurts. Does it help to have me admit it?"

"I wasn't trying to score points," she replied quietly. "I didn't get to say so in the café, but I'm sorry you got hurt."

His own eyes were pointed on the scar that ran the length of her cheek. "I'm sorry you did," he said gruffly. "You mentioned coffee?"

There it was again, that bluntness that had frightened her so much at eighteen. Despite the eight years in between, he still intimidated her.

She moved into the small kitchen, visible from the living room, and filled the pot with water and a premeasured coffee packet. After she'd started it dripping, and had laid a tray with cups, saucers and the condiments, she rejoined him.

"Are you settling in?" he asked a minute after she'd dropped down onto the sofa.

"Yes," she said. "It's strange, after being away for so many years. And I miss Dad. But I always loved this house. Eventually it will be comforting to live here. Once I get over the worst of the grieving."

He nodded. "We lost both our parents at once, in a flood," he said tersely. "I remember how we felt."

He looked around at the high ceilings and marked walls, and the open fireplace. He nodded toward it. "That isn't efficient. You need a stove in here."

"I need a lot of things in here, but I have to eat, too," she said with a faint smile. She pushed back her short, wavy platinum hair and curled up on the sofa in her jeans and gray sweatshirt and socks. Her shoes were under the sofa. Even in cold weather, she hated wearing shoes around the house.

He seemed to notice that and found it amusing, judging by the twinkle in his pale eyes.

"I hate shoes," she said.

"I remember."

That was surprising. She hardly remembered the girl she'd been eight years ago. It seemed like a lifetime.

"You had a dog, that damned little spaniel, and you were out in the front yard washing him one day when I drove by," he recalled. "He didn't like a bath, and you were soaked, bare feet, cutoffs, tank top and all." His eyes darkened as he looked at her. "I told you to go in the house, do you remember?"

"Yes." The short command had always puzzled her, because he'd seemed angry, not amused as he did now.

"I never said why," he continued. His face tautened as he looked at her. "You weren't wearing anything under that tank top and it was plastered to you," he added quietly. "You can't imagine what it did to me... And there was that damned Bobby Harris standing on the sidewalk gawking at you."

Bobby had asked her out later that day, and she'd refused, because she didn't like him. He was an older boy; her father never had liked him.

"I didn't realize," she said, amazed that the memory should be so tame now, when his odd behavior had actually hurt in the past. She actually flushed at the thought that he'd seen her that way so early in their relationship.

"I know that, now, eight years too late," he said abruptly.

She cocked her head, studying him curiously.

He saw her gaze and lifted his eyes. "I thought you were displaying your charms brazenly for my benefit, and maybe even for Bobby's," he said with a mocking smile. "That's why I acted the way I did that last night we dated."

Her face thinned with distress. "Oh, no!"

"Oh, yes," he said, his voice deep with bitterness. "I thought you were playing me for a sucker, Dorie. That you were pretending to be innocent because I was rich and you wanted a wedding ring instead of an affair."

The horror she felt showed in her wan face.

"Yes, I know," he said when she started to protest. "I only saw what I wanted to see. But the joke was on me. By the time I realized what a hell of a mistake I'd made about you, you were halfway on a bus out of town. I went after you. But I couldn't manage the right words to stop you. My pride cut my throat. I was never that wrong about anyone before."

She averted her gaze. "It was a long time ago. I was just a kid."

"Yes. Just a kid. And I mistook you for a woman." He studied her through narrow lids. "You don't look much older even now. How did you get that scar?"

Her fingers went to it. The memories poured over her, hot and hurting. She got to her feet. "I'll see about the coffee."

She heard a rough sound behind her, but apparently it wasn't something he wanted to put words to. She escaped into the kitchen, found some cookies to put in a bowl and carried the coffee back to the coffee table on a silver tray.

"Fancy stuff," he mused.

She knew that he had equally fancy stuff at his place. She'd never been there, but she'd certainly heard about the Hart heirlooms that the four brothers displayed with such pride. Old Spanish silver, five generations old, dating all the way back to Spain graced their side table. There was crystal as well, and dozens of other heirlooms that would probably never be handed down. None of the Harts, it was rumored, had any ambitions of marrying.

"This was my grandmother's," she said. "It's all I had of her. She brought this service over from England, they said."

"Ours came from Spain." He waited for her to pour the coffee. He picked up his cup, waving away cream and sugar. He took a sip, nodded and took another. "You make good coffee. Amazing how many people can't."

"I'm sure it's bad for us. Most things are."

He agreed. He put the cup back into the saucer and studied her over its rim. "Are you planning to stay for good?"

"I guess so," she faltered. "I've had stationery and cards printed, and I've already had two offers of work."

"I'm bringing you a third—our household accounts. We've been sharing them since our mother died. Consequently each of us insists that it's not our turn to do them, so they don't get done."

"You'd bring them to me?" she asked hesitantly.

He studied her broodingly. "Why shouldn't I? Are you afraid to come out to the ranch and do them?"

"Of course not."

"Of course not," he muttered, glaring at her. He sat forward, watching her uneasy movement. "Eight years, and I still frighten you."

She curled up even more. "Don't be absurd. I'm twenty-six."

"You don't look or act it."

"Go ahead," she invited. "Be as blunt as you like."

"Thanks, I will. You're still a virgin."

Coffee went everywhere. She cursed roundly,

amusing him, as she searched for napkins to mop up the spill, which was mostly on her.

"Why are you?" he persisted, baiting her. "Were you waiting for me?"

She stood up, slamming the coffee cup to the floor. It shattered with a pleasantly loud crash, and she thanked goodness that it was an old one. "You son of a…!"

He stood up, too, chuckling. "That's better," he mused, watching her eyes flash, her face burn with color.

She kicked at a pottery shard. "Damn you, Corrigan Hart!"

He moved closer, watching her eyelids flutter. She tried to back up, but she couldn't go far. Her legs were against the sofa. There was no place to run.

He paused a step away from her, close enough that she could actually feel the heat of his body through her clothing and his. He looked down into her eyes without speaking for several long seconds.

"You're not the child you used to be," he said, his voice as smooth as velvet. "You can stand up for yourself, even with me. And everything's going to be all right. You're home. You're safe."

It was almost as if he knew what she'd been through. His eyes were quiet and full of secrets, but he smiled. His hand reached out and touched her short hair.

"You still wear it like a boy's," he murmured. "But it's silky. Just the way I remember it."

He was much too close. He made her nervous. Her hands went out and pressed into his shirtfront, but instead of moving back, he moved forward. She shivered at the feel of his chest under her hands, even with the shirt covering it.

"I don't want a lover," she said, almost choking on the words.

"Neither do I," he replied heavily. "So we'll be friends. That's all."

She nibbled on her lower lip. He smelled of spice and leather. She used to dream about him when she first left home. Over the years, he'd assumed the image of a protector in her mind. Strange, when he'd once frightened her so much.

Impulsively she laid her cheek against his chest with a little sigh and closed her eyes.

He shivered for an instant, before his lean hands pressed her gently to him, in a nonthreatening way. He stared over her head with eyes that blazed, eyes that he was thankful she couldn't see.

"We've lost years," he said half under his breath. "But Christmas brings miracles. Maybe we'll have one of our own."

"A miracle?" she mused, smiling. She felt ever so safe in his arms. "What sort?"

"I don't know," he murmured, absently stroking

her hair. "We'll have to wait and see. You aren't going to sleep, are you?"

"Not quite." She lifted her head and looked up at him, a little puzzled at the familiarity she felt with him. "I didn't expect that you'd ever be comfortable to be around."

"How so?"

She shrugged. "I wasn't afraid."

"Why should you be?" he replied. "We're different people now."

"I guess."

He brushed a stray hair from her eyebrow with a lean, sure hand. "I want you to know something," he said quietly. "What happened that night…I wouldn't have forced you. Things got a little out of hand, and I said some things, a lot of things, that I regret. I guess you realize now that I had a different picture of you than the one that was real. But even so, I wouldn't have harmed you."

"I think I knew that," she said. "But thank you for telling me."

His hand lay alongside her soft cheek and his metallic eyes went dark and sad. "I mourned you," he said huskily. "Nothing was the same after you'd gone."

She lowered her eyes to his throat. "I didn't have much fun in New York at first, either."

"Modeling wasn't all it was cracked up to be?"

She hesitated. Then she shook her head. "I did better as a stenographer."

"And you'll do even better as a financial expert, right here," he told her. He smiled, tilting up her chin. "Are you going to take the job I've offered you?"

"Yes," she said at once. Her gaze drew slowly over his face. "Are your brothers like you?"

"Wait and see."

"That sounds ominous."

He chuckled, moving slowly away from her to retrieve his cane from the chair. "They're no worse, at least."

"Are they as outspoken as you?"

"Definitely." He saw her apprehension. "Think of the positive side. At least you'll always know exactly where you stand with us."

"That must be a plus."

"Around here, it is. We're hard cases. We don't make friends easily."

"And you don't marry. I remember."

His face went hard. "You have plenty of reason to remember that I said that. But I'm eight years older, and a lot wiser. I don't have such concrete ideas anymore."

"You mean, you're not still a confirmed bachelor?" She laughed nervously. "They say you're taken with the gay divorcée, just the same."

"How did you hear about her?" he asked curtly.

His level, challenging gaze made her uneasy. "People talk," she said.

"Well, the gay divorcée," he emphasized, his expression becoming even more remote, "is a special case. And we're not a couple. Despite what you may have heard. We're friends."

She turned away. "That's no concern of mine. I'll do your bookkeeping on those household accounts, and thank you for the work. But I have no interest in your private life."

He didn't return the compliment. He reached for his hat and perched it on his black hair. There were threads of gray at his temples now, and new lines in his dark, lean face.

"I'm sorry about your accident," she said abruptly, watching him lean heavily on the cane.

"I'll get by," he said. "My leg is stiff, but I'm not crippled. It hurts right now because I took a toss off a horse, and I need the cane. As a rule, I walk well enough without one."

"I remember the way you used to ride," she recalled. "I thought I'd never seen anything in my life as beautiful as you astride a horse at a fast gallop."

His posture went even more rigid. "You never said so."

She smiled. "You intimidated me. I was afraid of you. And not only because you wanted me." She averted her eyes. "I wanted you, too. But I hadn't been raised to believe in a promiscuous life-style. Which," she added, looking up at his shocked face, "was all you were offering me. You said so."

"God help me, I never knew that your father was a minister and your mother a missionary," he said heavily. "Not until it was far too late to do me any good. I expected that all young women were free with their favors in this age of no-consequences intimacy."

"It wouldn't be of no consequence to me," she said firmly. "I was never one to go with the crowd. I'm still not."

"Yes, I know," he murmured dryly, giving her a long, meaningful glance. "It's obvious."

"And it's none of your business."

"I wouldn't go that far." He tilted his hat over his eyes. "I haven't changed completely, you know. I still go after the things I want, even if I don't go as fast as I used to."

"I expect you do," she said. "Does the divorcée know?"

"Know what? That I'm persistent? Sure she does."

"Good for her."

"She's a beauty," he added, propping on his stick. "Of an age to be sophisticated and good fun."

Her heart hurt. "I'm sure you enjoy her company."

"I enjoy yours as much," he replied surprisingly. "Thanks for the coffee."

"Don't you like cookies?" she asked, noting that he hadn't touched them.

"No," he said. "I don't care for sweets at all."

"Really?"

He shrugged. "We never had them at home. Our mother wasn't the homey sort."

"What was she like?" she had to ask.

"She couldn't cook, hated housework and spouted contempt for any woman who could sew and knit and crochet," he replied.

She felt cold. "And your father?"

"He was a good man, but he couldn't cope with us alone." His eyes grew dark. "When she took off and deserted him, part of him died. She'd just come back, out of money and all alone, from her latest lover. They were talking about a reconciliation when the flood took the house where she was living right out from under them." His face changed, hardened. He leaned heavily on the cane. "Simon and Cag and I were grown by then. We took care of the other two."

"No wonder you don't like women," she murmured quietly.

He gave her a long, level look and then dropped his gaze. She missed the calculation in his tone when he added, "Marriage is old-fashioned, anyway. I have a dog, a good horse and a houseful of modern appliances. I even have a housekeeper who can cook. A wife would be redundant."

"Well, I never," she exclaimed, breathless.

"I know," he replied, and there was suddenly a wicked glint in his eyes. "You can't blame that on me," he added. "God knows, I did my best to bring you into the age of enlightenment."

While she was absorbing that dry remark, he tipped his hat, turned and walked out the door.

She darted onto the porch after him. "When?" she called after him. "You didn't say when you wanted me to start."

"I'll phone you." He didn't look back. He got into his truck laboriously and drove away without even a wave of his hand.

At least she had the promise of a job, she told herself. She shouldn't read hidden messages into what he said. But the past he'd shared with her, about his mother, left her chilled. How could a woman have five sons and leave them?

And what was the secret about the fifth brother, Simon, the one nobody had ever seen? She wondered if he'd done something unspeakable, or if he was in trouble with the law. There had to be a reason why the brothers never spoke of him much. Perhaps she'd find out one day.

Chapter Three

It was the next day before she realized she hadn't thanked Corrigan for the flowers he'd brought. She sent a note out to the ranch on Monday, and got one back that read, simply, "You're welcome." So much for olive branches, if one had been needed.

She found plenty to keep her busy in the days that followed. It seemed that all her father's friends and the people she'd gone to school with wanted her to come home. Everyone seemed to know a potential client. It wasn't long before she was up to her ears in work.

The biggest surprise came Thursday morning when she heard the sound of many heavy footsteps and looked up from her desk to find three huge, intimidating men standing on her porch just beyond the glass-fronted door. They'd come in that big double-cabbed pickup that Corrigan usually drove, and she wondered if these were his brothers.

She went to open the door and felt like a midget when they came tromping inside her house, their spurs jingling pleasantly on boots that looked as if they'd been kept in a swamp.

"We're the Harts," one of them said. "Corrigan's brothers."

As she'd guessed. She studied them curiously. Corrigan was tall, but these men were giants. Two were dark-haired like Corrigan, and one had blond-streaked brown hair. All were dark-eyed, unlike him. None of them would have made any lists of handsome bachelors. They were rugged-looking, lean and tanned, and they made her nervous. The Hart boys made most people nervous. The only other local family that had come close to their reputations for fiery tempers were the Tremayne boys, who were all married and just a little tamer now. The Harts were relative newcomers in Jacobsville, having only been around eight years or so. But they kept to themselves and seemed to have ties to San Antonio that were hard to break. What little socializing they did was all done there, in the city. They didn't mix much in Jacobsville.

Not only were they too rugged for words, but they also had the most unusual first names Dorie could remember hearing. They introduced themselves abruptly, without even being asked first.

Reynard was the youngest. They called him Rey. He had deep-set black eyes and a thin mouth and, gossip said, the worst temper of the four.

The second youngest was Leopold. He was broader than the other three, although not fat, and the tallest. He never seemed to shave. He had blond-streaked brown hair and brown eyes and a mischievous streak that the others apparently lacked.

Callaghan was the eldest, two years older than Corrigan. He had black eyes like a cobra. He didn't blink. He was taller than all his brothers, with the exception of Leopold, and he did most of the bronc-breaking at the ranch. He looked Spanish, more than the others, and he had the bearing and arrogance of royalty, as if he belonged in another century. They said he had the old-fashioned attitudes of the past, as well.

He gave the broader of the three a push toward Dorie. He glared over his shoulder, but took off his hat and forced a smile as he stood in front of Dorie.

"You must be Dorothy Wayne," Leopold said with a grin. "You work for us."

"Y…yes, I guess I do," she stammered. She felt

surrounded. She moved back behind the desk and just stared at them, feeling nervous and inadequate.

"Will you two stop glaring?" Leopold shot at his taciturn brothers. "You're scaring her!"

They seemed to make an effort to relax, although it didn't quite work out.

"Never mind," Leopold muttered. He clutched his hat in his hand. "We'd like you to come out to the ranch," he said. "The household accounts are about to do us in. We can't keep Corrigan still long enough to get him to bring them to you."

"He came over Saturday," she said.

"Yeah, we heard," Leo mused. "Roses, wasn't it?"

The other two almost smiled.

"Roses," she agreed. Her gray eyes were wide and they darted from one giant to another.

"He forgot to bring you the books. The office is in a hel…heck of a mess," Leo continued. "We can't make heads nor tails of it. Corrigan scribbles, and we've volunteered him to do it mostly, but we can't read his writing. He escaped to a herd sale in Montana, so we're stuck." He shrugged and managed to look helpless. "We can't see if we've got enough money in the account to buy groceries." He looked hungry. He sighed loudly. "We'd sure appreciate it if you could come out, maybe in the morning, about nine? If that's not too early."

"Oh, no," she said. "I'm up and making breakfast by six."

"Making breakfast? You can cook, then?" Leopold asked.

"Well, yes." She hesitated, but he looked really interested. "I make biscuits and bacon and eggs."

"Pig meat," the one called Reynard muttered.

"Steak's better," Callaghan agreed.

"If she can make biscuits, the other stuff doesn't matter," Reynard retorted.

"Will you two shut up?" Leopold asked sharply. He turned back to Dorie and gave her a thorough appraisal, although not in the least sexual. "You don't look like a bookkeeper."

"Nice hair," Reynard remarked.

"Bad scar on that cheek," Callaghan remarked. "How did it happen?"

Heavens, he was blunt! She was almost startled enough to tell him. She blurted that it had been in an accident.

"Tough," he said. "But if you can cook, scars don't matter much."

Her mouth was open, and Leopold stomped on his big brother's foot, hard.

Callaghan popped him one on the arm with a fist the size of a ham. "Cut it out!"

"Don't insult her, she won't come!"

"I didn't!"

Reynard moved forward, elbowing the other two out of the way. He had his own hat in his hand. He tried to smile. It looked as if he hadn't had much practice at it.

"We'd like you to come tomorrow. Will you?"

She hesitated.

"Now see what you've done!" Leopold shot at Callaghan. "She's scared of us!"

"We wouldn't hurt you," Reynard said gently. He gave up trying to smile; it was unnatural anyway. "We have old Mrs. Culbertson keeping house for us. She carries a broomstick around with her. You'll be safe."

She bit back a laugh. But her eyes began to twinkle.

"She carries the broomstick because of him," Reynard added, indicating Leopold. "He likes to…"

"Never mind!" Leopold said icily.

"I was only going to say that you…"

"Shut up!"

"If you two don't stop, I'm going to lay you both out right here," Callaghan said, and looked very much as if he meant it. "Apologize."

They both murmured reluctant apologies.

"All right, that's that." He put his hat back on. "If you can come at nine, we'll send one of the boys for you."

"Thank you, I'd rather drive my own car."

"I've seen your car. That's why I'm sending one of the boys for you," Callaghan continued doggedly.

Her mouth fell open again. "It's a…a nice old car! And it runs fine!"

"Everybody knows Turkey Sanders sold it to you," Callaghan said with a disgusted look. "He's a pirate. You'll be lucky if the wheels don't fall off the first time you go around a curve."

"That's right," Rey agreed.

"We'll stop by on our way out of town and talk to him," Leopold said. "He'll bring your car back in and make sure it's perfectly safe to drive. He'll do it first thing tomorrow."

"But…"

They put their hats back on, gave her polite nods and stomped back out the way they'd come.

Callaghan paused at the front door, with the screen open. "He may talk and act tough, but he's hurt pretty bad, inside where it doesn't show. Don't hurt him again."

"Him?"

"Corrigan."

She moved forward, just a step. "It wasn't like that," she said gently. "He didn't feel anything for me."

"And you didn't, for him?"

She averted her gaze to the floor. "It was a long time ago."

"You shouldn't have left."

She looked back up, her eyes wide and wounded. "I was afraid of him!"

He let out a long breath. "You were just a kid. We tried to tell him. Even though we hadn't seen you, we knew about you from other people. We were pretty sure you weren't the sort of girl to play around. He wouldn't listen." He shrugged. "Maybe we corrupted him. You might ask him sometimes about our parents," he added coldly. "Kids don't grow up hating marriage without reason."

There was a lot of pain in his lean face. He was telling her things she'd never have dared ask Corrigan. She moved forward another step, aware of the other two talking out on the porch in hushed whispers.

"Is he still…like that?"

His eyes were cold, but as they looked into hers, they seemed to soften just a little. "He's not the same man he was. You'll have to find out the rest for yourself. We don't interfere in each other's lives, as a rule." His gaze went over her wan face. "You've been to hell and back, too."

He was as perceptive as his brother. She smiled. "I suppose it's part of becoming an adult. Losing illusions and dreams and hope, I mean." She locked her fingers together and looked up at him quietly. "Growing up is painful."

"Don't let go," he said suddenly. "No matter what he says, what he does, don't let go."

Her surprise widened her eyes. "Why?"

He pulled his hat lower over his forehead. "They don't make women like you anymore."

"Like me?" She frowned.

His dark eyes glittered. He smiled in a way that, if she hadn't been half-crazy about Corrigan, would have curled her toes. "I wish we'd met you before," he said. "You'd never have gotten on that bus." He tilted the hat. "We'll send Joey for you in the morning."

"But..."

The door closed behind him. He motioned to the other two and they followed him down the steps to the four-door pickup truck. It had a big cab. It was streamlined and black, and it had a menacing look not—unlike Corrigan Hart's brothers!

She wondered why they'd all come together to ask her to go out to the ranch, and why they'd done it when Corrigan was gone. She supposed she'd find out. She did wonder again about the fifth brother, the mysterious one that Corrigan had mentioned. None of these men were named Simon.

Later, the telephone rang, and it was Turkey Sanders. "I just wanted you to know that I'm going to have that car I sold you picked up in the morning and put to rights," he said at once. "I guarantee, it's going to be the best used car you've ever driven! If you would, just leave the keys in it, and I'll have it picked up first thing. And if there's anything else I can do for you, little lady, you just ask!"

He sounded much more enthusiastic than he had when he'd sold her the rusty little car. "Why, thank you," she said.

"No problem. None at all. Have a nice day, now."

He hung up and she stared blankly at the receiver. Well, nobody could say that living in Jacobsville wasn't interesting, she told herself. Apparently the brothers had a way with other businessmen, too. She'd never have admitted that the car had worried her from the time Turkey had talked her into buying it, for what seemed like a high price for such a wreck. She had a driver's license, which she had to have renewed. But never having owned a car in New York, it was unique to have one of her own, even if it did look like ten miles of bad road.

It was a cold, blustery morning when a polite young man drove up in a black Mercedes and held the door open for her.

"I'm Joey," he told her. "The brothers sent me to fetch you. I sure am glad you took on this job," he added. "They won't give me any money for gas until that checkbook's balanced. I've been having to syphon it out of their trucks with a hose." He shook his head ruefully as he waited for her to move her long denim skirt completely out of the door frame so that he could close the door. "I hate the taste of gasoline."

He closed the door, got in under the wheel and took off in a cloud of dust.

She smiled to herself. The brothers were strange people.

The ranch was immaculate, from its white wood fences to the ranch house itself, a long elegant brick home with a sprawling manicured lawn and a swimming pool and tennis court. The bunkhouse was brick, too, and the barn was so big that she imagined it could hold an entire herd of horses.

"Big, huh?" Joey grinned at her. "The brothers do things on a big scale, but they're meticulous—especially Cag. He runs the place, mostly."

"Cag?"

"Callaghan. Nobody calls him that in the family." He glanced in her direction, amused. "They said you're the reason Corrigan never married."

Her heart jumped. "No kidding?"

"Oh, yeah. He doesn't even look at women these days. But when he heard that you were coming back, he shaved and bought new clothes." He shook his head. "Shocked us all, seeing him without a beard."

"I can't imagine him with one," she said with some confusion.

"Pity about his leg, but he's elegant on a horse, just the same."

"I think he gets around very well."

"Better than he used to." He pulled up in front of the house, turned off the engine and went around to help her out.

"It's right in here."

He led her in through the front door and down a carpeted hall to a pine-paneled office. "Mrs. Culbertson will be along any minute to get you some coffee or tea or a soft drink. The brothers had to get to work or they'd have been here to meet you. No worry, though, Corrigan's home. He'll be here shortly and show you the books. He's trying to doctor a colt, down in the barn."

"Thank you, Joey."

He tipped his hat. "My pleasure, ma'am." He gave her a cursory appraisal, nodded and went back out again.

He'd no sooner gone than a short, plump little woman with twinkling blue eyes and gray hair came in, rubbing her hands dry on her apron. "You'd be Miss Wayne. I'm Betty Culbertson," she introduced herself. "Can I get you a cup of coffee?"

"Oh, yes, please."

"Cream, sugar?"

"I like it black," she said.

The older woman grinned. "So do the boys. They don't like sweets, either. Hard to get fat around here, except on gravy and biscuits. They'd have those every meal if I'd cook them."

The questions the brothers had asked about her cooking came back to haunt her.

"None of them believe in marriage, do they?" she asked.

Mrs. Culbertson shook her head. "They've been bachelors too long now. They're set in their ways and none of them have much to do with women. Not that they aren't targeted by local belles," she added with a chuckle. "But nobody has much luck. Corrigan, now, he's mellowed. I hear it's because of you."

While Dorie flushed and tried to find the right words to answer her, a deep voice did it for her.

"Yes, it is," Corrigan said from the doorway. "But she isn't supposed to know it."

"Oops," Mrs. Culbertson said with a wicked chuckle. "Sorry."

He shrugged. "No harm done. I'll have coffee. So will she. And if you see Leopold…"

"I'll smash his skull for him, if I do," the elderly woman said abruptly, and her whole demeanor changed. Her blue eyes let off sparks. "That devil!"

"He did it again, I guess?"

She made an angry noise through her nose. "I've told him and told him…"

"You'd think he'd get tired of having that broomstick thrown at him, wouldn't you?" Corrigan asked pleasantly.

"One of these days he won't be quick enough," Mrs. Culbertson said with an evil smile.

"I'll talk to him."

"Everybody's already talked to him. It does no good."

"What does he do?" Dorie asked curiously.

Mrs. Culbertson looked at Corrigan, who'd started to answer, with eyes that promised culinary retribution.

"Sorry," he said abruptly. "I can't say."

Mrs. Culbertson nodded curtly and smiled at Dorie. "I'll just get that coffee. Be back in a jiffy."

She left and Corrigan's dark eyes slid over Dorie's pretty figure.

"You look very nice," he said. His eyes lifted to her wavy hair and he smiled appreciatively. "I always loved your hair. That was a first for me. Usually I like a woman's hair long. Yours suits you just as it is."

Her slender hand went to the platinum waves self-consciously. "It's easy to keep like this." She shifted to the other foot. "Your brothers came to the house yesterday and asked me to come out here and look at the household accounts. They say they're starving."

"They look like it, too, don't they?" he asked disgustedly. "Good God, starving!"

"They were very nice," she continued. "They talked to Turkey Sanders and he's repairing my car."

"His *mechanic's* repairing your car," he told her. "Turkey's having a tooth fixed."

She knew she shouldn't ask. But she had to. "Why?"

"He made a remark that Cag didn't like."

"Cag. Oh, yes, he's the eldest."

He brightened when he realized that she remembered that. "He's thirty-eight, if you call that old." Anticipating her next question, he added blithely, "Leo's thirty-four. I'm thirty-six. Rey's thirty-two."

"So Cag hit Turkey Sanders?"

He shook his head.

"Then who broke his tooth?"

"Leo."

"Cag got mad, but Leo hit Turkey Sanders?" she asked, fascinated.

He nodded. "He did that to save him from Cag."

"I don't understand."

"Cag was in the Special Forces," he explained. "He was a captain when they sent him to the Middle East some years back." He shrugged. "He knows too much about hand-to-hand combat to be let loose in a temper. So we try to shield people from him." He grinned. "Leo figured that if he hit Turkey first, Cag wouldn't. And he didn't."

She just shook her head. "Your brothers are… unique," she said finally, having failed to find a good word to describe them.

He chuckled. "You don't know the half of it."

"Do they really hate women?"

"Sometimes," he said.

"I'll bet they're sought after," she mentioned, "especially when people get a good look at this ranch."

"The ranch is only a part of the properties we own," he replied. "Our people are fourth-generation Texans, and we inherited thousands of acres of land and five ranches. They were almost bankrupt when the old man died, though," he mused. "He didn't really have a head for figures. Broke Grandad's heart. He saw the end of his empire. But we pulled it out of the fire."

"So I see," she agreed.

"The only problem is, none of us are married. So if we don't have descendants, who's going to keep the empire going?"

She thought of the most terrible answer to that question, and then got the giggles.

He raised an eyebrow.

She put a hand over her mouth until she got herself

back under control. "Sorry. I was only thinking of that movie about the man who got pregnant…!"

He gave her a level look, unsmiling.

She cleared her throat. "Where are the accounts?"

He hesitated for a minute, and then opened the desk drawer and took out a set of ledgers, placing them on the spotless cherry wood desk.

"This is beautiful," she remarked, stroking the silky, high-polished surface.

"It was our grandfather's," he told her. "We didn't want to change things around too much. The old gentleman was fond of the office just the way it is."

She looked around, puzzled by the plain wood paneling. There were no deer heads or weapons anywhere. She said so.

"He didn't like trophies," he told her. "Neither do we. If we hunt, we use every part of the deer, but we don't have the heads mounted. It doesn't seem quite sporting."

She turned as she pulled out the desk chair, and looked at him with open curiosity.

"None of your brothers are like I pictured them."

"In what way?"

She smiled. "You're very handsome," she said, averting her eyes when his began to glitter. "They aren't. And they all have very dark eyes. Yours are gray, like mine."

"They favor our mother," he said. "I favor him." He nodded toward the one portrait, on the wall behind the desk. It looked early twentieth century and featured a man very like Corrigan, except with silver hair.

"So that's what you'll look like," she remarked absently.

"Eventually. Not for a few years, I hope."

She glanced at him, because he'd come to stand beside her. "You're going gray, just at the temples."

He looked down into her soft face. His eyes narrowed as he searched every inch of her above the neck. "Gray won't show in that beautiful mop on your head," he said quietly. "It'll blend in and make it even prettier."

The comment was softly spoken, and so poetic that it embarrassed her. She smiled self-consciously and her gaze fell to his shirt. It was open at the collar, because it was warm in the house. Thick black hair peered over the button, and unwanted memories of that last night they'd been together came flooding back. He'd taken his shirt off, to give her hands total access to his broad, hair-roughened chest. He liked her lips on it…

She cleared her throat and looked away, her color high. "I'd better get to work."

His lean hand caught her arm, very gently, and he pulled her back around. His free hand went to the snaps that held the shirt together. He looked into her startled eyes and slowly, one by one, he flicked the snaps apart.

"What…are you…doing?" she faltered. She couldn't breathe. He was weaving spells around her. She felt weak-kneed already, and the sight of that broad chest completely bare drew a faint gasp from her lips.

He had her by the elbows. He drew her to him, so that her lips were on a level with his collarbone. She could hear his heartbeat, actually hear it.

"It was like this," he said in a raw, ragged tone. "But I had your blouse off, your breasts bare. I drew you to me, like this," he whispered unsteadily, drawing her against the length of him, "and I bent, and took your open mouth under my own…like this…"

It was happening all over again. She was eight years older, but apparently not one day less vulnerable. He put her cold hands into the thick hair on his chest and moved them while his hard mouth took slow, sweet possession of her lips.

He nudged her lips apart and hesitated for just a second, long enough to look into her eyes and see the submission and faint hunger in them. There was just the hint of a smile on his lips before he parted them against her soft mouth.

Chapter Four

She had no pride at all, she decided in the hectic seconds that followed the first touch of his hard mouth. She was a total washout as a liberated woman.

His hands had gone to her waist and then moved up to her rib cage, to the soft underside of her breasts. He stroked just under them until she shivered and moaned, and then his hands lifted and took possession; blatant possession.

He felt her mouth open. His own answered it while he touched her, searched over her breasts and found the hard nipples that pushed against his palms.

His mouth grew rougher. She felt his hands move

around her, felt the catch give. Her blouse was pushed up with a shivering urgency, and seconds later, her bare breasts were buried in the thick hair that covered his chest and abdomen.

She cried out, dragging her mouth from his.

He looked into her eyes, but he wouldn't let her go. His hard face was expressionless. Only his eyes were alive, glittering like gray fires. He deliberately moved her from side to side and watched her face as he did it, enjoying, with a completely masculine delight, the pleasure she couldn't hide.

"Your nipples are like rocks against me." He bit off the words, holding her even closer. "I took your breasts inside my mouth the night we made love, and you arched up right off the bed to give them to me. Do you remember what you did next?"

She couldn't speak. She looked at him with mingled desire and fear.

"You slid your hands inside my jeans," he whispered roughly. "And you touched me. That's when I lost control."

Her moan was one of shame, not pleasure. She found his chest with her cheek and pressed close to him, shivering. "I'm sorry," she whispered brokenly. "I'm so sorry…!"

His mouth found her eyes and kissed them shut. "Don't," he whispered roughly. "I'm not saying it to shame you. I only want you to remember why it ended the way it did. You were grass green and I didn't know it. I encouraged you to be uninhibited, but I'd never have done it if I'd known what an innocent you were." His mouth slid over her forehead with breathless tenderness while his hands slid to her lower back and pulled her even closer. "I was going to take you," he whispered. His hands contracted and his body went rigid with a surge of arousal that she could feel. His legs trembled. "I still want to, God help me," he breathed at her temple. "I've never had the sort of arousal I feel with you. I don't even have to undress you first." His hands began to tremble as he moved her sensually against his hips. His mouth slid down to hers and softly covered it, lifting and touching and probing until she shivered again with pleasure.

"I thought you knew," she whimpered.

"I didn't." His hands moved to the very base of her spine and lifted her gently into the hard thrust of his body. He caught his breath at the wave of pleasure that washed over him immediately. "Dorie," he breathed.

She couldn't think at all. When he took one of her hands and pressed it to his lower body, she didn't even have the will to protest. Her hand opened and she let him move it gently against him, on fire with the need to touch him.

"Eight years," she said shakily.

"And we're still starving for each other," he whispered at her mouth. His hand became insistent. "Harder," he said and his breath caught.

"This…isn't wise," she said against his chest.

"No, but it's sweet. Dorie…!" He cried out hoarsely, his whole body shuddering.

Her hand stilled at once. "I'm sorry," she whispered frantically. "Did I hurt you?"

He wasn't breathing normally at all. His face was buried in her throat and he was shaking like a leaf. She brushed her mouth over his cheek, his chin, his lips, his nose, whispering his name as she clung to him.

His hand gripped her upper thigh, and it was so bruising that she was afraid she was going to have to protest. He fought for sanity, embarrassed by his weakness.

She was still kissing him. He felt her breasts moving against his chest, intensifying the throbbing, hellish ache below his belt.

He held her firmly in place with hands that shook.

She subsided and stood quietly against him. She knew now, as she hadn't eight years ago, what was wrong with him. She felt guilty and ashamed for pushing him so far out of control.

Her fingers touched his thick, cool hair lovingly. Her lips found his eyelids and brushed softly against them. He was vulnerable and she wanted to protect him, cherish him.

The tenderness was doing strange things to him. He still wanted her to the point of madness, but those comforting little kisses made his heart warm. He'd never been touched in such a way by a woman; he'd never felt so cherished.

She drew back, and he pulled her close again.

"Don't stop," he whispered, calmer now. His hands had moved up to the silken skin of her back, and he smiled under the whisper of her lips on his skin.

"I'm so sorry," she whispered.

His fingers slid under the blouse again and up to explore the softness of her breasts. "Why?" he asked.

"You were hurting," she said. "I shouldn't have touched you…"

He chuckled wickedly. "I made you."

"I still can't go to bed with you," she said miserably. "I don't care if the whole world does it, I just can't!"

His hands opened and enfolded her breasts tenderly. "You want to," he murmured as he caressed them.

"Of course I want to!" Her eyes closed and she swayed closer to his hands. "Oh, glory," she managed to say tightly, shivering.

"Your breasts are very sensitive," he said at her

lips. "And soft like warm silk under my hands. I'd like to lay you down on my grandfather's desk and take your blouse off and put my lips on you there. But Mrs. Culbertson is making coffee." He lifted his head and looked into her dazed, soft gray eyes. "Thank God," he whispered absently as he searched them.

"Thank God for what?" she asked huskily.

"Miracles, maybe," he replied. He smoothed the blouse up again and his eyes sketched her pretty pink breasts with their hard dark pink crowns. "I could eat you like taffy right now," he said in a rough tone.

The office was so quiet that not a sound could be heard above the shiver of her breath as she looked up at him.

His pale eyes were almost apologetic. "I think I have a death wish," he began huskily as he bent.

She watched his mouth hover over her breast with a sense of shocked wonder. Her eyes wide, her breath stopped in her throat, she waited, trembling.

He looked up, then, and saw her eyes. He made a sound in the back of his throat and his mouth opened as he propelled her closer, so that he had her almost completely in that warm, moist recess.

She wept. The pleasure grew to unbearable heights. Her fingers tangled in his hair and she pulled him closer. She growled sharply at the sensations she felt. Her hips moved involuntarily, searching for his body.

The suction became so sweet that she suddenly arched backward, and would have fallen if it hadn't been for his supporting arm. She caught her breath and convulsed, her body frozen in an arc of pure ecstasy.

He felt the deep contractions of her body under his mouth with raging pride. His mouth grew a little rough, and the convulsions deepened.

Only when he felt her begin to relax did he lift his head and bring her back into a standing position, so that he could look at her face.

She couldn't breathe. She sobbed as she looked up into his pale eyes. The tears came, hot and quick, when she realized what had happened. And he'd seen it!

"Don't," he chided tenderly. He reached for a handkerchief and dried her red eyes and wiped her nose. "Don't be embarrassed."

"I could die of shame," she wept.

"For what?" he asked softly. "For letting me watch you?"

Her face went red. "I never, never…!"

He put a long forefinger against her lips. "I've never seen a woman like that," he whispered. "I've never known one who could be satisfied by a man's mouth suckling at her breast. It was the most beautiful experience I've ever had."

She wasn't crying now. She was staring at him, her eyes wide and soft and curious.

He brushed back her wild hair. "It was worth what I felt earlier," he murmured dryly.

She colored even more. "I can't stay here," she told him wildly. "I have to go away..."

"Hell, no, you don't," he said tersely. "You're not getting away from me a second time. Don't even think about running."

"But," she began urgently.

"But what?" he asked curtly. "But you can't give yourself to me outside marriage? I know that. I'm not asking you to sleep with me."

"It's like torture for you."

"Yes," he said simply. "But the alternative is to never touch you." His hand slid over her blouse and he smiled gently at the immediate response of her body. "I love this," he said gruffly. "And so do you."

She grimaced. "Of course I do," she muttered. "I've never let anyone else touch me like that. It's been eight years since I've even been kissed!"

"Same here," he said bluntly.

"Ha! You've been going around with a divorcée!" she flung at him out of frustration and embarrassment.

"I don't have sex with her," he said.

"They say she's very pretty."

He smiled. "She is. Pretty and elegant and kind.

But I don't feel desire for her, any more than she feels it for me. I told you we were friends. We are. And that's all we are."

"But…but…"

"But what, Dorie?"

"Men don't stop kissing women just because they get turned down once."

"It was much worse than just getting turned down," he told her. "I ran you out of town. It was rough living with that, especially when your father took a few strips off me and told me all about your past. I felt two inches high." His eyes darkened with the pain of the memory. "I hated having made an enemy of him. He was a good man. But I'd never had much interest in marriage or let anyone get as close to me as you did. If you were afraid, so was I."

"Cag said your parents weren't a happy couple."

His eyebrow lifted. "He never talks about them. That's a first."

"He told me to ask you about them."

"I see." He sighed. "Well, I told you a little about that, but we're going to have to talk more about them sooner or later, and about some other things." He lifted his head and listened and then looked down at her with a wicked grin. "But for the present, you'd better fasten your bra and tuck your blouse back in and try to look as if you haven't just made love with me."

"Why?"

"Mrs. Culbertson's coming down the hall."

"Oh, my gosh!"

She fumbled with catches and buttons, her face red, her hair wild as she raced to put herself back together. He snapped his shirt up lazily, his silvery eyes full of mischief as he watched her frantic efforts to improve her appearance.

"Lucky I didn't lay you down on the desk, isn't it?" he said, chuckling.

There was a tap on the half-closed door and Mrs. Culbertson came in with a tray. She was so intent on getting it to the desk intact that she didn't even look at Dorie.

"Here it is. Sorry I took so long, but I couldn't find the cream pitcher."

"Who drinks cream?" Corrigan asked curiously.

"It was the only excuse I could think of," she told him seriously.

He looked uneasy. "Thanks."

She grinned at him and then looked at Dorie. Her eyes were twinkling as she went back out. And this time she closed the door.

Dorie's face was still flushed. Her gray eyes were wide and turbulent. Her mouth was swollen and when she folded her arms over her chest, she flinched.

His eyes went to her blouse and back up again.

"When I felt you going over the edge, it excited me, and I got a little rough. Did I hurt you?"

The question was matter-of-fact, and strangely tender.

She shook her head, averting her eyes. It was embarrassing to remember what had happened.

He caught her hand and led her to the chairs in front of the desk. "Sit down and I'll pour you a cup of coffee."

She looked up at him a little uneasily. "Is something wrong with me, do you think?" she asked with honest concern. "I mean, it's unnatural…isn't it?"

His fingers touched her soft cheek. He shook his head. "People can't be pigeonholed. You might not be that responsive to any other man. Maybe it's waiting so long. Maybe it's that you're perfectly attuned to me. I might be able to accomplish the same thing by kissing your thighs, or your belly."

She flushed. "You wouldn't!"

"Why not?"

The thought of it made her vibrate all over. She knew that men kissed women in intimate places, but she hadn't quite connected it until then.

"The inside of your thighs is very vulnerable to being caressed," he said simply. "Not to mention your back, your hips, your feet," he added with a gentle smile. "Lovemaking is an art. There are no set rules."

She watched him turn and pour coffee into a ceramic cup. He handed it to her and watched the way her fingers deliberately touched his as he drew them away.

He wanted her so much that he could barely stand up straight, but it was early days yet. He had to go slowly this time and not push her too hard. She had a fear not only of him, but of real intimacy. He couldn't afford to let things go too far.

"What sort of things are we going to talk about later?" she asked after she'd finished half her coffee.

"Cabbages and kings," he mused. He sat across from her, his long legs crossed, his eyes possessive and caressing on her face.

"I don't like cabbage and I don't know any kings."

"Then suppose we lie down together on the sofa?"

Her eyes flashed up to see the amusement in his and back down to her cup. "Don't tease. I'm not sophisticated enough for it."

"I'm not teasing."

She sighed and took another sip of coffee. "There's no future in it. You know that."

He didn't know it. She was living in the past, convinced that he had nothing more than an affair in mind for them. He smiled secretively to himself as he thought about the future. Fate had given him a second chance; he wasn't going to waste it.

"About these books," he said in a businesslike tone. "I've made an effort with them, but although I can do math, my penmanship isn't what it should be. If you can't read any of the numbers, circle them and I'll tell you what they are. I have to meet a prospective buyer down at the barn in a few minutes, but I'll be somewhere close by all day."

"All right."

He finished his coffee and put the cup back on the tray, checking his watch. "I'd better go." He looked down at her with covetous eyes and leaned against the arms of her chair to study her. "Let's go dancing tomorrow night."

Her heart jumped. She was remembering how it was when they were close together and her face flushed.

His eyebrow lifted and he grinned. "Don't look so apprehensive. The time to worry is when nothing happens when I hold you."

"It always did," she replied.

He nodded. "Every time," he agreed. "I only had to touch you." He smiled softly. "And vice versa," he added with a wicked glance.

"I was green," she reminded him.

"You still are," he reminded her.

"Not so much," she ventured shyly.

"We both learned something today," he said quietly. "Dorie, if you can be satisfied by so small a caress, try to imagine how it would feel if we went all the way."

Her eyelids flickered. Her breath came like rustling leaves.

He bent and drew his mouth with exquisite tenderness over her parted lips. "Or is that the real problem?" he asked at her mouth. "Are you afraid of the actual penetration?"

Her heart stopped dead and then ran away. "Corrigan!" She ground out his name.

He drew back a breath so that he could see her eyes. He wasn't smiling. It was no joke.

"You'd better tell me," he said quietly.

She drew her lower lip in with her teeth, looking worried.

"I won't tell anyone."

"I know that." She took a long breath. "When my cousin Mary was married, she came to visit us after the honeymoon was over. She'd been so happy and excited." She grimaced. "She said that it hurt awfully bad, that she bled and bled, and he made fun of her because she cried. She said that he didn't even kiss her. He just...pushed into her...!"

He cursed under his breath. "Didn't you talk to anyone else about sex?"

"It wasn't something I could discuss with my

father, and Mary was the only friend I had," she told him. "She said that all the things they write about are just fiction, and that the reality is just like her mother once said—a woman deals with it for the pleasure of children."

He leaned forward on his hands, shaking his head. "I wish you'd told me this eight years ago."

"You'd have laughed," she replied. "You didn't believe I was innocent anyway."

He looked up into her eyes. "I'm sorry," he said heavily. "Life teaches hard lessons."

She thought about her own experience with modeling. "Yes, it does."

He got to his feet and looked down at her with a worried scowl. "Don't you watch hot movies?"

"Those women aren't virgins," she returned.

"No. I don't guess they are." His eyes narrowed as he searched her face. "And I don't know what to tell you. I'd never touched an innocent woman until you came along. Maybe it does hurt. But I promise you, it would only be one time. I know enough to make it good for you. And I would."

"It isn't going to be that way," she reminded him tersely, denying herself the dreams of marriage and children that she'd always connected with him. "We're going to be friends."

He didn't speak. His gaze didn't falter. "I'll check back with you later about the books," he said quietly.

"Okay."

He started to turn, thought better of it and leaned down again with his weight balanced on the chair arms. "Do you remember what happened when I started to suckle you?"

She went scarlet. "Please…"

"It will be like that," he said evenly. "Just like that. You won't think about pain. You may not even notice any. You go in headfirst when I touch you. And I wasn't even taking my time with you today. Think about that. It might help."

He pushed away from her again and went to the desk to pick up his hat. He placed it on his head and smiled at her without mockery.

"Don't let my brothers walk over you," he said. "If one of them gives you any trouble, lay into him with the first hard object you can get your hands on."

"They seem very nice," she said.

"They like you," he replied. "But they have plans."

"Plans?"

"Not to hurt you," he assured her. "You should never have told them you could cook."

"I don't understand."

"Mrs. Culbertson wants to quit. They can't make biscuits. It's what they live for, a plateful of homemade buttered biscuits with half a dozen jars of jam and jelly."

"How does that concern me?"

"Don't you know?" He perched himself against the desk. "They've decided that we should marry you."

"We?"

"We're a family. Mostly we share things. Not women, but we do share cooks." He cocked his head and grinned at her shocked face. "If I marry you, they don't have to worry about where their next fresh biscuit is coming from."

"You don't want to marry me."

"Well, they'll probably find some way around that," he said pointedly.

"They can't force you to marry me."

"I wouldn't make any bets on that," he said. "You don't know them yet."

"You're their brother. They'd want you to be happy."

"They think you'll make me happy."

She lowered her eyes. "You should talk to them."

"And say what? That I don't want you? I don't think they'd believe me."

"I meant, you should tell them that you don't want to get married."

"They've already had a meeting and decided that I do. They've picked out a minister and a dress that they think you'll look lovely in. They've done a rough draft of a wedding invitation…"

"You're out of your mind!"

"No, I'm not." He went to the middle desk drawer,

fumbled through it, pulled it farther out and reached for something pushed to the very back of the desk. He produced it, scanned it, nodded and handed it to her. "Read that."

It was a wedding invitation. Her middle name was misspelled. "It's Ellen, not Ellis."

He reached behind him for a pen, took the invitation back, made the change and handed it back to her.

"Why did you do that?" she asked curiously.

"Oh, they like everything neat and correct."

"Don't correct it! Tear it up!"

"They'll just do another one. The papers will print what's on there, too. You don't want your middle name misspelled several thousand times, do you?"

She was all but gasping for breath. "I don't understand."

"I know. Don't worry about it right now. There's plenty of time. They haven't decided on a definite date yet, anyway."

She stood up, wild-eyed. "You can't let your brothers decide when and who you're going to marry!"

"Well, you go stop them, then," he said easily. "But don't say I didn't tell you so."

He pulled his hat over his eyes and walked out the door, whistling softly to himself.

Chapter Five

First she did the accounts. Her mind was still reeling from Corrigan's ardor, and she had to be collected when she spoke to his brothers. She deciphered his scribbled numbers, balanced the books, checked her figures and put down a total.

They certainly weren't broke, and there was enough money in the account to feed Patton's Third Army. She left them a note saying so, amused at the pathetic picture they'd painted of their finances. Probably, the reason for that was part of their master plan.

She went outside to look for them after she'd done the books. They were all four in the barn, standing close together. They stopped talking the minute she came into view, and she knew for certain that they'd been talking about her.

"I'm not marrying him," she told them clearly, and pointed at Corrigan.

"Okay," Leo said easily.

"The thought never crossed my mind," Rey remarked.

Cag just shrugged.

Corrigan grinned.

"I'm through with the books," she said uneasily. "I want to go home now."

"You haven't eaten lunch," Rey said.

"It's only eleven o'clock," she said pointedly.

"We have an early lunch, because we work until dark," Cag volunteered.

"Mrs. Culbertson just left," Rey said. He sighed. "She put some beef and gravy in the oven to warm. But she didn't make us any biscuits."

"We don't have anything to put gravy on," Leo agreed.

"Can't work all afternoon without a biscuit," Cag said, nodding.

Corrigan grinned.

Dorie had thought that Corrigan was making up that story about the brothers' mania for biscuits. Apparently it was the gospel truth.

"Just one pan full," Leo coaxed. "It wouldn't take

five minutes." He eyed her warily. "If you can really make them. Maybe you can't. Maybe you were just saying you could, to impress us."

"That's right," Rey added.

"I can make biscuits," she said, needled. "You just point me to the kitchen and I'll show you."

Leo grinned. "Right this way!"

Half an hour later, the pan of biscuits were gone so fast that they might have disintegrated. Leo and Corrigan were actually fighting over the last one, pulled it apart in their rush, and ended up splitting it while the other two sat there gloating. They'd had more than their share because they had faster hands.

"Next time, you've got to make two pans," Corrigan told her. "One doesn't fill Leo's hollow tooth."

"I noticed," she said, surprisingly touched by the way they'd eaten her biscuits with such enjoyment. "I'll make you a pan of rolls to go with them next time."

"Rolls?" Leo looked faint. *"You can make homemade rolls?"*

"I'll see about the wedding rings right now," Rey said, wiping his mouth and pushing away from the table.

"I've got the corrected invitation in my pocket," Cag murmured as he got up, too.

Leo joined the other two at the door. "They said they can get the dress here from Paris in two weeks," Leo said.

Dorie gaped at them. But before she could say a word, all three of them had rushed out the door and closed it, talking animatedly among themselves.

"But, I didn't say…!" she exclaimed.

"There, there," Corrigan said, deftly adding another spoonful of gravy to his own remaining half of a biscuit. "It's all right. They forgot to call the minister and book him."

Just at that moment, the door opened and Leo stuck his head in. "Are you Methodist, Baptist or Presbyterian?" he asked her.

"I'm…Presbyterian," she faltered.

He scowled. "Nearest Presbyterian minister is in Victoria," he murmured thoughtfully, "but don't worry, I'll get him here." He closed the door.

"Just a minute!" she called.

The doors of the pickup closed three times. The engine roared. "Too late," Corrigan said imperturbably.

"But didn't you hear him?" she burst out. "For heaven's sake, they're going to get a minister!"

"Hard to get married in church without one," he insisted. He gestured toward her plate with a fork to the remaining chunk of beef. “Don’t waste that. It’s one of our own steers. Corn fed, no hormones, no antibiotics, no insecticides. We run a clean, environmentally safe operation here.”

She was diverted. “Really?”

“We’re renegades,” he told her. “They groan when they see us coming at cattle conventions. Usually we go with Donavan. He’s just like us about cattle. He and the Ballenger brothers have gone several rounds over cattle prods and feed additives. He’s mellowed a bit since his nephew came to live with him and he got married. But he likes the way we do things.”

“I guess so.” She savored the last of the beef. “It’s really good.”

“Beats eating pigs,” he remarked, and grinned.

She burst out laughing. “Your brother Cag had plenty to say on that subject.”

“He only eats beef or fish. He won’t touch anything that comes from a pig. He says it’s because he doesn’t like the taste.” He leaned forward conspiratorially. “But I say it’s because of that movie he went to see. He used to love a nice ham.”

“What movie?”

“The one with the talking pig.”

“Cag went to see *that?*”

“He likes cartoons and sentimental movies.” He shrugged. “Odd, isn’t it? He’s the most staid of us. To look at him, you’d never know he had a sense of humor or that he was sentimental. He's like the others in his lack of conventional good looks, though. Most women can't get past that big nose and those eyes."

"A cobra with a rabbit," she said without thinking.

He chuckled. "Exactly."

"Does he hate women as much as the rest of you?"

"Hard to tell. You haven't seen him in a tuxedo at a social bash. Women, really beautiful women, followed him around all night dropping their room keys at his feet."

"What did he do?"

"Kept walking."

She put down her fork. "What do you do?"

He smiled mockingly. "They don't drop room keys at my feet anymore. The limp puts them off."

"Baloney," she said. "You're the handsomest of the four, and it isn't just looks."

He leaned back in his chair to look at her. His eyes narrowed thoughtfully. "Does the limp bother you?"

"Don't be ridiculous," she said, lifting her gaze. "Why should it?"

"I can't dance very well anymore."

She smiled. "I don't ever go to dances."

"Why not?"

She sipped coffee. "I don't like men touching me."

His eyes changed. "You like me touching you."

"You aren't a stranger," she said simply.

"Maybe I am," he murmured quietly. "What do you know about me?"

She stared at him. "Well, you're thirty-six, you're a rancher, you've never married, you come from San Antonio."

"And?"

"I don't know any more than that," she said slowly.

"We were a couple for several weeks before you left town. Is that all you learned?"

"You were always such a private person," she reminded him. "You never talked about yourself or your brothers. And we never really talked that much when we were together."

"We spent more time kissing," he recalled. "I was too wrapped up in trying to get you into bed to care how well we knew each other," he said with self-contempt. "I wasted a lot of time."

"You said that we shouldn't look back."

"I'm trying not to. It's hard, sometimes." He moved forward to take her hands under his on the table. "I like classical music, but I'm just as happy with country or pop. I like a good chess game. I enjoy science fiction movies and old Westerns, the silent kind. I'm an early riser, I work hard and I don't cheat on my tax returns. I went to college to learn animal husbandry, but I never graduated."

She smiled. "Do you like fried liver?"

He made a horrible face. "Do you?"

She made the same face. "But I don't like sweets very much, either," she said, remembering that he didn't.

"Good thing. Nobody around here eats them."

"I remember." She looked around at the comfortably big kitchen. There was a new electric stove and a huge refrigerator, flanked by an upright freezer. The sink was a double stainless-steel one, with a window above it overlooking the pasture where the colts were kept. Next to that was a dishwasher. There was plenty of cabinet space, too.

"Like it?" he asked.

She smiled. "It's a dream of a kitchen. I'll bet Mrs. Culbertson loves working in here."

"Would you?"

She met his eyes and felt her own flickering at the intensity of his stare.

"If you can make homemade bread, you have to be an accomplished cook," he continued. "There's a high-tech mixer in the cabinet, and every gourmet tool known to man. Or woman."

"It's very modern."

"It's going to be very deserted in about three weeks," he informed.

"Why is Mrs. Culbertson quitting?"

"Her husband has cancer, and she wants to retire and stay at home with him, for as long as he's got," he said abruptly. He toyed with his coffee cup. "They've been married for fifty years." He took a sharp breath, and his eyes were very dark as they met hers. "I've believed all my life that no marriage could possibly last longer than a few years. People change. Situations change. Jobs conflict." He shrugged. "Then Mrs. Culbertson came here to work, with her husband. And I had to eat my words." He lowered his eyes back to the cup. "They were forever holding hands, helping each other, walking in the early morning together and talking. She smiled at him, and she was beautiful. He smiled back. Nobody had to say that they loved each other. It was obvious."

"My parents were like that," she recalled. "Dad and Mom loved each other terribly. When she died, I almost lost him, too. He lived for me. But the last thing he said on his deathbed—" she swallowed, fighting tears "—was her name."

He got up from the table abruptly and went to the window over the sink. He leaned against it, breathing heavily, as if what she'd said had affected him powerfully. And, in fact, it had.

She watched him through tears. "You don't like hearing about happy marriages. Why?"

"Because I had that same chance once," he said in a low, dull tone. "And I threw it away."

She wondered who the woman had been. Nobody had said that any of the Hart brothers had ever been engaged. But there could have been someone she hadn't heard about.

"You're the one who keeps saying we can't look back," she remarked, dabbing her eyes with her napkin.

"It's impossible not to. The past makes us the people we are." He sighed wearily. "My parents had five of us in ten years. My mother hadn't wanted the first child. She didn't have a choice. He took away her checkbook and kept her pregnant. She hated him and us in equal measure. When she left it was almost a relief." He turned and looked across the room at her. "I've never been held with tenderness. None of us have. It's why we're the way we are, it's why we don't have women around. The only thing we know about women is that they're treacherous and cold and cruel."

"Oh, Corrigan," she said softly, wincing.

His eyes narrowed. "Desire is a hot and unmanageable thing. Sex can be pleasant enough. But I'd gladly be impotent to have a woman hold me the way you did in my office and kiss my eyes." His face went as hard as stone. "You can't imagine how it felt."

"But I can," she replied. She smiled. "You kissed my eyes."

"Yes."

He looked so lost, so lonely. She got up from the table and went to him, paused in front of him. Her hands pressed gently against his broad chest as she looked up into his eyes.

"You know more about me than I've ever told anyone else," he said quietly. "Now don't you think it's time you told me what happened to you in New York?"

She sighed worriedly. She'd been ashamed to tell him how stupid she'd been. But now there was a bigger reason. It was going to hurt him. She didn't understand how she knew it, but she did. He was going to blame himself all over again for the way they'd separated.

"Not now," she said.

"You're holding back. Don't let's have secrets between us," he said solemnly.

"It will hurt," she said.

"Most everything does, these days," he murmured, and rubbed his thigh.

She took his hand and held it warmly. "Come and sit down."

"Not in here."

He drew her into the living room. It was warm

and dim and quiet. He led her to his big armchair, dropped into it and pulled her down into his arms.

"Now, tell me," he said, when her cheek was pillowed on his hard chest.

"It's not a nice story."

"Tell me."

She rubbed her hand against his shirt and closed her eyes. "I found an ad in the paper. It was one of those big ads that promise the stars, just the thing to appeal to a naive country girl who thinks she can just walk into a modeling career. I cut out the ad and called the number."

"And?"

She grimaced. "It was a scam, but I didn't know it at first. The man seemed very nice, and he had a studio in a good part of town. Belinda had gone to Europe for the week on an assignment for the magazine where she worked, and I didn't know anyone else to ask about it. I assumed that it was legitimate." Her eyes closed and she pressed closer, feeling his arm come around her tightly, as if he knew she was seeking comfort.

"Go ahead," he coaxed gently.

"He gave me a few things to try on and he took pictures of me wearing them. But then I was sitting there, just in a two-piece bathing suit, and he told me to take it off." His breathing stilled under her ear. "I couldn't," she snapped. "I just couldn't let him look at me like that, no matter how good a job I could get, and I said so. Then he got ugly. He told me that he was in the business of producing nude calendars and that if I didn't do the assignment, he'd take me to court and sue me for not fulfilling the contract I'd signed. No, I didn't read it," she said when he asked. "The fine print did say that I agreed to pose in any manner the photographer said for me to. I knew that I couldn't afford a lawsuit."

"And?" He sounded as cold as ice.

She bit her lower lip. "While I was thinking about alternatives, he laughed and came toward me. I could forget the contract, he said, if I was that prudish. But he'd have a return for the time he'd wasted on me. He said that he was going to make me sleep with him."

"Good God!"

She smoothed his shirt, trying to calm him. Tears stung her eyes. "I fought him, but I wasn't strong enough. He had me undressed before I knew it. We struggled there on the floor and he started hitting me." Her voice broke and she felt Corrigan stiffen against her. "He had a diamond ring on his right hand. That's how he cut my cheek. I didn't even feel it until much later. He wore me down to the point that I couldn't kick or bite or scream. I would never have been able to get away. But one of his girls, one of the ones who didn't mind posing nude, came into the studio. She was his lover and she was furious when she saw him with me…like that. She started screaming and throwing things at him. I grabbed my clothes and ran."

She shivered even then with the remembered humiliation, the fear that he was going to come after her. "I managed to get enough on to look halfway decent, and I walked all the way back to Belinda's apartment." She swallowed. "When I was rational enough to talk, I called the police. They arrested him and charged him with attempted rape. But he said that I'd signed a contract and I wasn't happy with the money he offered me, and that I'd only yelled rape because I wanted to back out of the deal."

He bit off a curse. "And then what?"

"He won," she said in a flat, defeated tone. "He had friends and influence. But the story was a big deal locally for two or three days, and he was furious. His brother had a nasty temper and he started making obscene phone calls to me and making threats as well. I didn't want to put Belinda in any danger, so I moved out while she was still in Europe and never told her a thing about what had happened. I got a job in New Jersey and worked there for two years. Then Belinda moved out to Long Island and asked me to come back. There was a good job going with a law firm that had an office pretty close to her house. I had good typing skills by then, so I took it."

"What about the brother?" he asked.

"He didn't know where to find me. I learned later that he and the photographer were having trouble with the police about some pornography ring they were involved in. Ironically they both went to prison soon after I left Manhattan. But for a long time, I was even afraid to come home, in case they had anyone watching me. I was afraid for my father."

"You poor kid," he said heavily. "Good God! And after what had happened here…" His teeth ground together as he remembered what he'd done to her.

"Don't," she said gently, smoothing out the frown between his heavy eyebrows. "I never blamed you. Never!"

He caught her hand and brought it to his mouth. "I wanted to come after you," he said. "Your father stopped me. He said that you hated the very mention of my name."

"I did, at first, but only because I was so hurt by the way things had worked out." She looked at his firm chin. "But I would have been glad to see you, just the same."

"I wasn't sure of that." He traced her mouth. "I thought that it might be as well to leave things the way they were. You were so young, and I was wary of complications in my life just then." He sighed softly. "There's one other thing you don't know about me."

"Can't you tell me?"

He smiled softly. "We're sharing our deepest secrets. I suppose I might as well. We have a fifth brother. His name is Simon."

"You mentioned him the first time you came over, with that bouquet."

He nodded. "He's in San Antonio. Just after you left town, he was in a wreck and afterward, in a coma. We couldn't all go back, and leave the ranch to itself. So I went. It was several weeks before I could leave him. By the time I got back, you weren't living with Belinda anymore and I couldn't make her tell me where you were. Soon after that, your father came down on my head like a brick and I lost heart."

"You called Belinda?"

"Yes."

"You wanted to find me?"

He searched her eyes quietly. "I wanted to know that you were safe, that I hadn't hurt you too badly. At least I found that much out. I didn't hope for more."

She traced his eyebrows, lost in the sudden intimacy. "I dreamed about you," she said. "But every time, you'd come toward me and I'd wake up."

He traced the artery in her throat down to her collarbone. "My dreams were a bit more erotic." His eyes darkened. "I had you in ways and places you can't imagine, each more heated than the one before. I couldn't wait to go to bed, so that I could have you again."

She blushed. "At first, you mean, just after I left."

His hand smoothed onto her throat. "For eight years. Every night of my life."

She caught her breath. She could hardly get it at all. His eyes were glittering with feeling. "All that time?"

He nodded. He looked at her soft throat where the blouse had parted, and his face hardened. His fingers trailed lightly down onto her bodice, onto her breast. "I haven't touched a woman since you left Jacobsville," he said huskily. "I haven't been a man since then."

Her wide eyes filled with tears. She had a good idea of what it would be like for a man like Corrigan to be incapable with a woman. "Was it because we fought, at the last?"

"It was because we made love," he whispered. "Have you forgotten what we did?"

She averted her eyes, hiding them in embarrassment.

"You left a virgin," he said quietly, "but only technically. We had each other in your bed," he reminded her, "naked in each other's arms. We did everything except go those last few aching inches. Your body was almost open to me, I was against you, we were moving together…and you cried out when you felt me there. You squirmed out from under me and ran."

"I was so afraid," she whispered shamefully. "It hurt, and I kept remembering what I'd been told..."

"It wouldn't have hurt for long," he said gently. "And it wouldn't have been traumatic, not for you. But you didn't know that, and I was too excited to coax you. I lost my temper instead of reassuring you. And we spent so many years apart, suffering for it."

She laid her hot cheek against his chest and closed her eyes. "I didn't want to remember how far we went," she said through a mist. "I hurt you terribly when I drew back..."

"Not that much," he said. "We'd made love in so many ways already that I wasn't that hungry." He smoothed her soft hair. "I wanted an excuse to make you leave."

"Why?"

His lips touched her hair. "Because I wanted to make you pregnant," he whispered, feeling her body jump as he said it. "And it scared me to death. You see, modern women don't want babies, because they're a trap. My mother taught me that."

Chapter Six

"That's not true!" She pressed closer. "I would have loved having a baby, and I'd never have felt trapped!" she said, her voice husky with feeling. Especially your baby, she added silently. "I didn't know any of your background, especially anything about your mother. You never told me."

His chest rose and fell abruptly. "I couldn't. You scared me to death. Maybe I deliberately upset you, to make you run. But when I got what I thought I wanted, I didn't want it. It hurt when you wouldn't even look at me, at the bus stop. I guess I'd shamed you so badly that you couldn't." He sighed. "I thought you were modern, that we'd enjoy each other and that would be the end of it. I got the shock of my life that last night. I couldn't even deal with it. I lost my head."

She lifted her face and looked into his eyes. "You were honest about it. You'd already said that you wanted no part of marriage or a family, that all you could offer me was a night in your arms with no strings attached. But I couldn't manage to stop, or stop you, until the very last. I was raised to think of sleeping around as a sin."

His face contorted. He averted his eyes to keep her from seeing the pain in them. "I didn't know that until it was much too late. Sometimes, you don't realize how much things mean to you until you lose them."

His fingers moved gently in her hair while she stood quietly, breathing uneasily. "It wasn't just our mother who soured us on women. Simon was married," he said after a minute. "He was the only one of us who ever was. His wife got pregnant the first time they were together, but she didn't want a child. She didn't really want Simon, she just wanted to be rich. He was crazy about her." He sighed painfully. "She had an abortion and he found out later, accidentally. They had a fight on the way home from one of her incessant parties. He wrecked the car, she died and he lost an arm. That's why he doesn't live on the ranch. He can't do the things he used to do. He's embittered and he's withdrawn from the rest of us." He laughed a little. "You think the four of us hate women. You should see Simon."

She stirred in his arms. "Poor man. He must have loved her very much."

"Too much. That's another common problem we seem to have. We love irrationally and obsessively."

"And reluctantly," she guessed.

He laughed. "And that."

He let her go with a long sigh and stared down at her warmly. "I suppose I'd better take you home. If you're still here when the boys get back, they'll tie you to the stove."

She smiled. "I like your brothers." She hesitated. "Corrigan, they aren't really going to try to force you to marry me, are they?"

"Of course not," he scoffed. "They're only teasing."

"Okay."

It was a good thing, he thought, that she couldn't see his fingers crossed behind his back.

He took her home, pausing to kiss her gently at the front door.

"I'll be along tomorrow night," he said softly. "We'll go to a movie. There's a new one every Saturday night at the Roxy downtown."

She searched his eyes and tried to decide if he was doing this because he wanted to or because his brothers were pestering him.

He smiled. "Don't worry so much. You're home, it's going to be Christmas, you have a job and plenty of friends. It's going to be the best Christmas you've ever had."

She smiled back. "Maybe it will be," she said, catching some of his own excitement. Her gaze caressed his face. They were much more like friends, with all the dark secrets out in the open. But his kisses had made her too hungry for him. She needed time to get her emotions under control. Perhaps a day would do it. He was throwing out broad hints of some sort, but he hadn't spoken one word of love. In that respect, nothing had changed.

"Good night, then," he said.

"Good night."

She closed the door and turned on the lights. It had been a strange and wonderful day. Somehow, the future looked unusually bright, despite all her worries.

The next morning, Dorie had to go into town to Clarisse's shop to help her with the bookkeeping. It was unfortunate that when she walked in, a beautiful woman in designer clothes should be standing at the counter, discussing Corrigan.

"It's going to be the most glorious Christmas ever!" she was telling the other woman, pushing back her red-gold hair and laughing. "Corrigan is taking me to the Christmas party at the Coltrains' house, and afterward we're going to Christmas Eve services at the Methodist Church." She sighed. "I'm glad to be home. You know, there's been some talk about Corrigan and a woman from his past who just came back recently. I asked him about it, if he was serious about her." She laughed gaily. "He said that he was just buttering her up so that she'd do some bookkeeping for him and the brothers, that she'd run out on him once and he didn't have any intention of letting her get close enough to do it again. I told him that I could find it in my heart to feel sorry for her, and he said that he didn't feel sorry for her at all, that he had plans for her…"

Clarisse spotted Dorie and caught her breath. "Why, Dorothy, I wasn't expecting you…quite so soon!"

"I thought I'd say hello," Dorie said, frozen in the doorway. She managed a pasty smile. "I'll come back Monday. Have a nice weekend."

"Who was that?" she heard the other woman say as she went quickly back out the door and down the street to where she'd parked the car Turkey Sanders had returned early in the morning, very nicely fixed.

She got behind the wheel, her fingers turning white as she gripped it. She could barely see for the tears. She started the engine with shaking fingers and backed out into the street. She heard someone call to her and saw the redhead standing on the sidewalk, with an odd expression on her face, trying to get Dorie's attention.

She didn't look again. She put the car into gear and sped out of town.

She didn't go straight home. She went to a small park inside the city and sat down among the gay lights and decorations with a crowd that had gathered for a Christmas concert performed by the local high-school band and chorus. There were so many people that one more didn't matter, and her tears weren't as noticeable in the crush of voices.

The lovely, familiar carols were oddly soothing. But her Christmas spirit was absent. How could she have trusted Corrigan? She was falling in love all over again, and he was setting her up for a fall. She'd never believe a word he said, ever again. And now that she'd had a look at his beautiful divorcée, she knew she wouldn't have a chance with him. That woman was exquisite, from her creamy skin to her perfect figure and face. The only surprising thing was that he hadn't married her years ago. Surely a woman like that wouldn't hang around waiting, when she could have any man she wanted.

Someone offered her a cup of hot apple cider, and she managed a smile and thanked the child who held it out to her. It was spicy and sweet and tasted good against the chill. She sipped it, thinking how horrible it was going to be from now on, living in Jacobsville with Corrigan only a few miles away and that woman hanging on his arm. He hadn't mentioned anything about Christmas to Dorie, but apparently he had his plans all mapped out if he was taking the merry divorcée to a party. When had he been going to tell her the truth? Or had he been going to let her find it out all for herself?

She couldn't remember ever feeling quite so bad.

She finished the cider, listened to one more song and then got up and walked through the crowd, down the long sidewalk to where she'd parked her car. She sat in it for a moment, trying to decide what to do. It was Saturday and she had nothing planned for today. She wasn't going to go home. She couldn't bear the thought of going home.

She turned the car and headed up to the interstate, on the road to Victoria.

Corrigan paced up and down Dorie's front porch for an hour until he realized that she wasn't coming home. He drove back to town and pulled up in front of Tira Beck's brick house.

She came out onto the porch, in jeans and a sweatshirt, her glorious hair around her shoulders. Her arms were folded and she looked concerned. Her frantic phone call had sent him flying over to Dorie's house hours before he was due to pick her up for the movie. Now it looked as if the movie, and anything else, was off.

"Well?" she asked.

He shook his head, with his hands deep in his jacket pockets. "She wasn't there. I waited for an hour. There's no note on the door, no nothing."

Tira sighed miserably. "It's all my fault. Me and my big mouth. I had no idea who she was, and I didn't know that what I was telling Clarisse was just a bunch of bull that you'd handed me to keep me from seeing how much you cared for the woman."

She looked up accusingly. "See what happens when you lie to your friends?"

"You didn't have to tell her that!"

"I didn't know she was there! And we had agreed to go to the Coltrains' party together, you and me and Charles Percy."

"You didn't mention that you had a date for it, I guess?" he asked irritably.

"No. I didn't realize anyone except Clarisse was listening, and she already knew I was going with Charles."

He tilted his hat farther over his tired eyes. "God, the webs we weave," he said heavily. "She's gone and I don't know where to look for her. She might have gone back to New York for all I know, especially after yesterday. She had every reason to think I was dead serious about her until this morning."

Tira folded her arms closer against the cold look he shot her. "I said I'm sorry," she muttered. "I tried to stop her and tell her that she'd misunderstood me about the party, that I wasn't your date. But she wouldn't even look at me. I'm not sure she saw me. She was crying."

He groaned aloud.

"Oh, Corrigan, I'm sorry," she said gently. "Simon always says you do everything the hard way. I guess he knows you better than the others."

He glanced at her curiously. "When have you seen Simon?"

"At the cattle convention in San Antonio last week. I sold a lot of my Montana herd there."

"And he actually spoke to you?"

She smiled wistfully. "He always speaks to me," she said. "I don't treat him like an invalid. He feels comfortable with me."

He gave her an intent look. "He wouldn't if he knew how you felt about him."

Her eyes narrowed angrily. "I'm not telling him. And neither are you! If he wants me to be just a friend, I can settle for that. It isn't as if I'm shopping for a new husband. One was enough," she added curtly.

"Simon was always protective about you," he recalled. "Even before you married."

"He pushed me at John," she reminded him.

"Simon was married when he met you."

Her expression closed. She didn't say a word, but it was there, in her face. She'd hated Simon's wife, and the feeling had been mutual. Simon had hated her husband, too. But despite all the turbulence between Tira and Simon, there had never been a hint of infidelity while they were both married. Now, it was as if they couldn't get past their respective bad marriages to really look at each other romantically. Tira loved Simon, although no one except Corrigan knew it. But Simon kept secrets. No one was privy to them anymore, not even his own brothers. He kept to himself in San Antonio. Too much, sometimes.

Tira was watching him brood. "Why don't you file a missing persons report?" she suggested suddenly.

"I have to wait twenty-four hours. She could be in Alaska by then." He muttered under his breath. "I guess I could hire a private detective to look for her."

She gave him a thoughtful look and her eyes twinkled. "I've got a better idea. Why not tell your brothers she's gone missing?"

His eyebrows lifted, and hope returned. "Now that's a constructive suggestion," he agreed, nodding, and he began to grin. "They were already looking forward to homemade biscuits every morning. They'll be horrified!"

And they were. It was amazing, the looks that he got from his own kinfolk when he mentioned that their prized biscuit maker had gone missing.

"It's your fault," Rey said angrily. "You should have proposed to her."

"I thought you guys had all that taken care of," Corrigan said reasonably. "The rings, the minister, the gown, the invitations..."

"Everything except the most important part," Cag told him coldly.

"Oh, that. Did we forget to tell her that he loved her?" Leo asked sharply. "Good Lord, we did! No wonder she left!" He glared at his brother. "You could have told her yourself if you hadn't been chewing on your hurt pride. And speaking of pride, why didn't you tell Tira the truth instead of hedging your bets with a bunch of lies?"

"Because Tira has a big mouth and I didn't want the whole town to know I was dying of unrequited love for Dorie!" he raged. "She doesn't want to marry me. She said so! A man has to have a little pride to cling to!"

"Pride and those sort of biscuits don't mix," Rey stressed. "We've got to get her back. Okay, boys, who do we know in the highway patrol? Better yet, don't we know at least one Texas Ranger? Those boys can track anybody! Let's pool resources here…"

Watching them work, Corrigan felt relieved for himself and just a little sorry for Dorie. She wouldn't stand a chance.

She didn't, either. A tall, good-looking man with black hair wearing a white Stetson and a Texas Ranger's star on his uniform knocked at the door of her motel room in Victoria. When she answered it, he tipped his hat politely, smiled and put her in handcuffs.

They were halfway back to Jacobsville, her hastily packed suitcase and her purse beside her, before she got enough breath back to protest.

"But why have you arrested me?" she demanded.

"Why?" He thought for a minute and she saw him scowl in the rearview mirror. "Oh, I remember. Cattle rustling." He nodded. "Yep, that's it. Cattle rustling." He glanced at her in the rearview mirror.

"You see, rustling is a crime that cuts across county lines, which gave me the authority to arrest you."

"Whose cattle have I rustled?" she demanded impertinently.

"The Hart Brothers filed the charges."

"Hart...Corrigan Hart?" She made a furious sound under her breath. "No. Not Corrigan. Them. It was them! Them and their damned biscuits! It's a put-up job," she exclaimed. "They've falsely accused me so that they can get me back into their kitchen!"

He chuckled at the way she phrased it. The Hart brothers and their mania for biscuits was known far and wide. "No, ma'am, I can swear to that," he told her. His twinkling black eyes shone out of a lean, darkly tanned face. His hair was black, too, straight and thick under that wide-brimmed white hat. "They showed me where it was."

"It?"

"The bull you rustled. His stall was empty, all right."

Her eyes bulged. "Didn't you look for him on the ranch?"

"Yes, ma'am," he assured her with a wide smile. "I looked. But the stall was empty, and they said he'd be in it if he hadn't been rustled. That was a million-dollar bull, ma'am." He shook his head. "They could shoot you for that. This is Texas, you know. Cattle rustling is a very serious charge."

"How could I rustle a bull? Do you have any idea how much a bull weighs?" She was sounding hysterical. She calmed down. "All right. If I took that bull, where was he?"

"Probably hidden in your room, ma'am. I plan to phone back when we get to the Hart place and have the manager search it," he assured her. His rakish grin widened. "Of course, if he doesn't find a bull in your room, that will probably mean that I can drop the charges."

"Drop them, the devil!" she flared, blowing a wisp of platinum hair out of her eyes. "I'll sue the whole damned state for false arrest!"

He chuckled at her fury. "Sorry. You can't. I had probable cause."

"What probable cause?"

He glanced at her in the rearview mirror with a rakish grin. "You had a hamburger for lunch, didn't you, ma'am?"

She was openly gasping by now. The man was a lunatic. He must be a friend of the brothers, that was the only possible explanation. She gave up arguing, because she couldn't win. But she was going to do some serious damage to four ugly men when she got back to Jacobsville.

The ranger pulled up in front of the Harts' ranch house and all four of them came tumbling out of the living room and down to the driveway. Every one of them was smiling except Corrigan.

"Thanks, Colton," Leo said, shaking the ranger's

hand. "I don't know what we'd have done without you."

The man called Colton got out and opened the back seat to extricate a fuming, muttering Dorie. She glared at the brothers with eyes that promised retribution as her handcuffs were removed and her suitcase and purse handed to her.

"We found the bull," Cag told the ranger. "He'd strayed just out behind the barn. Sorry to have put you to this trouble. We'll make our own apologies to Miss Wayne, here."

Colton stared at the fuming ex-prisoner with pursed lips. "Good luck," he told them.

Dorie didn't know where to start. She looked up at Colton and wondered how many years she could get for kicking a Texas Ranger's shin.

Reading that intent in her eyes, he chuckled and climbed back into his car. "Tell Simon I said hello," he called to them. "We miss seeing him around the state capital now that he's given up public office."

"I'll tell him," Cag promised.

That barely registered as he drove away with a wave of his hand, leaving Dorie alone with the men.

"Nice to see you again, Miss Wayne," Cag said, tipping his hat. "Excuse me. Cows to feed."

"Fences to mend," Leo added, grinning as he followed Cag's example.

"Right. Me, too." Rey tipped his own hat and lit out after his brothers.

Which left Corrigan to face the music, and it was all furious discord and bass.

She folded her arms over her breasts and glared at him.

"It was their idea," he said pointedly.

"Arrested for rustling. Me! He…that man…that Texas Ranger tried to infer that I had a bull hidden in my motel room, for God's sake! He handcuffed me!" She held up her wrists to show them to him.

"He probably felt safer that way," he remarked, observing her high color and furious face.

"I want to go home! Right now!"

He could see that it would be useless to try to talk to her. He only made one small effort. "Tira's sorry," he said quietly. "She wanted to tell you that she's going to the Coltrains' party with Charles Percy. I was going to drive, that's all. I'd planned to take you with me."

"I heard all about your 'plan.'"

The pain in her eyes was hard to bear. He averted his gaze. "You'd said repeatedly that you wanted no part of me," he said curtly. "I wasn't about to let people think I was dying of love for you."

"Wouldn't that be one for the record books?" she said furiously.

His gaze met hers evenly. "I'll get Joey to drive you home."

He turned and walked away, favoring his leg a little. She watched him with tears in her eyes. It was just too much for one weekend.

* * *

Joey drove her home and she stayed away from the ranch. Corrigan was back to doing the books himself, because she wouldn't. Her pride was raw, and so was his. It looked like a complete stalemate.

"We've got to do something," Cag said on Christmas Eve, as Corrigan sat in the study all by himself in the dark. "It's killing him. He won't even talk about going to the Coltrains' party."

"I'm not missing it," Leo said. "They've got five sets of Lionel electric trains up and running on one of the most impressive layouts in Texas."

"Your brother is more important than trains," Rey said grimly. "What are we going to do?"

Cag's dark eyes began to twinkle. "I think we should bring him a Christmas present."

"What sort of present?" Rey asked.

"A biscuit maker," Cag said.

Leo chuckled. "I'll get a bow."

"I'll get out the truck," Rey said, shooting out the front door.

"Shhh!" Cag called to them. "It wouldn't do to let him know what we're up to. We've already made one monumental mistake."

They nodded and moved more stealthily.

Corrigan was nursing a glass of whiskey. He heard the truck leave and come back about an hour later, but he wasn't really interested in what his brothers were doing. They'd probably gone to the Christmas party over at Coltrain's ranch.

He was still sitting in the dark when he heard curious muffled sounds and a door closing.

He got up and went out into the hall. His brothers looked flushed and flustered and a little mussed. They looked at him, wide-eyed. Leo was breathing hard, leaning against the living-room door.

"What are you three up to now?" he demanded.

"We put your Christmas present in there," Leo said, indicating the living room. "We're going to let you open it early."

"It's something nice," Cag told him.

"And very useful," Leo agreed.

Rey heard muffled noises getting louder. "Better let him get in there. I don't want to have to run it down again."

"Run it down?" Corrigan cocked his head. "What the hell have you got in there? Not another rattler…!"

"Oh, it's not that dangerous," Cag assured him. He frowned. "Well, not quite that dangerous." He moved forward, extricated Leo from the door and opened it, pushing Corrigan inside. "Merry Christmas," he added, and locked the door.

Corrigan noticed two things at once—that the door was locked, and that a gunnysack tied with a ribbon was sitting in a chair struggling like crazy.

Outside the door, there were muffled voices.

"Oh, God," he said apprehensively.

He untied the red ribbon that had the top securely tied, and out popped a raging mad Dorothy Wayne.

"I'll kill them!" she yelled.

Big booted feet ran for safety out in the hall.

Corrigan started laughing and couldn't stop. Honest to God, his well-meaning brothers were going to be the death of him.

"I hate them, I hate this ranch, I hate Jacobsville, I hate you...*mmmfff!*"

He stopped the furious tirade with his mouth. Amazing how quickly she calmed down when his arms went around her and he eased her gently out of the chair and down onto the long leather couch.

She couldn't get enough breath to continue. His mouth was open and hungry on her lips and his body was as hard as hers was soft as it moved restlessly against her.

She felt his hands on her hips and, an instant later, he was lying between her thighs, moving in a tender, achingly soft rhythm that made her moan.

"I love you," he whispered before she could get a word out.

And then she didn't want to get a word out.

His hands were inside her blouse and he was fighting his way under her skirt when they dimly heard a key turn in the lock.

The door opened and three pair of shocked, delighted eyes peered in.

"You monsters!" she said with the last breath

she had. She was in such a state of disarray that she couldn't manage anything else. Their position was so blatant that there was little use in pretending that they were just talking.

"That's no way to talk to your brothers-in-law," Leo stated. "The wedding's next Saturday, by the way." He smiled apologetically. "We couldn't get the San Antonio symphony orchestra to come, because they have engagements, but we did get the governor to give you away. He'll be along just before the ceremony." He waved a hand at them and grinned. "Carry on, don't mind us."

Corrigan fumbled for a cushion and flung it with all his might at the door. It closed. Outside, deep chuckles could be heard.

Dorie looked up into Corrigan's steely gray eyes with wonder. "Did he say the governor's going to give me away? Our governor? The governor of Texas?"

"The very one."

"But, how?"

"The governor's a friend of ours. Simon worked with him until the wreck, when he retired from public office. Don't you ever read a newspaper?"

"I guess not."

"Never mind. Just forget about all the details." He bent to her mouth. "Now, where were we…?"

The wedding was the social event of the year. The governor did give her away; along with all four brothers, including the tall, darkly distinguished

Simon, who wore an artificial arm just for the occasion. Dorie was exquisite in a Paris gown designed especially for her by a well-known couturier. Newspapers sent representatives. The whole world seemed to form outside the little Presbyterian church in Victoria.

"I can't believe this," she whispered to Corrigan as they were leaving on their Jamaica honeymoon. "Corrigan, that's the vice president over there, standing beside the governor and Simon!"

"Well, they sort of want Simon for a cabinet position. He doesn't want to leave Texas. They're coaxing him."

She just shook her head. The Hart family was just too much altogether!

That night, lying in her new husband's arms with the sound of the ocean right outside the window, she gazed up at him with wonder as he made the softest, sweetest love to her in the dimly lit room.

His body rose and fell like the tide, and he smiled at her, watching her excited eyes with sparks in his own as her body hesitated only briefly and then accepted him completely on a gasp of shocked pleasure.

"And you were afraid that it was going to hurt," he chided as he moved tenderly against her.

"Yes." She was gasping for air, clinging, lifting to him in shivering arcs of involuntary rigor. "It's… killing me…!"

"Already?" he chided, bending to brush his lips

over her swollen mouth. "Darlin', we've barely started!"

"Barely...? Oh!"

He was laughing. She could hear him as she washed up and down on waves of ecstasy that brought unbelievable noises out of her. She died half a dozen times, almost lost consciousness, and still he laughed, deep in his throat, as he went from one side of the bed to the other with her in a tangle of glorious abandon that never seemed to end. Eventually they ended up on the carpet with the sheet trailing behind them as she cried out, sobbing, one last time and heard him groan as he finally shuddered to completion.

They were both covered with sweat. Her hair was wet. She was trembling and couldn't stop. Beside her, he lay on his back with one leg bent at the knee. Incredibly he was still as aroused as he'd been when they started. She sat up gingerly and stared at him, awed.

He chuckled up at her. "Come down here," he dared her.

"I can't!" She was gasping. "And you can't...you couldn't...!"

"If you weren't the walking wounded, I sure as hell could," he said. "I've saved it all up for eight years, and I'm still starving for you."

She just looked at him, fascinated. "I read a book."

"I'm not in it," he assured her. He tugged her down

on top of him and brushed her breasts with his lips. "I guess you're sore."

She blushed. "You *guess?*"

He chuckled. "All right. Come here, my new best friend, and we'll go to sleep, since we can't do anything else."

"We're on the floor," she noted.

"At least we won't fall off next time."

She laughed because he was outrageous. She'd never thought that intimacy would be fun as well as pleasurable. She traced his nose and bent to kiss his lips. "Where are we going to live?"

"At the ranch."

"Only if your brothers live in the barn," she said. "I'm not having them outside the door every night listening to us."

"They won't have to stand outside the door. Judging from what I just heard, they could hear you with the windows closed if they stood on the town squa… Ouch!"

"Let that be a lesson to you," she told him dryly, watching him rub the nip she'd given his thigh. "Naked men are vulnerable."

"And you aren't?"

"Now, Corrigan…!"

She screeched and he laughed and they fell down again in a tangle, close together, and the laughter gave way to soft conversation. Eventually they even slept.

When they got back to the ranch, the three brothers

were gone and there was a hastily scrawled note on the door.

"We're sleeping in the bunkhouse until we can build you a house of your own. Congratulations. Champagne is in the fridge." It was signed with love, all three brothers—and the name of the fourth was penciled in.

"On second thought," she said, with her arm around her husband, "maybe those boys aren't so bad after all!"

He tried to stop her from opening the door, but it was too late. The bucket of water left her wavy hair straight and her navy blue coat dripping. She looked at Corrigan with eyes the size of plates, her arms outstretched, her mouth open.

Corrigan looked around her. On the floor of the hall were two towels and two new bathrobes, and an assortment of unmentionable items.

He knew that if he laughed, he'd be sleeping in the barn for the next month. But he couldn't help it. And after a glance at the floor—neither could she.

* * * * *

A Man of Means

Chapter One

Meredith Johns glanced around her worriedly at the out-of-control Halloween partygoers in their colorful costumes. Meredith was wearing an outfit left over from college days. She made a good salary at her job, but there was no money for little luxuries like Halloween costumes. She had to budget just to be able to pay the utility bill in the house she shared with her father.

The past few months had been traumatic, and the wear was telling on her. She needed to get out of the house, Jill, one of her colleagues, had said firmly—especially after her most agonizing experience at home. Meredith was reluctant. Her father was only just back at their house after three days. But Jill was insistent. So she'd put on the only costume she had, a bad choice in many ways, and walked the three blocks to her friend's downtown apartment. She grimaced at her surroundings. What an idiot she'd been to come to this wild party.

But it really had been a tumultuous week for Meredith and she'd wanted to get her mind off her troubles. Her father's violent behavior at the house they shared was unnerving. They were both still grieving, but her father had taken the tragedy much harder. He felt responsible. That was why a scholarly, conservative college professor had suddenly retired from his job and turned into an alcoholic. Meredith had tried everything she could think of to get him into treatment, but he refused to go on his own accord and the treatment facilities which would have taken him wouldn't unless he went voluntarily. Only a violent episode that had landed him in jail had temporarily spared her of this saddening experience. But he was out three days later and he had a new bottle of whiskey. She still had to go home after the party. He'd warned her not to be late. Not that she ever was.

Her grey eyes were sad as she sipped her soft drink. She had no head for alcohol, and she was as out of place here as a cup of tea. Not only that, her costume was drawing unwanted attention from the men. So was her long blond hair. It had been a bad costume choice, but it was the only thing she had to wear on the spur of the moment. Going to a Halloween party in her street clothes would have made her stand out, too.

She moved away from a slightly tipsy colleague who wanted to show her around Jill's bedroom and unobtrusively put her glass on a table. She found Jill, pleaded a headache, thanked her for a "good" time and headed out the front door as fast as she could. Once on the sidewalk, she drew in a long, sweet breath of fresh air.

What a bunch of wild people! She coughed delicately, remembering the unmistakable smell of that smoke that had been thick enough to obstruct clear vision inside. She'd thought it would be fun to go to a party. She might even meet a man who would be willing to take her out and cope with her father. And cows might fly, she told herself. She hadn't been out on a date in months. She'd invited one prospective date to her home for supper. But after a good look at her father, who was mean when he drank, the prospective suitor took off. Her heart wasn't in it, anyway. Recently she'd given up trying to attract anyone. She had her hands full already. Her grief was still fresh, too.

An odd noise attracted her attention as she started back toward her own house. She felt self-conscious in her getup, and remembering the lewd remarks she'd drawn from a man who was normally very polite and gentlemanly, she was sorry she hadn't had a coat to wear. Her clothes were mostly old, because by the time she made the mortgage payment and took care of the bills, there wasn't much left over. Her father couldn't work and wouldn't get help, and she loved him too much to desert him. It was becoming a costly proposition.

She wrapped her arms around herself and hoped she was covering up enough skin to discourage stalkers. But her skirt was very short and tight, and she was wearing fishnet hose, very high heels, a low-cut blouse and a flaming pink feather boa. Her blond hair was loose around her shoulders and she was wearing enough makeup to do justice to a ballet recital. She winced, hoping she hadn't been noticed. She'd gone to the party as a burlesque dancer. Sadly she looked more like a professional hooker in her garb.

She rounded a corner and saw two shadowy figures bending over what looked like a man on the ground.

"Hey! What do you think you're doing there?" she yelled, making as much noise as possible. Then she started running toward them and waving her arms, yelling threats as she went.

As she expected, the surprise of her aggressive presence shocked them into retreat. They jumped up and ran away, without even looking back. The best defense, she thought with faint amusement, was always a good offense. It was a calculated bluff, but she'd seen it work for women smaller in stature than she was.

She ran to the downed man and examined him the best she could in the dim glow of the streetlights.

Concussion, she thought, feeling his head and encountering a metallic smelling wetness. Blood. He'd been hit on the head by his assailants, and probably robbed as well. She felt around under the jacket he was wearing and her hand touched something small and square on his belt. She pulled it out.

"Aha," she said with a triumphant grin. A man dressed as well as he was could be expected to have a cell phone. She dialed 911 and gave the operator her location and the condition of her patient, staying on the line while the dispatcher got an ambulance en route.

While she waited for it, she sat down on the pavement beside the man and held his hand.

He groaned and tried to move.

"Don't do that," she said firmly. "You'll be okay. You mustn't move until the EMTs get here. I haven't got anything to treat you with."

"Head…hurts."

"I imagine it does. You've got a heck of a bump. Just lie still. Feel sick, sleepy…?"

"Sick," he managed weakly.

"Lie still." She lifted her head to listen for the ambulance, and sure enough, a siren sounded nearby. The hospital was less than two blocks from her home, maybe four from here. Lucky for this guy, whoever he was. Head injuries could be fatal.

"My…brothers," the man was whispering brokenly. "Hart…Ranch. Jacobsville, Texas."

"I'll make sure they're contacted," she promised.

He gripped her hand, hard, as he fought not to lose consciousness. "Don't…leave me," he ground out.

"I won't. I promise."

"Angel," he whispered. He took a long, shaky breath, and went back into the oblivion he'd left so briefly. That wasn't a good sign.

The ambulance rounded the corner, and the headlights spilled out onto Meredith and her patient. She got to her feet as two EMTs, one male and one female, piled out the doors and rushed to the downed man.

"Head wound," she told them. "Pulse is slow, but steady. He's coherent, some nausea, his skin is cold and clammy. Blunt force trauma, probably mild concussion…"

"Don't I know you?" the female EMT asked. Her face brightened. "Got you! You're Johns!"

"That's me," Meredith said with a grin. "I must be famous!"

"Sorry, not you—your dad." She winced at the look on Meredith's face.

Meredith sighed. "Yes, he spends a lot of time on ambulances these days."

"What happened here?" the woman asked quickly, changing the subject. "Did you see anything?"

"I yelled and scared off two guys who were bending over him," she volunteered. "I don't know if they were the ones who hit him or not. What do you think?" she added as the woman gave him a professional once-over.

"Concussion, definitely," she agreed. "Nothing broken, but he's got a lump the size of the national debt here on his head. We'll transport him. Coming along?"

"I guess I should," Meredith said, waiting until they loaded him onto the gurney. He was still unconscious. "But I'm not exactly dressed for visiting a hospital."

The EMT gave her a speaking glance. "Should I ask why you're dressed like that? And does your boss know you're moonlighting?" she added wickedly.

"Jill Baxley had a Halloween party. She thought I should come."

The other woman's eyebrows levered up. "Jill's parties are notorious for getting out of control. I've never even seen you take a drink."

"My father drinks enough for both of us," came the reply. "I don't drink or use drugs, and I need my head examined for going to that party. I escaped early, which is how I found this guy."

"Lucky for him," the woman murmured as they loaded him into the back of the ambulance. "Judging by his condition, he could have died if he hadn't been found in time."

Meredith climbed up into the back and sat down on the bench while the driver got in under the wheel and the female EMT called the hospital emergency room for orders. It was going to be a long night, Meredith thought worriedly, and her father was going to be very upset when she got home. He and her mother had been really close, but her mother had been fond of going to parties and staying out until the early morning; sometimes with other men. Recent events had made him dwell on that behavior. Her father seemed to have transferred that old contempt to her. It made her uneasy to think of arriving home in the wee hours. Anything could happen. On the other hand, how could she leave this man? She was the only person who knew who to contact for him. She'd promised to stay with him. She couldn't let him down.

He was examined by the resident on duty in the emergency room, who diagnosed concussion. He'd been unconscious most of the way to the hospital, but he'd come out of it just once to look up at Meredith and smile, tightening his big hand around the fingers that were holding it.

His family had to be notified, and Meredith was coaxed into making the call to Jacobsville for the harassed and overworked emergency room staff.

She was given a phone and a telephone directory which also listed Jacobs County, of which Jacobsville was the county seat. She looked through it until she found a listing for Hart Ranch Properties, Inc. That had to be it.

She dialed the number and waited. A deep, drawling voice answered, "Hart Ranch."

"Uh, I'm calling for a Mr. Leo Hart," she said, having found his driver's license in the wallet his assailants hadn't had time to steal. "He's at Houston General…"

"What happened?" the voice asked impatiently. "Is he all right?"

"He was mugged. He has a concussion," she added. "He can't give the staff any medical information…"

"Who are you?"

"I'm Meredith Johns. I work…

"Who found him?"

"I did, actually. I called the ambulance on his cell phone. He said to call his brothers and he told me where they were…"

"It's two o'clock in the morning!" the voice pointed out angrily.

"Yes, I am aware of that," she began. "It only happened a little while ago. I was walking down the street when I saw him on the sidewalk. He needs his family—"

"I'm his brother, Rey. I'll be there in thirty minutes."

"Sir, it's a long way to Houston from where you are. If you drive that fast…!" she said at once.

"We have an airplane. I'll get the pilot out of bed right

now. Thanks." He added that last word as if it hurt him, and hung up.

Meredith went back to the waiting room. Ten minutes later, she was admitted to the room where the victim had been examined.

"He's conscious," the attending physician told her. "I'm going to admit him overnight, just to be sure. Any luck with his family?"

"His brother is on the way, in his own plane, apparently," she said. "I didn't get a thing out of him. Sorry."

"People get upset and they don't think," the resident said with a weary smile. "How about staying with him? We're understaffed because of that respiratory virus that's going around, and he shouldn't be alone."

"I'll stay," she said with a grin. "It's not as if I have a hectic social life."

The resident pursed his lips and smirked at her outfit.

"Halloween party," she said, grimacing. "And next time I get invited, I'll have a broken leg, I swear it!"

Forty-five minutes later, there was a problem. It was six feet tall, had black hair and dark eyes and it erupted into the hospital cubicle like an F-5 tornado, dressed in jeans and boots and a fringed rawhide jacket thrown carelessly over what looked like a beige silk shirt. The wide-brimmed hat slanted over those threatening eyes was a Stetson, one of the most expensive made, with its distinctive feathered logo pin on the hatband. He looked impressively rich, and excessively angry.

The man was livid when he saw his big brother, still drifting in and out of consciousness, on the examining table. He gave Meredith a scrutiny that could have peeled paint off old furniture, his eyes narrowing contemptuously on her costume.

"Well, that explains why you were on the street at two in the morning," he snarled angrily. "What happened? Did you feel guilty and call for help after you tried to roll him?" he added sarcastically.

"Look here," she began, rising.

"Save it." He turned to the big man on the table and laid a lean, strong hand on his brother's broad chest. "Leo. Leo, it's Rey! Can you hear me?" he asked in a tone that combined affection with concern.

The big man's eyes blinked and opened. He stared blankly up at the leaner man. "Rey?"

"What happened to you?" Rey Hart demanded gently.

Leo grinned wearily. "I was thinking about new forage grasses and wasn't paying attention to my surroundings," he murmured drowsily. "Something hit me in the head and I went down like a brick. Didn't see a thing." He winced and felt clumsily in his pockets. "Damn! My wallet's gone. So's my cell phone."

Meredith started to tell him that she had the phone and wallet in her purse for safekeeping, but before she could speak, Rey Hart gave her a furious, speaking glance and walked out of the cubicle like a man hunting a fight.

His brother drifted off again. Meredith stood beside him, wondering what to do. Five minutes later, Rey Hart walked back in accompanied by a tall man in a police uniform. He looked familiar, but Meredith couldn't quite place him. She knew she'd seen him before.

"That's her," Rey told the policeman, indicating Meredith. "I'll sign anything necessary as soon as I see that my brother's going to be okay. But get her out of here."

"Don't worry. I'll handle it," the policeman said quietly. He handcuffed Meredith with easy efficiency and pulled her out of the cubicle before she could protest.

"I'm being arrested?" she exclaimed, stunned. "But, why? I haven't done anything!"

"Yes, I know, I've heard it all before," the officer told her in a bored tone when she tried to explain what had happened. "Nobody's ever guilty. Honest to God, dressed like that, out on the streets alone after midnight, you were bound to be up to no good. What did you do with his cell phone and his wallet?"

"They're in my pocketbook," she began.

He confiscated it from her shoulder and propelled her out of the building. "You're going to be in a lot of trouble. You picked the wrong man to rob."

"See here, I didn't mug him! It was two men. I didn't see their faces, but they were bending over him as I came down the sidewalk."

"Soliciting is a felony," he pointed out.

"I wasn't soliciting anything! I'd just come from a Halloween party dressed as a burlesque dancer!" she raged, furious that she was being punished for having done someone a good turn. She read his name tag. "Officer Sanders, you have to believe me!"

He didn't say a word. He drew her with him, firmly but gently, and put her into the back seat of the police car.

"Wait," she told him before he could close the door. "You get my wallet out of my purse and look in it. Right now," she insisted.

He gave her an impatient look, but he did what she asked. He looked through the plastic inserts in her wallet and glanced at her with a changed expression. "I thought you looked familiar, Johns," he murmured, using her last name, as most people she knew at work did.

"I didn't mug Mr. Hart," she continued. "And I can prove where I was when he was being mugged." She gave him her friend Jill's address.

He gave in. He drove to Jill's apartment, went to the door, spoke to an obviously intoxicated and amused Jill and came back to the squad car. He let Meredith out of the back of the squad car and took off the handcuffs. It was cool in the night air, and Meredith felt self-conscious and uncomfortable in her garb, even though the police officer knew the truth now.

"I'm really sorry," he told her with a grimace as he met her grey eyes. "I didn't recognize you. All I knew was what Mr. Hart told me, and he was too upset to think straight. You have to admit, you don't look very professional tonight."

"I do realize that. Mr. Hart cares about his brother, and he doesn't know what happened," she pointed out. "He walked in and saw his brother on the table and me dressed like this," she indicated her clothing, "and his brother said his wallet and cell phone were missing. He doesn't know me from a stump. You can't blame him for thinking the worst. But those two men who hit him would have gotten his wallet if I hadn't come along, and they're still on the loose."

"Can you show me where you found him?" he asked.

"Of course. It was just down the sidewalk, that way."

She led and he followed her, with his big wide-angle flashlight sweeping the sidewalk and the grass as they walked. She pointed to an area of flattened grass. He left her on the sidewalk and gave the area a thorough scrutiny, looking for clues. He found a candy wrapper and a cigarette butt.

"I don't guess you know if Mr. Hart smokes or likes candy?" he asked.

She shook her head. "Sorry. All he told me was his brothers' names and where they lived. I don't know anything more about him."

He stood up. "I'll ask his brother later. Wait here while I call for one of the technicians to bag this evidence," he told her.

"Okay," she said agreeably, drawing the feather boa closer. It was getting cold standing around briefly clad, waiting for crime scene investigators. "Somebody's going to love being turned out of bed to come look at a cigarette butt and a candy wrapper," she stated with helpless amusement.

"You'd be surprised at what excites those guys," he chuckled. "Catching crooks isn't exactly a chore to them. It's high drama."

"I hope they catch these two," she said firmly. "Nobody should have to be afraid to walk down the streets at night. Even after dark, dressed like this, alone," she added pointedly, indicating her clothes.

"Good point," he was fair enough to admit.

He called in his location and requested crime scene technicians. Meredith was ready to go home, but she couldn't leave until she'd given the policeman a statement for his report. She sat in his car, with the overhead lights on, writing out what she knew of the attack on Leo Hart. It didn't take long, because she didn't know much.

She handed it back to him. "Can I go home now?" she asked. "I live with my father and he's going to be upset because I'm coming home so late. I can walk. It's only about three blocks from here."

He frowned. "Your father is Alan Johns, isn't he?" he asked. His expression changed. "Do you want me to go with you?"

She didn't usually flinch at facing her irate parent. She was gutsy, and she could handle herself. But tonight, she'd been through a lot. "Would you?" she asked, uneasy because her fear was visible.

"No problem. Get in."

He drove her to her house and went to the door with her. The house was dark and there was no movement inside. She let out a sigh of relief. “It’s okay. If he was awake, the lights would be on. Thanks, anyway,” she said with a smile.

“If you need us, call,” he said. “I’m afraid I’ll be in touch again about this. Rey Hart already reminded me that his brother is our state attorney general. He’s not going to let this case go until it’s solved.”

“I don’t blame him. Those guys are a menace and they’re probably still running around looking for easy targets to rob. Take care.”

“You, too. And I’m sorry about the handcuffs,” he added, with the first smile she’d seen on his lean face since her ordeal began.

She smiled back. “My fault, for wearing a costume like this on the streets,” she admitted. “I won’t do it again. Thanks for the ride.”

Back at the hospital, Rey Hart sat by his brother’s bedside until dawn, in the private room he’d obtained for him. He was worried. Leo was the hardiest one of the lot, and the most cautious as a rule. He was the prankster, always playing jokes, cheering them up in bad times. Now, he lay still and quiet and Rey realized how much his sibling meant to him.

It infuriated him that that woman had thought nothing of robbing his brother while he was sick and weak and helpless. He wondered what she’d hit him with. She wasn’t a big woman. Odd, that she’d been able to reach as high as Leo’s head with some blunt object. He recalled with distaste the way she’d been dressed. He was no prude, but in his early twenties he’d had a fling with a woman he later found out was a private call girl. He’d been infatuated with her, and thought she loved him. When he learned her profession and that she'd recognized him at once and knew how wealthy he was, it had soured him on women. Like his married brothers had been, and Leo still was, he was wary of females. If he could find a man who could bake biscuits, he told himself, he'd never let even an old woman into the house ever again.

He recalled their latest acquisition with sorrow. He and Leo had found a retired pastry chef who'd moved in with them—the last of the Hart bachelors—to bake their beloved biscuits. She'd become ill and they'd rushed to the drugstore to get her prescriptions, along with candy and chocolates and a bundle of flowers. But her condition had worsened and she'd told them, sadly, that the job was just too much in her frail state of health. She had to quit. It was going to be hard to replace her. There weren't a lot of people who wanted to live on an isolated ranch and bake biscuits at all hours of the day and night. Even want ads with offers of a princely salary hadn't attracted anyone just yet. It was depressing; like having Leo lying there under white sheets, so still and quiet in that faded striped hospital gown.

Rey dozed for a few hours in the deep night, used to sleeping in all sorts of odd positions and places. Cattle ranchers could sleep in the saddle when they had to, he thought amusedly, especially when calving was underway or there was a storm or they were cutting out and branding calves and doing inventory of the various herds.

But he came awake quickly when Sanders, the police officer who'd arrested that woman last night, came into the room with a murmured apology.

"I'm just going off shift," Officer Sanders told Rey. "I thought I'd stop by and tell you that we've gone over the scene of the attack and we have some trace evidence. The detectives will start looking for other witnesses this morn ing. We'll get the people responsible for the attack on your brother."

Rey frowned. "Get 'them'?" he queried. "You've already got her. You arrested her!"

Officer Sanders averted his eyes. "Had to turn her loose," he said uneasily. "She had an alibi, which was confirmed. She gave me a statement and I took her home."

Rey stood up, unfolding his intimidating length, and glared at the officer. "You let her go," he said coldly. "Where's my brother's cell phone?" he added as an afterthought.

The policeman grimaced. "In her purse, along with his wallet," he said apologetically. "I forgot to ask her for them when I left. Tell you what, I'll swing by her house and get them on my way home..."

"I'll go with you," he said curtly. "I still think she's guilty. She's probably in cahoots with the guys who attacked Leo. And she could have paid someone to lie and give her an alibi."

"She's not that sort of woman," the policeman began.

Rey cut him off angrily. "I don't want to hear another word about her! Let's go," he said, grabbing his hat, with a last, worried glance at his sleeping brother. He wondered how the policeman could make such a statement about a woman he'd just met, but he didn't really care. He wanted her in jail.

He drove his rental car, with the off-duty policeman beside him, to Meredith's home, following the directions Officer Sanders gave him. It was in a run-down neighborhood, and the house was in poor condition. It only intensified Rey's suspicions about her. She was obviously poor. What better way to get money than to rob somebody?

He went to the door, accompanied by the policeman, and knocked. Hard.

He had to do it three times, each with more force and impatience, before someone answered the door.

Meredith Johns was disheveled and white-faced. She was clutching a bulky washcloth to her face and wearing a robe over the clothes she'd had on the night before.

"What do you want now?" she asked huskily, her voice slurred and jerky.

"Been drinking, have you?" Rey Hart asked in a blistering tone.

She flinched.

Officer Sanders knew what was going on. He read the situation immediately. He stepped past Rey, grim and silent, grimacing when he saw Meredith's face. He went by her and into the living room and began looking around.

"Hard night, I gather? It must be a continual risk, in your profession," Rey said insinuatingly, with a speaking glance at her dress in the opening of the old, worn robe. "Do your marks make a habit of beating you up?" he added with cold contempt.

She didn't answer him. It was hard to talk and her face hurt.

Officer Sanders had gone into the bedroom. He came back two minutes later with a tall, disheveled but oddly dignified-looking man in handcuffs. The man, who'd been quiet before, was now cursing furiously, accusing Meredith of everything from prostitution to murder in a voice that rose until he was yelling. Rey Hart looked at him with obvious surprise. His eyes went to Meredith Johns, who was stiff as a poker and wincing every time the man yelled at her. The policeman picked up the telephone and called for a squad car.

"Please, don't," Meredith pleaded, still clutching the ice-filled cloth to her face. "He's only just got out..."

"He isn't staying. This time, he's going to be in jail for longer than three days," the officer said firmly. "You get to the hospital and let one of the residents look at you, Miss Johns. How bad is it? Come on, show me," he demanded, moving closer.

Rey stood by, silent and confused, watching as Meredith winced and moved the bulky cloth away from her face. His breath was audible when he saw the swelling and the growing purple and violet discoloration around her eye, cheek and jaw.

"God Almighty," Rey said harshly. "What did he hit you with?"

"His fist," the policeman replied coldly. "And it isn't the first time. You have to face facts, Miss Johns," he told her. "He isn't the man he used to be. When he drinks, he doesn't know what he's doing. He'll kill you one night when he's like this, and he won't even remember doing it!"

"I won't press charges," she said miserably. "How can I? He's my father! He's the only family I have left in the world...."

The policeman looked at her with compassion. "You don't have to press charges," he told her. "I'll provide them myself. You'd better phone your boss and tell him you won't be in for a few weeks. He'll have kittens if you walk into the office looking like that."

"I suppose he would." Tears ran down her pale cheeks, all the more eloquent for being silent. She looked at her raging, cursing father and sadness claimed her features. "He wasn't like this before, honest he wasn't," she told them. "He was a kind, loving, caring man."

"Not anymore," Officer Sanders replied grimly. "Get to

the hospital and have your face seen about, Miss Johns. I'll take your father outside until the unit comes…"

"No," she groaned. "Please, spare us that! I can't bear to have the whole neighborhood watching, hearing him… like that, again!"

He hesitated. "Okay. I'll watch for them out the window. The unit can drop you by the hospital, since it's going there first…."

"I'll take her," Rey said at once, without wondering why he should do such an about-face. He didn't trust the woman, or even totally believe her story. But she did look so pitiful. He couldn't bear to leave her in that condition to get to the hospital. Besides, whatever her motives, she had gotten help for Leo. He could have died if he hadn't been cared for.

"But…" she began.

"If," he added coldly, "you change clothes first. I am *not* being seen in public with you in that rig!"

Chapter Two

Meredith wished she felt up to a fight. Her long blond hair was down in her face, her grey eyes were sparking fire. But she was sick to her stomach and bruised. She would rather have gone to bed if these stubborn men would just have let her alone. But her face could have broken or shattered bones. She knew that. She grimaced, hoping her insurance would cover a second "accident" in as many months.

When the unit arrived, Meredith turned away from the sight of her raging father being carried off and closed the door. Probably it wasn't surprising to the neighbors anymore, it happened so often. But she hated having everyone know.

"I'll get dressed," she said in a subdued tone.

Rey watched her go and then shoved his hands into his pockets and looked around the room. It was shabby. The only bright things in it were books—hundreds of them, in bookcases and boxes and stacked on tables and chairs. Odd, he thought. They were apparently short of cash, judging by the worn old furniture and bare floor. There was only a very small television and a portable stereo. He glanced at the CD case and was surprised to find classical music dominating the discs. What a peculiar family. Why have so many books and so little else? He wondered where the woman's mother was. Had she left the father, and was that why he drank? It would have explained a lot. He knew about missing parents, especially missing mothers—his had left the family while the five Hart boys were young, without a backward glance.

Minutes later, Meredith came back, and except for the bruised face, he might not have recognized her. She was wearing a beige sweater set, with a tweed coat over it. Her blond hair was in a neat bun and her face devoid of makeup. She wore flat-heeled shoes and carried a purse that looked new.

"Here's your brother's cell phone and his wallet," she said, handing it to him. "I forgot to give them to Officer Sanders."

He glared at them and put them in his pocket. He wondered if she'd have given them back at all if he hadn't come here. He didn't trust her, regardless of what the policeman had said. "Let's go," he said stiffly. "The car's outside."

She hesitated, but only for a minute. She wasn't going to be able to avoid a checkup. She knew the problems that negligence could cause. Even a relatively minor problem could become major.

Unexpectedly Rey opened the car door for her. She slid in, surprised to find herself in a new luxury car. She fastened her seat belt. His brother, Simon Hart, was state attorney general. Rey owned a ranch. She remembered how his injured brother, Leo, had been dressed last night, and her eyes went to Rey's expensive hat and boots and silk shirt. Of course, they were a wealthy family. Considering her state of dress—or undress—the night before, she could understand his misgivings about her character.

She sat wearily beside him, the ice-filled cloth still in her hand. She held it to the side of her face that was bruised and hoped that it would spare her some of the swelling. She didn't need a doctor to tell her that it was a bad blow. The pain was almost unbearable.

"I took a hit to the face a few years ago in a brawl," he volunteered in his deep, slow drawl. "It hurt like hell. I imagine your face does, too."

She swallowed, touched by the faint concern. Tears threatened, but she never cried now. It was a weakness she couldn't afford.

He glanced at her, puzzled. "Nothing to say?"

She managed to get her voice under control. "Thank you for taking me to the hospital," she said huskily.

"Do you usually dress like that when you go out at night?" he asked belatedly.

"I told you. There was…a Halloween party," she said. It hurt to talk. "It was the only costume I had."

"Do you like parties?" he asked sarcastically.

"My first one…in almost four years," she managed to say. "Please…hurts…to talk."

He glanced at her and then was quiet. He didn't like her. He didn't trust her. Why was he taking care of her? There was something unexpectedly vulnerable about her. But she had spirit.

He walked her into the emergency room. She filled out forms and was ushered back into a treatment cubicle while Rey sat in the waiting room between a squalling toddler and a man coughing his head off. He wasn't used to illness. He'd never seen much of it, and he didn't know how to cope with it. Accidents, sure, he was a good hand in an emergency, and there were plenty on a ranch. But he hated hospitals.

Meredith came back a good thirty minutes later with a prescription and a frown.

"What did he say?" he asked conversationally.

She shrugged. "He gave me something…for pain," she said, waving the prescription.

"They sent me to a plastic surgeon," he volunteered as they went through the automatic door.

She didn't speak.

"I had a shattered bone in my cheek that they couldn't repair," he persisted.

"I'm not…going…to any damned…plastic surgeon!"

His eyebrows arched. "Your face could be distorted."

"So what?" she muttered, wincing because it really did hurt to speak. "It's not…much of a face, anyway."

He scowled. She wasn't pretty, but her face had attractive features. Her nose was straight and elegant, she had high cheekbones. Her mouth was like a little bow, perfect. Her eyes, big and gray, fascinated him.

"You should go," he said.

She ignored him. "Can you…drive me by the pharmacy?"

"Sure."

She gave him directions and he waited while she had the prescription filled. He drove her back to her house and left her there reluctantly.

"I'll be at the hospital with Leo if you need anything," he said as if it pained him to say it.

"I don't need any help. Thanks," she added stiffly.

His eyebrows arched. "You remind me of me," he murmured, and a thin smile touched his lips—a kind one. "Proud as Lucifer."

"I get by. I really am…sorry about your brother. Will he be all right?" she asked at her door.

He nodded. "They want to keep him for two or three days. He'll want to thank you."

"No need. I would have done it for anyone."

He sighed. She was going to look bad for a long time, with her face in that condition. She'd been beaten and he felt responsible, God knew why. He took a breath. "I'm sorry I had you arrested," he said reluctantly.

She pursed her lips. "I'll bet…that hurt."

"What?"

"You don't apologize much, do you?" she asked, as if she knew.

He scowled down at her, puzzled.

She turned away. "No sweat. I'll live. So long."

She went in and closed the door. Rey, who'd done without companionship for a number of years, suddenly felt alone. He didn't like the feeling, so he shoved it out of his mind and drove back to the hospital. He wouldn't see her again, anyway.

Leo came back to himself with a vengeance late that afternoon. He had Rey lever the head of his bed up and he ate dinner with pure enjoyment.

"It's not bad," Leo murmured between mouthfuls. "But I wish I had a biscuit."

"Me, too," Rey said on a sigh. "I guess we could buy a restaurant, as a last resort," he added dejectedly. "One that serves breakfast."

"Who was that woman who came in with me?" he asked Rey.

"You remember her?" Rey was surprised.

"She looked like an angel," he mused, smiling. "Blonde and big-eyed and all heart. She held my hand and sat down on the sidewalk in the cold and talked to me until the ambulance got there."

"You were unconscious."

"Not all the time. She even came in with me on the ambulance," he said. "She kept telling me I was going to be all right. I remember her voice." He smiled. "Her name was Meredith."

Rey's heart jumped. He felt uneasy. Leo usually didn't pay much attention to strange women. "Meredith Johns," he agreed.

"Is she married?" Leo asked at once.

Rey felt threatened; it irritated him. "I don't know," he said.

"Do you think you could find somebody who knows how to get in touch with her?" his brother persisted. "I want to thank her for saving me."

Rey got up from the chair where he'd been sitting and walked to the darkened window, peering out through the blinds while he played for time. "She lives near the place where you were attacked," he said finally, unable to lie.

"What does she do for a living?"

"I don't know," Rey said, feeling uncomfortable. He couldn't get her father's accusing remarks out of his mind. She'd said she was dressed up for a party, she'd even found someone to give her an alibi, but Rey didn't completely believe her. What if that whole defense was a lie? What if she was some sort of prostitute? He didn't want his brother getting mixed up with a woman like that. He didn't trust women, especially strange women. Then he remembered her poor, bruised face and he felt bad about his suspicions.

"I'll ask one of the nurses," Leo said abruptly.

"No need," Rey told him. He turned back around with his hands in his pockets. "If you're determined, I'll go get her in the morning and bring her in to see you."

"Why not tonight?"

Rey let out an impatient breath. "Her father roughed her up because she got home late last night. I took her to the emergency room this morning before I came back here."

Leo's eyes narrowed and went cold. "Her father beat her? And you took her back home to him?" he said angrily.

"He wasn't there. They took him off to jail," he said. His face hardened even more. "She'll have a hell of a bruise. They said she couldn't go back to work for a few weeks." He moved one shoulder restlessly. "Considering the way they live, I don't know how she'll manage," he added reluctantly. "They don't seem to have much. Apparently the old man doesn't work and she's the only one bringing home any money." He didn't volunteer his opinion of how she made it.

Leo leaned back against the pillows. His big frame was without its usual vibrance. His dark eyes were dull, and his lean face was drawn. His blond-streaked brown hair was unkempt, and looked odd in the back where they'd had to shave it to put stitches in. It was a reminder of how tricky head wounds were. Leo was very lucky not to have brain damage. Rey thought about the assailants and his eyes blazed.

"I'm going to phone Simon tonight," he told Leo. "I'm sure the local police will do all they can to catch the guys who waylaid you, but they'll work even harder if they get a call from the state attorney general."

"There you go again, pulling strings," Leo mused.

"It's for a good cause."

"Did you find my wallet and my cell phone?" Leo asked.

"The woman had them. They're in my pocket."

"Good. I didn't think she had anything to do with mugging me. Don't forget your promise to bring Meredith here in the morning," he said.

Now it was "Meredith." Rey didn't like the whole idea of having Leo around the woman, but he didn't have a legitimate reason for keeping her from Leo's side. It would sound even more suspicious if Rey started throwing out sarcastic remarks about her. Leo did love to pull his chain.

"Okay," he said reluctantly.

"Good man," Leo replied with a wan grin. "Nothing like family to look after you."

"Next time, watch your back instead of daydreaming about forage grasses," Rey said firmly. Then he leaned forward in the chair. "So, tell me what sort of grasses the Cattleman's Association is advocating."

Rey got a hotel room near the hospital, so that he could have a bath and get some rest. The night staff had the phone number, so they could call him immediately if he was needed.

He phoned Simon before he went to bed.

"Leo's been mugged?" Simon exclaimed. "And you didn't call me last night?"

That tone was still intimidating, even though Rey was thirty-one. Simon was the eldest of the five brothers, and the bossiest, next to Cag.

"I was too upset to phone anybody," Rey returned, "and too busy trying to handle…another problem that cropped up. He's all right. Honest. I didn't find out until the early hours of the morning, and it's been a long day. He was already out of danger before it occurred to me that I needed to let you know."

"All right," Simon said, sounding as if he was more relaxed. "Do they have a suspect?"

"No. I thought we did, but it turned out to be a dead end," he added, without going into details about Meredith Johns. "There were two of them, and they haven't been caught. It's a miracle he wasn't killed, and that they were stopped in time before they robbed him. You might give the local police chief a call. Just to let him know we're all interested in solving the case."

"You want me to use my influence for personal gain?" Simon drawled.

"Hell, yes, I do!" Rey shot back. "This is our brother, for God's sake! If a big, strong man like Leo can get mugged in a residential neighborhood, so can anybody else! It doesn't say a lot for the security in this area."

"No, it doesn't," Simon agreed. "I'll point that out to the police commissioner, first thing tomorrow. Then I'll run down to Jacobsville and get Cag and Corrigan and we'll be right up to see about Leo."

Rey chuckled. It was the first bit of humor he'd felt so far. The five brothers rarely went so far as to gang up on people, but considering the size and reputation of them, they got results when they did. This was an emergency, anyway. They could have lost a brother. The perpetrators had to be caught.

"They should be home by now," Rey replied. "I couldn't phone them because they were showing those Japanese businessmen around the ranch and the town."

"I'll see how much luck they had. Japan is very careful about its import beef. The fact that we run organically raised cattle will certainly go in our favor," Simon said.

"Yes, it will. Get some sleep. And don't worry about Leo. He's fine. I'd never have left the hospital if I'd had one doubt about that."

"I'll stop worrying."

"Give my love to Tira and the boys," Rey added.

"I'll do that. See you tomorrow."

Rey hung up, thinking about Simon and his family. Tira was redheaded and gorgeous, and the boys favored both of them, although they had Simon's dark eyes and hair. Corrigan and Dorie had a boy and a girl. Cag and Tess had just a boy, but they were talking about how nice a daughter would be. Meanwhile, Rey and Leo enjoyed being uncles, but had no interest in joining the ranks of the married.

If it wasn't for those biscuits, Rey thought miserably. It was going to be expensive to have the local café make biscuits for them every day until they employed a new biscuit maker, but if they got desperate enough, and offered enough of an incentive, they could probably manage it.

Turning his attention elsewhere, Rey gave a thought to poor Leo with his stitches and his headache, and another to Meredith Johns's bruised face. Tomorrow, he'd have to deal with Leo's request to see her, and he wasn't looking forward to it. He wished he knew why.

Rey went to Meredith Johns's house the next morning after he'd had breakfast. It took her a minute or two to answer the door, and for an instant, he thought that perhaps she might not be in any condition to answer it. She'd been badly bruised.

But she opened the door and peered up at him bravely, even though she looked like a refugee from a bar brawl. Her left eye was swollen shut completely now.

"Leo wants to see you," he said easily, noticing how the top of her blond head only came to his shoulder. She wasn't tall. Even bruised, her face had a beautiful complexion. Her mouth was pretty. He shook himself mentally. "He wants to thank you for what you did. He remembers that you rode in on the ambulance with him. You didn't tell me that," he added with faint accusation.

"I wasn't thinking," she said. "I was worried about what would happen when I came home late."

"Have you heard any more about your father this morning?" he asked grimly.

"They're going to charge him with simple battery," she said heavily. "I can't afford a lawyer. He'll have a public defender and he'll probably have to stay in jail for a few weeks." She looked up at him. "It will be a godsend, you know, because he'll dry out completely."

He hated the compassion he felt. "Did your mother leave him?" he asked.

She averted her face. She couldn't bear to talk about it yet. "In a way," she said huskily. "Are you going to drive me?" she added, glancing at him over her shoulder. "The bus doesn't run for another thirty minutes."

"Sure," he agreed.

"Then I'll get my jacket and purse."

She went into another room and came back quickly, leading the way out the door. "Is he conscious now?"

"Very," he murmured dryly. "When I left him, he was telling a nurse what she could do with the wash basin, and how far."

She chuckled. "He didn't seem like that kind of man," she murmured. "I had him figured for a gentleman, not a renegade."

"We're all that kind of man," he replied.

"All?"

He led her to the car and put her into the passenger seat. "There are five of us. The other three are coming up this morning to have a talk with the police."

"I remember. You said that your brother was the attorney general."

"He is," he replied. "We tend to stick together."

Her eyes went to his hands on the steering wheel. He had nice hands, very lean and strong with neat, clean fingernails. He was a tough-looking man, like a cowboy.

"How's your face?" he asked unexpectedly.

She shrugged. "It still hurts. It will for a while, but I'll be fine."

"You should see that plastic surgeon."

"Why?" she asked heavily. "My insurance won't pay for cosmetic surgery, and there's not much chance that they can do any major repair on tiny shattered bones."

"You're not a doctor. Stop giving yourself medical advice."

She stared at him for a long moment and started to speak, then lost the opportunity when he pulled up in the hospital parking lot, cut off the engine and got out.

Rey waited for her and led her up to the floor where his brother's room was located.

Leo wasn't alone. Three other men were with him, one big and dark and missing an arm, the other lean and light-eyed and handsome, and a third big one with black eyes and a threatening face towering over both the others.

"That's Cag," Rey indicated the black-eyed man. "Corrigan," he nodded toward the light-eyed man, "and that's Simon," he finished, smiling at the one-armed man. "This is Meredith Johns. She rescued Leo."

"Nice to see you and know who you are," Leo said, alert now and interested as his dark eyes swept over the neat woman just inside the door. "Miss Johns, I presume?"

She smiled self-consciously, because everybody was looking at her bruised face. "Yes," she said.

Simon Hart frowned when he got a good look at her. "What the hell happened to you?" he demanded.

"Her father," Rey said for her. "She got in late and he beat her up."

Leo looked suddenly as intimidating as the other three. "Where is he?" he asked.

"In jail," Meredith said heavily. "For several weeks, at least, and he'll have time to dry out."

"Good." Leo looked toward Simon. "Maybe you can find a way to get him into rehab before he gets out."

"I'll look into it," Simon said at once.

"And some counseling wouldn't come amiss," Rey put his two cents worth in.

"I'll see about that, too," Simon replied. "Nice to meet you, Miss Johns. We're all grateful for what you did for Leo."

"You're all very welcome," she replied. She clutched her purse, intimidated by the group of brothers.

"Come here," Leo said, holding out his hand. "They're big and they look tough, but they're really marshmallows. You don't have to feel threatened. I'll protect you."

"She doesn't need protecting from us!" Rey snapped.

The others gaped at him. It wasn't like Rey to act that way.

He cleared his throat. He didn't want them asking themselves embarrassing questions about his attitude. He shoved his hands into his pockets. "Sorry. I didn't sleep much last night," he explained.

Meredith went to stand beside Leo, who took one of her small, cold hands in his and looked up at her with interest.

"Have you seen a doctor?" he asked.

"Your brother took me to the emergency room yesterday," she said.

"Rey. His name's Reynard, but he's called Rey," Leo informed her.

She smiled. "You look much better today. Head hurt?"

"A bit, but my vision's clear and I'm not disoriented," he said, quoting the doctor. "I have a good prognosis."

"That's nice to hear. You were in pretty bad shape."

"I'd have been in a lot worse shape, but for you," Leo said. "I hear that you can't work out in public for a while, until your face heals," he added. "Can you cook?"

She blinked. "Of course," she said at once.

"Can you make bread?"

She frowned. "Bread?"

"More specifically, biscuits," he added, and had the oddest expression on his face.

She shifted her purse in the hand he wasn't holding. "Well, yes, those and rolls and loaf bread," she said, as if everybody could do it.

Leo shot a glance at Rey, who was just staring at him without daring to say a word. He knew what was coming, and he couldn't decide how he felt about it. He didn't want to think about it.

"How would you like a brief stay in Jacobsville, Texas, in a big sprawling ranch house where your only job would be to make biscuits every morning?" Leo asked with his best smile.

Rey and the other brothers were staring at her, waiting. She wondered why. And Rey was frowning, as if he didn't like the idea at all. Probably he still secretly thought she was a hooker. He couldn't seem to credit her with any sense of decency.

She thought about his attitude for a few seconds, and decided that it wouldn't be a bad idea to take the job, and show him that you really couldn't judge a book by its cover. It wouldn't hurt that arrogant cowboy to be taken down a step or two, and she was just the girl who could do it.

She smiled. It hurt her face, but what was a little pain for a good cause? She turned back to Leo. “Mr. Hart, I think I’d like that job very much!”

Chapter Three

"Good for you!" Leo exclaimed, animated and smiling. "You won't be sorry, Meredith. Honest."

She smiled back at him. He was nice, like a big brother. She liked him already. "I can do housekeeping, too," she told him. "I'll earn my keep."

"You'll go on salary, of course," he insisted. "It won't be a holiday."

"Nothing is a holiday with those two," Simon murmured dryly. "They aren't kidding about biscuits. They'll run you crazy baking them."

Rey and Leo gave their brother a disgusted look.

Meredith grinned. "I don't mind," she assured Simon. "I love to cook."

"It won't be that hard," Leo promised, with another speaking glance at Simon. "We just love biscuits. But we'll make you feel right at home. Anything you need, you can have—a new stove…" he added mischievously.

She thought about her father and her job, and her smile faltered. "I have to wrap up a few loose ends first," she began.

"No problem," Leo assured her. "I can't get out of here for another day at least, or so that doctor said," he added with impatience.

"You'll stay until he lets you out," Rey said firmly. "Concussions are tricky. You know that."

Leo grimaced. "I guess so. I hate hospitals."

"I'm not too wild about them myself," Rey had to agree.

"It would be a very sad world without them," Meredith spoke up.

She seemed irritated, Rey thought, and wondered why. "I'll run you back home when you're ready," Rey told her. "We'll be in touch before we're ready to leave."

"All right." She held Leo's hand again and squeezed it gently, to the amusement of all the Harts except Rey. "You get better. I'll see you soon."

"Thanks again," Leo told her with genuine gratitude.

"It was nothing." She gave him another smile, tugged her hand free, and let Rey herd her out the door after a quick goodbye to the other brothers.

"I thought your brother was big until I saw all of you together. Goodness, you're all huge!" she exclaimed when they were outside in the parking lot. She gave him a long scrutiny. "And there doesn't seem to be an extra ounce of fat on any of you."

"We don't sit behind desks. We're ranchers, not office workers, and we work hard, right alongside our cowboys," he said. His dark eyes cut sideways. "Leo likes you."

She smiled. "I'm glad, because I like him, too."

That set him off and he tried not to let it show. He didn't want her to like Leo. He wished he knew why. He glanced at her as he wove skillfully through traffic toward her house. "Do you have family besides your father?" he asked.

"A cousin or two near Fort Worth," she said. She glanced out the window, absently rubbing the ring finger of her left hand, trying not to choke up over the question. "What is Jacobsville like?" she asked to divert him from any further questions.

"It's small," he said easily. "There are a lot of ranches in the area. We have good pasture and soil, and we get enough rain to manage healthy crops." He grinned. "A lot of us are heavily into organic cattle raising. And with the industry under threat right now, we'll probably keep our financial heads above water when some other ranchers are going under."

"I like organic food," she said. "It may have a few more blemishes and bug bites, but if it doesn't kill bugs, it won't kill me," she added with a grin.

He chuckled. "Good point. Do you like animals?"

"I love them. I'd like to have a cat, but it's not possible. Dad's allergic to them." She sighed wearily, leaning her head back against the headrest. Her bruises were still giving her a lot of pain. Her hand went to them and she winced.

"You should see that plastic surgeon," he reminded her.

She shook her head. "Can't afford it. Even if I could, I don't want to go through weeks of surgery."

He hesitated and then he shrugged. "Have it your way."

"I'll heal." She touched her cheek again self-consciously. "I'm not sure going to work for you is a good idea. I mean, people might think the five of you beat me up!"

He laughed wholeheartedly. "Nobody who knows us would ever think that. Especially," he added, "if you can bake. Simon was right. I'm afraid we're famous locally for our addiction to biscuits."

Actually they were famous a lot further out than Jacobsville, but he didn't want to make her think they were loopy.

She took the words at face value. "I like to cook."

He glanced at her again, taking in her very conservative way of dressing. "You don't look like the same woman I met just after Leo was assaulted."

"I almost never dress up," she confided. "And it really was a costume," she pointed out. "I wasn't lying. I don't make my living on the streets."

"How old are you?"

Her eyebrows arched. "Old enough."

"Are you over twenty-one?" he persisted.

"I'm twenty-three, almost twenty-four," she replied.

"And not married?"

"I've had responsibilities for the past few years," she said distantly, staring out the windshield. "My father has become the largest of them. I've been afraid to leave him alone."

"He's obviously dangerous when he drinks."

She hesitated, fingering her purse. "He seemed to lose himself in the bottle overnight. I thought I could handle him, control him, break the cycle. I couldn't even get help for him. My father doesn't think he has a drinking problem, so nobody would take him." She looked over at him. "I'm very grateful to your brother for his help. As I mentioned the night he was arrested, my father has only been like this for the past few months. It's not a long-standing problem. But I couldn't solve it alone."

"You're going to work for us," Rey said. "And it's not that much of a problem for Simon. He's good at his job."

"Is it a big ranch?" she asked unexpectedly.

"Enormous," he replied, "and one of five ranches we own as a family. Things get hectic during roundup, as you'll find out if you're still there next Spring."

"I won't be," she said with some certainty. "When I heal, I have to get back to my job."

"What do you do?" he asked curiously. "Is it housecleaning or working as a cook in a restaurant?"

She almost bit her tongue at the demeaning comment. "You don't think I'm qualified to do anything else?"

He averted his eyes to the road. "I don't know you, Miss Johns," he commented carelessly. "But you seem pretty domestic to me."

She didn't feel well enough to retaliate. But one day, she promised herself, she was going to make him eat those condescending words.

"I've made beds and done light cleaning," she said, talking around her actual profession.

"Aren't you ambitious?" he persisted, with a faint frown. "Most women are, these days."

"That sounded bitter," she commented. "Did you get thrown over by an ambitious woman?"

"By a couple of them," he said curtly, and his expression became hard.

She hadn't thought of him that way. They'd been adversaries from the first contact. But it occurred to her as she gave him a quick, covert scrutiny, that he was a sensuous man. He wasn't handsome—except for Corrigan Hart, the rest of the brothers seemed cursed by a lack of conventional good looks.

But Rey had a lithe, graceful stride, and a strong face. He had good hands, clean and long-fingered. She liked the blackness of his straight hair, the high cheekbones, the long, thin, chiseled mouth. He was the sort of man who could have attracted women, except for his personality. The Harts didn't strike her as particularly gregarious or good mixers from her brief acquaintance with them. Leo was the one with the warmest personality. He made her feel at ease. The man beside her made her uncomfortable, insecure, nervous. She wasn't usually so strung-out by a man's proximity. Not that she'd had a lot to do with men in very recent years. Her father's overprotective, possessive nature had seen to that. He'd been so certain that she was going to end up like her mother.

She closed her eyes briefly, hating the memories.

"If you want to go and see your father before we leave for Jacobsville, I'll ask Simon to arrange it."

She stiffened. "I don't want to see him again until he's sober," she replied. "We both need time to get over what happened."

"Is your face the only place he hit you?" he asked unexpectedly.

"He got me in the back and the side, too, but those were only bruises. The doctor checked me over thoroughly." She sighed wearily. "I'm so tired," she murmured absently.

"I'm not surprised. You can get some rest. I'll phone you tomorrow, when we'll know more about Leo's condition and when he'll be released."

"Okay."

He stopped in front of her house and parked the car, walking to the door with her. He looked down at her while she fumbled the key into the lock. She was, in some ways, the most vulnerable woman he'd ever met. But there was steel in her makeup. He sensed that she wasn't like this usually, that she was fiery and independent and determined.

"This isn't the first time your father's laid into you, is it?" he asked suddenly.

She glanced at him, surprised. "No. But until this happened, it was more humiliating than painful." She frowned. "How did you know?"

He seemed concerned. "When I was in school, I had a couple of friends whose fathers got violent during binges. There's an…attitude, a posture, that people get when they've been beaten. I can't explain it, but I recognize it when I see it."

"Do you want to know what it is?" she asked with a world-weary smile. "It's a feeling of futility, of knowing that no matter what you do, you can't hold out physically against a man who's enraged and bent on hurting you. Because you know if you fight back, it will be even worse, maybe fatally worse. I don't like it," she added, her pale eyes beginning to glow, "and he's never getting the chance to do this again. He's my father. I love him, and I feel sorry for him. But I'm nobody's victim. Not even his."

He pushed his hands into his slacks' pockets and smiled at her. Her face was bright with color, and her eyes were alive, like peridots in sunlit water. He remembered her long blond hair around her shoulders and he wondered what she'd look like in pink silk. The thought shocked him and he scowled.

"Did I glue my nose on upside down?" she asked, raising her eyebrows.

He let out a short laugh. "No. I had a wild thought. Do you need an advance on your salary? I mean, is there anything you have to get for the trip that you can't afford?"

"I don't have a car," she began, and hated remembering why.

He glared. "I didn't say you were going to have to get to Jacobsville on your own. You'll go with Leo and me. Simon drove my car up from Jacobsville."

"Do I get to ride in the car, or have you got me earmarked for the trunk?" she returned.

He pursed his lips. Odd feelings were kindling inside him. "Keep that up and you'll be riding on the back bumper."

She wrinkled her nose. "Nice. Real nice. I can see you're going to be a great boss."

"If you don't burn the biscuits, I will be," he said.

"I'll stick close to your brother," she promised. "He'll protect me."

He didn't like that, but he wasn't going to let it show. "Leo's a tease," he said flatly. "Don't get your hopes up. He's not a marrying man. Neither am I," he added deliberately.

Her eyes widened. "Well, gee whiz, that's a major disappointment! And to think, I was only willing to take the job because of the marriage prospects!"

His face shuttered. "Sarcasm doesn't get you any points with me. I'm just making the position clear. We need a cook, not a prospective soul mate."

"Speak for yourself," she told him, turning back to her door. "I think Leo likes me already."

"I just told you…!"

She opened the door and looked back at him with pure irreverence. "Your brother can speak for himself. You don't own him, and you don't own me. I'll do what I please."

"Damn it…!"

"With charm like that, it's no surprise to me that you're still single," she said as she walked into the house.

"I can be charming when I've got a reason to be," he said icily. "But that's something you'll never know!"

"Lucky me!"

He started to speak, closed his lips tight, and walked back to his car.

She closed the door quickly and leaned back against it, almost shivering with anger. Of all the conceited, infuriating men she'd ever met, that one took the cake!

* * *

The next day, Rey phoned her midmorning to tell her that he and Leo would pick her up at one for the drive down to Jacobsville.

She had her suitcase packed and the house closed up when the big luxury car pulled into the driveway. It was a late-model car, and it looked odd, sitting in front of the shabby little house.

As she walked to the car, Meredith saw curtains fluttering and knew that the neighbors were getting an eyeful. They probably thought she was being carried off by the mob. That amused her and she smiled, glad that something diverted her mind from her father and her pain, and the misery of the past few months.

"We hadn't planned to ask you to help us move cattle," Rey drawled when he saw how she was dressed, in jeans and a striped shirt and boots.

"I haven't volunteered, either," she assured him. "But I didn't think you'd want me to do housework in a dress." She gave him a wry glance. "Those old black-and-white sitcoms weren't historically accurate, you know. I never saw a woman vacuum the carpet wearing a dress and high heels and pearls!"

"You can do housework in a suit for all I care, as long as you can bake me a pan of biscuits every morning," Rey said, taking the suitcase and putting it in the trunk.

"Good morning," Leo called from the open window of the front seat, grinning as Rey opened the back door and helped her inside.

"Good morning," she said brightly. "You look much better."

"I feel better, except for the headache." He gave her a long look. "You aren't in very good shape yourself. Face hurt?"

"Yes. I guess we're both like walking wounded, huh?" she asked with a grin as she leaned back into the warm leather seat.

"Maybe we should take a nurse with us," Rey muttered as he got in and started the car.

Meredith cleared her throat, but before she could speak, Leo turned to his brother. "I don't need nursing, thank you very much!" Leo said curtly.

"Neither do I!" Meredith agreed.

Rey glanced at them as he pulled out into the street. "I've seen accident victims who looked better than the two of you."

"Don't let him insult you, Meredith," Leo told her. "I'll tell you all about his weak spots so that you can deal with him."

She wouldn't have expected Rey to have any of those, but she was keeping her mouth shut and her options open for the time being. Her new boss looked formidable, and even Leo seemed curious about his lack of warmth.

"Are you all from Jacobsville originally?" Meredith changed the subject.

"No, we're from San Antonio," Leo said. "We inherited the Jacobsville property and it needed a lot of work, so we made it our headquarters. It's convenient to Houston and San Antonio, and frankly, it's isolated and gives us some privacy. We don't like cities as a rule."

"Neither do I," she said, recalling her grandmother's beautiful flower garden at the old place near Fort Worth. She smiled. "I wish Dad hadn't taken the job in Houston in the first place."

"What does he do?" Leo asked.

"He's retired," she said, not wanting to go into specifics. 't hurt to talk about her family. Her father was a sore spot st now, anyway.

"Simon talked to the authorities," Rey interrupted. "They're going to make sure he gets counseling and he won't be released until he's kicked the alcohol habit." He glanced over the seat at her, his dark eyes intent. "They think it will be better if you don't have any contact with him for a few weeks, until he's through the worst of the withdrawal symptoms."

"I know about withdrawal," she replied, absently smoothing her hand over her jeans. "Bad habits are hard to break, even new ones."

"You two must read a lot," Rey replied. "I never saw so many books in one place as I did at your house. Even our library isn't that stuffed, and we all read."

"I love reading," she agreed. "We have a television, but neither of us had much time to watch it. Until recently," she added reluctantly, and winced at the thoughts that went through her mind. "I hope they get those men who mugged you, Mr. Hart," she told Leo fervently.

"Leo," he corrected. "It's really Leopold, but nobody calls me that," he added with a grin. "We're pretty informal with our employees."

"Do you have a lot?" she asked curiously.

"A good many in Jacobsville," he replied. "Although we don't have a full-time vet, we do have several accountants, livestock managers, computer programmers, salesmen... you name it, we've got one. It's big business these days to run cattle. We even have a man who does nothing but keep up with legislation that may impact us."

"Do you have dogs and cats?" she asked.

"Always," Rey replied. "We have border collies that help us herd cattle, and we keep cats in the barn to help handle the rats."

"We had a cat in the house," Leo added, "but it was Cag and Tess's, and they took it with them when they move into their new house. At least she won't have to cope with Herman," he told his brother, and laughed.

Rey smiled involuntarily. "You might not have wanted to work for us if we still had Herman."

"Who's Herman?" she wanted to know.

"He was Cag's albino python," he told her. "He weighed a hundred and ten pounds and lived in a cage in Cag's bedroom. He gave Herman up when he married Tess. He said it would be crazy to keep an animal that big and dangerous around their son. They're still over the moon about that little boy."

"Yes, but there are people who don't even consider things like that," Meredith murmured absently. "I remember a little girl who had to have plastic surgery because she was bitten in the face by her father's pet boa constrictor."

"Herman didn't bite, but Tess almost had a heart attack when she first came to work for us and found him in the washing machine."

"I can sympathize with her," Meredith said. "I haven't come across many snakes. I'm not sure I want to."

"We have rattlers and water moccasins around the place," Rey told her. "You have to watch where you walk, but we've only had one person bitten in recent years. Snakes are always going to be a hazard in open country. You can't be careless."

"I'll remember."

"We've got a big garage apartment," Leo told her. "It's got picture windows and a whirlpool bath. Tess lived there until she and Cag married. I think you'll like it."

"I don't mind where I stay," she said easily. "I'm grateful to have a job at all. I really couldn't go to work in Houston looking like this. It would have been embarrassing for my boss."

"You won't have people staring at you on the ranch," Leo

assured her. "And it won't take too long for those bruises to heal."

"I'll be fine, but you'll have to take it easy for a few days still, I'm sure they told you that," she returned at once. "No violent exertion. Concussion is tricky."

"I know that," Leo told her. "We had a man who was kicked in the head by a horse. He dropped dead three days later while he was walking into the corral. It was a hard lesson about head injuries. None of us ever forgot it."

She averted her eyes. She didn't like thinking about head injuries just now.

"I've got to stop for gas," Rey said as they reached the outskirts of the city and he pulled into a self-service gas station. "Anybody want something to drink?"

"Coffee for me," Leo said. "Meredith?"

"I'd like a small coffee, black, please."

"I'll go get it after I fill the tank," Rey said. He got out and started pumping gas.

Leo leaned his arm over the backseat and looked at Meredith openly, his dark eyes quiet and gently affectionate.

"You're still having a hard time with Rey, aren't you?" he asked her.

"He doesn't really like me," she confessed with a wry smile. "And I have to admit, he puts my back up, too. He seems to want to think the worst of me. He was convinced that I mugged you."

He chuckled. "You aren't tall enough to have knocked me out," he said. "But Rey doesn't like women much. He had a bad time of it with a young woman who turned out to be a call girl," he added, noticing absently how stunned Meredith seemed to be at that remark. "He had the ring bought, the honeymoon spot picked out, and then he found out the truth about her. It took him years to get over it. He was crushed."

"I guess so," she said heavily. "Good Lord, no wonder he thought the worst when he saw how I was dressed."

Leo frowned. "I just barely remember the rig you had on. What was it, some sort of costume?"

"I'd been to a wild Halloween party and had just escaped when I saw those men bending over you," she told him. "I ran at them waving my arms and yelling, and frightened them off."

"That was taking a hell of a chance!" he exploded.

She shrugged. "I've done it before," she said. "I learned it from my…from my brother's best friend," she amended, forcing the words out. It was much too soon to try to talk about her tragedy. "He taught karate in the military. He said that sometimes all it needed was a yell and the element of surprise to spook an attacker and make him run. It works."

"Not all the time," Leo said darkly, "and not for women. I'm all for equality, but most men are bigger and stronger than most women, and in hand-to-hand, you'd lose. You can't count on a man running, loud noise or not."

"Well, it worked for you," she amended, and smiled at him. "I'm glad, because I couldn't have wrestled those guys down."

He nodded. "See that you remember it," he told her. "Don't take chances. Get help."

"Some help those partygoers would have been," she scoffed. "Half of them were drunk, and the other half probably wouldn't have walked across the street to save a grandmother from a mugging!"

"Then why were you at a party with them?" he asked reasonably.

She picked at a fingernail. "A girl I know from work said I needed a night off and insisted that I come. I wore an old costume, the only one I had, and thought I'd enjoy myself. I don't do drugs or drink, and one of the men made a blatant pass at me." She wrapped her arms around her body in a defensive posture that betrayed her fear. "I was anxious to get away from the whole mess, luckily for you," she added with a grin.

"I don't like parties much, either," he said. "Getting drunk isn't my idea of a good time."

She glanced out the window. Rey had finished pumping gas and was inside the convenience store now. "Does he drink?" she asked.

"Very rarely. I've been known to, under provocation, but Rey's levelheaded and sober. He can be mean, and he's got the blackest temper of all of us, but he's a good man to have on your side when the chips are down."

"He doesn't like me," she repeated.

"He'll come around, give him time," Leo told her. "Meanwhile, you've got a job and a place to stay while your face heals. We all have hard times," he added gently. "But we get through them, even when we don't expect to. Give yourself time."

She smiled. "Thanks," she said huskily. "You really are a nice man."

"Nice, clean, sober, modest and incredibly handsome," he added with a wicked grin. "And I haven't even gotten to my best points yet!"

"Compared to your brothers," she began, "you—"

The door opened before she could hang herself, and Rey shoved a cup of coffee at her before he handed the second one to Leo.

"It's hot," he told them as he slid in and took the soft drink out of his jacket pocket and put it in the cup holder.

"Cold caffeine," Leo said, shuddering. "Why can't you drink coffee like a normal man?"

"I drink coffee at breakfast," Rey told him haughtily.

"So do I, but you don't have to have rules on when to drink it!"

Rey started the engine with a speaking glance.

"See that look?" Leo indicated it to Meredith. "When he looks like that, you've already lost whatever argument you're in the middle of. We call it 'the look.' I once saw him break up a fistfight with it."

"I don't plan to argue," Meredith promised.

Rey gave her "the look," and it lingered before his attention turned back to the windshield.

Meredith sat back against the leather seat and wondered suddenly if she wasn't making the biggest mistake of her life.

Chapter Four

The Hart Ranch was almost as Meredith had pictured it, with neat wooden fences concealing electrified fencing, improved pasture land and cattle everywhere. There were also pastures with horses, and there was a barn big enough to store a commercial jet. But she loved the house itself, with its graceful arches reminiscent of Spanish architecture, and the incredible number of small trees and shrubs around it. In the spring, it must be glorious. There were two ponds, a decorative one in the front of the house and a larger one behind the house in which a handful of ducks shivered in the November sun.

"Do you have goldfish in the pond?" she asked excitedly as Rey stopped the car in front of the house on an inlaid stone driveway.

"Goldfish and Koi," he answered, smiling reluctantly at her excitement. "We have a heater in the pond to keep them comfortable during the winter. There are water lilies in there, too, and a lotus plant."

"Does the other pond have goldfish, too, where the ducks are?" she wondered.

Leo chuckled. "The other one is because of the ducks. We had to net this pond to keep them out of it so we'd *have* some goldfish. The ducks were eating them."

"Oh, I see." She sighed. "It must be beautiful here in the spring," she said dreamily, noting the gazebo and the rose garden and stone seats and shrubs around the goldfish pond.

"It's beautiful to us year-round," Leo told her with lazy affection. "We all love flowers. We've got some more roses in a big flower garden around the back of the house, near a stand of pecan trees. Tess is taking courses in horticulture and she works with hybrids."

"I love roses," Meredith said softly. "If I had time, I'd live in a flower garden."

"I suppose cleaning rooms is time-consuming," Rey murmured sarcastically as he got out of the car and went in the front door of the house.

Leo glanced at her curiously while Rey was out of earshot. "You clean rooms?"

"I don't," she told him with a sharp grin. "But I'm living down to your brother's image of my assets."

Leo pursed his lips. "Now, that's interesting. You sound like a woman with secrets."

"More than you'd guess," she told him heavily. "But none that I'm ashamed of," she added quickly, just in case he got the wrong idea.

"Rey doesn't like you, does he?" he murmured, almost to himself. "I wonder why? It's not like him to pick on sick people."

"I'm not sick," she assured him. "I'm just battered, but I'll heal."

"Sure you will," Leo promised, smiling. "You'll be safe here. The only real chore you'll have is baking. By the time you're completely back on your feet, your father will be sober and in counseling, and your home life will have changed drastically."

"I hope so," she said huskily.

He watched her eyes grow tragic and haunted. He frowned. "Meredith," he said slowly. "If you need to talk, ever, I can listen without making judgments."

She met his clear dark eyes. "Thanks, Leo," she said with genuine gratitude. "But talking won't change a thing. It's a matter of learning to live with…things."

"Now I'm intrigued."

"Don't push," she said gently. "I'm not able to talk about my problems yet. They're too fresh. Too painful."

"And more than just your father, or I'm a dirt farmer," he drawled.

She shrugged. "Perhaps."

"Anyway, just take your time and let the world pass you by. You're going to love it here. I promise."

"Am I?" She watched Rey come back out of the house with an elderly lady in tow, wringing her hands on her apron.

"That's Mrs. Lewis," Leo told her. "We talked her into coming back to bake biscuits for us, even though she'd retired, but now we're losing her to arthritis. She's going to show you the ropes. But not right now," he added quickly.

"No time like the present," Meredith disagreed with a smile. "Busy hands make busy minds."

"I know how that works," Leo murmured drolly.

Rey opened the back door and helped Meredith out. "Mrs. Lewis, this is Meredith Johns, our new cook. Meredith,

Annie Lewis. She's retiring. Again." He made it sound like a shooting offense.

"Oh, my, yes, I'm losing the use of my hands, I'm afraid," Mrs. Lewis said. "Glad to meet you, Miss Johns."

"Glad to meet you, too, Mrs. Lewis," Meredith replied.

"I'll take your bag to your room, while Mrs. Lewis shows you around the house," Rey added.

"She just got here," Leo protested.

"And there's no time like the present to show her the house," Rey replied.

"That's just what she said," Leo sighed.

Rey glanced at Meredith, who gave him a wicked grin and followed along behind Annie Lewis, who was making a valiant effort not to ask about the terrible bruises on Meredith's face.

"It's a big, sprawling house, and it takes a lot of cleaning," Mrs. Lewis said as she led Meredith down the long hall and opened doors to the very masculine bedrooms both with dark, heavy Mediterranean furniture and earth tones in the drapes and carpets. "The men aren't messy, thank God, but they track in all that mud and dust and animal fur! They had beige carpeting when I came here." She glanced at Meredith with a shake of her head. "Red mud just won't come *out* of beige carpet!"

"Or anything else," Meredith added on a soft laugh.

"They work hard, and they're away a lot. But the foreman lives in the bunkhouse with a couple of bachelor cowboys, and they'll look out for you."

"I don't know that I'll be here very long," Meredith replied quietly. "They offered me the job so that I can have time for these to heal." She touched her face, and looked straight at the older woman, who was struggling not to ask the question in her eyes.

"Nobody will hurt you here," Mrs. Lewis said firmly.

Meredith smiled gently. "My father got drunk and beat me up, Mrs. Lewis," she explained matter-of-factly. "He's a good and kind man, but we've had a terrible tragedy to work through. He hasn't been able to cope with it except by losing himself in a bottle, and now he's gone too far and he's in jail." She sighed. "I tried so hard to help him. But I couldn't."

Mrs. Lewis didn't say a word. She put her arms around Meredith and rocked her in them. The shock of it brought the tears that she'd held back for so long. She wept until her body shook with sobs.

Rey, looking for her, stopped dead in the doorway of his bedroom and met Mrs. Lewis's misty eyes over Meredith's bowed shoulders. It shocked him to see that feisty, strong woman collapsed in tears. It hurt him.

Mrs. Lewis made a gesture with her eyebrows and a severe look. Rey acknowledged it with a nod and a last glance at the younger woman as he walked back down the hall.

Supper was riotous. Meredith had made a huge pan of homemade biscuits and ferreted out all sorts of preserves to go with them. For an entrée, she made fajitas with lean beef and sliced vegetables, served with wild rice and a salad. Dessert was fresh fruit and fresh whipped cream, the only concession besides the biscuits that she made to fat calories. She'd also found some light margarine to set out.

"This is good," Rey commented as he glanced at her. "We usually have broiled or fried steak with lots of potatoes."

"Not bad once a week or so, but terrible for your cholesterol," she pointed out with a smile as she finished her salad. "Lean beef is okay for you, but not in massive doses."

"You sound like a dietician," Leo chuckled.

"Modern women have to keep up with health issues,"

she said evasively. “I’m responsible for your health while I’m working for you. I have to be food-conscious.”

“That’s fine,” Rey told her flatly, “but don’t put tofu and bean sprouts in front of me if you want to stay here.”

Her eyebrows arched. “I hate tofu.”

“Thank God,” Leo sighed as he buttered another biscuit. “I got fed tofu salad the last time I went to Brewster’s for supper,” he added with absolute disgust. “I ate the olives and the cheese and left the rest.”

“I can’t say that I blame you,” Meredith said, laughing because he looked so forlorn.

“Janie Brewster thinks tofu is good for him,” Rey commented. “But she thinks he needs therapy more. He doesn’t like fish. She says that has some sort of connection to his fear of deep water.” He glanced at his brother with wicked affection. “She’s a psychology major. She already has an associate degree from our local junior college.”

“She’s twenty,” Leo said with a twist of his lower lip. “She knows everything.”

“She just got her associate degree this spring,” Rey added.

“Good. Maybe she’ll get a job in New York,” Leo said darkly.

“Why New York?” Meredith asked curiously.

“Well, it’s about as far east as she can go and find her sort of work,” Leo muttered. “And she’d be out of my hair!”

Rey gave him a covert glance and finished his fajitas.

Meredith finished her own meal and got up to refill coffee cups. She had a feeling that Leo was more interested in the nebulous Brewster girl than he wanted to admit.

“We need groceries,” she told them when she’d served dessert and they were eating it. “Mrs. Lewis made me a list.”

"You can use one of the ranch trucks to drive to town," Leo suggested carelessly.

Her fingers toyed with her fork. "I haven't driven in several months."

"You don't drive?" Rey exclaimed, shocked.

She couldn't meet his eyes. "I take buses." Cars made her feel guilty.

"Why?"

She remembered a day she should have driven. The memories were horrible…

"Meredith, it's all right," Leo said gently, sensing something traumatic about her behavior. "I'll drive you. Okay?"

"You won't," Rey replied. "You're in worse shape than she is. Which brings up another point. You don't need to be walking around town like that," he told her.

She wasn't offended; it was a relief. She even smiled. "No, I don't guess I do. Will you do the shopping?" she asked him, her wide, soft eyes steady on his.

He felt wild little thrills shooting through his body at the impact. It had been years since he'd been so shaken by eye contact alone. He didn't move. He just stared at her, his dark eyes unblinking, curious. His body rippled with vague hunger.

Leo, watching the eye contact, tried not to grin. He cleared his throat, and Rey seemed to remember that he had a forkful of fruit halfway to his mouth. He took it the rest of the way and chewed it carefully before he spoke.

"I'll get the groceries," Rey volunteered. He glared at both of them, noting the shaved place where Leo had stitches near the back of his head. "Obviously I'm the only one here who can walk around without drawing curious stares from bystanders!"

Leo buttered another biscuit. "That sounds like sour

grapes to me. If you want attention, try walking around without your pants."

"I didn't say I wanted attention," Rey returned hotly.

"Good thing." He glanced at Meredith with a mischievous smile. "He looks like hell without his pants," he said conversationally. "Hairiest legs of the bunch."

"That's debatable," Rey shot back. "Yours aren't much better."

"What a good thing you two aren't Scottish," Meredith said demurely.

It took a minute for them to get it, then Leo burst out laughing, trying to picture his younger brother in a kilt. Rey lifted a corner of his thin mouth, but he wasn't in a smiling mood. It bothered him, that Meredith had been crying in Mrs. Lewis's arms, that she didn't drive, that she was so mysterious about her life. She was twenty-three, almost twenty-four. Most women by that age had been involved in a serious relationship, some more than one. Many had been married.

His heart skipped. Was that her secret? He remembered watching her rub her ring finger in the car. He glanced at it curiously. She didn't wear a ring, and there was no sign that she'd been wearing one there. She didn't act married. She hadn't talked about having a husband. She was single, apparently by choice. But had there been men in her past? He was still carrying scars from his one great love affair, from the deception he'd endured. Meredith had gone out walking to a party in a rig that made her look like a prostitute, and she'd been comfortable doing that. It wasn't something an innocent girl would have considered.

Knowing that, he looked at her in a different way, speculatively. She had a nice figure and she wasn't all flushing smiles like Janie Brewster when Leo was around. Meredith was oddly mature for her age, almost matronly. She seemed to be used to giving instructions, too. She was a puzzle that disturbed him. What if she was hiding something sordid in her past? He and Leo had taken her in on faith and pity, but now he wondered if they'd made a terrible mistake. If she were in league with the men who'd robbed Leo, they might have a dangerous situation developing. What if she'd planned the whole thing as a means to an end?

Basically Rey didn't trust her. He wasn't going to let down his guard, either, no matter if looking at her did raise his blood pressure. She wasn't going to know that she did. And he'd keep his eyes open, all the time, just in case.

The days turned to a week. Meredith's painful bruises faded slowly. She lost some of the brooding sadness that seemed to cling to her like the jeans she wore around the house when she was working. She found the slower, easier pace strange, and she missed the urgency of her daily routine. But as the days went by lazily, she realized that she hadn't really given herself time to think. She'd avoided it, ignored it, hoping that the past would vanish. Now she was face to face with it, forced to reflect on what had happened.

She sat beside the fishpond one sunny afternoon, between chores, and watched the goldfish under the surface of the dark water as they moved sluggishly. The water wasn't frozen, but it was cold. The pond heater only kept a small area heated, so the fish were limited in movement. She could imagine how it would be to sit here in the summer and watch them move around in their watery world, with flowers blooming all around.

She'd loved planting flowers. She missed her home, her bulbs and shrubs, the familiar things that she'd accumulated around her. Now it was all gone, sold without a second thought to make the memories bearable. It was too late, and she wished she'd been more sensible. There were things she should have kept. Mike's stupid baseball cap, the one he always wore on the rare occasions when he wasn't working, and when he went fishing. She missed her mother's collection of small silk Chinese boxes and her pretty evening gowns. She'd thrown all those things away. At the time, it had seemed reasonable to cut all the ties with the past. It didn't now.

The sound of a truck pulling up to the front door caught her attention. Rey and Leo had been out of town for two days, attending another cattle convention, this time in Denver.

They climbed out of the cab of the big six-wheeled pickup truck and retrieved their suitcases from the back, waving as the ranch truck pulled right out again and took off down the road.

Meredith got up and went to join them.

"Want some coffee and pie?" she asked with a smile.

"That would really hit the spot," Leo said, returning the smile. "I hate commercial flights."

"You're the smart guy who said our jet needed to be overhauled," Rey reminded him.

"It did," Leo replied.

Rey was looking at Meredith openly. "The bruises are fading," he remarked. "You have more color, too."

"I've been getting out in the sunlight," she replied easily. "I like to watch the fish, even though they don't move much."

"We might put a big aquarium inside," Rey remarked, unaware of his brother's quick, curious glance. "I like fish myself."

"They've done studies," Meredith volunteered as they stood aside to let her enter the house first. "They say watching fish swim is calming. It helps relieve stress."

"God knows, we could use some of that," Leo chuckled. "Especially when cattle prices fall and feed prices go through the roof."

"Cattle raising must be a complex process," she remarked.

"Very complex," Rey said. He frowned as he watched her walk. "Hip sore?" he asked.

She laughed self-consciously. "Well, yes, it is. How did you know?"

"You've got a light limp on the right side. Barely noticeable."

She rubbed her hip self-consciously. "I fell on that side, the night Dad hit me," she told him. "The floor's pretty hard."

"There's a whirlpool bath in your bedroom," Rey reminded her. "It'll help the soreness."

"I discovered that," she said, grinning. "What a luxury! We only have a shower at home, and it's temperamental."

Rey gave her a long look. "When we've had time to catch our breath, I'll see what I can find out about your father, if you'd like."

Her face brightened. "That would be nice."

He smiled slowly, liking the way her pale eyes seemed to glow when she was pleased. She wasn't bad-looking at all, and her figure was just about perfect. He wondered how she could have remained single for so long, with her homemaking skills, not to mention her sweet personality and that knockout body.

She was watching him with equal appreciation, and totally unaware of it. He had a lithe, powerful physique that made her think of rodeo. He walked with a unique sort of grace, and he didn't stoop or slouch, ever. She liked his eyes best of all. They were almost a liquid-brown, and they had black rims around the pupils. He was rugged and sensuous and she looked at his wide thin mouth and wondered for the first time how it would feel to kiss it.

Her thoughts horrified her. She dragged her eyes away and excused herself in an absolute fluster to go make coffee.

Leo lifted both eyebrows and stared at his brother after she was out of earshot. "Well, well," he murmured. "You do seem to be making an impression on her."

"Cut it out," Rey said testily.

"And vice versa," came the irritating reply.

Rey made a rough sound in his throat and stomped off down the hall to his room. He put down his suitcase, took off his suit and dress shirt and got into jeans and a checked long-sleeved work shirt. He glanced at himself in the mirror as he buttoned it, his eyes blank as he recalled the wild flush on Meredith's cheeks. It shouldn't please him. He didn't trust her. She could be trying to play them all for suckers. But he smiled, just the same.

Meredith had coffee and cherry pie in saucers on the table by the time the brothers were changed and walking into the kitchen.

"Coffee's fresh," she said.

"Aren't you having any?" Rey asked.

"I have to get the clothes into the dryer," she excused herself with a quick smile. "Yell if you need anything."

She was gone in a flash.

Rey stared broodingly at his pie and frowned. She didn't want to have coffee with them. Why?

"You make her nervous," Leo said, answering the unspoken question. "She knows you don't trust her."

Rey frowned as he nibbled at his pie and sipped coffee. "I don't know her," he replied. He gave his brother a speaking glance. "We've always done background checks on employees," he added firmly. "I don't think we should make an exception of her, even though she's temporary."

"Translated, that means you want to know more about her than you do," Leo drawled, grinning.

"Maybe I do," Rey confessed. "But she's in a position to do a lot of damage if she isn't what she seems. You could have been killed, or suffered brain damage," he added quietly. "If she's in cahoots with the guys who mugged you..." He let the sentence trail off meaningfully.

Leo grimaced. "I don't like poking into peoples' private business," he replied. "But you're right. It's risky not to check her out."

"I'll get the agency on it first thing tomorrow," Rey said. He took another bite of the pie. "She's a hell of a good cook," he murmured.

"Makes good coffee, too," Leo commented.

They looked at each other and grimaced. It was going to upset Meredith if she found out what they were up to. But it was too much of a gamble not to find out what they could about her background and character. On the other hand, Leo promised himself, he was going to intercept that background check before Rey had a chance to see it. If Meredith had secrets she was hiding for a good reason, he wasn't going to give her away to Rey.

It took several days for the private detective to get to the case and send a report to the Harts.

Rey was out of town at a one-day seminar on a new spreadsheet computer program the brothers were using for herd records when the report arrived. Leo carried the report into his office and closed the door while he read it.

When he finished, he let out a harsh breath. So that was Meredith's secret. No wonder her father drank. No wonder she was so reticent and quiet about her past. He smiled as he considered her true profession, and he was determined that Rey wasn't going to know about it until disclosure was inevitable. Rey was too prone to conclusion-jumping and rushing to judgment. It was about time he had a set down, and Meredith was just the woman to give it to him. Meanwhile, he'd let Rey work on hanging himself. Obviously Meredith was enjoying her anonymity, and considering the high-powered pressures of her daily job, it wasn't surprising that she found mundane housekeeping a nice change. It wouldn't hurt to let her enjoy the vacation from stress, without probing into her feelings. No doubt she still felt the grief, even after several months.

He touched the report with idle fingers, frowning as he recognized one of the names on it. Mike had been a Houston policeman. He was also a friend of Colter Banks, a Texas Ranger and cousin of the Harts, who worked out of the Houston ranger office. It really was a small world. He wanted to tell Meredith that he remembered Mike, but he didn't want to blow her cover. He also didn't want her to know that they'd been checking up on her.

He put the file into the filing cabinet, deliberately putting it under the wrong letter of the alphabet. If Rey asked, he'd just tell him that the agency was working on it but had other, more urgent cases to assign agents to first.

Meredith was alone in the house when Rey came in, late that night, from his business trip. Leo had gone to dinner at the Brewsters' house again, presumably at the invitation of Janie's father, to talk about a new breeding bull the Brewsters were trying to sell him.

She'd just started the dishwasher and was ready to turn the lights off in the kitchen when she heard Rey come in.

He paused in the kitchen doorway, a black Stetson slanted over one dark eye, wearing a grey vested suit that clung lovingly to the hard, muscular lines of his tall body. Meredith felt ragged by comparison in her jeans and red T-shirt, and barefoot. Her hair was disheveled because she'd been scrubbing the floor with a brush, and she wasn't wearing makeup. She hadn't expected to see either of the brothers before she went to bed.

Rey's dark eyes went to her pretty feet and he smiled. "You don't like shoes, do you?"

She grimaced. "No, and it's not good to go without them. No arch support." She studied his lean face. He had dark circles under his eyes. "Would you like some coffee and something to eat?"

"I would," he said heavily. "They gave me peanuts on the plane," he added with absolute disgust.

She chuckled. The sound was pleasant, and Rey was surprised at how it touched him to hear her laugh.

"I'll make you a nice thick low-fat ham sandwich with sauce."

"Thanks," he said, sliding a chair out so that he could straddle it. He tossed his hat into the chair beside him and ran a hand through his thick dark hair. "Make the coffee first, Meredith. I've got paperwork that has to be done tonight before the accountant comes to do the books in the morning."

"Can't it wait?" she asked gently. "You look worn to a frazzle. You need an early night."

His eyes searched hers intently. "I don't need mothering," he said, angered out of all proportion.

She flushed and turned away. She didn't apologize or say another word, but her hands shook as she filled the coffeepot and started it brewing.

Rey cursed himself silently for snapping at her. It was unkind, especially after she'd volunteered to feed him. She'd been working hard, too, he could see the spotless floor and the brush and bucket she'd been using on it. She must have done it on her hands and knees. It was a big kitchen, too. He wasn't the only one who was tired.

He got up from the chair and moved to stand just behind her. His lean hands caught her small waist and pulled her back against him. "I'm sorry," he said, his voice deep and husky with sudden emotion.

Her cold fingers came to rest on his and her whole body went rigid as a flash of white-hot pleasure shot through it. She caught her breath. He heard it. His own body tautened and the hands around her waist suddenly grew possessive, rough, insistent, as they pulled her tight against him.

He could hear her breathing change. He could feel the faint tremor of her hands over his. Impulsively he bent his head and his mouth touched the side of her neck.

Chapter Five

Meredith knew her knees were shaking. She hoped she wasn't going to fall on the floor at his feet with sheer excitement. It had been years since a man had made her feel such a rush of pleasure, and even then, it had been one-sided. She'd been crazy about a man who only saw her as a sort of unrelated sister. But even that wasn't as powerful as what she was feeling with Rey Hart.

His mouth became insistent as it moved slowly up her neck. He began to turn her, in the silence that was suddenly alive with passion. His hard lips traveled to the hollow of her throat, where a tiny pulse hammered, and then up to her chin. His teeth nibbled her chin, moving on to her lower lip. He tugged it away from the top one and tasted it with his tongue. All the while, his lean, strong hands were sliding up and down at her waist, smoothing her body completely against him.

His teeth nipped at her top lip with a sensual approac

that made her breath shiver in her throat. He was experienced, far more so than she was. For all her professional capability, in this way she was a novice, and it showed.

He noticed her lack of sensual response with absent curiosity. She was attracted to him, that was obvious, but it was as if she didn't know what to do.

He guided her hands to his vest and flicked open buttons while his lips teased around hers. She fumbled and he laughed softly, his nose rubbing against hers as he moved her hands and unfastened the buttons on his vest and shirt with deft efficiency. He coaxed her hands inside, against thick hair and hard, warm muscle, while his mouth began to bite at hers, tempting her lips to part. She was stiff, trying not to respond, but her body was hungry.

"Like this," he whispered gently, teaching her mouth the lazy, sensual rhythm he wanted from it. "Taste my mouth, the way I'm tasting yours. Don't fight what you're feeling."

She heard the words as if through a fog. She didn't understand what he was saying, but her body obeyed him. She was in a sensual limbo, her hands flat against his chest, her head lifted, her eyes slitted and looking up into his as he began to increase the teasing pressure of his mouth. She followed his lips. She relaxed into the curve of his powerful body with a little shiver.

He devoured her mouth roughly, again and then again, tempting her until her mouth followed his, returning the arousing pressure. She could see the glitter grow in his narrow eyes, feel the grip of his lean hands as he pushed her hips against the sudden hardness of him. She gasped with embarrassment and then lost all sense of it as his mouth opened and pushed down hard against her parted lips, drowning her in passion.

It was like flying, she thought dazedly. He hesitated for

an instant and her eyes opened, drowsy and curious. Her mouth was swollen, soft, tremulous. She looked at him with fascination, utterly helpless in his embrace. He felt an unfamiliar protectiveness toward her. It had been years since he'd kissed an innocent. Meredith's lack of experience was obvious. He was enjoying it.

"Yes," he murmured gruffly, and he bent again. His arms enfolded her, tender arms that no longer forced her into intimacy. His mouth was tender, too, exploring hers with slow mastery, careful not to overwhelm her.

She sighed into his hard mouth, relaxing against him. Her hands moved restlessly on his broad, bare chest, and contracted in the thick mat of hair that covered him.

He lifted his head, staring down into her wide eyes with somber delight. His hands smoothed hers deeper into his thick hair and hard muscle. He traced the edges of her short nails with his thumbs. His breath was jerky. He didn't like having her see that he was vulnerable. There were too many things he still didn't know about her, and he didn't trust her. She seemed innocent, but he couldn't forget the dress she'd been wearing and the accusations her father had made about her. He didn't dare trust her on such short acquaintance. On the other hand, his body was singing with pleasure from the long, hot contact with hers. He couldn't force himself to let her go. Not just yet.

"Why did you do that?" she asked huskily.

One dark eyebrow lifted. He didn't smile. "Why did you let me?" he shot back.

She felt uncomfortable. Despite the effort it took, she moved away from him. He let her go with no show of reluctance. He watched her struggle for composure while he refastened buttons with easy confidence, concealing the effect she had on him. He didn't even look ruffled.

"The coffee must be done by now," he pointed out when she seemed unable to move.

She turned stiffly and went to fill cups and put them, along with cream and sugar, on the table.

While he fixed his coffee, she made him two thick ham sandwiches with hands that slowly lost their tremor. She was devastated by a kiss that didn't seem to have disturbed him at all. She remembered the sudden hardness of his body, but she knew all about anatomy. A man couldn't help that reaction to anything feminine, it was part of his makeup. It wasn't even personal.

Somehow, it made things worse to know that. She felt his eyes on her back, and she knew he was measuring her up. She had no idea why he'd kissed her, but she didn't trust his motives. He didn't like her. She couldn't afford to let her guard down. Rey Hart would be hell on a woman who loved him. She knew that instinctively.

By the time she had the sandwiches made, her hands were steady again and she was able to put them on the table with a cool smile.

"I have to tidy up the living room…" she began.

He caught her hand as she started past him. "Sit down, Meredith," he said quietly.

She sat. He sipped coffee and studied her for a long moment. "I talked to Simon while I was away," he said. "Your father has been released from jail and placed in an alcohol treatment center. It's early days yet, but the prognosis is good. It helps that he hasn't been drinking that heavily for a long time."

She looked relieved and anxiously waited to hear what else Rey had to say about her father.

He continued. "The therapist wouldn't reveal any intimate details to Simon, you understand, but he was able to say that your father had been unable to deal with a family tragedy. Now that he's sober, he's extremely upset about what he did to you." He looked grim. "He doesn't remember doing it, Meredith."

She averted her eyes to her coffee cup. For something to do, she lifted it and took a sip of blistering black coffee, almost burning her lip. "That's common in cases of alcohol or drug abuse," she murmured absently.

He studied her over the rim of his coffee cup. "You won't be allowed to communicate with him until he's through the treatment program, but he wanted you to know that he's desperately sorry for what he did."

She ground her teeth together. She knew that. Her father wasn't a bad man. Until he'd started abusing alcohol, he'd been one of the gentlest men alive. But, like all human beings, he had a breaking point which he reached when tragedy erupted into his life.

"He isn't a bad man," she said quietly. "Although I know it must have seemed like it."

"I've seen drunks before," Rey replied. "My brothers have gone on benders a time or two." He smiled faintly. "In fact, Leo holds the current record for damage at Shea's Bar, out on the Victoria road. He doesn't cut loose often, but when he does, people notice."

"He doesn't seem the sort of man who would do that," she remarked, surprised.

"We're all the sort of men who would do that, given the right provocation," he told her.

She smiled. "Do you get drunk and wreck bars?" she couldn't resist asking.

"I don't drink as a rule," he said simply. "A glass of wine rarely, nothing stronger. I don't like alcohol."

She smiled. "Neither do I."

He leaned back in his chair and studied her quietly. His hair was still faintly disheveled where her hands had caught in it when he was kissing her, and his lower lip was swollen from the pressure of her mouth. She knew she must look almost as bad. Her hand went unconsciously to her unruly hair.

"Take it down," he said abruptly.

"Wh…what?"

"Take your hair down," he said huskily. "I want to see it."

She'd just gotten her wild heart under control, and now it was galloping all over again from that sultry tone, from the dark, intent caress of his eyes on her face.

"Listen, I work for you," she began with a tremor in her voice.

He got up from the chair and moved toward her with a lazy, almost arrogant stride. He drew her up in front of him and started pulling out hairpins. Her hair, unbound, fell in soft waves down her back, almost concealing one eye.

"It's hard to manage when it's down," she said self-consciously.

"I love long hair." He tangled his lean hands in it and coaxed her face up to his. He searched her eyes at point-blank range. "I've kissed girls years younger than you who knew even more than I do. Why are you still a novice?"

She swallowed hard. He was making her knees weak again. She couldn't quite get a whole breath of air into her lungs. Her hands rested on his chest lightly and she felt her heart choking her with its rapid beat as she stared into his narrowed, dark eyes.

"What?" she asked, barely having heard much less understood the question.

His hands were exploring the cool length of her hair with fascination. "You're not bad-looking, Meredith. Surely you've dated."

"Yes," she said, disconcerted. "But I'm old-fashioned."

Both eyebrows went up over a cynical smile. "That's a pitiful excuse in this day and age."

"Why?" she asked, her clear grey eyes staring up into his with no thought of subterfuge. "The whole reason for the women's movement is so that women can have the freedom to do as they please. I'm not promiscuous. Why should I need an excuse?"

He blinked. She made his question sound unreasonable. "I thought sexual liberation was the soul of the movement," he drawled.

"Being chaste is sexual liberation, in my book," she replied. "You'd be amazed how many women in my graduating class practiced abstinence."

"In high school, I gather," he said absently, tracing the length of her hair with his hands.

She almost corrected him, but then, she really mustn't destroy the illusions he had about her as a domestic. "Yes. In high school."

He moved closer to her, his lean body a sensual provocation that made her breath catch. He laughed softly. "Care to test the hypothesis?" he murmured softly.

"I work for you," she repeated, playing for time.

"So?"

"So it's not wise to mix business…"

"…with pleasure?" He caught her waist and drew her close. "It's been a while since I found a woman so desirable," he whispered, bending to her mouth. "Experience bores me. You," he bit off against her soft lips, "are a challenge."

"Thank you, but I don't want to be," she whispered, trying to pull away.

He lifted his head and searched her eyes. "No curiosity about the great unknown?" he taunted.

"No desire to treat it as a sophisticated game," she corrected abruptly.

He hesitated, but only for an instant. His lean hands contracted and then released her. He went back to his chair and sat down. "Touché," he said with a curious glance. "All right, Meredith, I'll sit here and eat my sandwiches and we'll pretend that we're still strangers physically."

"Good idea," she approved. She reached down for her half-empty coffee cup and put it in the sink.

He was halfway through a sandwich when she excused herself and went to fluff up the pillows in the living room and put magazines and books back in their places. Leo had left things strewn about before he'd gone to the Brewsters'. She was glad, because it gave her a valid reason not to sit next to Rey with her emotions in turmoil.

By the time she'd gone back to the kitchen, Rey had finished his sandwiches and coffee and was coming out the door.

"You're safe," he drawled. "I'm going to change and get to work in the study. Where's Leo?"

"Having supper at the Brewsters' house," she told him. "He said he'd be early."

"That means he'll be late," he mused. "Janie Brewster will have found twenty excuses to keep him talking to her father. She's one determined young lady, but Leo's equally determined. He doesn't want ties."

"Doesn't that sound familiar?" she murmured wickedly.

His eyes slid up and down her body in a silence that teemed with tension. "I never said I didn't want ties," he corrected. "I said I didn't want marriage. There's a difference."

"Don't look at me," she said carelessly. "I don't have time for relationships."

"Of course. All that cleaning must demand a lot of you," he said deliberately.

She flushed. He had no idea what her life was like on a daily basis, and she wanted very badly to tell him. But he was so almighty arrogant and condescending that he put her back up. She wasn't going to tell him a thing. He'd find out soon enough.

She put her hands on her hips and stared at him. "And what's wrong with being a housekeeper?" she demanded, going on the offensive. "Where would you and your brother be right now if there weren't women you could hire to bake and clean for you? I guess you'd have to get married then, or learn to cook, wouldn't you?"

He glared at her. "I could cook if I wanted to."

"You're the sort of man who makes a woman wish she didn't have a culinary skill to her name," she said icily. "You are so 'lord of the manor-ish,' Mr. Hart!"

"It isn't a manor," he pointed out. "They have those in England. We call this a ranch."

She glared at him.

He grinned. "You really do rise to the bait beautifully," he murmured, and something flashed in his dark eyes. "The sandwiches were good," he added.

She looked surprised. "Nothing but ham and a home-made sauce," she faltered.

"You do that a lot with food," he remarked gently. "I like the way you experiment with dishes. I even like the way you garnish the plates. You make things look appetizing."

She didn't realize that he'd even noticed. "I learned that from a dietician," she said without thinking. "If food is decorative, sometimes it makes up for bulk."

He smiled quizzically. "You can't decorate biscuits," he teased. "But you make really good ones."

"Thanks." She smiled back. "I'll tidy up the kitchen if you're through."

"I am. Don't stay up too late," he added and his eyes wer

suddenly bright with mischief. "You need plenty of rest so that you can make biscuits for breakfast!"

"Okay. I'll get an early night." She laughed and went on past him to the kitchen.

He stared after her for several long seconds with an expression that he was glad she didn't see. He liked the taste of her. That hadn't been wise, kissing her that way. He was going to have to make sure it didn't happen again. He didn't need complications.

Nothing was the same between Meredith and Rey after that day. They were aware of each other. It wasn't blatant, but she could feel tingling in her spine when Rey was in a room. It was instinctive. Her eyes followed him like puppies, and she flushed wildly when he caught her at it and gave her that amused, worldly glance.

Leo noticed, too, and it worried him that Rey was encouraging Meredith. He knew Rey too well to think he'd had a change of heart toward his bachelor status.

"You're leading her on," Leo accused his brother one evening when they were alone in the study with the door closed. "Why?"

Rey gave him a surprised glance. "You make it sound like a crime to flirt with her."

"In your case, it is," his brother said flatly. "You're a rounder. She isn't."

Rey shrugged. "She's not exactly off-limits," he told his brother. "Not at her age."

"And what do you have in mind? Seduction?" Leo persisted irritably. "She's already been damaged enough by what happened with her father. The bruises are barely healed, and the mental scars are still there. Don't play games with her."

"Aren't you self-righteous all of a sudden?" Rey shot

back angrily. “You’ve been stringing Janie Brewster along for weeks, and we both know you don’t have any intention in hell of getting serious about her. All you want is first chance at that damned seed bull they’re thinking of selling! Does she know?” he added maliciously.

Leo’s eyes began to glitter. “Janie is a child,” he said furiously. “I pick at her, and not because of any damned bull. I’m certainly not hell-bent on seduction!”

“She’s not a child,” Rey countered. “You’re leading her down a blind alley, when you know full well she’s in love with you.”

Leo looked shocked. “She’s not in love with me! Maybe she’s got a crush. That’s all!”

“You don’t see the way she looks at you, do you?” Rey replied solemnly.

Leo cleared his throat. “We’re talking about Meredith,” he said firmly.

Rey’s eyes narrowed. “Meredith is an adult.”

“And she works for us,” Leo went on relentlessly. “I’m not going to stand by and let you make an amusement of her.”

“Jealous?” his brother taunted.

Leo was very still. “Is that the draw?” he asked softly. “Are we competing for a woman again?”

Rey’s eyes flashed. “I would never have known about Carlie if you hadn’t started propositioning her in front of me. Do you think I can forget that?”

“I keep hoping you will someday. She would have taken you for the ride of your life,” Leo said quietly. “You’re my brother. I couldn’t stand by and do nothing.”

Rey turned away with a muttered curse. Leo was right; he had saved him from even worse heartache, but the memory was still raw enough to hurt.

"Don't try to take it out on Meredith," Leo told him firmly. "She's had enough tragedy. Let her do her job."

Rey glanced at him over his shoulder. "I would, if she'd remember why she's here," he said venomously. "It's not my fault that every time I turn around, she's drooling over me! A saint could be tempted by a woman whose eyes worship him like that. I'm only human!"

"Don't raise your voice," Leo cautioned.

"Why? Do you think she's standing outside the door eavesdropping?" Rey drawled sarcastically. "What if she did hear me? It's the truth. She wants me. A blind man could see it."

"That's no reason to take advantage of her. She's not like your usual women."

"No, she's not. She has no ambition, no intellect. Besides that, she's so inexperienced, it's unreal. I never thought kissing a woman could be boring, until she came along," Rey added coldly, trying not to let Leo see how attracted he was to their housekeeper. "She's so naive, it's nauseating."

Outside the door, Meredith stood poised like a statue with a cup of coffee in a saucer shaking in her hands. She'd come to offer it to Rey, and overheard words that had never been meant for her ears. She fought tears as she turned around and went quickly and silently back down the hall to the kitchen.

Hearts couldn't really break, she told herself firmly, as she dabbed at the tears with a paper towel. She was just feeling the aftereffects of her devastating experience at home. It wasn't as if she was really drooling over Rey Hart.

She felt like sinking through the floor when she realized that she did spend an inordinate amount of time staring at him. He was handsome, sensuous, attractive. She liked looking at him. And maybe she was infatuated, a little. That didn't give him the right to say such horrible things about her.

If she hadn't been listening, she'd never have known about them in the first place. She'd have gone right ahead, mooning over him and having him know it and be amused by it. Her pride felt tattered. She'd never been one to wear her heart on her sleeve, but Rey had kissed her as if he enjoyed it, and she'd built dreams on those kisses. She realized now how truly naive it had been. The first man who paid her any attention in years, and she fell head over heels for him. Seen in that context, perhaps it wasn't surprising after all. She'd heard Leo accuse him of being a rounder, and she had to admit that his experience ran rings around hers. Apparently he was accustomed to playing sensual games with women. That was all those devastating kisses that had brought her to her knees had meant to him—just a game. And she'd taken it seriously!

Well, she told herself firmly, he needn't worry that she'd throw herself at his feet again. From now on, she was going to be the perfect employee, polite and courteous and eager to please—but she'd never stare at him longingly again. Thank God she'd overheard what he said to Leo. It had spared her a terrible humiliation. A little hurt now was far better than being wrung out emotionally down the road because she'd been ignorant of the facts. Wasn't she herself always telling people that the truth, however brutal, was always best in the long run? It was time to take her own advice.

When Rey and Leo came in to breakfast the next morning, she put bacon and eggs and biscuits on the table with a cool, professional smile.

Rey was oddly subdued. He didn't give her the arrogant scrutiny that had become force of habit in recent days. I fact, he didn't look at her at all. Leo kept up a pleasant conversation about the day's chores. They were moving some sick cattle into a pasture near the house so the vet could examine them, and stock was being shifted into closer quarters as well, within easier reach of the hay barn.

"I thought you had those big round bales of hay?" Meredith asked curiously.

"We do," Leo agreed. "But we still bale it the old-fashioned way and stack it in the barn. You lose some of the round bales through weathering by sun and rain. The hay that's kept dry in the barn has less deterioration and better nutrition."

"But you feed more than hay?"

Leo chuckled. He buttered a second biscuit. "You are sharp. Yes, we have a man who mixes feeds for better nutrition. No animal proteins, either," he added. "We're reactionaries when it comes to ranching. No artificial hormones, no pesticides, nothing except natural methods of pest control and growth. We're marketing our beef under the Hart Ranch label, as well, certifying it organic. We've already got several chain supermarkets carrying our product, and we've just moved onto the internet to extend our distribution."

"That's amazing," Meredith said with genuine interest. "It's like having custom beef," she added, nodding.

"It is custom beef," Leo told her. "We're capitalizing on the move toward healthier beef. Quick profit methods are going to fail producers in the long run, especially with the current attitude toward hormones and antibiotics and animal-product proteins for feed. We think that once organic beef catches on, the market will justify the added expense."

"Word of mouth will take you far, too," Meredith said. Hospitals teach nutrition these days, not only to patients but to the community. Tailored beef will find a market among consumers with heart problems, who'll pay the extra cost for healthier cuts of meat grown organically."

Rey was listening. He finished his biscuit and poured himself another cup of coffee from the carafe on the table. "J.D. Langley pioneered that organic approach locally," he remarked. "He and the Tremayne boys got into terrific fights with other producers at seminars for a while. Then we saw the disasters overseas and suddenly everybody else was jumping on the bandwagon."

"They'll be glad they did, I think," Meredith said.

"Which reminds me," Leo said, eyeing her. "Mrs. Lewis said her larder hadn't been opened since you came here. So…what are you making these biscuits with?"

She gave them a wary glance. "Light olive oil," she said slowly.

Rey gaped at his biscuit as if it had suddenly sprouted hair. "Olive oil?" he gasped.

"Listen," she said quickly, aware of horrified stares, "olive oil is so healthy that people who live on a Mediterranean diet have only a fraction of the vascular problems we have in abundance in this country. The fat content is still there, but it's a vegetable fat, and it's actually good for you. Until I told you, you didn't even know you'd given up great gobs of animal fat in those biscuits!"

The brothers looked at each other. "Well," Leo had to admit, "they taste just as good as the others did."

"That's true," Rey agreed reluctantly.

"And we're getting older," Leo continued. "We don't want clogged arteries giving us heart attacks and strokes."

"Or bypass surgery," Rey sighed.

"So I guess olive oil isn't so bad, after all," Leo concluded, with a grin at Meredith.

She grinned back. "Thank goodness. I had visions of being tarred and feathered," she confessed.

"I'm not giving up butter, though," Rey told her firmly, dipping his knife into the tub next to the biscuit basket. "Nothing tastes like real butter on a biscuit."

Meredith didn't look at him. She couldn't confess that what he was eating was not butter, but rather a light margarine that actually lowered cholesterol levels. She only smiled and poured herself another cup of coffee.

Leo and Rey had started moving bulls into the lower pasture, where new forage grasses were thriving even in autumn, when a mangy old longhorn bull suddenly jerked his head and hooked Leo in the shoulder.

Leo yelled and threw a kick at him, but the aggravating animal was already trotting nonchalantly into the new pasture without a backward glance.

"How bad is it?" Rey asked, leaving the cowboys to work the cattle alone while he looked at his brother's shoulder.

"Probably needs stitches," Leo said through his teeth. "Drive me to the house and let me change shirts, then you can take me to Lou Coltrain."

"Damned bull," Rey muttered as he put his brother into the ranch truck and took off home.

Meredith was sweeping off the back steps when they drove up. She gave Leo's bloodstained shirt a quick glance.

"Come on in here, let me have a look," she said gently.

Disconcerted, Leo let her remove the shirt from his shoulder and bathe the blood away with a clean cloth.

She probed around the edges of the cut and nodded. "You'll need stitches. Here. Hold this tight against the cut until you get to town."

"I need to change shirts," he began.

"You need to get to the doctor. Which one do you use?" she persisted, picking up the mobile phone she kept on the table.

"Dr. Lou Coltrain," he said.

"I'll phone and tell them you're on the way," she said firmly.

Rey gave her a curious glance, but he hustled Leo out the door and into the truck again.

When they got to the office, Dr. Lou Coltrain's nurse, Betty, came right out to meet them and guide them back into a cubicle.

Lou walked in, took a professional look at the cut, and grinned. "Stitches," she said. "How about a tetanus jab?"

Leo grimaced. "Well…"

She patted him on the shoulder that wasn't injured. "We'll have you fixed up and out of here in no time."

He sighed, glancing at his brother. "I hate shots."

Rey shrugged. "You'd hate tetanus more," he told Leo. "Besides," he added, "I hear she gives sugarless gum to the good patients."

Leo made a face at him.

When Leo was stitched up and given his tetanus shot, Rey drove him back to the house, where Meredith made him a cup of coffee and cut him a slice of cherry pie, making sure he had a cushion for his back in the straight chair at the table.

Rey glared at the special treatment his brother was getting. "Maybe I should get gored," he commented drolly.

Meredith stared at him, and she didn't smile. "You'd get a vinegar dressing and a cup of cold coffee," she said.

He glared at her, too. He felt as if he'd been put in the corner without supper. It wasn't a feeling he liked. He gave them both a hard look and went back out the door, smoldering with bad temper.

Chapter Six

"I shouldn't have said that," Meredith said wryly when Rey was gone. "I set him off again."

"It won't hurt him to have one woman who doesn't fall all over herself when he's around," Leo told her flatly. "Sometimes too much success can ruin a good man."

She toyed with her coffee cup. "Women like him, I guess," she said.

He gave her a quick glance that she didn't see before he started on his pie. "He's had girlfriends since he was in grammar school. But there was only one serious one. She turned out to be a real loser," he added quietly. "She soured him on women."

She sipped coffee. "You can't judge an entire sex by one woman," she pointed out.

"Well, we had our mother as an example, too," he continued. "She left Dad with five young boys and never looked back. We haven't been overawed with sterling examples of womanhood, although Simon and Corrigan and Cag have made good marriages in spite of that."

She smiled absently as she looked at him. "I had a brother of my own," she said without thinking.

"Yes, I know," Leo replied, surprising her into silence. "His name was Michael Johns. He worked for Houston PD."

Her gasp was audible. "How…do you know about him?"

"Remember Colter Banks?"

"Yes. Colter was Mike's best friend."

"Well, Colter's our second cousin," he told her. "I knew Mike, too. I'm sorry."

She clenched one fist in her lap and tried not to give way to tears. "Do the others…know?"

"No, they don't," he replied. "They weren't that close to Colter, and they never met Mike. I haven't told them, and I'm not planning to."

She searched his dark eyes. "What else do you know about me, Leo?" she asked, because of the way he was watching her.

He shrugged. "Everything."

She let out a long breath. "And you haven't shared it with Rey."

"You wouldn't want me to," he murmured dryly. "He's having too much fun being condescending. When the time comes, he's got a few shocks coming, hasn't he?"

She laughed softly. "I hadn't meant to be cloak-and-daggerish. It's just that it still hurts too much to talk about," she said honestly.

"Colter told me the circumstances. It wasn't your fault," he replied. "Or your father's. I gather that he drinks because he feels responsible?"

She nodded. "We both dined out on 'what-if' just after it

happened," she confessed. "I know that it probably wouldn't have made any difference, but you can't help wondering."

"It doesn't do any good to torment yourself over things that are history," Leo said gently.

"I don't do it intentionally," she murmured.

"The first step was getting your father into treatment," he said. "Getting you out of your rut was the second. You don't have any memories to contend with here. I've noticed the difference in you just in the past week." He smiled. "You're changing already."

"I suppose so." She smiled back. "I've never even been on a ranch before. I could love it here. It's such a change of pace."

"When you're back to normal, we've got plenty of opportunity around here for your sort of job," he pointed out.

She chuckled. "Don't rush me. It's far too soon to think about leaving Houston." She didn't add that she didn't want to be that close to Rey, considering his opinion of her at the moment. "I've only been down here a week."

"Okay. I'll let it drop, for now." He leaned back in his chair and winced, favoring the arm he'd had stitched. "Damned bull," he muttered.

"Did they give you something for the pain?"

"No, and I didn't ask for anything. I have over-the-counter painkillers if it gets really bad. So far, it hasn't."

"You know, of course, that statistically farm and ranch work have the highest ratio of accidents," she said.

"Any job can be dangerous," he said easily.

She pursed her lips and lifted her coffee cup to them. "Your brother's a walking job hazard," she said thoughtfully.

"Oh? In what way, exactly?" he asked.

She wouldn't have touched that line with a pole. She laughed. "He's abrasive. I don't think he wants me here."

"I've noticed his attitude. I hope you haven't let it get to you?"

"I haven't. Anyway, he'll mellow one of these days," she said.

"He could use some mellowing. He's a disillusioned man."

She smoothed the lip of the cup. "Did he love her very much?"

He knew she was talking about Carlie. He sighed. "He thought he did. His pride suffered more than his heart." He hesitated. "I didn't help matters. I made a play for her deliberately, to show him what she was. That was a miscalculation. A bad one. He's never forgiven me for it. Now, if I pay any attention to a woman, he tries to compete with me..."

She noticed the way his voice trailed off, and she averted her eyes. "I get the picture," she said.

"It's not like that, not with you," he began.

She forced a smile. "He's not interested in me," she said bluntly. "And just in case you're worried that I might be falling all over him, there's no danger of that, either. I was outside the door when he was talking to you. I wasn't eavesdropping, but he was speaking rather loudly. I heard what he said. I'd have to be certifiable to lose my heart over a man like that."

He grimaced as he read the faint pain that lingered in her eyes. "I wouldn't have had you hear what he said for the world," he said deeply.

She managed a smile. "It's just as well. It will keep me from taking him seriously. Besides, I'm not really down here looking for a soul mate."

"Just as well, because Rey isn't any woman's idea of the perfect partner, not the way he is right now. I love him dearly, but I can afford to. It's another story for any woman who loses her heart to him." He studied her warily. "Just don't let him play you for a fool."

"I wouldn't dream of it," she said. "Even if I got the chance."

He nodded. He finished his pie and coffee and got to his feet. "I'd better change and get back to work. Thanks for running interference, by the way. You're a cool head in an emergency," he remarked with a smile.

"I've had lots of practice," she said modestly and grinned. "But try to stay away from horned things for a while."

"Especially my brother, the minor devil," he said, tongue-in-cheek, and grinned back when she got the reference and started laughing.

After Leo went back to work, Meredith went out to gather eggs. It seemed very straightforward. You walked into the henhouse, reached in the nest, and pulled out a dozen or so big brown eggs, some still warm from the chicken's feathered body.

But that wasn't what happened. She paused just inside the henhouse to let her eyes adjust to the reduced light, and when she moved toward the row of straw-laced nests, she saw something wrapped around one nest that wasn't feathered. It had scales and a flickering long tongue. It peered at her through the darkness and tightened its coils around its prey, three big brown eggs.

Meredith, a city girl with very little experience of scaly things, did something predictable. She screamed, threw the basket in the general direction of the snake, and left skid marks getting out of the fenced lot.

Annie Lewis, who was doing the laundry, came to the back door as fast as her arthritis would allow, to see what all the commotion was about.

"There's a…big black and white *snnnnnakkkkkke*…in

there!" Meredith screamed, shaking all over from the close encounter.

"After the eggs, I reckon," Annie said with a sigh. She wiped her hands on her apron. "Let me get a stick and I'll deal with it."

"You can't go in there alone with the horrible thing and try to kill it! It must be five feet long!"

"It's a king snake, not a rattler," Annie said gently, recognizing the description. "And I'm not planning to kill it. I'm going to get it on a stick and put in the barn. It can eat its fill of rats and poisonous snakes and do some good out there."

"You aren't going to kill it?" Meredith exclaimed, horrified.

"It's a king snake, dear," came the gentle reply. "We don't like to kill them. They're very useful. They eat rattlesnakes, you know."

"I didn't know." Meredith shivered again. "I've never seen a snake except in a zoo, and it was a python."

"You'll see lots of them out here in the country. Just remember that if one rattles at you, it means business and it will strike. Rattlesnakes are venomous."

Meredith looked around as if she expected to be mobbed just at the mention of them.

"You can finish the washing," Annie said, trying not to grin. "I'll take care of the snake."

"Please be careful!"

"I will. After all, you get used to things like..."

Rey drove up and stopped the truck just short of the two women, exiting it with his usual graceful speed.

"What's going on?" he asked as he pulled a box of assorted bovine medicines out of the boot of the truck.

"There's a snake in the henhouse!" Meredith exclaimed.

He stopped with the supplies in his arms and stared at her curiously. "So?" he asked.

"I'm just going to move it for her, Rey," Mrs. Lewis said with a grin. "It sounds like a king snake. I thought I'd put him in the barn."

"I'll get him for you." He put the box on the hood of the truck. "Scared of snakes, are you?" he scoffed.

"I'd never seen one until a few minutes ago," she said huffily, and flushed. He was looking at her as if she were a child.

"There's a first time for everything," he said, and his eyes made a very explicit remark as they lingered on her breasts.

She gave him a glare hot enough to fry bacon, which he ignored. He walked right into the chicken lot and, then, into the henhouse.

Barely a minute later, he came back out with the snake coiled around one arm, its neck gently held in his other hand.

"Would you look at this, it's Bandit!" he exclaimed, showing it to a fascinated Mrs. Lewis. "See the scar on his back where he got caught in the corn sheller that time?"

"So it is!" she said. "Hello, old fella!" She actually petted the vile thing under the chin.

"How can you touch that thing?" Meredith groaned. "It's a snake!"

Mrs. Lewis glanced at Rey. "Reckon we should tell her that he used to live in the house?"

"Probably not," Rey suggested, aware of her white face. "I'll just stick him up in the loft. Come on, Bandit, I'll put you in a safe place."

Meredith was holding both chill-bump laden arms with 'er hands and shivering.

"There, there," Annie said gently. "He wouldn't bite you unless you provoked him. He's very gentle."

"If you say so."

"I do. Now you go back in there and get the eggs. Don't let Rey see how frightened you are. Trust me, he'll take advantage of it. You'll find rubber snakes in the refrigerator, the blender, the washer…"

"No!" Meredith exclaimed, horrified.

"Just grit your teeth and go back in the henhouse," Annie suggested. "Quick, before he comes back out."

Meredith took a quick breath and gave Annie a miserable glance, but she did as she was told.

Her skin crawled when she had to pick up the basket and gather the eggs, especially the ones the snake had been curled around. Now, every time she went to the henhouse, she'd be shivering with apprehension.

You've looked at gunshot wounds, accident victims, every sort of horror known to human eyes, she told herself firmly. *The snake wasn't even lacerated! So get it done and move on.*

She did, walking back out into the sunlight with a full basket of eggs and a forced look of composure on her soft face.

Rey was waiting for her, leaning against the bumper of the truck with his arms crossed and his hat pulled low over his eyes.

She didn't dare look at him for long. In that indolent pose, his lean, muscular body was shown to its very best advantage. It made her tingle to think how it had felt to be held against every inch of that formidable frame, to be kissed by that long, hard mouth.

"You get thrown, you get right back on the horse," he said with approval. "I'm proud of you, Meredith. It would b hard for even a ranch-born girl to go back into a henhouse where a snake had been lurking."

She took a slow breath. "We don't face things by running away from them, I guess," she agreed.

His eyes narrowed under the wide brim of the hat. "What are you running away from, Meredith? What is your father running away from?"

She clutched the basket to her chest. "That's nothing that you need to concern yourself with," she said with quiet dignity.

"You work for me," he replied.

"Not for long," she pointed out. "In another week or so, I'll be a memory."

"Will you?" He lurched away from the bumper and went to stand just in front of her, a tall and sensual threat. His fingers touched her soft mouth lightly. "Those bruises still look pretty fresh," he pointed out. "And you did ask for a month's leave, or so you said. Did you?"

She grimaced. "Well, yes, but I don't have to stay here all that time."

"I think you do," he returned. He bent and drew his mouth slowly over hers, a whisper of a contact that made her breath catch. He smiled with faint arrogance as he stood up again. "Anything could happen," he drawled. "You might like ranch life."

"I don't like snakes already."

"That was a fluke. They're generally hibernating by November, but it's been unseasonably warm. Spring is generally when you have to watch where you put your hands. But you don't need to worry. I'll protect you from snakes. And other perils."

"Who'll protect me from you?" she asked huskily.

He raised any eyebrow. "Why would you need protection?" he asked. "You're well over the age of consent."

"I've lived a very sheltered life," she said flatly.

He pursed his lips as he studied her, examining the statement. "Maybe it's time you walked out of the cocoon."

"I'm not in the market for an affair."

"Neither am I." He smiled slowly. "But if you worked at it, you might change my mind."

"I don't think so," she said. Her eyes were cool as they met his. "I wouldn't want you to think I was 'drooling' over you," she added deliberately.

His face changed. He knew immediately that she'd overheard what he'd said to Leo. He was sorry, because it wasn't true. He'd been desperate to throw Leo off the track. He didn't want his brother to know how attracted he was to her.

"Eavesdroppers never hear anything good about themselves, don't they say?" he asked quietly.

"Never," she agreed. "Now, if you'll excuse me, I'll go wash the eggs."

"I said something else that you'll remember with sordid ease," he murmured as she started past him. He caught her by the shoulder and tugged her close, bending to drag his mouth roughly across hers. "But I didn't mean that, either," he whispered against her parted lips. "Your innocence makes my head spin. I lay awake at night thinking of all sorts of delicious ways to relieve you of it."

"You'd be lucky!" she exclaimed, shocked.

He laughed softly as he let her go. "So would you," he drawled. "I've been called 'sensual hell' in bed, and I can assure you it wasn't meant to be a derogatory remark."

"Rey Hart!" she burst out.

"But why take anyone else's word for it?" he teased. "I'll be glad to let you see for yourself, anytime you like."

"If you think…I have never…of all the…!"

"Yes, it does tend to make women flustered when I mention what a great lover I am," he said with a wicked grin.

She couldn't get one coherent sentence out. She stomped her foot hard, turned around, and stormed into the kitchen, almost knocking herself down with the door in the process. It didn't help that Rey stood out there laughing like a predator.

If she expected Rey to be apologetic about what he'd said, she was doomed to disappointment. He watched her with narrow, assessing eyes as she went about her household duties. He didn't harass her, or monopolize her. He just watched. The scrutiny made her so nervous that she fumbled constantly. Her heart ran wild at the attention from those dark, steady eyes.

"Why don't you want to do something else besides keep house?" Rey asked her one evening when she was putting supper on the table. Leo, as usual, was late getting in. Rey had volunteered to set the table while she fixed Mexican corn bread and chili.

"Keeping house has less stress than most outside jobs," she said, not looking at him.

"It pays lousy wages," he continued, "and you could get into a lot of trouble in some households, with men who'd see you as fair game."

"Do you see me that way?" she asked, wide-eyed.

He glowered at her. "No, I don't. The point is, some other man might. It isn't a safe career. In a profession, there are more laws to protect you."

"Most professional people have degrees and such. Besides, I'm too old."

"You're never too old to go back to school," he replied.

She shrugged. "Besides, I like cooking and cleaning."

He eyed her curiously. "You're very good at handling

injured people," he said suddenly. "And you're remarkably calm in an emergency."

"It's good practice for when I have kids," she said.

He drew in a short breath. "You like being mysterious, don't you?"

"While it lasts, it's fun," she agreed.

His eyes narrowed. "What dark secrets are you keeping, Meredith?" he asked quietly.

"None that should bother you, even if you found them out," she assured him. She smiled at him from the stove. "Meanwhile, you're getting fresh biscuits every day."

"Yes, we are," he had to agree. "And you're a good cook. But I don't like mysteries."

She pursed her lips and gave him a teasing glance over her shoulder. "Too bad."

He put the last place setting on the table and sat down at his place, just staring at her, without speaking. "You know," he said after a minute, frowning, "there's something familiar about your last name. I can't quite place it, but I know I've heard it somewhere."

That wasn't good, she thought. He might remember Leo talking about her brother. She didn't want to have to face the past, not just yet, when she was still broken and bruised and uncomfortable. When she was back on her feet and well again, there would be time to come to grips with it once and for all—as her poor father was already doing.

"Think so?" she asked with forced nonchalance.

He shrugged. "Well, it may come back to me one day."

Fortunately Leo came in and stopped his train of thought. Meredith put supper on the table and sat down to eat it with the brothers.

The next morning, Rey came out to the kitchen with a bright silver metal gun case. He set it down besi the counter, out of the way, before he started eating his breakfast.

"Going hunting?" Meredith asked impishly.

He gave her a wary glance. "Skeet shooting," he corrected. "The season's over, but I practice year-round."

"He won two medals at the World championships in San Antonio, this year," Leo told her with a grin. "He's an A class shooter."

"Which gauge?" she asked without thinking.

Rey's face became suspicious. "All of them. What do you know about shotguns?"

"I used to skeet-shoot," she volunteered. "My brother taught me how to handle a shotgun, and then he got me into competition shooting. I wasn't able to keep it up after I grad…after high school," she improvised quickly. She didn't dare tell him she gave it up after she finished college. That would be giving away far too much.

He watched her sip coffee. "You can shoot, can you?" he asked, looking as if he were humoring her. He didn't seem to believe what she claimed.

"Yes, I can," she said deliberately.

He smiled. "Like to come down to the range with me?" he asked. "I've got a nice little .28 gauge I can bring along for you."

By offering her his lowest caliber shotgun, he was assuming that she couldn't handle anything heavier.

"What's in the case?" she asked.

"My twelve gauge," he said.

She gave him a speaking glance. "I'll just shoot that, if you don't mind sharing it. Uh, it doesn't have a kick or anything…?" she added, and had to bite her tongue to keep from grinning at her innocent pose.

He cleared his throat. He didn't dare look at Leo. "No," said carelessly. "Of course it doesn't have a kick."

In truth, it would kick worse than any other of the four gauges, but Rey was planning to call her bluff. She was putting on an act for his benefit. He was going to make her sorry she tried it.

"Then I'll be just fine with that gun," she said. "More apple butter?" She offered him an open jar and spoon.

"Thanks," he replied smugly, accepting the jar. He put it down and buttered another biscuit before he spooned the apple butter into it. "Don't mind if I do. Leo, want to come along?" he asked his brother.

Leo was also trying not to grin. "I think I will, this time," he told his brother. This was one shooting contest he wasn't about to miss. He knew that Mike Johns was a champion shooter. If he'd been the one who taught his sister, Meredith would shock Rey speechless when she got that shotgun in her arms. He was going along. He didn't want to miss the fun.

"The more the merrier, I always say," Rey chuckled.

"Funny thing, that's just what I was thinking," Leo replied, tongue-in-cheek.

Meredith didn't say another word. She finished her breakfast, waited until they finished theirs, and put the dishes in the dishwasher. Then she dressed in jeans, boots, and a long-sleeved flannel shirt with a down-filled vest and a bib cap, and went off to let Rey show her how to shoot a shotgun.

The target range was unusually busy for a lazy Friday afternoon in November. It was a cool day, with a nice nip in the air. Meredith felt good in the down vest. It was one she'd often worn when she went to the firing range with Mike in cold weather. Coats were cumbersome and often got in the way of a good, quick aim.

Rey and Leo stopped to pass the time of day with t

elderly shooters, both of whom gave Meredith a warm welcome.

"This is Jack, and that's Billy Joe," Rey introduced the white-haired men, one of whom was tall and spare, the other overweight and short. The short one had walked briskly the short distance from the red pickup truck parked at the clubhouse, and he was out of breath already. "We all go to district, state and national shoots as a team from our club."

"But we get honorable mention, and Rey wins the medals," Billy Joe, the shorter man, chuckled, still trying to catch his breath. "We don't mind. We're just happy that somebody from our club breaks records!"

"Amen to that," Jack agreed, smiling.

"All right, let's get to shooting," Billy Joe said, turning back to his truck. "Stay where you are, Jack. I'll bring your gun, too!"

He turned back toward the truck, rushing and still breathless. Meredith frowned. His cheeks were unnaturally pink, and it wasn't that cold. His complexion was almost white. He was sweating. She knew the symptoms. She'd seen them all too often.

"You might go with him," Meredith said abruptly, interrupting Jack's banter with Rey.

"Excuse me?" Jack asked.

Just at that moment, Billy Joe stopped, stood very still for a minute, and then buckled and fell forward into a crumpled heap at the door of his truck.

Meredith took off at a dead run. "Somebody get me a cell phone!" she called as she ran.

Leo fumbled his out of the holder on his belt and passed it to her as she knelt beside Billy Joe.

"Get his feet elevated. Find something to cover him with," she shot at the other men. She was dialing while she spoke. She loosened the man's shirt, propping the phone against her ear—the worst way to hold it, but there was no other way at the moment—and felt down Billy Joe's chest for his diaphragm. "Get his wallet and read me his weight and age from his driver's license," she added with a sharp glance in Leo's direction.

Leo dug out the wallet and started calling out information, while Rey and Jack stood beside the fallen man and watched with silent concern.

"I want the resident on duty in the emergency room, stat," she said. "This is Meredith Johns. I have a patient, sixty years of age, one hundred and eighty pounds, who collapsed without warning. Early signs indicate a possible myocardial infarction. Pulse is thready," she murmured, checking the second hand of her watch as she took his pulse with her fingertips, "forty beats a minute, breathing shallow and labored, grey complexion, profuse sweating. I need EMTs en route, I am initiating cardiopulmonary resuscitation now."

There was a long pause, and a male voice came over the line. With her voice calm and steady, Meredith gave the information again, and then handed the phone to Leo as she bent over the elderly man and did the spaced compressions over his breastbone, followed by mouth-to-mouth breathing.

Rey was watching, spellbound at her proficiency, at the easy and quite professional manner in which she'd taken charge of a life-or-death emergency. Within five minutes, the ambulance was screaming up the graveled road that led to the Jacobsville Gun Club, and Billy Joe was holding his own.

The EMTs listened to Meredith's terse summary of events as they called the same resident Meredith had been talking to.

"Doc says to give you a pat on the back." The female EMT grinned at Meredith as they loaded Billy Joe into the ambulance. "You sure knew what to do."

"Yes," Rey agreed, finding his tongue at last. "You've obviously had first-aid training."

He probably meant it as praise, but it hit Meredith in the gut. She glared at him. "What I've had," she emphasized, "is five years of college. I have a master's degree in nursing science, and I'm a card-carrying nurse practitioner!"

Chapter Seven

Rey stared at his new cook as if she'd suddenly sprouted feathers on her head. His summation of her abilities was suddenly smoke. She was someone he didn't even know. She was a health-care professional, not a flighty cook, and certainly not the sort of woman to streetwalk as a sideline.

She nodded solemnly. "I figured it would come as a shock," she told him. She turned her attention back to the EMTs. "Thanks for being so prompt. Think he'll be okay?"

The female EMT smiled. "I think so. His heartbeat's stronger, his breathing is regular, and he's regaining consciousness. Good job!"

She grinned. "You, too."

They waved and took off, lights flashing, but without turning on the sirens.

"Why aren't the sirens going?" Rey wanted to know "He's not out of danger yet, surely?"

"They don't like to run the sirens unless they have to," Meredith told him. "Some people actually run off the road and wreck their cars because the sirens rattle them. They use the lights, but they only turn on the sirens if they hit heavy traffic and have to force their way through it. Those EMTs," she added with a smile, "they're the real heroes and heroines. They do the hardest job of all."

"You saved Billy Joe's life," Jack said huskily, shaking her hand hard. "He's the best friend I got. Thank you."

She smiled gently and returned the handshake. "It goes with the job description. Don't try to keep up with the ambulance," she cautioned when he went toward Billy Joe's truck, which still had the key in the ignition. The two men had come together.

"I'll be careful," the older man promised.

"Whew!" Leo let out the breath he'd almost been holding, and put up his cell phone. "You're one cool lady under fire, Meredith."

She smiled sadly. "I've had to be," she replied. She glanced at Rey, who looked cold and angry as it occurred to him, belatedly, that she'd played him for a fool. "I can see what you're thinking, but I didn't actually lie to you. You never asked me exactly what I did for a living. Of course, you thought you already knew," she added with faint sarcasm.

He didn't reply. He gave her a long, contemptuous look and turned away. "I've lost my taste for practice," he said quietly. "I want to go on to the hospital and see about Billy Joe."

"Me, too," Leo added. "Meredith…?"

"I'll go along," she said. "I'd like to meet that resident I spoke with. He's very good."

Rey glanced toward her. "You'll get along. He keeps secrets, too," he said bitterly, and got behind the wheel.

Leo made a face at Meredith, opening the third door of the big double-cabbed truck so that she could sit in back. He put the gun cases in the boot, in a locked area, and climbed in beside Rey.

The resident turned out to be a former mercenary named Micah Steele. He was married to a local girl, and he'd gone back to school to finish his course of study for his medical license.

"I couldn't very well carry a wife and child around the jungles with me," Micah told her with a grin. He was tall and big, and not at all bad-looking. She could picture him with a rifle in one arm. But now, in a white lab coat with a stethoscope thrown carelessly around his neck, he seemed equally at home.

"When's Callie due?" Leo asked.

"Any minute," he said, tongue-in-cheek. "Can't you see me shaking? I'm the soul of self-confidence around here, but one little pregnant woman makes me a basket case!"

"Callie's quite a girl," Rey agreed, smiling at the big man.

Micah gave him a look. "Yes, and isn't it lucky for me that you hardly ever went into her boss Kemp's office for legal advice, while she was still single?"

Rey pursed his lips. "Kemp eats scorpions for breakfast, I hear. I like my lawyers less caustic."

"Last I heard, the local bar association had you down as a contagious plague and was warning its members to avoid you at all costs," Micah replied wickedly.

"I never hit any local lawyers." Rey looked uncomfortable. "It was that Victoria lawyer, Matherson," he muttered. "And I didn't even hit him that hard. Hell, he's lucky I wasn't sober at the time! Otherwise, he'd have had twice the number of stitches!"

Meredith listened to the repartee with wide, fascinated eyes, but Rey wouldn't meet her eyes and Micah, too, cleared his throat and didn't pursue the subject.

"Matherson took a client who accused us of assault," Leo volunteered. "Cag had hit him, several times, after he got drunk and assaulted Tess, who's now Cag's wife. But the bounder swore that he was the injured party, that we falsely accused him and all took turns pounding him. He convinced a jury to award him damages. Not a lot of money," Leo added solemnly, "but the principle was what set Rey off. He was in a bad mood already and he had a few too many drinks at Shea's Bar, out on the Victoria road. To make a long story short," he added with a chuckle, "Matherson was having a quiet beer when Rey accused him of handling the ex-employee's case for spite because he lost an argument with us over Tess when he was handling her inheritance. Matherson took exception to Rey's remarks, and the two of them set about wrecking the pretty stained-glass window that used to overlook the parking lot."

"Used to?" Meredith fished, sensing something ominous.

"Yes, well, Matherson made a rather large hole in it when Rey helped him into the parking lot the hard way," Leo concluded.

Micah Steele looked as if it was killing him not to burst out laughing.

"He," Leo jerked his thumb toward Steele, "had to remove quite a number of glass particles from Matherson's rear end. *And* we got sued again, for that!"

"But the jury, after hearing Kemp's masterful summation of our grievances," Rey interrupted, "decided that Matherson was only entitled to the cost of the repair job on his butt. Shea had insurance that replaced the stained-glass window with one of comparable age and exclusivity." Rey smiled smugly. "And the judge said that if she'd been sitting on the first case, the rat Matherson was representing would have gotten a jail sentence."

Leo chuckled. "Only because Kemp put Tess on the stand and had her testify about what really happened the night Matherson's client took her on a date. The jury felt that Rey was justifiably incensed by the former verdict." He glanced at Meredith wryly.

"Yes, but I understand that Shea's two bouncers meet Rey at the door these days and won't let him in if he's not smiling," Micah contributed.

Rey shrugged. "I never get drunk anymore. I've learned to handle aggression in a nonphysical manner."

The other two men actually walked down the hall. Meredith noticed their shoulders vibrating.

Rey took a step toward Meredith, half irritated by the character assassination job his brother and Micah Steele had just done on him, and even more put out by Meredith's unmasking.

"You knew I had no idea about your education," Rey accused Meredith. "Why didn't you say something at the outset, when Leo first went to the hospital?" he demanded in a low, deep tone. "I may have jumped to conclusions, but you provided the springs, didn't you?"

She grimaced. "I guess so. But it was only a little jump from telling you about my job to talking about the reason Daddy started drinking. It's…still very fresh in my mind," she added huskily. "It's only been six months. The memories are—" she swallowed and looked away "—bad."

Unexpectedly he reached out and caught her fingers in his, tugging her closer. The hall was deserted. In the background there were muted bell-tones and announcements and the sound of lunch trays being distributed. "Tell me," he said gently

She bit her lower lip hard and lifted her tormented eyes to his curious ones. "Not…yet," she whispered tightly. "One day, but…not yet. I can't."

"Okay," he said after a minute. "But I'd like to know how you learned to shoot."

"My brother, Mike, taught me," she said reluctantly, staring at his broad chest. She wanted to lay her head on it and cry out her pain. There hadn't been anyone to hold her, not when it happened, not afterward. Her father withdrew into his own mind and started drinking to excess at once. Her job was all that had kept Meredith sane. She hadn't been able to let out her grief in any normal way.

Rey's mind was working overtime. He stared down at her, still holding her fingers entwined tightly with his own, and he frowned as bits and pieces of memory began fitting themselves together.

"Mike. Mike Johns." His eyes narrowed. "Our cousin Colter's best friend, and one of Leo's acquaintances. He was killed…!"

She tried to tug her fingers away. He wouldn't let her. He pulled her into his arms, holding her there even when she struggled. But a few seconds of resistance were all she had. She laid her flushed cheek against his broad chest and let the tears flow.

Rey's arms contracted roughly. He smoothed his hand over her nape, caressing, soothing. "There was a bank robbery in Houston," he recalled quietly. "Mike was a cop. He was at the bank with your mother. It was Saturday. He was off duty, but he had his service revolver under his jacket." His arms tightened as her sobs grew painful to hear. "He drew and fired automatically, and one of the robbers sprayed fire from one of those damned little automatic rifles in his general direction. He and your mother died instantly…"

Meredith's fingers dug into his wide back. He rocked her, barely aware of curious glances from passersby.

"Both men were caught. You don't kill a cop and get away with it in Texas," he added softly. "They were arraigned and treated to a speedy trial just a month ago. You and your father testified. That was when your father really went off the deep end, wasn't it, when he had to see the autopsy photos..."

Micah and Leo came back down the hall, frowning when they saw the condition Meredith was in. Even as they watched, her eyes rolled back and she would have fallen to the floor except for Rey's strong arms lifting her.

Later, she wouldn't recall much except that she was hustled into a cubicle and revived. But when she started sobbing hysterically, they'd given her a shot of something that put her out like a light. She came to back at the ranch, in her own little garage apartment.

She opened her eyes, and there was Rey, sitting by the bed, still wearing the same jeans and shirt and boots he'd worn to the shooting range. Meredith was aware of the bedspread covering her up to her waist. Her boots were off, but she was also wearing the same clothes she'd started out in that morning.

"What time is it?" she asked in a husky, slightly disoriented tone.

"Five hours past the time you flaked out on me," he said, smiling gently. "Micah knocked you out. He thought some sleep might help." The smile faded into quiet concern. "You don't sleep much, do you, Meredith?" he asked surprisingly.

She sighed, brushed back her disheveled blond hair, and shook her head. "When I go to sleep, I have nightmares. I wake up in a cold sweat, and I see them, lying there on the floor, just the way they looked in those vivid crime scen photos." She closed her eyes and shivered. "People look so fragile like that, they look like big dolls, sprawled in pitiful disarray on the floor. Everybody stares at them…"

He brushed back her hair with a lean, gentle hand. "They got the guys who did it," he reminded her. "Including the trigger man. He'll serve life without any hope of parole. He'll pay for it."

Her pale eyes were tormented as they met his. "Yes, but it won't bring them back, will it?" she asked. "And do you know why they said they did it? For a bet. For a stupid bet, they killed two innocent people!"

"They also ruined their own lives," he reminded her, "and the lives of their own families."

She looked at him blankly, scowling.

"Don't you ever think about that?" he asked softly. "Criminals have families, too. Most of them have loving, decent parents who took care of them and disciplined them and blame themselves for what their children do. It must be pure hell, to have your child kill someone, and feel responsible for it."

"I haven't considered that," she admitted.

He continued. "When I was in high school, one of my best friends was arrested for murder. He killed the old man next door in the process of stealing his wallet. He wanted to buy his girl a diamond necklace she liked, and he didn't have any money. He figured the man was old and didn't need money anyway, so he might as well take it. He was sorry about it, but he never figured on killing the man or getting caught."

"Was he a good friend?" she asked.

He looked at their linked fingers. He nodded. "We were pals since grammar school. He wasn't quite as bright as some of the other boys, but he had a gentle nature. Or so we thought." He met her eyes. "His mom and dad always had a houseful of other peoples' kids. They were everybody's mom and dad. It shattered them when Joey went to prison. Even the children of the old man felt sorry for them."

"Funny," she mused. "I never even thought of how it would feel to have a child or a parent or a sibling who broke the law in some terrible way." She met his eyes. "I guess I'd feel guilty, too."

"Most kids are raised right. But some of them have a wild streak that nobody can tame, others have poor impulse control. Many are handicapped. Nobody goes to jail because he wants to."

"I never thought of you as a sensitive man," she blurted out, and then flushed at the insult.

His eyebrows lifted. "Who, me? I stop to pick worms out of the highway so my tires won't bruise their little bodies, and you think I'm insensitive?"

It took a minute for the words to make sense, and then she burst out laughing.

"That's better," he said. He smiled and squeezed her fingers. "You're going to be okay. You've had a lot of traumatic experiences just lately. No wonder you caved in."

"Lucky for you," she shot back.

"Me? Why?"

"Because if we'd unpacked those shotguns, I'd have destroyed your ego," she said with a smug smile. "At Mike's gun club, they used to call me 'dead-eye.'"

"Oh, they did, did they?" he challenged. "Well, we'll see about that when you step up to my gun range."

She studied his lean face. He wasn't handsome, but he had strong, stubborn features. He was familiar to her now, almost necessary. She thought about going back to Houston with real panic.

He touched her cheek where the bruises were a mixture of purple and yellow, much less vivid now. "He reall knocked you around," he said, and his face hardened visibly. "I don't care if a man is drunk, there's no excuse for hitting a woman."

"Shades of primitive man," she chided with a smile.

"Women are the cradles of life," he said simply. "What sort of man tries to break a cradle?"

"You have a unique way of putting things."

"We had Spanish ancestors," he told her. "They were old-world men, conquerors, adventurers. One of them made his way to Texas and was given a huge tract of land under a Spanish land grant, for services to the crown of Spain." He noticed a start of surprise on her face. "Do you know the legend of the Cid?"

"Yes!" she exclaimed. "He was a great Spanish hero. *Cid* is for the Arabic *Sidi* which means *Lord.*"

"Well, our ancestor wasn't El Cid," he said on a chuckle. "But he fought his way through hostile neighbors to claim his land, and he held it as long as he lived. Our family still holds it, through our late uncle, who left us this ranch."

"This is the original grant?" she exclaimed.

He nodded. "It isn't nearly as big as it was a couple of hundred years ago, but it's no weekend farm, either. Didn't you notice the antique silver service in the dining room?"

"Yes, I've been afraid to touch it. It looks very old."

He smiled. "It came from Madrid. It's over two hundred years old."

"An heirloom!" she breathed.

"Yes. Like the ranch itself." He tilted his head and studied her for a long time. "Now I understand. Your father wasn't violent until the killer's trial, was he?"

"No, he wasn't." She looked down at Rey's big, warm hand wrapped around her own. It made her feel safe. "He told Mike to drive Mama to the bank," she added reluctantly. "He had papers to grade. He couldn't spare the time, he said, and he snapped at her when she protested that Mike was spending his day off, carting her all over Houston." She glanced at him. "I was called in to work at a clinic my boss holds in the Hispanic community every Saturday. There's a regular nurse, but she was at home with a sick child. I went to stand in for her." Her eyes fell to his broad chest. "I could have asked someone to go in my place. I didn't. So he and I both have our guilt."

"Because you lived and they didn't," Rey said bluntly.

She gasped. "No, that's not true!"

"It is true." His black eyes held hers relentlessly. "The same thing happens to people who survive airplane crashes, automobile wrecks, sinking ships. It's a normal, human reaction to surviving when other people don't. It's worse when the victims include close relatives or friends."

"Where did you learn that?" she asked.

"From Janie Brewster," he said.

She frowned. "That name sounds familiar."

"We've mentioned her to you. She's the daughter of a neighboring cattleman," he related. "She got her associate degree in psychology from our community college, and now she's studying it in Houston," he added with a grin. "She's almost twenty. They let her take college courses while she was still in high school, so she's ahead."

"Oh."

"She's not hard on the eyes, either," he murmured, avoiding her eyes. "She and her father live alone. Leo and I have a standing dinner invitation, any time we care to show up."

She started to say "oh" again, and realized how juvenile she was behaving. She straightened her shoulders against the pillow that was propping her up, and tugged at the hand Rey still held. "Then if she can bake biscuits, you're saved when I leave, aren't you?" she asked coolly.

"Well, she can't exactly bake stuff," Rey had to admit

"Why?"

"She has no sense of time. She sets the timer and it goes off, and she never hears it. So the chicken bounces, the heat-and-serve rolls usually come out black, and I won't even mention what happens to vegetables she tries to cook on *top* of the stove." He gave her a sad look. "She did try to make us a pan of biscuits once." He actually shuddered.

"Not a successful try?" she fished.

"We had to take the damned things home, or her father would never have let us near the Salers heifers he was offering for sale." He glanced at her. "Leo just bought us a big Salers bull, and we needed purebred heifers to breed to him. Purebred breeding stock brings a big price, especially if you show cattle and win ribbons." He shrugged. "So we took the biscuits home."

"Did you eat them?" she persisted.

He shook his head and he shuddered again.

"Then what did you do with them?" she asked, thinking he probably fed them to the cattle dogs or some livestock.

"Well, actually, we took them out to the skeet field and used them for clay pigeons," he confessed with a grin. "They were the best damned targets we ever had, but we didn't dare say where we got them!"

She put her face in her hands and burst out laughing. "Oh, the poor girl!" she chuckled.

"Don't worry, we'd never tell her," he promised. "But we did ask her for another pan of biscuits, without telling her why." He sighed. "That woman has a ready-made profession as a target maker, and we haven't got the guts to tell her so. Hell of a shame!"

She brushed at her eyes with the hem of her blouse. Poor Janie. And she'd been jealous.

"What does she look like?" she asked, curious.

"She comes up to my shoulder. She's got light brown

hair, longer than yours, and her eyes are green. If she didn't know everything, and tell you so every time you saw her, she might get married one day."

"You don't want to marry her?" she teased. "Not even for an inexhaustible supply of skeet targets?"

"I don't want to marry anybody," he said bluntly, and he looked her straight in the eye when he said it. "I love my freedom."

She sighed and smiled. "So do I," she confessed. "I don't think I could ever settle for diapers and dishes. Not with my background."

"You were a science major, weren't you?" he asked abruptly.

"Yes. Chemistry and biology, genetics—stuff like that. I made good grades, but it was hard work. Then I went right to work for my boss, straight out of college. I need to be two people, just to catch up. I run my legs off. The stress is pretty bad sometimes."

"No wonder keeping house and baking biscuits seemed like a holiday to you," he said to himself.

"It's been fun," she agreed. "I love to cook. I do it a lot, at home. I used to when Mama was alive," she recalled. "She hated housework and cooking. I came home from work and did it all."

"I've read about the sort of work you do," he commented, recalling articles he'd seen in the daily newspaper. "You're second only to a physician in authority. The only thing you can't do is write a prescription without his supervision."

"That's true." She smiled.

He studied her slender body, her exquisite figure nicely outlined by the garments she was wearing. "All those years, nothing but textbooks and exams and, then, a hectic career. No men?" he added, with a calculating stare.

"I dated," she replied. "I just couldn't afford to get seriou about anybody. My father scraped and begged and borrowed to get the money to finance my nursing education," she told him. "Even Mike…contributed to it." She drew in a steadying breath and locked her fingers together on her lap. "It would have been so petty of me to throw all that up, just so I could go to parties and get drunk with the other students."

"Surely there wasn't much of that, at a community college?"

She laughed. "You'd be surprised. There was all too much, for my taste. But I didn't live on campus. I lived at home and commuted." She met his searching gaze. "That party I was at, when Leo was attacked—the woman who gave it was a college classmate who works for a doctor in our practice. I knew she sort of had a reputation. I guess I should have realized how wild things would get, but I was so depressed that I let her pressure me into going to the party. It was a mistake."

"A lucky mistake, for my brother," Rey said gently. "He might have been killed, if you hadn't come along when you did." He scowled. "You said, you ran at the attackers, waving your arms."

She nodded. "Mike taught me about shock tactics," she said sadly. "I was afraid it wouldn't work, but I had no weapon, no other way of stopping them. So I took the risk."

"I'm grateful that you did." He shook his head slowly. "But it was an act of lunacy, Meredith. You could have been lying on the grass next to Leo."

"But I wasn't." She hunched her shoulders as if she felt a chill. "I think there might be a force behind every single chain of events," she said thoughtfully. "I don't believe in chaos," she elaborated. "The body is such a messy, beautiful miracle. A single cell has chemical processes that are so complex, so meticulously crafted, that I can't believe life is an accident. If it isn't accidental, it has to be planned." She shrugged. "That's simple logic. That's why I don't think God is a myth."

They were silent for a moment. "You're the most intriguing woman I've ever met," he murmured, and his dark eyes fell to her soft, full mouth.

"Surely not?" she asked demurely. "I don't have any secrets left."

"That's what you think," he said in a soft, low tone.

She looked up and he moved toward her, one hand catching the wooden headboard as he levered his hard mouth down against her soft one.

Her hands instinctively went to his chest, but its muscular warmth was fascinating. She'd never done anything really intimate with her infrequent dates, having been completely turned off by men with fast reputations. She preferred gentlemen to rounders. She knew that Rey had been a rounder. She wanted to draw away. She really did.

But Rey Hart was completely out of her experience. He wasn't aggressive and insistent, as one of Meredith's rare dates had been. He didn't rush at her. He didn't insist. He wasn't insulting with the speed of his advances. He simply bent and kissed her, slowly and gently, with nothing more intimate than his hard, tender lips touching hers. He nibbled her upper lip and lifted his mouth slowly.

"You're doing a surfboard imitation," he murmured. "There's no need. I'm too good a cattleman to rush my fences."

She was trying to understand the slow, sensuous speech when his lips came down on hers again and caressed her upper lip. Her hands pressed flat against his muscular chest. She liked the way he felt. She could feel the quick strong pulse of his heart under her palms. She could feel the growing rise and fall of his breathing.

His teeth nibbled her lips again, tenderly, and she found her hands moving under his arms and around him. She wanted to be held close, tight. She wanted him to envelop her against him. She wanted something more than this torturous teasing of his mouth on hers.

She made a husky, high-pitched little cry into his mouth and her nails bit into the solid muscles of his back.

"What do you want?" he whispered just above her lips.

"Kiss me," she moaned huskily.

"Kisses are dangerous, didn't you know?" he murmured, smiling against her responsive mouth. "They can be very addictive."

She was following his lips mindlessly. Her body was on fire. She'd never felt such headlong desire. Belatedly she realized that his hands were at her rib cage. Whether by accident or design, they were moving slowly up and down, up and down, so that his long fingers just lightly brushed the underswell of her breasts. It was extremely provocative. It was arousing.

She caught her breath as they moved ever closer to entrapment, and her eyes locked into his.

"Don't you like it this way?" he asked at her lips, brushing his mouth against them.

"Like…it?" she murmured mindlessly. Her body was reaching up toward those tormenting hands. She was shivering with every pulsating motion of her body, trembling with new and exciting surges of pleasure.

He laughed softly, sensuously. "Never mind." He lifted a hand to her hair and tugged out the hairpins, so that her beautiful long hair fell down around her shoulders. He tugged aside the top she was wearing, so that her shoulder was bare. Then he bent to it with his mouth, and she felt the warm, moist press of his lips right in the hollow of her shoulder.

Her nails dug into him. She lifted toward his mouth with a hoarse moan as she felt the slow tracing of his tongue against skin that had never known a man's touch. She was on fire. She was going to go up in flames right here. She didn't want to think, see, hear anything. She only wanted Rey to keep on touching her, to keep on holding her, to never, never stop…!

Chapter Eight

Just when the world was spinning away in a warm, pleasurable oblivion, the sound of loud, urgent footsteps echoed down the hall and brought Rey upright.

He looked at her with narrow, blank eyes as the sound grew louder. He cursed under his breath and got to his feet, keeping his back to her as he moved to the window, gripped the curtains and stared out at the pasture beyond.

Meredith dragged the bedspread up under her arms, over her clothes, and tried to steady her breathing. When she remembered what she and Rey had been doing, she blushed.

The door, ajar, was pushed completely open, and Leo came in with a tray. On it were a china cup and saucer, with a silver coffeepot, a silver cream and sugar service and a napkin and spoon. On a china plate were some dainty little chicken salad sandwiches.

"I thought you might be hungry," Leo said with a gentle

smile as he put the tray on her lap. It had legs, so it would stand alone over her lap. "Mrs. Lewis came over to fix supper, and I had her make you these."

"Thank you!" she exclaimed. "And thank Mrs. Lewis, too. I was just starting to feel empty!"

Rey made an odd sound and she reached for a tiny sandwich very quickly, not daring to glance at him after the enthusiastic and unwise remark she'd just made.

Leo turned his eyes toward his brother. "Something wrong with you?" he asked curiously.

"Stomach cramp," Rey said without turning. "I had chili and salsa for lunch. Heartburn's killing me!"

"You should go and take an antacid tablet," Leo advised. "And drink some milk."

"I guess I'd better." Rey took a long breath and turned around, feeling more normal, finally. He glanced at Meredith. "I'm glad you're okay."

"I'll be fine. Thanks for the conversation," she said, and wouldn't meet his eyes. But she smiled shyly.

He just looked at her. Suddenly his dark eyes began to burn. He studied her intently, as if something had just happened that shocked him.

"Are you all right?" she asked impulsively.

He took a slow breath. He was still staring at her, to his brother's covert amusement. With her hair around her shoulders like that, sitting up in bed, smiling at him, he felt as if his whole life had just shifted five degrees. She was uncommonly pretty with her hair down. She had a warm, kind heart. She'd put her life on the line for a total stranger. Why hadn't that occurred to him in Houston, when they first told him that she'd saved his brother from attackers?

"Leo probably owes you his life," Rey said carefully. "But it bothers me that you risked your own to save him.

"Wouldn't you have done that same thing, even for a total stranger?" she mused.

He hesitated. "Yes," he said after deliberating for a few seconds. "I suppose I would have."

"See? You have all sorts of potential as a prospective husband," she added with a wicked smile, which got wider when he reacted. "You're sexy, you're rich, you drive a nice car, and besides all that, you like animals." She began nodding her head. "Definite potential."

His high cheekbones flushed and he glared at her. "I don't want to get married."

"Don't worry about it," she said soothingly. "It's perfectly natural for a bachelor to resist matrimony. But you'll come around." She wiggled both eyebrows. "If you get me a ring, I'll let you see my collection of used chewing-gum wrappers and bottle caps."

He was still glaring.

Leo chuckled. "I'd love to see your used chewing-gum wrappers, Meredith," he said enthusiastically. "In fact, I may start collecting right now!"

Rey stared a hole through his brother while, inside him, something froze.

"I'll even consider marrying you," Leo added wickedly.

She laughed, not taking him seriously. "Sorry. It's Rey or nobody. My heart's set on him." She frowned. "Pity I couldn't trade you something for him," she murmured to Leo.

Rey was getting angrier by the second, and uncomfortable at the idea that Leo was trying to cut him out.

"Make me an offer," Leo told her. "But he can't cook, and he has a temper worse than a sunburned rattler. Besides hat, you can't domesticate him. He wears his spurs to the nner table."

"So do you!" Rey accused.

"I sit more daintily than you do," Leo said imperturbably.

Rey rammed his hands into the pockets of his jeans and glared at Meredith again. "You can't give people away."

"I'm not trying to give you away," Leo said calmly. "I want to make a profit." He scowled suddenly and his eyes widened as he looked at his brother's boots.

Meredith was staring at them, too. She pursed her lips and exchanged a look with Leo.

Rey glared back at them belligerently. "What?" he demanded hotly.

Both Leo's eyebrows went up, along with both hands, palms out. "I didn't say a word!"

"Neither did I," Meredith assured him.

Rey looked from one to the other and finally looked down. There, on one of his feet, was a dainty little foot sock with a tassel on it, covering the steel toe of his brown cowboy boot. He'd unknowingly picked it up under Meredith's bed while he was kissing her.

Rey jerked it off, cursed royally, shot a furious glance at Meredith and his brother, who were trying valiantly not to look at him, and stomped out.

Helpless laughter erupted from the two people left in Meredith's room, and the sound of it infuriated Rey.

Leo was obviously ready to set up shop with their recently disclosed nurse, and Rey didn't like it. Leo was the plague of housekeepers everywhere, but he was also easier on the eyes than the other brothers, and he was charming. Rey had never learned how to use charm. He always looked uncomfortable when he smiled. Especially with women like Meredith, who was painfully shy and naive. He wasn't used to such women. But what made it so much worse was the dropping sensation in his stomach that he'd experienced when he'd stared at Meredith. He hadn't had anything like that since Carlie, who made his pulse race almost as fast as Meredith did when he kissed her.

He could still taste Meredith on his mouth. She didn't know much, but she made up for her lack of knowledge with enthusiasm and curiosity. He thought about carrying the lessons much farther, about baring her to the waist. His heart began to slam into his throat as he tried to imagine what she looked like under her blouse. He already knew that the skin of her shoulder was warm and soft, like silk. He remembered her husky moan when he'd kissed her there, the way her fingers had bitten into his back like little sharp pegs.

He'd been away from women for a long time, but he still knew what to do with one, and his imagination was working overtime just now. Meredith had attracted him when she was just his cook. Now that he knew about the intelligent, capable woman underneath the flighty camouflage, he was fascinated with her. She was everything a man could wish for.

Not that she wanted him, oh, no. She'd made it plain. But that teasing speech about marriage had unnerved him. His freedom was like a religion. He didn't want to get married. Of course he didn't!

But it was natural to think of Meredith with children. He could picture her baking biscuits for him every morning and holding a child in her arms at night while they watched television. He could picture her playing catch with a little boy out in back, or picking wildflowers with a little girl at her skirts. She was kind and sweet. She'd make a wonderful mother.

There was her job, of course. He knew something about her profession, that it was supposed to be high pressure. She'd be called upon to make life and death decisions, to comfort the sick and grieving, to make herself involved in the daily lives of her patients so that she should counsel them on how to maintain good health. Besides all that, she had a college degree.

Rey was college educated, too, with a degree in management and a minor in marketing. He was the mind behind the business decisions, the coordinator of the labor pool, and the director of marketing for the brothers' cattle cooperative. He was good at what he did. He enjoyed conversations with other educated people, and he'd convinced himself that Meredith wouldn't know Degas from Dali, Domingo from Dwight Yoakum, Hemingway from Dr. Seuss. Now he knew better, and his respect for her increased.

She'd saved Billy Joe's life at the gun club. He recalled that she must have known what to do for Leo as well, when she'd found him after he was mugged. Leo really did owe her his life. She was competent, confident, and she wasn't hard on the eyes, either. She had wonderful qualities.

But he didn't want to marry her. He wasn't sure about Leo. His eyes narrowed as he recalled the way Leo conspired with her. Leo had known all about her already. Obviously they'd been talking together since her arrival at the ranch, because Leo hadn't been a bit surprised when she rushed over to manage Billy Joe's heart attack.

Why hadn't he noticed that? Leo had called for Meredith when he was in the hospital. He was obviously fond of her. Maybe he was interested in her romantically, too. He'd been interested in Tess, before Cag had walked off with her, but Tess hadn't realized it. Or if she had, she'd ignored it. Leo wasn't hard on the eyes, either, and when it came to charm, he had his share and Rey's as well.

As he walked down to the barn to talk to one of his men, Rey had a terrible premonition that Leo had been serious when he joked about being willing to marry Meredit

Would she be desperate enough, lonely enough, frightened enough, to marry Leo and give up her job and living with her father? Her father had beaten her badly. She might be looking for a way out of the torment, and there was Leo, successful and handsome and charming, just ready to take her in and protect her.

Rey felt himself choke on dread. He couldn't imagine living in a house with Meredith if she was married to his brother. He'd rather throw himself headfirst into a cement mixer!

But, then, Leo had been teasing. Leo was always teasing. Rey forced himself to breathe normally and at least give the appearance of someone who was relaxed. Sure, it was just a joke. He didn't have to worry about the competition. There wasn't any. He pulled his hat lower over his eyes and walked on down the aisle to the man who was doctoring a heifer.

Several days later, Meredith received a huge bouquet of assorted roses from Billy Joe, now out of the hospital and back on the shooting range. She put them in water in the kitchen, along with the card, which the brothers blatantly read.

"He'd marry you," Rey drawled with pure acid in his tone as he dragged out a chair and sat down to lunch. "He's been widowed twenty years."

Meredith gave Leo a mischievous glance and fiddled with putting biscuits in a linen-lined basket. "He's not bad-looking for a man his age, and it wouldn't hurt him to have a nurse under his roof." She glanced at Rey's eloquent back. "But can he cook?"

Rey sipped coffee noisily.

"And does he slurp his coffee?" she added without missing a beat.

"That was done deliberately, to show you that I don't give a damn about manners!" Rey growled.

"All right, just don't expect me to take you to any nice restaurants while we're courting," she said easily, setting the basket of biscuits on the table.

"Lady, you aren't taking me as far as the mailbox," he said curtly.

He looked ferocious. That black temper was already kindling. Meredith studied his bent head curiously. You never knew about men. She'd seen some very mild-mannered ones come to the emergency room with wives who'd been beaten within an inch of their lives. It didn't hurt to see how far a man would go when he got mad. Especially after her experience with her father.

"You'll have to learn to scrape the mud off those enormous boots, too," she went on in a conversational tone. "And not slurp your soup. Your hair could use a good trim…"

"Damn it!"

He shot to his feet, eyes blazing in a rigid face, with a dusky flush creeping along his high cheekbones with all the warning color of a poisonous reptile.

Meredith stood her ground, watching him clench those big fists at his side.

"Rey," Leo cautioned abruptly, and started to get to his feet.

Meredith went right up to Rey, looking him in the eyes, quiet, still—waiting.

Rey was breathing through his nostrils. His jaw was clenched with fury. But intelligence won easily over bad temper. His chin raised slowly. "You're testing me," he said out of the blue. "You want to know if I'll hit you."

"It's something a woman needs to know about a man," she said very quietly. "And she needs to find it out where she can get help if she needs it." She didn't look at Leo but Rey knew that was what she meant. She smiled gently. "No, you don't hit," she said in a soft, quizzical tone. "You do have a temper, but it's not a physical one."

He was still breathing through his nose. "If you were a man, it might be," he told her bluntly.

"But I'm not a man," she replied.

Her eyes were almost glowing with feeling. He got lost in those soft, warm, grey eyes. He hated the way he felt when he was near her. He'd been fighting it ever since he carried her up to her garage apartment after she'd fainted at the hospital. He liked the feel of her in his arms. He liked kissing her. He liked the way she picked at him and teased him. No woman had ever done that before. As his older brothers had been before they married, he was taciturn and uncommunicative most of the time. His very attitude put most women off.

It didn't put Meredith off. She wasn't afraid of his temper, either. She made him into a different person. It wasn't something he could easily explain. He felt comfortable with her, even while she was stirring him to passion. He could imagine just sitting in front of the television with her and holding hands, late at night.

The image intimidated him. He sat back down, ignoring Meredith, and started putting butter and strawberry preserves on four biscuits.

Leo gave him a measuring look. "Don't eat all the biscuits."

"I'm only getting my share. She," he jerked his thumb towards Meredith, "didn't make but eight this morning. That's one for her, four for me, and three for you."

"And why do you get four?" Leo asked belligerently.

"Because she proposed to me," he said with pure smug arrogance, and a look that made Leo's teeth snap together.

"I did not," Meredith said haughtily, sitting down across

from him. "I said I was thinking of you as a marriage prospect, not that I actually wanted to go through with a ceremony." She cleared her throat. "I'll have to see how you work out."

Rey smiled faintly. "That sounds interesting."

He didn't necessarily mean what it sounded like he meant. She mustn't jump to any conclusions here. But her cheeks were getting very rosy.

He noticed that. It was a devilish game they were playing, and he could do it better. He stared pointedly at her soft mouth as he put a cube of fresh pear into his mouth, slowly and deliberately.

She felt very uncomfortable in odd places when he did that. She ate her beef and gravy and tried to ignore him.

"I like having fresh fruit," Rey said with a slow smile. He speared a grape with his fork and eased it slowly between his lips.

She moved restlessly in her chair. "It's healthy stuff."

"No wonder you were trying to get us to eat right," Leo said, trying to break the growing spell Rey was casting on her. "You teach nutrition, I suppose."

"In a way. I'm supposed to counsel patients on changing bad habits and making lifestyle changes when they're warranted," she explained. If only her hand didn't shake while she was holding the stupid fork. Rey saw it and knew why, and she hated that damned smug smile on his lean face!

He picked up a piece of perfectly cooked asparagus spear and slowly sucked it into his mouth, using his tongue meaningfully.

"I have to fix dessert," Meredith choked, jumping to her feet so quickly that she knocked her chair winding and had to right it.

"I saw that chair jump right out and trip you, Meredith," Rey commented dryly. "You ought to hit it with a stick."

"I ought to hit *you* with a stick instead!" she raged at him, flushed and flustered and out of patience.

"Me?" Both eyebrows arched. "What did I do?"

She pictured hitting him across the jaw with the biggest frying pan she had. It was very satisfying. Pity she couldn't do it for real.

She went to the cupboard and drew out the ingredients for an instant reduced fat pudding. She had some low-fat whipped cream in the freezer that she could top it with. Meanwhile, Rey would finish his meal and stop using fruits and vegetables to torment her with. She could have kicked him.

Behind her, Rey was talking comfortably to Leo about some new equipment they were ordering, and about routine chores that had to be completed before Thanksgiving this month and the Christmas holidays next month. Most of the ranch hands would have Thanksgiving, the day after, and that weekend free. Next month, they'd have Christmas Eve and Christmas Day free, along with four days before or after, depending on the schedule. Some of the men had families in far-flung locations and they had to travel a distance for the holidays. The Harts made a practice of giving the men time off to go home during the holiday season by staggering work schedules, so that there was an adequate crew here to work when days off were assigned.

Then they moved on, naturally, to a discussion about Thanksgiving dinner.

"You're going to stay until after Thanksgiving, aren't you?" Rey asked Meredith.

She had her back to them. "Yes, I'd like to," she said, because she'd already been planning special menus and light, noncaloric desserts for it. "Unless you're planning to go away for it," she added quickly.

"The family has a Christmas party, when we all get

together. We sort of save Thanksgiving for just us, so the others can have the day with their wives and kids," Leo told her. "It's been sort of hit and miss since Mrs. Lewis has been plagued with arthritis. As you know, we got her to come back to work just briefly, but her hands won't hold out to make bread and do any scrubbing with them, despite medicine. She has her children up from Corpus Christi for the holidays and cooks for them. We sort of got leftovers."

She grimaced. "Well, I'll make sure you have a big Thanksgiving dinner this year," she said gently. "With all the trimmings. Including biscuits," she added when they both looked her way.

She finished whipping the pudding, and put it in bowls in the refrigerator to chill before she sat back down. "That will make us a nice dessert tonight," she commented. "I don't suppose you want it any sooner?"

They shook their heads. "I've got a meeting with our marketing staff in half an hour," Rey said, checking his multifunction watch.

"And I've got to go over the new equipment list with our mechanic and see if we've got everything ready to order," Leo added.

"How about a nice Greek salad for supper?" Meredith asked. "I make it with feta cheese and black olives and eggs. I bought the ingredients yesterday at the store. Except for the eggs, of course. I'll get those out of the henhouse."

"Sounds nice," Leo said with a grin.

"Watch where you put your hands," Rey murmured without looking right at her. "I haven't seen my pet snake in the barn lately."

She gave him a cold look. "If I see him, I'll get him on a stick and put him right back in the barn," she said with pure bravado.

Rey glanced at her with dancing dark eyes. "I'd pay real money to see you do that," he chided.

So would I, she thought, but she didn't say it. She just smiled smugly.

The brothers finished their last swallows of coffee and went out the door still talking business.

Later, Meredith went out to the henhouse to gather the eggs, with her straw basket on her arm. Rey had unnerved her with his comment about the damned snake. Now she was sure it was in there, waiting for a gullible victim to frighten.

She took a deep breath and walked carefully into the dim confines of the henhouse. She bit her lower lip and approached the nest slowly. She stopped dead. There was actually a snake in there. He was wrapped around the eggs. He was licking his snaky lips.

She shivered with fear, but she wasn't going to let the stupid thing make her a laughingstock twice.

She saw a long, thick stick on the straw-covered floor. She put her basket down, still watching the snake, and picked up the stick.

"It's okay, old fellow," she said to the snake. "It's okay. I'm just going to ease you out of the nest. Don't get mad, now. I won't hurt you. It's okay."

While she was talking, softly, she eased the stick under its coils and very carefully lifted it. It was very still, not moving its head except to hiss. So far, so good. She had it up on the stick. It was heavy.

As she pulled it out of the nest, she noticed that it was really quite long. It really didn't look much like that black and white one Rey had put in the barn. This one had a pretty brown pattern on its back and had a white underbelly. But, then, it wasn't striking at her or anything, so she wasn't worried.

She held it far out in front of her and stepped carefully out of the henhouse into the bright light. As she did, the snake hung from the stick, looking rather bored by the whole thing.

She carried it through the yard and out toward the barn. One of the men was standing by a truck, watching her progress. His jaw fell. She wondered what was wrong with him. Maybe he'd never seen a woman carry a snake around before.

"Nice day," she called to him.

He didn't answer. She shrugged and kept walking.

The barn was empty, except for the bales of hay that were stacked neatly on the bottom and the loft of the huge structure. Over against one wall there was a corn crib with stacks and stacks of dried corn, and a machine that shelled them.

"Here we go, old fellow," she told the snake. She eased him over the wooden box and slid him down into the piles of unshelled corn.

He drew back in a threatening pose and hissed at her again.

Odd, the shape of his head, she thought, frowning as she studied him. It looked like an arrowhead. That other snake's head had been rounded.

Well, it might be some other species of king snake, she supposed. Weren't there several?

She walked back out of the barn into the daylight, whistling softly to herself as she started back to the henhouse. She was so proud of herself. She'd gotten the snake on the stick all by herself, without screaming once, and she'd carried him all the way to the barn and put him in the corn crib. She wasn't afraid of the snake anymore. As Rey had said, they were beneficial. It wasn't right to kill something just because you were afraid of it, she told herself.

The man who'd been standing by the truck was nowhere in sight, but the truck was still running and the driver's door was standing wide-open. She wondered where the driver had gone. He must have been in a hurry for some reason.

Meredith went back to the henhouse, put the stick down, picked up her basket and went to gather eggs. There were no more snakes, but there were plenty of eggs. She could boil several to go in her nice Greek salad. The spinach she'd bought to make it with was crisp and cold and almost blemishless. The brothers would love a salad if it had enough eggs and cheese and dressing.

She got the last egg into the basket and walked back out again, pausing to reach down and pet one of the big red hens who came right up to her and cocked its head curiously toward her face.

"Aren't you a pretty girl?" she said, smiling. She liked the way the chicken felt. Its feathers were very smooth and silky, and the chicken made the sweetest little noises when she petted it. She'd never been around farm creatures. She found that she enjoyed the chickens and the cattle dogs and the endless cats that hung around outside begging for handouts.

Two other hens came up to her, curious about the tall creature in jeans and tank top. She petted them, too, laughing as they crowded close. But then one started to peck the eggs, and she stood up again.

She turned back toward the house, her mind on the snake and her bravery. She'd have to remember to tell Rey and Leo about it...

"Meredith!"

The loud, urgent deep voice sent her spinning around. Rey was running toward her, bare-headed, with the cowhand who'd been next to the running pickup truck at his heels.

"Hi, Rey," she said hesitantly. "What's wrong?"

He stopped just in front of her. He caught her a little roughly by the arms and took the basket away from her, setting it aside, while he looked at every inch of her bare arms and hands. He was breathing rapidly. He seemed unnaturally pale and tight-lipped.

"It didn't bite you?" he demanded.

"What?"

"The snake! It didn't bite you?" he snapped.

"No, of course not," she stammered. "I just got it on a stick, like you did, and put it in the corn crib."

"Get my Winchester," Rey told the other man in a harsh tone. "Load it and bring it back here. Hurry!"

"I don't understand," Meredith said with noticeable confusion. "What's wrong with you? Why do you need a gun?"

"Oh, baby," he whispered hoarsely. He pulled her against him and bent to kiss her in view of the whole outfit, his mouth hard and rough against hers. "Baby!"

She had no idea what was wrong, but she loved the faint tremor in his hard arms as they crushed her against his body. And she loved the way he was kissing her, as if he couldn't get enough of her mouth. He'd called her "baby…"

She held on and moaned under the crush of his lips.

He drew back. "I'm sorry. It was such a shock. I was scared out of my wits, I didn't even stop to grab my hat when Whit came into the office…!"

Her mouth was pleasantly swollen. She looked up at him dreamily and smiled.

"You don't have a clue, do you?" he asked huskily, searching her soft grey eyes.

"Mmm. About what?" she murmured, only half hearing him.

The other man came out with a rifle. He handed it to Rey. "Safety's on," the man advised.

"Thanks, Whit."

He moved back from Meredith. "I'll go kill it."

"Kill it?" Meredith exclaimed. "You can't! It will eat the rats, it's harmless…!"

"Sweetheart," he said very gently, "you were carrying a copperhead moccasin."

"Yes?" She stared at him blankly.

"It's one of the most poisonous snakes in Texas!"

She stood looking after him with her mouth open and her heartbeat choking her. She'd been carrying the damned thing on a stick, with it hissing at her. She felt the blood leave her head. Seconds later, she was lying on the hard ground. Fortunately she missed the basket of eggs on the way down.

Chapter Nine

"You're making a habit of this lately," Rey murmured as he carried Meredith up the stairs to the garage apartment. "I never figured you for a fainter, Meredith," he added dryly.

He was still bare-headed, but he wasn't grim now. He was smiling.

"Of course I fainted! I picked up a poisonous snake!" she gasped, still in shock.

"Well, you've got guts, woman, I'll give you that," he said with a slow smile, shifting her a little closer. "Picked up a poisonous snake with a stick and carried it all the way to the barn, and it didn't bite you. Now I've heard everything."

"It did hiss a little," she recalled, shivering.

"It had eaten three eggs," he murmured. "Probably it was too busy digesting to care where it went at the time. Lucky for you."

She laid her cheek against his broad, strong shoulder and held on tight. She had a sudden thought. "It didn't bite you?" she asked worriedly.

"It didn't get the chance. Didn't you hear the shot? I got it as it was crawling down from the corn bin onto the floor." He chuckled. "If I hadn't gotten it, though, Bandit would have. King snakes are natural enemies of any poisonous snake. They eat them. I hate to kill even a copperhead, but we can't have poisonous snakes around the livestock, or the men. Or, especially," he added with a warm glance at her, "in the henhouse. At the very least, a bite from one can put a man in the hospital."

She shivered, and her arms tightened around Rey's neck. "I was so proud of myself," she murmured. "I had no idea I was taking my life in my hands. It didn't look exactly like the other snake, but the patterns were sort of similar. I know about snake bites because I've helped treat them, but I don't know one snake from another unless I see pictures of them!" she added defensively.

"You'll learn." He kissed her forehead with breathless tenderness. "My brave girl," he whispered. "You'll never know how scared I was when Whit came running to tell me what you were doing."

It made soft little ripples of pleasure run through her body when he said that. He was being protective about her. She closed her eyes and drank in the warm nearness of him, the easy strength of his arms as he carried her. She felt safe as she'd never felt in her whole life. It was nice to lean on somebody strong, just for a little while.

He felt the vulnerability. He told himself that he wouldn't take advantage of it, but who was he kidding? She was soft and cuddly like this, and it was almost an involuntary action when his mouth slowly moved over hers as he reached her door.

The pressure was light, comforting. She sighed under the warmth and delight of it, and her lips parted, just the least little bit.

His whole body contracted with desire at that faint response. He looked down into her half-closed, misty eyes with growing hunger.

The look was as new as the tenderness. She couldn't tear her eyes away from that dark hunger in his. She forgot the snake, the scare, the people outside in the yard, everything. He bent back to her, and she met his mouth hungrily with her own, her arms clinging fiercely to his shoulders.

He groaned aloud. It was too soon, but he didn't care. He managed to open the door and close it behind them, making a beeline for the neatly made-up bed. He barely took time to put her down on the coverlet before his body slid against and over her own, his arms under her, taking his weight while his mouth made new, insistent demands on her innocence.

He lifted his head a torturous few seconds later, and his eyes blazed into her own. One lean hand slid deliberately under the hem of her tank top. At the same time, one long, powerful leg eased between both of hers and his hard mouth began to tease around the corners of hers.

"Danger will do it every time," he murmured deeply.

"Will…do what?" she asked, burning with new longings as his hand began to move up her rib cage toward the lacy little bra she was wearing under the top.

"This." His mouth opened on hers and became quickly insistent. While he kissed her, his fingers found the catch on her bra and flicked it open. She jumped when she felt his hand on flesh that had never known a man's touch before. He lifted his head and looked into her eyes. "I know. It's new territory," he said gently. His fingers stroked the delicate, warm flesh as lightly as a breeze. "Try to think of it as a rite of passage."

She felt strange new sensations. There was a tightening, a swelling, in her breasts as he touched them. She lifted involuntarily, and her eyes mirrored her surprise.

"Innocence is a rare, rare thing these days," he said at her lips. "I respect it. And you'd better thank your lucky stars that I do," he added as his mouth bit hungrily at hers. "Because with an experienced woman, I'd lock the door and I wouldn't hesitate a minute."

She felt the words like the caress of his hands on her body. She moaned huskily under the demanding crush of his mouth. She felt his tongue tracing her lips, teasing under them, darting and touching and withdrawing. She felt his teeth, too, in a sensual caress that only intensified the new sensations he was teaching her to feel.

She felt her back arch again as he traced around the curves of her breast without ever touching the hard, taut nipple. She wanted him to touch it. Her body ached to have him touch it. She didn't understand why it should be such a violent, aching need…!

He laughed in a soft, sexy way against her lips. "Is this what you want?"

He caught the nipple between his thumb and forefinger and she lifted off the bed with a sharp cry. Heat spread over her, through her. Her short nails dug into his back fiercely and she gasped with pleasure.

"Baby," he groaned roughly, aroused by her unexpectedly ardent response. "Baby, you turn me on so hard…!"

The top was suddenly around her collarbone and his mouth—his mouth!—was right on her nipple, suckling her while his tongue tasted the hardness with a subtle caress that made her shiver. Her hands caught in the thick strands of his dark hair and held him to her body while he explored it with his mouth. She'd never imagined that she was capable of so much passion, and so unexpectedly swift. He could do anything to her, and she didn't have the willpower to stop him. Even a simple "no" was beyond her now. She wanted more. She wanted his eyes on her, his hands on her. She wanted his body closer.

As if he knew that, both lean hands smoothed up from her waist and onto her soft breasts. His fingers were rough from hard work, but their touch was pure heaven. She caressed his nape, moving rhythmically with each slow brush of his fingers, lost in pleasure.

He lifted his head to look at what he'd uncovered. She was beautiful, not too big or too small. She was just right. He loved the way her body moved when he touched it. He loved knowing how innocent she was. He'd never been with an innocent. Making love to one was a whole new experience, with levels of pleasure he'd never tasted. Her soft little moans excited him as much as those enthusiastic fingers caressing his back.

She felt his eyes and she opened hers, looking up at him. "Am I doing it right?" she whispered breathlessly.

His body tautened even more. "Yes," he whispered. "Just right."

He bent and drew his mouth gently over hers with a soft, cherishing pressure. He felt it open under his, felt her arms pulling at him. It wasn't a good idea to let this go any farther than it already had. While he was thinking it, he was moving slowly between her long legs until his body rested in the fork of hers. He eased down against her, letting her feel the slow burgeoning of his body against her belly.

She caught her breath.

He heard it, and lifted his head. His eyes were smoldering with desire, his body was rigid with it. He was getting little surges of insistent pleasure that ran the length of his spine. Her hips moved as if they were responding helplessly to the touch of him. She was making him ache like hell.

His hand moved to her hip and bit into the soft flesh, stilling the faint motion of her hips instantly while he rested on the elbow of his other arm. "Meredith," he said softly. "That will get you seduced. Right now."

She felt hot all over. Her mind seemed barely under her control. She searched his dark eyes with wonder. Her hands were against his shirt, right on the buttons. She felt him against the lower part of her body, and it felt right. It felt wonderful. She wanted to writhe under him and tempt him into intimacy.

His hand contracted and he gave her a wise, challenging stare as he read the look on her face. "Don't do it," he said huskily. "I'm years ahead of you in experience, but I can still lose my head. You don't want me to do that. Not really."

She pulled at a stabilizing breath. Her heart was still whacking around at the walls of her chest, as if she'd been running a race. "Are you sure I don't want you to do that? I mean, if you get pregnant, I'll marry you," she said breathlessly, and with deathbed humor. "Honest!"

He looked at her as if he couldn't believe his ears. The passion drained out of him, replaced by howling amusement. He started laughing. "Damn you, that wasn't fair!" he accused.

"Well, I like that! You're laughing, and here I've made you a solemn promise," she persisted, eyes twinkling.

"Hell!" He rolled away from her and sat up on the edge of the bed to run a lean hand through his disheveled hair. He glared down at her. "Now you've got fingerprints and lipstick and perfume all over me. The men will laugh themselves sick if I go to work smelling like a flower garden."

She tugged down her top and gave him an impish grin. "We could rush into my bathroom and shower it off, together," she offered wickedly.

He laughed again. He'd never laughed as much in his life as he did with her. Was this the way she'd been, before the tragedies of the past year that had marred her life? She'd said she didn't date much, but how in the world could men ignore a sweet, pretty little woman like that?

"I can't believe you spend your weekends watching television with your father," he murmured.

"I don't. I work."

He frowned. "On the weekends?"

She sat up, reaching under her blouse to refasten the bra he'd unsnapped. She wondered why she didn't feel embarrassed. "Seven days a week, for the past six months," she said honestly. "Before that, six days a week, and I had to rest on Sunday. I usually work ten-hour days, sometimes longer if we have an emergency."

He didn't like that. "You don't have any free time, do you?"

She shook her head. "I've been dedicated to the job since I got out of college."

"And no men," he murmured with a speculative glance.

She grimaced. "Well, there was one I liked very much. We went out together for four months, and I was very nearly in love with him. But he never touched me. I thought he was building up to it, or something." She sighed. "Then I saw him, with another man." She shrugged. "He thought of me as a friend. I thought of him as a boyfriend. I sort of lost confidence in myself after that."

"It happens, in the modern world," he replied quietly.

"Before that, I had crushes on boys who never noticed me, except to ask me to help them with math or chemistry."

She searched his eyes. "Of course, I didn't exactly look like this until last year."

"How did you look?" he asked curiously.

She got off the bed, went to get her purse, and took out a plastic insert. She pulled a photo from behind a credit card and handed it to him.

His eyes widened. "Good heavens!"

She winced. "I was sixty pounds overweight, and I couldn't lose it at all. I guess I tried every diet known to man. Then I took nutrition classes and learned how to get it off the sensible way. That's why I know so much about low-fat cooking."

He looked from the photo to her face and smiled. "You were pretty before, too," he said slowly. "You know, Meredith, it's not the outside that attracts people. It's what you are, how you treat other people, that makes friends of them. You risked your life to save my brother, then you stayed with him until his family came. I wasn't very flattering to you when we first met, but I've had a lot of time to think about what you did. You're good people. Really good people."

She flushed and cleared her throat. "Thanks." She gave him a mischievous look. "So, would you like to get married Friday, or is Monday better for you?" she added with a grin.

He chuckled. "Sorry, I have to wash my dogs."

She sighed. "Rejected again."

He pursed his lips and let his eyes run over her slowly. "You could lie back down and we could discuss it again."

"Absolutely not. I only have so much willpower. You shouldn't throw yourself at women that way unless you're asking to be seduced. It's unfair."

"You're not bad yourself, kid," he murmured with a warm smile. He got up. "I've got to go back to work. Come here."

She went to him. "Changed your mind?" she asked. "I can get a ring today…"

He put a finger over her mouth. "How do I smell?"

"Is that all you want?" she exclaimed. "Good Lord, you got me all the way over here to *smell* you?"

He bent and kissed her hungrily, pulling her so close that she could feel him against every cell of her body. But before she could cling, he put her away. "How do I smell?" he persisted.

She sniffed him. "You smell like aftershave."

He bent and sniffed her, and frowned. "You're not wearing perfume, are you?"

She shook her head. "I'm allergic to most strong fragrances."

"You smell like flowers."

She smiled. "Herbal shampoo. Flowers don't bother me. Well, real ones do sometimes, but not flowery scent. I can use scented shampoos and wear one or two colognes, but no perfumes. They're too strong."

"At least I don't smell womanly," he said with mocking relief. "I'd never live that down."

She cocked her head and stared up at him. "There goes the shower," she sighed.

He tapped her nose. "Now, cut that out." His fingers traced the fading bruises on her cheek and jaw and his eyes narrowed. "He'll never touch you again, I swear he won't," he said in a low, dangerous tone.

Her heart lifted at the look on his face. "Oh, my, aren't we getting possessive?" she teased.

He didn't smile. "Careful," he told her quietly. "I'm not teasing."

Her eyes widened with something like wonder.

"Hasn't anyone ever stood up for you?" he asked curiously.

"Just my brother. But he never had to protect me from Daddy. I know it looks really bad, but my father was the most gentle man on earth until we lost Mama and Mike. He goes crazy when he drinks, and he never remembers what he did." Her eyes fell to his chest. She toyed with his shirt buttons, wondering absently how it would feel to smooth her fingers over his bare chest. "I miss my brother terribly," she added simply.

"I'm sure you do. And your mother."

She grimaced. "She and I weren't really very close," she confessed. She searched his eyes. "You see, what Daddy yelled about her that night you were at the house was pretty much true. She was a very attractive woman, and she had lovers." She winced. "I hated knowing that. You can't imagine what it did to Daddy. She even bragged about them."

"She doesn't sound like much of a wife," he murmured.

"She didn't act like one, either. She did love to spend money, though. That's why she picked rich lovers." Her face clouded. "I was so ashamed of her. I guess she saw herself as a modern woman. I'm not. There's a big difference between sleeping with someone you truly love, and jumping into bed with anyone who has some money."

He nodded and touched her soft, swollen mouth. "She's soured you on men, hasn't she?"

"Sort of. Until you came along, at least," she admitted, without looking at him. She stared at his shirt button. "Bad temper and all, you've got some wonderful qualities."

He gave her a wry look. "I'll have to tell my brothers. They didn't know."

She chuckled. "Thanks for letting me come here to heal, anyway."

He felt uneasy. "That sounds like goodbye, Meredith."

She sighed. Her fingers stilled on his buttons. "I can't stay much longer," she said sadly. "Even though I'd like to. My boss is shorthanded as it is, and the woman filling in for me doesn't like leaving her kids in day care. She retired when she had the second one."

"Retired?"

"Yes. She said keeping two kids in day care ate up her whole paycheck." She lifted her eyes to his. "Since her husband got a raise, it was actually cheaper for her to stay home with the kids than it was to work. She loves it."

There was a strange look on his face. He rubbed his fingertips over her short fingernails absently. "Would you want to stay home with your kids?"

She stared up at him, transfixed. "Yes, I would. Those first few years are so important. If I could find any way to do it, I would, even if I had to sacrifice some little luxuries."

"That would be tricky. You're a highly trained professional."

"One of my friends was a highly trained doctor," she replied. "She gave up her job and stayed home with her little boy until he was in kindergarten. Even then, she arranged her schedule so that she'd be there when he got home in the afternoons."

He was frowning, and his fingers were still smoothing over hers. He wanted to ask if she thought she could get used to ranch life and snakes. He was afraid to say it. The act of commitment was still very new to him. He couldn't rush her.

He sighed, troubled. "What does your father do, by the way?" he asked suddenly.

"Oh, he teaches in the veterinary department of his college in Houston."

His hand stilled on hers. "He's a veterinarian?"

"He has a doctorate in veterinary medicine, yes. Why?"

Wheels were turning in his head. He stared at her thoughtfully. "Will he have a job to go back to, after all the trouble he's had with the law?"

"You're very perceptive," she said after a minute. "Actually, no, he won't. The college phoned before his last bender and told him not to come back. You can't blame them, either," she added sadly. "What would it do to the college's image, to have an alcoholic on staff with a dangerous temper?"

"Not much," he had to admit. "Did he drink before the shooting?"

"Never. Not even a beer," she replied. "But he's set records in the past six months. I couldn't get him near a treatment center. At least he's in one, now."

"Not only in it, but improving by the day," Rey said unexpectedly. "He'd like you to come see him. I can run you up there Sunday, if you'd like to go."

That was surprising. "You've spoken to him?" she asked.

He nodded. "I had Leo phone Colter. He has contacts who helped arrange it." He drew in a deep breath. "Your father seems pretty rational right now. Of course, he isn't drinking, either." His eyes darkened. "I meant exactly what I said. He'll never touch you again in anger."

"When he's sober, he never would. I can't believe…he really wants to see me?" she asked haltingly.

He brushed his hand against her cheek. "He loves you. I'm sure you love him, too. You don't throw people away because they make a mistake—even a bad one. You get help for them."

"I tried."

"Sure you did. But it's better this way. When he comes home, we'll decide where to go from there. For now, I'll drive you to Houston on Sunday to see him. Want to go?"

"Oh, yes," she said. Her expression was soft, wondering. "You'd do that, for me?"

He smiled. "Anything you want, kiddo," he murmured. "It's the least I can do for the only woman who's ever proposed to me."

She pursed her lips and gave him an impish look. "We could lie down and talk about it."

"No, we couldn't," he told her firmly, and chuckled as he removed her hands from his shirt. "I have to get back to work. I was in the middle of a meeting when you did your snake charmer routine. I left twelve employees sitting in the boardroom with glasses of water and no ashtrays. At least six of them smoke, despite all the regulations. I expect they've attacked the other six with chairs by now, or vice versa. I've got to get back. Quick."

"I'd love to go Sunday," she said.

"Fine. I'll run you up there Sunday afternoon. We can go to church first."

Her eyebrows lifted. "I'm Methodist."

He grinned. "So are we. It's a date." He opened the door. Before he went out it, he glanced back over his shoulder. "And stay out of the henhouse for the rest of the day, will you?"

"Anything for my prospective fiancé," she said with a theatrical gesture of her arm.

He shook his head and walked out, still chuckling.

Later, she wondered what he'd meant, about making decisions when her father got out of rehab. She didn't dare think too hard about it. But it sounded very much as if he wanted to go on looking out for her.

She was a modern woman. She could look out for herself. But it was kind of nice to have a man act protective and possessive, especially one like Rey, who didn't seem the sort to do it habitually. She remembered the hunger in his lean body when he held her, when he kissed her. She remembered the strange tenderness he reserved for her. It was an adventure, just being around him. They'd known each other such a short time, really, but she felt as if she'd known him all her life. The thought of going back to Houston without him was suddenly frightening.

She did the routine things until Sunday, except that when she gathered eggs, she was overly cautious about going into the henhouse. She'd learned from Rey that snakes often traveled in pairs, so she was careful to look before she stepped anywhere that the ground was covered.

She'd become something of a legend among the Hart ranch hands already. They removed their hats when she walked by, and they spoke to her in respectful tones.

"It's really strange," she remarked at the dinner table on Saturday evening, glancing from Leo to Rey. "The men seem sort of in awe of me."

Rey chuckled and exchanged an amused look with his brother. "They are. None of them has ever picked up a copperhead on a stick."

"It let me," she reminded him.

"That's the awesome thing," Leo remarked. "You see, Meredith, copperheads have a nasty reputation for attacking without provocation. It's kind of mystic, what you did." He pursed his lips and gave her a teasing glance over his buttered biscuit. "Any snake charmers in your family?"

"No, but Mike had a pet boa for a while, until it ate one of the neighbor's rabbits," she sighed.

"Yuccch!" Rey said, and shivered.

"It was an accident," Meredith insisted. "It escaped out the window and was gone for three weeks. We figured it was starving, because it hadn't been fed in so long. Besides that," she added, "the rabbit was vicious. It attacked everybody who opened the cage."

"Why did the neighbor keep rabbits?"

"He sold them for meat to a specialty grocery store."

Rey chuckled. "Maybe the boa was a reincarnated taste-tester," he mused.

Leo made a face. "I wouldn't eat a rabbit if I was starving. On the other hand, snake's not so bad. Remember when we were in Arizona on that hunting trip, camping out, and our guide caught that big, juicy rattler?"

"Sure do," Rey agreed, nodding. "Tasted just like chicken!"

Obviously that was a private joke, because the brothers looked at each other and burst out laughing.

"What became of the boa?" Leo asked, interested.

"Mike had just sold it to a breeder," she recalled sadly. "He was engaged to the sweetest, kindest girl I ever knew. It devastated her when he was killed. They had to sedate her for two days, and she couldn't even go to the funeral." She shook her head. "I felt as sorry for her as I did for Dad and me."

"What happened to her?" Leo asked.

She finished her coffee. "She became a missionary and went to South America with a group of them." She winced. "She had the worst luck…it was that plane that was mistaken for drug smugglers and shot down. I think she was one of the survivors, but she didn't come back to America with the others."

"Poor kid," Rey said.

"Colter was upset over the shooting for a long time, too," Leo recalled. "Just between you and me, he was sweet o

Mike's girl, but too much a gentleman to do anything about it. He thought the sun rose and set on Mike."

"I never knew," Meredith said softly.

"Neither did Mike. Or the girl," Leo added with a smile. "Colter's a clam. He never talks."

"Is he still with the Texas Rangers?" Meredith asked.

Leo nodded. "Got promoted to lieutenant just recently. He's good at his job."

She pushed back from the table. "If you two are through, I'll just wash up. Rey's going to drive me up to see my dad tomorrow."

"What a sweet guy!" Leo exclaimed with a wide-eyed look at his brother.

"He's being nice to me, because I'm the only woman who ever proposed to him," Meredith volunteered with a wicked grin. "He feels guilty because he turned me down."

"Good. I'll marry you, Meredith," Leo volunteered at once. "You just name the time and place, and I'll buy a new suit…!"

"Shut the hell up!" Rey said curtly, and hit his brother with his Stetson.

Leo protected his shoulder. "Meredith, he's picking on me!" he wailed.

"Do you want biscuits for breakfast?" she asked Rey.

He stopped flogging his brother. "All right. But only for biscuits," Rey said. He got up and deliberately bent and kissed Meredith, right in front of Leo. "Don't stay up too late. Leo and I have to check the livestock in the barn."

"Okay. Wear a jacket," she said, smiling up at him.

He bent and brushed his mouth against hers one more time. "It's not cold."

"It is. Wear a jacket," she insisted.

He sighed and made a face, but he picked up his lightweight denim jacket from the hat stand by the back door as he went out.

Leo followed him, but with a new expression on his face. He'd seen something he hadn't expected during that teasing exchange. He wondered if Rey realized that he was in love with that sweet little biscuit-making woman. And unless he missed his guess, it was mutual.

Chapter Ten

The next morning, Meredith sat next to Rey in church and felt his hand holding hers almost all the way through the service. She felt different with him than she'd ever felt with anyone else. Rey made her feel as if she could do anything. He made her feel strong and confident and safe.

She glanced up at him while they shared a hymnal and he forgot what he was singing. They searched each other's eyes slowly, until they realized that everybody else had stopped singing and were sitting down. Smiling sheepishly, Rey sat down and tugged her down beside him.

After the service, they got amused, affectionate looks from bystanders who knew Rey and had heard about his new cook.

But he didn't seem to be the least bit embarrassed by the attention. In fact, he made a point of introducing Meredith to several people, adding the little known information that she was a licensed nurse practitioner as well as a great biscuit chef.

Meredith flushed, because it sounded as if he were very proud of her, especially when he related how her quick thinking had probably saved Billy Joe's life at the target range. Billy Joe was well-known and liked locally, so that brought even more smiles. She clung to his hand with unashamed delight when they left.

"See, you're already a local celebrity," he teased. "And I didn't even get around to mentioning the snake."

"We should forget the snake," she said quickly.

He chuckled. "No, we shouldn't. It wins me points if I have a…cook who isn't even afraid of poisonous snakes."

She heard that hesitation before "cook," as if he wanted to say something else instead. It made her tingle all over. She couldn't stop smiling, all the way to the Jaguar convertible he drove when he wasn't working.

"This is a very flashy car," she commented as he put her in on the passenger side.

"I like sports cars," he said with a grin.

"So do I," she confessed. She didn't even put on a scarf. In fact, she pulled the pins out of her hair and let it fall around her shoulders.

"Won't it tangle in the wind?" he asked when they were seat-belted in place.

"I don't care." She looked at him and smiled warmly. "I like to feel the wind."

"Me, too."

He started the car, put it in gear, and pulled out onto the highway. When they were on the interstate, heading toward Houston, he let the powerful car do its best.

"Now this is a HORSE!" he called over the roar of the wind.

She laughed with pure delight. It was the most wonderful day of her life. She even forgot where they were going in the excitement of being with him in the elegant vehicle.

* * *

But all too soon, they were pulling up at an impressive brick building with its function discreetly labeled on a metal plate near the door. It was a substance abuse rehabilitation center, three stories tall, and staffed impressively with psychologists, psychiatrists, and health professionals, including physicians.

Rey held her hand to the information desk and then up to the second floor waiting room, where her father would be brought to visit with them.

"They don't like visitors the first week," Rey explained to her. "You probably knew that," he added, remembering her profession.

"I've never had anybody in here," she said quietly. She was nervous and she looked it.

He caught her fingers in his again and held them tight. "It's going to be all right," he said firmly.

She met his eyes and took a deep breath. "Okay," she said after a minute, and her body lost some of its rigidity.

There were footsteps and muffled voices. A minute later, her father came in the door, wearing slacks and a knit shirt, and behind him was a uniformed woman with a clipboard.

"Miss Johns? I'm Gladys Bartlett," the woman introduced herself with a firm handshake. "I'm the staff psychologist on your father's case."

"Hello, Merry," her father said hesitantly. He winced when he noticed the faded bruises on her face. "I'm sorry, my dear," he choked.

Meredith let go of Rey's hand and went forward to hug her father warmly. Mr. Johns closed his eyes and hugged her back, hard. His lips trembled as he forced them together, ut tears ran down his lean, pale cheeks. "I'm so sorry," he bbed.

She patted him on the back and tears fell hotly from her own eyes. "It's okay, Daddy," she whispered brokenly, comforting him the way he'd once comforted her and Mike when they were little, and something had hurt them. He'd been a wonderful father. "It's okay," she said again. "You're going to be fine. We both are."

"My son. My boy!" He shook all over. "I said I was too busy to take her to the bank. I asked him…I *asked* Mike… to go instead. He'd be alive, but for me!"

"Now, Mr. Johns," the counselor said gently, "we've been over this several times already. You can't assume blame for the lawless acts of other people. Ninety-nine times out of a hundred, nothing would have happened if you'd asked your son to go to the bank on your behalf."

"But this was the one out of a hundred," he husked. "And I can't live with the guilt!"

"I've had my own problems with it," Meredith confessed. "I could have refused to go in to work that day and taken her instead."

"And you'd be lying dead instead of Mike," her father replied curtly. "And I'd be just as eaten up with guilt!"

"You're both missing the point," Rey said, standing up. "You can't control life. Nobody can."

They all looked at him. He stood quietly, his hands deep in his slacks pockets, and stared back. "Einstein said that God didn't play dice with the universe, and he was right. Even in seeming chaos, there's an order to things, a chain of events that leads inevitably to conclusions. People are links in the chain, but people don't control the events. Life has a pattern, even if we don't see it."

"You've studied philosophy," Mr. Johns said quietly.

Rey nodded. "Yes, I have."

The older man, with thinning hair and glasses and a faintly stooped posture, moved away from Meredith ar smiled. "I took several courses in it, myself. You have a degree, haven't you?"

"I do, in business. A master's, from Harvard," Rey volunteered, something that Meredith hadn't even known.

"Mine is in medicine. Veterinary medicine. I'm..."

"I know. You're Dr. Alan Johns," Rey said, shaking hands. "Your daughter is staying with us on the ranch in Jacobsville, baking biscuits, while she recovers."

Dr. Johns winced and flushed. "They told me what I did to you," he said, glancing shamefaced at his daughter. "I swear before God, I'll never take another drink as long as I live!"

"You won't get the chance," Rey said. "I intend to watch you like a red-tailed hawk."

"Excuse me?" Dr. Johns stammered.

Rey studied his boots. "We don't have a vet on staff. We have to call one down from Victoria, because our vets are overworked to death. It would be nice to have our own vet. We pay competitive salaries and you'd have your own house."

Dr. Johns sat down quickly. "Young man, I...!"

Rey lifted his head and stared him in the eyes. "You made a mistake. People do. That's why they put erasers on pencils. You can work for us. We'll keep you straight, and you won't have to take some sort of menial job in Houston just to make ends meet. You'll like the ranch," he added. "We have a good crew."

"Someone might know what I did," Dr. Johns stammered.

"Everybody knows already," Rey said, and shrugged. "It's no big deal to us. We've got one man who came back from cocaine addiction—let me tell you, that was a story nd a half—and another one who was a habitual DWI for x years until we hired him and helped him get straight."

He smiled. "We don't hold a man's past against him, as long as he's willing to stay straight and work hard."

Dr. Johns was having a hard time keeping control of himself, and it was obvious. "Young man, I'll work without a salary, if that's what it takes. And I promise, you'll never have cause to regret giving me a job."

"Not unless you keep calling me 'young man,'" Rey said with a grin. "I'm Reynard Hart, but everybody calls me Rey."

"Glad to meet you," the older man said. "Rey."

Rey nodded. "How much longer will they keep you?" he asked, and glanced at the woman with the clipboard.

"Another week should do it," she said with a big smile. "And how nice, to see him with a settled environment to look forward to the day he leaves! I believe in minor miracles, but I don't see many. This is certainly one."

Rey gave her a complacent smile. "Miracles only happen for people who believe in them," he said, chuckling.

"Thanks, Rey," Meredith said huskily.

He only shrugged. "How could I ignore the father of the only woman who ever proposed to me?" he said, matter-of-factly, and with a smile that made her blush.

"You proposed to him?" her father asked with raised eyebrows.

"Several times," she said with mock disgust. "But he has to wash his dogs, so he can't marry me."

Dr. Johns laughed heartily.

The counselor relaxed. This was going to work out. Dr. Johns was never going to end up in rehab again, she was certain of it. She only wished she could say the same for more of her poor patients.

On the drive back to Jacobsville, Meredith was on top of the world. "Not only does he get a new job, but or doing what he always loved best, working around large animals."

"He likes cattle, does he?" Rey asked absently, enjoying Meredith's animated company.

"He grew up on a cattle ranch in Montana," she explained. "He was even in rodeo for six or seven years before he went to college."

Rey expelled a breath. This was going to work out even better than he'd dreamed. Amazing, he thought, how a single act of kindness could expand like ripples around a rock dropped into a pond.

"He's not much good on a horse anymore," she continued chattily, "but he really knows veterinary medicine."

"He might go back to teaching one day. Not in Houston," he added gently. "But Texas is a big state, and when he's been away from alcohol a couple of years, who knows?"

"The ranch will be good for him. You did mean it, didn't you?" she added quickly. "It wasn't something you said to help him want to get better?"

"I very rarely say things I don't mean, Meredith," he replied. "Well," he added with a frown, "I wasn't exactly telling the truth about washing the dogs."

"Excuses, excuses." She toyed with her purse. "Rey, thank you for giving him a second chance."

He laughed gently. "I've got an ulterior motive," he murmured dryly. "When you come to the ranch to visit him, you can make me a pan of biscuits."

"Just you? Not one to share with Leo?"

He shifted behind the wheel. "He can go find someone to make him biscuits," he said. "Surely, somewhere in Texas, there's a woman who'd do it just for him."

"Your other brothers, do their wives bake?"

"Dorie and Tess do," he said. "But Tira hasn't got a clue how to," he added on a sigh. "Simon doesn't mind. They have a cook who can. Although he's really not much on biscuits, so it doesn't matter." He grinned. "You should see him with his sons. Two of them now. They're still toddlers, and he's a whiz at fatherhood. Dorie and Corrigan have a boy and a girl and Cag and Tess have a son. That makes me an uncle five times over! Christmas is going to be a real treat this year."

She thought about Christmas. It was going to be a lonely one for her, with her father down here on the ranch.

He saw the look on her face and reached out to catch her hand in his. "Hey," he said softly, "you're invited for Christmas, you know. We'll pack up the kids and go over to the annual Christmas party at the Doctors Coltrain. They have huge layouts of Lionel trains that they run every year, especially with a little boy of their own who'll be big enough to play with them in a couple of years. Draws a big crowd. Do you like train sets?"

She smiled. "I do." It lifted her heart to know that she was going to be included in the family get-together. She loved children. It would make the season less traumatic for her and her father, because they were missing two members of their immediate family.

"We'll make it a happy Christmas," he said softly.

She tangled her fingers into his. "I'll have that to look forward to, when I go back."

"It's premature right now, but if you decide to move down here, too, I'd bet good money that Micah Steele would offer you work."

She looked at his big, warm hand holding hers. "I like Jacobsville."

His fingers grew possessive. "I like *you*."

"Thanks. I like you, too, and if you'll loan me your cell phone, I'll call the minister right now and we can set a date," she added with wicked haste.

He chuckled. "Hold on, tiger, I may have been lying about washing the dogs, but marriage is a big step. You have to look out for me. I know you can tame snakes and handle heart attacks, and you bake good biscuits. But how do you look in a suit, and can you dance?"

"I look great in a suit," she said firmly, "and I can do Latin dances."

He grimaced. "I can't. How about a nice, slow two-step?"

"I can do that, too!"

He glanced at her. "What do you like to read?" he asked.

The next few minutes were spent in gleeful harmony, going over things they had in common. They liked the same basic forms of relaxation, and they even thought alike on politics and child-raising. It was a very good start. Meredith had seen far too many relationships start out with nothing more than sex for a foundation, and they didn't last. It took common interests, common beliefs, friendship, to make a lasting marriage.

Marriage. That word, once so warily approached, now seemed as natural as letting Rey hold her hand all the way back to Jacobsville. She wondered where they were going together in the future, and hoped it was someplace nice.

She had to go back to work the following week. Friday morning she had her suitcase packed. She was wearing her tailored beige suit with her blond hair in a neat ponytail when she followed Rey out the front door. He carried her suitcase to his car and put it in the trunk.

"I'll be back late this afternoon," he told Leo. "If you need me, I'll be on my cell phone." He patted the cell phone carrier on his belt.

"Oh, I think I can cope," Leo drawled with a wink at

Meredith. "Don't be a stranger, Meredith," he added. "We'll miss you. But thanks for making us all those pans of frozen biscuits!"

"It's a good thing you have a walk-in freezer, is all I can say," she mused, chuckling. "But don't forget the directions on how to cook them," she added. "They're only dough until then."

"I'll have it all down pat in no time," Leo promised. "Meanwhile," he added, rubbing his big hands together with visible delight, "there are still six biscuits left over from breakfast!"

"No use asking you to save me a couple, is there?" Rey asked on a sigh.

"Blood is thicker than water, except where biscuits are involved," Leo shot back. "Sorry."

Rey got in the car and started the engine without another word.

Meredith was quiet most of the way to Houston. She was oddly reluctant to go back to work, although she loved her job. She was going to miss Rey and Leo and Mrs. Lewis. She was even going to miss the chickens.

"You can come down anytime you want to," Rey reminded her, when he noticed that she was brooding. It had been hard, but he'd kept his hands to himself for the duration of her stay at the ranch. He was planning a frontal assault in the near future. This wasn't the time, though.

"I know." She stared out the window at the bare trees and chilly flat landscape. "Thanksgiving comes along pretty soon."

"Your father will be working for us by then. You can come and spend a few days while you're off."

"I might still be on call," she worried.

He was grim and silent himself, after she said that. Th

rest of the way to Houston, he had the radio on, letting it fill the cool silence.

He dropped her off at her father's house. It looked cold and unwelcoming as she unlocked the front door so that he could sit her suitcase inside.

She turned back to him, her grey eyes wide and sad as they met his dark ones. He hadn't removed his hat, and it was hard to see his face in the shadow of it.

"Well, thanks for everything," she began.

He stared down at her with a sense of loss. After their ride up to Houston to visit her father, there seemed to be a curtain between them. They'd been very close that Sunday. But he'd gotten cold feet, he admitted to himself, and he'd drawn back. He felt the threat of her in his heart and he was trying to run from it. Suddenly it was like trying to run from himself.

"You'll be here alone," he said quietly. "Make sure you keep your door locked. We haven't had any reports that they caught the guys who rolled Leo. Just in case, don't let your guard down."

"I'll be fine," she promised him.

She looked so small and vulnerable standing there. He hated leaving her.

"You wear your jacket when it's cold like this," she told him firmly, noticing that he was standing in the cold wind in just the shirtsleeves of his chambray shirt.

"And my raincoat when it's raining," he said with a mocking smile. "You wear yours, too."

She hesitated. "Well, goodbye," she said after a minute.

"You and I won't ever say goodbye, Meredith," he replied. "It's 'so long.'"

She forced a smile to her lips. "So long, then."

He was still hesitating. His face was absolutely grim.

"I know where a jeweler's is open this early," she said suddenly, with mischievous enthusiasm.

It warmed him to hear her tease, to see that wonderful smile. "Do you, really?"

She nodded. "You can even have a diamond. But it would have to be a small one."

His dark eyes twinkled. "You just hold that thought," he said gently. "One of these days we might talk about this marriage hang-up of yours. Meanwhile, I've got to..."

"If you say 'wash the dogs,'" she interrupted, "I'll slug you!"

He chuckled. "I wasn't going to say that. I've got to get back and finish my marketing strategy for the next year before we have our year-end board meeting."

"I guess that's pretty complicated."

"No more than treating diseases and plotting nutrition," he replied. He studied her quietly. "I'll miss you. Don't stay away too long."

"Why?" she prodded.

"You have to save me from attacks on my virtue from hordes of amorous, sex-crazed women," he said without cracking a smile. "Who knows when I might weaken and give in to one of them, and then where would we be?"

"I've got my heart set on a virgin," she informed him.

He laughed helplessly. "Sorry, honey, you missed the boat by a decade or so."

She snapped her fingers. "Damn!"

"On the other hand, I didn't," he said in a deep, soft voice, and moved closer. He framed her face in his lean hands and studied it hungrily for several seconds. "You make me ache every time I touch you," he whispered, bending. "I'll starve to death before you get back."

"Starve...?" She wasn't thinking. She was watching his long, hard mouth come closer. She held her breath until i settled, ever so softly, on her parted lips. And then she didn't think at all for several long, tempestuous seconds.

Too soon, he caught her by the arms and pushed her away. "You stop that," he muttered breathlessly. "I refuse to be seduced on the front lawn."

She was trying to catch her own breath. "No problem. There's a nice soft carpet just five steps this way," she indicated the hall.

"I'm not that kind of man," he said haughtily.

She made a face at him.

He chuckled and kissed her one last time, teasingly, before he pulled back and started toward his car. "I'll call you."

"That's what they all say!" she cried after him.

"Then you call me, honey," he said in that deep, sexy voice that made her melt. "You've got my number, even if you don't know it yet." He winked and went on to the car. He didn't look back, even as he drove away. Meredith's eyes followed the car until it was out of sight. She didn't cry until she was inside, behind the closed door.

She was back at work and going crazy in no time, overrun by people with everything from stomach viruses to the flu. She had a good immune system, and she didn't catch any of the ailments, but she missed Rey terribly.

Three days before Thanksgiving, her father telephoned her from the ranch, full of excitement about his new job. He seemed like a different person. He told her he was still going to therapy sessions, but in Jacobsville with a psychologist. He was doing much better, and he was going to make everything up to his daughter, he swore it. And wasn't she coming for Thanksgiving?

It took real nerve to tell him the truth, that she hadn't een able to get off because of the time she'd already missed. There was simply nobody available to replace her. She'd have Thanksgiving Day, but nothing more.

She'd tried to beg the time off to have a long weekend, but her boss hadn't been pleased and he refused. He wanted her on call that weekend, and she couldn't be and go to Jacobsville. The office held a huge clinic for the local immigrant population on Saturdays, as well as Sunday afternoons, and Meredith was competently bilingual in medical terms. It made her indispensable. Not that she minded. These people were desperately in need of even the most basic health care, and Meredith was a whiz at preventive medicine. She counseled them, advised them on nutrition and wellness, and tried not to let her heart break at the sight of little children with rotting teeth and poor vision and a dozen other ailments that money could have corrected easily. The disparity between the rich and the poor was never more evident than in minority communities.

But the fact was, she had one day off for Thanksgiving and no real time for herself. It was a reminder of just how pressured her job really was, and how demanding. She loved what she did, but she hated being made to feel guilty when she asked for time off—something she hadn't done since her brother's and mother's untimely deaths. Actually it had been a battle royal to get time off for bereavement leave, and the funerals, and she'd had to go right back to work the day after the burials. It had been too soon, but she'd thought work would be good medicine.

Perhaps it had been, but she was living on nerves. The weeks at the Hart ranch had given her a taste of a whole other life. It was one she recalled with joy and missed every day. Most of all, she missed Rey. Now she wouldn't even see him. Her father said that he'd ask someone to loan him a vehicle, and he'd come to have Thanksgiving with her. Th cheered her up a little, but it would mean she wouldn't see Rey. It was a bad blow. She told her father that she'd make dinner, which cheered him up as well.

Thanksgiving Day came, and Meredith got up before daylight to start cooking. She was determined that she and her father were going to have the best Thanksgiving dinner she could manage. She'd bought a turkey and a small ham, and raw ingredients to make dressing and sweet-potato soufflé, green beans, ambrosia, homemade rolls and cherry and pumpkin pies.

She'd just taken the last pie out of the oven when she heard a car pull up in front of the house. She didn't stop to take off her apron or run a brush through her disheveled hair. She ran to the front door and opened it, just in time to see her father and Rey come up on the porch.

"Happy Thanksgiving, Merry," her father said, and hugged her warmly.

Rey grinned. "We thought you might like company to help you eat all that food," he told her.

"I didn't make any biscuits," she said worriedly. "Just homemade rolls."

"I love rolls." He held out his arms. "Well, come on," he chided when she hesitated. "You can't treat a red-hot matrimonial prospect like me to the cold shoulder! You'll never get me to say 'yes' from arm's length!"

Her father coughed. "I'll just, uh, check on the turkey," he said with an impish smile and went into the kitchen.

Rey nudged Meredith back inside the house, closed the door, and kissed her to within an inch of her life. He barely stopped to breathe before he was kissing her again, enfolding her in a bearish embrace while he made up for what seemed like years of abstinence.

"You'll smother me," she complained weakly.

"Stop complaining and kiss me," he murmured against her swollen lips. He kissed her ever harder.

"I'm not…complaining!" she gasped when he finally stopped.

He bit her lower lip ardently. "I am," he groaned. "Come on, woman, ravish me!"

"Here?" she exclaimed, wide-eyed.

"Well, give your father a quarter and send him to the store for cigarettes!" he asked with comical desperation between kisses.

"Nobody here smokes," she pointed out.

"Excuses, excuses," he murmured against her lips, using her own favorite complaint. His arms tightened and he only stopped when he had to breathe. "What a long, dry spell it's been, Merry," he whispered huskily. "Come back here…"

She kissed him and kissed him with no thought of the future. It was wonderful to be held and cuddled and wanted. She thought she'd never felt so much joy in her whole life as she did here, in Rey's hard arms.

"There's that carpet you mentioned when I left here last time," he said breathlessly, indicating the floor. He wiggled both eyebrows. "We can lock your father in the kitchen and you can ravish me, right here!"

"Not on your life." She linked her arms around his neck. "I won't ravish you until you agree to marry me," she managed unsteadily.

"Is that a proposal?" he murmured huskily.

"Sure. You can have a ring. I think there's a ten-year-old cigar around here somewhere with a band on it…"

He was still kissing her between words. "I'll phone the minister first thing tomorrow. You can have a blood test at work. I already had Micah Steele do one on me. He said he'd love to have a nurse practitioner of his very own, by th way, if you're interested. We can have a Christmas wedding in Jacobsville."

Her mind was spinning. She couldn't quite understand what he was saying. Of course, he was kissing her and she could hardly think at all. "Blood test…work for Micah… Christmas wedding?" she murmured.

"Mmm-hmm," he whispered, kissing her again. "You can get me a ring whenever you like, but I got you one already." He fumbled in his jacket pocket and pulled out a velvet-covered jeweler's box. He opened it and showed it to her. Inside was a glorious emerald solitaire, and a diamond and emerald wedding band. "If you don't like it, we can throw it in the fishpond and go buy you something else…"

"I love it!" she exclaimed, flustered by the sudden turn of events.

"Good. Here." He took out the engagement ring, pocketed the box and slid it gently onto her ring finger. "Now it's official. We're engaged. Remember what you just promised," he added with a wicked grin. "The minute your father leaves, I'll let you ravish me on the carpet!"

Chapter Eleven

"But, Rey, Daddy won't leave," she whispered. "There's a turkey in the kitchen!"

"He can take it with him," he said generously.

She laughed and hugged him very hard. "I can't believe this."

"Neither can I," he said, nuzzling his cheek against hers. His arms tightened. "Even when I was suspicious of you, I couldn't bear you out of my sight. I still can't. This past week has been endless. I thought we could cool it for a few weeks, while I got things into perspective. But the only thing I got into perspective was how lonely I was without you." He lifted his head and looked down into her wide, rapt eyes. "I love my freedom. But not as much as I love you."

"And I love you, Rey," she said huskily. "I was lonely, too. I feel as if I've known you for centuries."

"Same here," he replied. "We're going to make a good marriage."

"A very good marriage," she agreed, and lifted her face so that he could kiss her again. He did, at length and very nicely, until her father came out of the kitchen with a turkey leg in one hand and asked if there were plans to take the dressing out of the oven before it got any blacker. Rey told him their news while Meredith took off at a dead run to rescue dinner.

Meredith worked out a two-week notice and gave up her job, to the dismay and regret of her boss, who hadn't wanted to lose her. He did see that she couldn't have a husband in Jacobsville and a job in Houston, however, and he made them a wedding present of a beautiful faceted crystal bowl.

Micah Steele offered her a job at his office, which she accepted with pleasure, on the understanding that she could work three days a week instead of six. Micah understood being a newlywed, since he and his Callie were still newlyweds as well, even with a baby on the way.

The only hitch was that all Rey's brothers got together and took over the wedding plans, to his dismay and Meredith's horror.

"It's going to be a humdinger of a wedding," Leo promised with relish, rubbing his hands together. "Cag had this great idea for entertainment."

"I don't want to hear it," Rey said firmly.

"You'll love this," Leo continued, unabashed. "He's got this great hard-rock band from Montana coming down to play their new hit record. They just had a hit single about getting married," he added with a rakish grin. "And they're having a caterer from San Antonio bring down the buffet ınch. The wedding gown is coming from one of the couture uses in Paris..."

"But you don't even know my size!" Meredith protested breathlessly.

"We looked in your dresses," he said imperturbably. "Got your shoe size, too, and we also looked in your drawers and got the, ahem, other sizes." He grinned sheepishly. "Everything is couture, and silk. Only the best for our new sister-in-law," he added sweepingly.

Meredith didn't know whether to laugh or scream.

"We booked you a room at a five-star hotel for your honeymoon," he continued, glancing at Rey. "You still speak French, don't you?"

"French?" Meredith gasped.

"Well, your rooms are in Nice," he said. "The French Riviera. You've got a suite, overlooking the beach. Monaco is just on down the beach from there."

Rey whistled. "Not bad, for a rush job."

"We try to be efficient," Leo said, and his eyes twinkled. "We even ordered her a trousseau with formal gowns and casual clothes. Lots of pinks and blues and soft beige colors. We thought pastels would suit her."

Her mouth was open. She was trying to take it all in without fainting. She was only beginning to realize that the horror stories she'd heard from Tess about weddings and the brothers were true.

"You did kidnap Dorie and tie her in a sack with ribbon and carry her home to Corrigan!" she gasped.

"He didn't have a Christmas present," Leo explained patiently. "We gave him one. Look how well it worked out!"

"You hooligans!"

"Our hearts are all in the right place," Leo protested. "Besides, Dorie could bake. Which brings us to Tess, who could also bake…"

"You blackmailed Callaghan into marrying her, I heard!" Meredith was getting her second wind now.

"He's very happy. So is Tess."

"And poor Tira," she continued, unabashed. "You arranged her wedding and she didn't even get to choose her own gown, either!"

"She was pregnant. We had to hurry, there was no time," Leo explained matter-of-factly.

"I am not pregnant!" she exclaimed, red-faced.

Leo gave Rey a quick, speculative glance. "Yet," he replied. He grinned.

"If you would just give me a little time to organize my own wedding," she began, exasperated, and thought, I'm being nibbled to death by ducks…!

Leo checked his watch. "Sorry, I'm running late. The printer is waiting for me to check the proofs."

"Of what?" she burst out.

"Oh, just the wedding invitations. We're overnighting them to the people we invited. The governor's coming, so is the lieutenant governor. The vice president wanted to come, but he has to be in Singapore…" He frowned and checked his back pocket. "There they are! I almost forgot the interview questions. Here." He handed Rey two folded sheets of paper. "You'll have time to look them over before the camera crews move in."

Meredith and Rey exchanged wide glances. "What camera crews?" she asked.

"Just a few reporters," Leo waved them away with a lean hand. "You know, CNN, Fox, the international press…got to run!"

"International press!" Meredith choked.

"We've just signed an important export deal with Japan, didn't I mention it?" Leo called back. "They love organic beef, and we've got some. I mentioned it to our public relations people and they called the news people for us. Your father's writing the statement we're giving them. He's sure got a way with words, hasn't he?"

He waved again, climbed into his truck and sped off.

"Invitations," Meredith said haltingly. "Clothes. Honeymoons. Reporters."

"Now, now," he said, pulling her into his arms. "Just think of all the work they've saved you. You'll have nothing to do but dress and say yes, and fly off to the Riviera with your brand-new husband!"

"But, but," she blurted.

"I want to marry you right away," he added. "You're a qualified health professional, and I have a terrible pain that you can cure in only one night."

She got the idea, belatedly, and hit him.

He chuckled, bending to kiss her gently. "It's no use trying to stop them," he said. "Besides, they're very good at it. I used to be, too." He scowled. "Somehow, it's not as much fun being on the receiving end, though."

She just shook her head.

The wedding was beautiful, despite her misgivings. Meredith wore the most gorgeous gown she'd ever seen, with yards and yards of exquisite lace over satin, with a long veil made of the same lace and a bouquet of pure white roses. Her father gave her away, and all four of Rey's brothers were best men. Tess, Cag's wife, stood with Meredith as her matron of honor. In a very short time, the two women had become close friends.

Most of Jacobsville turned out for the affair, but Meredith had eyes only for her handsome husband, who was dressed to the hilt as well. They exchanged rings and Rey lifted the veil very slowly. He'd been romantic and gentle and teasing over the days before the wedding. But when he looked at her now, his eyes were quiet and loving and very solemn

He bent and kissed her with such tenderness that she knew she'd remember the moment for the rest of her life.

They clasped hands and ran down the aisle and out of the church together, laughing gaily as they were pelted with rice and rose petals. At the waiting limousine, Meredith turned and tossed her bouquet. Surprisingly it was caught by Janie Brewster, notorious locally for her rubber chicken dinners and trying to catch Leo Hart's eye. She blushed vividly and clutched the bouquet, her eyes on it and not on anyone nearby. Which was as well, because Leo looked suddenly homicidal as the ranch foreman elbowed him and grinned.

The newlyweds waved and dived into the limousine, already packed and ready to take them to the airport. They'd already announced that the reception would have to go on without them, to the brothers' shock and dismay.

"I hated for us to miss it," Rey told her on the way to the airport, "but I know my brothers. They'd have found some way to embarrass us."

She chuckled, snuggling close to him. "Well, we're safe now."

The flight to France was long and boring. They held hands and couldn't sleep as the little computers above the seats marked the long trail on a map, showing the progress of the flight. When the jumbo jet finally landed, they walked like zombies into the airport to go through passport control and then on to wait for their luggage so that they could get through customs and to the waiting car that would take them to their hotel. The driver, holding a sign that read Hart Newlyweds had met them at the gate and arranged to meet them at customs. Meredith was yawning visibly when they found the driver and followed him and the wheeled luggage out the door. He and Rey exchanged comments that went right over Meredith's head.

"I don't speak French," she said worriedly when they were in the car. "I took a double minor in German and Spanish."

"No Latin?" he teased.

"There's a special course of it for nursing students," she replied with a smile. "Fortunately you don't have to learn the whole language anymore, although I wouldn't have minded. I'm so tired!"

"We'll have a nice long rest when we get to the hotel." He pulled her close. "I could use a little sleep myself!"

The car pulled up under the covered entrance and a bellboy came out to get the luggage. Rey paid the driver and made arrangements to contact him when they were ready to go sightseeing in a day or two.

Meredith followed Rey and the luggage to the desk clerk and waited while he got the key to their suite.

It didn't take long. Rey unlocked the door and opened it. And the bellhop burst into helpless laughter.

There, on the bed, very obviously courtesy of the Hart boys, were two life-size blow-up dolls, a blonde female and a dark-haired male, in the midst of a garden of thornless roses of every color known to man. They were obviously engaged in a notorious newlywed ritual.

Rey tipped the bellhop and opened the door himself, waving the man out while he tried not to bend over double laughing.

When he closed the door again, Meredith was removing the dolls and roses with tears of mirth running down her cheeks.

"Just wait until they break something, anything," she threatened. "We can have them put in body casts for a sprained ankle...!"

He came up behind her and caught her around the waist. "And I'll help you. But, later, sweetheart," he added in a soft, hungry tone as he turned her into his arms. "Much, much…later!"

She was a professional health care worker. She knew all the mechanics of marriage. In fact, she counseled young wives in them. This was totally out of her experience.

Rey undressed her with slow precision, while he kissed every soft inch of skin as he uncovered it. He never rushed. He seemed to have committed the whole night to her arousal, and he went about it like a soldier with a battle plan.

She was teased, caressed, kissed until she felt as if there wasn't a bed under her at all. The roses were scattered over the carpet by now, along with half the bed linen. She was under him and then over him as he increased the insistence of his hands and mouth on her body. She heard high-pitched little cries of pleasure and barely realized that they were coming from her own throat.

One particularly enthusiastic embrace landed them on the carpet, cushioned by the sheet and blanket and, under them, the thick comforter.

"The bed," she whispered, trembling with unsatisfied hunger.

"It will still be there when we're finished," he replied breathlessly as his mouth bent again to her taut, arching breasts. "Yes, do that again, sweetheart!" he added when she pulled his head down to her.

He guided her hands along his lean, fit body to his hips and pressed them there as he suddenly shifted between her soft legs and his mouth ground into hers with intent.

The abrupt shift in intensity took her by surprise and sened the sharp pain of his possession of her. His hard mouth absorbed the tiny cry that pulsed out of her tight throat, and his hands moved under her hips to caress her.

After a few seconds, she began to relax. He shifted again and found the place, and the pressure, that made her lift toward him instead of trying to escape the downward rhythm of his hips.

She clung to his damp shoulders as the little bites of pleasure became great, shivering waves. She could feel him in every cell of her body, and she wanted to look at him, to see his face, but she was intent on some distant goal of pleasure that grew by the second. Her mouth opened against the hollow of his shoulder and she moaned, her eyes closed, her body following the lead of his own as the heated minutes lengthened.

Her nails suddenly stabbed into his back and she gasped.

"Yes," he groaned at her ear. "Now, baby, now, now…!"

As if her body had given him some secret signal, his hips became insistent and the rhythm increased to madness. She reached, reached…reached…until the pleasure exploded inside her and began to spread in racking hot waves from her head to her toes. She rippled with him, sobbed against his skin, as the ecstasy she'd never known flamed through her with hurricane force.

"Rey!" She cried out pitifully as the wave peaked, and she felt her body go incandescent with joy.

His hands gripped her hips as he riveted her to his insistent hips. She heard his breathing become raspy and hoarse and then stop as he groaned endlessly against her throat and his entire body convulsed over her.

She felt him shake as the madness began to drift away.

"Are you all right?" she whispered urgently.

"I'm…dying," he choked.

"Rey!"

She held him close until the harsh contractions of h

body slowed and then stopped. He collapsed on her with his whole weight, his breathing as labored as his heartbeat. His mouth burrowed into her throat hungrily.

"Never like that, Mrs. Hart," he whispered huskily. "You just made me a whole man!"

"Did I, really?" she whispered with a silly giggle.

He laughed, too. "That's what it felt like." He sighed heavily and lifted his head to look at her. His hair was as damp as hers, and he looked exhausted. He brushed loose blond strands away from her cheeks. "I'm glad we waited. I hope you are."

"Yes." Filled with wonder, she touched his hard mouth, which was swollen from its long contact with hers. "I think I swallowed the sun," she whispered. "It was…glorious!" She hid her face in his throat, still shy of him, especially now.

He laughed again, lazily brushing his mouth over her closed eyes. "Glorious," he agreed with a long sigh. He rolled away from her gently, onto his back, and pulled her against him. "We fell off the bed," he remarked after a minute.

"I thought we were thrown off it," she murmured sleepily. "You know, by the hurricane."

"Hurricane." He kissed her forehead gently. "That's what it felt like."

"I'm sleepy. Is it normal?"

"Yes, it is, and it does worlds for my masculinity," he drawled. "Feel free to tell anyone you like that you ravished me to such an extent that I fell out of bed in my excitement, and you went to sleep from the tidal wave of pleasure!"

She managed one tired little chuckle. "I'll take out an ad in a magazine," she promised. She wrapped her arms and one leg around him, completely uninhibited now. "I love you, but I have to go to sleep now."

"Suit yourself, but I hope you're not throwing in the towel. I'm a brand-new bridegroom, remember, you can't just roll over and go to sleep once you've had your way with me… Meredith? Meredith!"

It was no use. She was sound asleep, worn-out by the pace of the wedding and her first passion. He lay watching her sleep, his eyes quiet and tender and loving. It had already been, he mused, one hell of a wedding night, even if they hadn't waited for it to get dark.

When she woke up, she was wearing a nightgown and lying on the bed, under the covers. Rey was sipping coffee and sniffing freshly cooked food under silver lids. He glanced up as Meredith sat up in bed and blinked her eyes sleepily.

"Supper?" she asked.

He grinned. "Supper. Come and eat something."

She pulled herself out of bed, feeling a little uncomfortable and grinning as she realized why. She sat down beside Rey, who was wearing a pair of blue silk pajama bottoms and nothing else, and looked under lids.

"Seafood," she sighed, smiling. "My favorite."

"Mine, too. Dig in, honey." He reached over and kissed her softly and gave her a wicked grin. "It's going to be a long, lovely night!"

And it was.

They came back to the ranch after several magical, wonderful days together to find the house deserted. There was a note propped up on the kitchen table, obviously left by Leo, because his name was signed to it.

"Goodbye, cruel world," it read. "Have run out of biscuits. No relief in sight. Can't go on. Have gone into Jacobsville to kidnap a cook or beg door-to-door for biscuits. If I fail, drag the river. P.S. Congratulations Meredith and Rey. Hope you liked the wedding present. Love, Leo."

"He wouldn't really kidnap a cook," Meredith said.

"Of course not," Rey agreed. But he had a very odd look on his face.

"Or beg door-to-door for a biscuit."

"Of course not," Rey repeated.

Meredith went to the telephone. "I'll call Dad."

He waited while she dialed the cottage her father occupied and tapped his foot while it rang and rang.

"Dad?" she asked suddenly. "Have you seen Leo?"

There was a pause, while Rey gestured with his hands for her to tell him something. She flapped a hand at him while she listened and nodded.

"Okay, Dad, thanks! Yes, we had a lovely honeymoon! We'll have you up for supper tomorrow. Love you, too!"

She hung up and sighed. "Well, Leo's gone to San Antonio."

"What the hell for?" he exclaimed.

"Apparently he walked out of Barbara's café with a cook in his arms and put him in the ranch truck…"

"Him?" Rey exclaimed.

"Him." She sighed. "The cook escaped out the other door and ran to get Chet Blake."

"The chief of police?" Rey looked horrified.

"Chet was laughing so hard that he didn't get to the café before Leo took off in a cloud of dust, barely escaping public disgrace. He tried to hire the little man to bake him some biscuits, but the cook refused, so Leo took harsh measures." She chuckled. "Dad said he phoned halfway to San Antonio and said he'd be back in a few days. He thinks he'll go to that genetics workshop until the heat dies down here."

"We'll never live that story down," Rey sighed, shaking his head.

"There is a solution," she remarked. "We can find him a nice wife."

He laughed even harder. "Leo's the one of us who'll have to be dragged to the altar behind a big horse," he told her. "For all that Janie Brewster is desperate to marry him, he's as elusive as smoke."

"Janie's pretty," she recalled, because the girl caught her bridal bouquet at the wedding.

"She's a doll, but she can't boil water," Rey told her. "He'd never get a biscuit if he married Janie. Besides, she's not mature enough for him."

"She could change."

"So could he, sweetheart," he drawled, pulling her close to kiss her. "But I wouldn't hold my breath in either case. Now here we are, at home, and all alone, and I'll give you one guess what I'd like you to do next," he whispered suggestively.

She smiled under his lips. "Would it have something to do with flour and olive oil and skim milk and a hot oven?" she whispered back.

He actually gasped. "Darling!" he exclaimed, and kissed her even harder.

She linked her arms around his neck. "So," she whispered, moving closer, "Just how badly do you want that pan of biscuits, sweetheart?" she teased.

Chuckling, he bent and lifted her clear of the floor and turned down the hall. "Let me show you!"

Eventually he got a pan of fresh biscuits and a whole jar of fresh apple butter to go on them—along with a nice pat of low-fat margarine. And he didn't even complain!

* * * * *